SOPHIE

DECEPTION

Enquiries to:
Robinson Publishing Ltd
7 Kensington Church Court
London W8 4SP

First published in the UK by Scarlet, 1996

A copy of the British Library Cataloguing in
Publication data is available from the British Library

ISBN 1-85487-481-0

Printed and bound in the EC

10 9 8 7 6 5 4 3 2 1

CHAPTER 1

It was a warm summer evening. Ashley Lawrence walked back slowly through the long shadows across the bridle path. Her dog Rusty raced ahead for an invigorating rummage through the undergrowth. Smiling, Ash stopped and surveyed the scene.

In the little copse the air was pleasantly cool on the back of her neck. The air was full of the scent of blossom and new leaves. Just visible through the woodland, quiet English fields stretched drowsily to the horizon. The prospect was utterly peaceful.

'So why do I feel so restless?' thought Ash, rubbing her neck viciously.

Her long curly hair felt sticky under her fingers. There were probably several straws in it, she thought ruefully. It had been a hard day at the animal centre and, as a volunteer, it fell to her to catch escaping patients. Today it had been a lop-eared rabbit. He had made his break for freedom still attached to a good deal of the straw in his cage. By the time Ash had caught him, he had transferred most of it to her.

She pulled a couple of straws out and resumed a brisk

1

pace. She enjoyed her work, perhaps more so because she only went to the centre three days a week. Normally when she walked home she was full of enthusiasm. And the harder the day the greater the fun.

So why was today different?

'You know,' she told herself. 'You just don't want to admit it.'

Rusty came tumbling back from his adventure. He was a long-coated golden retriever, a refugee at the centre whom no one had wanted. Ash had never had a dog. She had been hugely doubtful when Bob Cummings suggested she offer Rusty a home.

'Can I cope?' she asked doubtfully. 'I've never been responsible for anything like a dog.'

'Then it's time you were,' Bob said unanswerably. 'You know how to look after an animal. God knows you've handed out enough leaflets on it since you've been here.'

'That's different,' Ash protested.

He had grinned. 'You're so right. Now you find out what it's really like.'

So, with more trepidation than she was willing to admit, Ash had taken the boisterous puppy home. Since then she had learned exactly what it was really like. She adored it.

Now he plunged up to her and leaped up, getting both muddy paws squarely in the middle of her tee-shirt. Ash rubbed his head.

'Just as well for you this shirt is so dirty a few more paw marks won't make any difference,' she told him.

Rusty barked.

'Right you are,' said Ash as if he had spoken. 'Race you home.'

They both took off like rockets.

The Manor was a beautiful house, mainly Jacobean, set in a fold between three small hills. In the late evening sunlight the honey-coloured stone looked like very gentle gold. Normally just the sight of it filled Ash with content. Tonight, however, she was aware of a faint feeling of dread; as if she were not going to live in this beautiful place much longer.

'This is nonsense,' she said to herself. 'You're just feeling paranoid because . . .'

But she did not want to think about why she was feeling paranoid.

She took Rusty to the kitchen door and made him wait until she had hosed him down. He enjoyed that too. He danced round her, soaking them both before the water began to run clear. By the time she let him back into the kitchen the phone was ringing.

Just for a moment Ash stopped dead. She was aware of a cold little feeling in her throat like dread. Her heart began to race.

'Nonsense,' she told herself again. Aloud this time.

She marched through the kitchen door into the main house. The smell of lavender and beeswax and early roses met her like balm. Her heart quieted. She picked up the phone.

'Hayes Manor.'

She had learned a long time ago to say the name of the house instead of her own. When you have a famous name and your family are attracting public attention, you want all the anonymity you can get. Even though it was three years since Peter had died, she still retained the habit.

It was unnecessary. This was a voice she had known since school. 'Ash? Darling, how are you?'

Ten years ago Joanne had been one of her bridesmaids. Why was it, thought Ash, that bridesmaids always remembered your wedding anniversary, long after you would choose to forget it yourself?

She did not say that, of course. Instead she said with composure, 'Hi, Jo. Pretty bobbish, thank you. You?'

'Fine, fine.' Joanne was absent. She had not rung up to talk about herself. 'I wanted to drop in tonight but I'm still at the office.'

'Drop in?' Ash was genuinely taken aback. 'Jo, it's sixty miles from London.'

'Hour-and-a-half, max,' said Joanne airily. She was the sort of driver who liked to give motorway policemen new challenges. 'I really meant to. Only then this job came up and now I'm not going to get away for another hour at least. I wouldn't get to you till ten-thirty at the earliest. What do you think?'

'Don't even think about it,' said Ash firmly. She was touched, though. 'I'm fine. Really.'

'Are you?' Joanne did not sound convinced.

'Jo, it's a long time ago. Three years. And we were only married for seven. You can't mourn forever.'

'Exactly,' said her friend sharply.

Ash jumped. 'What?'

'Precisely my point,' Joanne went on as if she had not spoken. 'Sensible people don't keep company with ghosts.'

'Jo!' Ash was shocked.

'Well, I'm sorry,' said Joanne, modifying her tone. She sounded slightly ashamed of herself. 'I don't mean to be

4

unfeeling. I know you and Peter were the perfect couple. I know the accident was ghastly. Believe me, it's not that I don't sympathize. I *do*. But I can't bear to see you sinking under the cobwebs in that great barn of a house.'

'It's a lovely house,' said Ash, stung.

'Sure. For a family of ten. Not a woman on her own.'

'I'm not on my own. There's Rusty and the cats and the strays from the centre . . .'

Joanne made a trumpeting noise of disgust.

'You sound like a horse,' Ash said involuntarily.

'And you sound like a seriously peculiar old maid,' Joanne retorted. She sounded exasperated. 'You're twenty-eight, for God's sake. Not eighty-eight. Lighten up. Look around. Have some fun.'

'I do have fun,' Ash defended herself, half-laughing.

Joanne was a hard interrogator. 'When did you last go on the town? Have a meal with a man? Go to a show? Dance?'

'Not that sort of fun,' Ash admitted. 'But I love my garden and the animals . . .'

She was interrupted by a scream from the other end of the phone.

'Eighty-eight,' crowed Joanne, triumphant.

Ash was annoyed, but she had to laugh in spite of herself. 'You're mixing me up with yourself. I was never the one who did the dining and dancing, anyway.'

'Then it's about time you started.' Joanne gave a sharp sigh and her tone softened. 'Sorry, don't mean that either. I'm just a bit hyped up with work. Look, I just think you shouldn't be on your own all the time. Especially not – ' she hesitated, searching for the right word.

Ash said levelly, 'Especially not on my wedding anniversary.'

Joanne had been married within weeks of Ash. It had not lasted a year.

Now she said with feeling, 'Anniversaries can be bloody.'

'I know,' said Ash soberly.

Hurtful, guilt-making and altogether too complicated to be thought about, she added silently. There was a pause.

'It really is best not to be on your own,' Joanne burst out.

Ash sighed. She said honestly, 'Maybe for you. I'm best on my own, Jo.'

'So you can sit there and wallow in misery?'

'No, honestly. Like I said, it's a long time ago.'

'Are you trying to say you don't care any more?' Joanne did not sound as if she would believe her.

'Well, there's caring and caring. You get over things. And you grow up. I wouldn't say I care now in the way I probably once did,' Ash said carefully.

There was another pause.

'Oh Ash,' said Joanne. 'Nobody ever cared as much as you did.' She sounded full of pity.

This was deep water. Ash started to say something and found her throat was choked. She swallowed hard.

There was another, longer pause. Joanne started to say something. Then stopped. Ash could almost hear her friend making an effort to lighten up and be constructive.

'Well, as you say, with all those peculiar animals you're not exactly without company,' Joanne said at last.

'Or problems,' agreed Ash lightly. She felt a rush of

6

warmth. It was gratitude to Joanne for allowing them to paddle back into the shallows. 'Rusty likes the muddiest ditches and the palest upholstery. The trick is to make sure he doesn't go straight from one to the other.'

'That dog needs training,' said Joanne disapprovingly.

'No, just a regular bath.'

'Rather you than me,' said Joanne with feeling.

'That's why I'm here and you're there,' Ash agreed. 'I couldn't get out there every day hassling strangers.'

Joanne chuckled. 'My hassling days are long gone. I send other people out with the clipboards these days. I know you haven't noticed but I've become a big cheese in my own way.'

Ash was silenced. It was not true that she had not noticed. From the way Joanne's secretary was always saying apologetically that Ms Lambert was in conference when Ash rang, to the increasing difficulty with which Joanne could get away from London, it was obvious. If Joanne had accused her of not wanting to admit it, she would have been nearer the mark.

Ash did not like big business; and for good reasons. Joanne Lambert was her oldest friend. If Jo was turning out to be a success in the cut-and-thrust world of what Ash thought of as City piracy, then Ash felt she had in some sense lost her. She did not want to lose Joanne. They had shared too much.

Including the knowledge of what drove both of them.

Joanne said now in a dry tone, 'No need to go into mourning, Ash. I know it's not your cup of tea. But I'm having a hell of a good time. In fact you should try it some time.'

'Running a business?' Ash was appalled.

Joanne laughed. 'No need to go that far. But you might get out there and mix in a bit. Join the world.'

'I do voluntary work at the animal centre. That's as much of the world as I want,' said Ash firmly.

Jo made her derisive noise again. 'Oh, want! What about what's good for you?'

Ash chuckled. 'You sound like Miss Purves. Recommending eight o'clock netball, Jo?'

Joanne laughed too. 'All right. All right. I'll stop doing the Dutch uncle routine. You do what you want and I'll do what I want. Then we can both have a great time convinced the other is making a big mistake.'

'Done,' said Ash promptly.

It was a bargaining formula they had started at school. 'Done.' Down the phone Ash could hear Joanne grinning. 'No more lectures. Tell me what else is going down instead. Apart from the animal delinquency, that is.'

Ash searched her mind. She did not think Joanne would be interested in a wounded badger cub currently recovering in her garage or the preparations for the village fête. Joanne, as she occasionally announced when feeling particularly captious, usually to people she disliked, was a people person.

'Well, my father has got a widow after him. He came back from the Bahamas early and he won't admit it but she seems to be sticking to the chase.'

'I love your father,' said Joanne pleasurably. 'Power to his arm. What else?'

Ash sought wider. 'Someone has bought the Gate House at last. So I've got a neighbour nearer than three miles.' She added naughtily, 'Em is pleased. He doesn't seem to have a wife.'

Joanne was unimpressed. 'Then he'll have a boyfriend or crippling alimony payments. Or a chemical allergy to marriage.'

Ash said involuntarily, 'Then that would make two of us.'

Joanne sucked in her breath. At once Ash could have kicked herself. Why on earth had she said that? It might be true but all it would do would be to set Jo off on one of her lectures again.

So she said before Joanne could speak, 'And I've had some cowboys hounding me trying to buy the house.'

As a deflecting strategy it could not have been more successful. Joanne said blankly, 'Trying to buy the house? You mean your house? Hayes Manor? Who on earth? And *why*?'

'Some outfit called Dare Properties. As for why – well they wanted to buy Hayes Wood. When I said no, they offered me huge sums for the whole estate.'

'They *what*?'

'Irresistible amounts of money,' said Ash, deadpan.

'Good grief,' said Joanne blankly. 'Irresistible to whom?'

Ash's tone was dry. 'Ah, well there you have hit the nail on the head. It clearly dazzled the smooth piece of work they sent down to blag me into it.'

Joanne began to laugh. 'But not you. Oh boy, did they get the wrong customer there.'

'Yes, I thought it was a bit strange,' agreed Ash solemnly.

'Sounds to me as if they could use some decent market research. Haven't they worked out you don't give a toss about money? And that if you did, you could probably buy the whole county, if you wanted it?'

'I don't think,' said Ash with restraint, 'that Dare Properties is strong on noticing what other people are like. They just decide what is good for Dare Properties and then go after it with a bludgeon. And a cheque book, of course.'

'Well, they'll have got a new slant on things now,' said Joanne, chuckling. 'I suppose you gave them the Ashley Lawrence view of life, the world and the evils of greed in both.' She added thoughtfully, 'I almost feel sorry for them, whoever they are.'

Ash smiled. 'I was pretty crisp,' she agreed complacently. 'They won't be back.'

The London apartment was on the top floor of an Edwardian block. Interior decorators had stripped out internal walls but retained the high-definition relief work on the lofty ceilings along with the baronial fireplaces. Floors were inlaid woods imported from all round the world. Chairs were deeply cushioned and comfortable. The desk was a massive structure in Scandinavian wood lit by a lamp that looked like a robot designed by Giacommetti. The whole was starkly tidy and unmistakably masculine.

So was the only occupant. In the pool of light he looked remote, like a Renaissance prince. Yet even concentrating on the papers in front of him, there was an indefinable air of physicality about him, of male strength, compact and controlled, but none the less strong. You would not want to fight this man. Not in any arena. So it was surprising how many people seemed to want to do just that.

Or so thought the man who approached with a clipping noise across the polished floor. He was a tall, upright man in his sixties. He surveyed the concentrating figure for a moment. Then, when the man did not move, he coughed.

'Excuse me, sir. Your visitor has arrived. He is on his way up.'

Jake Dare looked up from his desk. He had a thin, clever face with intensely dark eyes. He was healthily tanned but just at the moment his face had a fine-drawn expression, as if he were exhausted, or even unwell. He frowned.

'What is it, Marriott?'

Marriott's face took on a masklike expression. 'His Highness, sir. He is here.'

'What? Is it that time already?'

Jake rubbed his eyes and cast a quick look out of the window. He was startled to see that some time while he was working it had got dark. The evening sky outside the penthouse was grey with the English summer twilight. Working under the light of his desk lamp, he had not noticed. How often was he not noticing the hours flying by these days? he wondered.

He stood up. 'Thank you, Marriott. OK. I'll be right there.'

Marriott inclined his head and retreated. Jake stood up and stretched. His shoulders felt cramped. That was the trouble with the life he was living at the moment, he thought.

He snapped off the light and went out to greet his guest.

There was a discreet buzz as the dedicated elevator came to a stop outside the penthouse. Marriott flung the door wide and stepped back.

'His Royal Highness, Prince Ahmed,' he announced.

Jake went forward, the thin face lighting up. The descendant of desert aristocrats and a boy from the wrong side of the Memphis tracks should have had nothing in common. Yet they had been friends from the first time Jake undertook a project for the prince's father. Neither of them was quite sure why, unless it was their shared pleasure in mountaineering.

It was six months since they had last met. The winter had been impossibly busy but, as Ahmed came in, Jake realized suddenly how much he had missed his friend's quirky views on life.

'Ahmed, great to see you. What are you doing in London?'

The prince had no truck with Anglo-Saxon handshakes. He hugged Jake enthusiastically.

'Stopping off to see you. I was in Paris. I gather I nearly missed you.' He held Jake away and looked at him critically. 'Just got back from Brazil, hmm? You look it.'

'Is that a compliment on my tan? Or pointing out that I have bags under my eyes?' asked Jake with a grin.

'You look a wreck,' his friend said frankly. 'What the hell are you doing to yourself, Jake?'

Marriott gave a discreet cough. He had moved to the drinks cabinet and was indicating that he was awaiting their orders. But there was no disguising that it was an approving cough.

'Mr Dare has been travelling a good deal, sir. Perhaps

excessively for his health and well-being.'

Jake groaned. 'Don't start.' He said to Ahmed, 'I thought English butlers were the last word in don't-give-a-shit superiority. Oh boy, did I draw the wrong one.'

Marriott inclined his head without apparent offence.

Jake relented. 'And he's got a point,' he said with a sigh. 'Too many airplanes and too many cities. Not enough days to go with them.'

'What you need,' said Ahmed, 'is a good hike up a bad mountain.'

'Not much chance of a decent climb at the moment,' Jake said sadly. 'For one thing I'm out of condition. For another – you should see the in-tray. No, a good evening's reminiscing will just have to do.'

'It is over a year since you took a holiday, sir,' Marriott remarked to the air.

'Vacations are harder work than work,' retorted Jake. He turned to Ahmed. 'See what I mean? In-your-face snootiness? Forget it. I might just as well have my mother living here.'

Ahmed had met Jake Dare's mother. His eyebrows rose. He had the impression she would neither know nor care when her only son had his last holiday. To Ahmed it had seemed that her only interest in Jake was that he continued to provide the funds to maintain an extravagant lifestyle.

'Really?' he murmured now.

Jake gave a wicked grin. 'The Mom I never had. Old-time, apple-pie style. These days I have the next best thing. Isn't that right, Marriott?'

Marriott ignored that. He said to Ahmed, 'May I offer you something to drink, sir?'

13

'Orange and soda water, please.'

Marriott poured it for him, replenished Jake's whisky and soda without asking and withdrew to the kitchen in a stately manner. Ahmed pursed his lips.

'Sound chap. If he thinks you ought to let up, I'm with Marriott.' He flung himself down in one of the deep chairs and raised his glass to Jake. 'Cheers.'

'Cheers.' Jake took a long swallow and felt the warmth course through him. He sat on the sofa and looked at his friend with pleasure. 'So how have you been? And what were you doing in Paris?'

But Ahmed was not going to waste time giving an account of himself. He said indifferently, 'Negotiations for the Foundation. The usual. What about you? Tan or no tan, you look like the walking dead.'

'Thank you,' said Jake, startled.

Ahmed swirled his drink round in his glass. Not looking at Jake, he said, 'Is this because of Rosie?'

That startled Jake even more. 'Rosie?' he echoed blankly.

Ahmed was not the sort of man to ask personal questions. Even if he had been, it was completely alien to the mutual irony of their relationship. As the head of his family's Charitable Foundation Ahmed had better things to do on his occasional visits to England than check up on the course of his friend's love life.

Ahmed frowned, still not looking up. 'I know you two are breaking up.'

'Now how the hell do you know that?' said Jake, torn between annoyance and amusement.

Ahmed shrugged. 'You're my friend. People know I'm interested. They hint. So then I asked.'

14

'Did you, by God?'

Ahmed looked up then. He seemed angry. 'Well, of course. That crazy day. I feel responsible.'

Eighteen months ago Ahmed had invited Jake to polo. It was a glorious day and the matches were exciting. But it was neither the weather nor the sport which made the day memorable to either of them. It was the fact that the lady Ahmed was escorting on that occasion took one look at Jake Dare and seemed to stop seeing any other man on the field.

There was no denying that for a while it had put a strain on the relationship. Ahmed had not been seriously involved with Rosalind Newman but he was handsome, rich and charming and used to being the object of feminine pursuit. He had never lost a girlfriend in that way before. Certainly not so publicly.

At first, Jake and Ahmed had met on their own from time to time for a game of squash. They would talk stiltedly about everything except themselves and each time they parted, thought sadly that they would probably not meet again. But then Jake and Rosie announced their engagement. Jake even started negotiations to merge his firm with that of Rosie's father. Ahmed sent them a magnificent engagement present and took them both to dinner. After that he started to behave, as Jake told him darkly, as if he had engineered the whole thing.

Now Jake said curtly, 'Crazy day, crazy relationship. One of those things. Forget it.'

Ahmed looked at him gravely. 'Like you have?'

Jake showed his teeth. 'Just one or two loose ends to tie up. Then I will.'

15

'Will you?'

'Sure.' He shrugged, looking impatient. 'Shouldn't have started and now it's over. End of story.'

Ahmed's eyes narrowed. 'Not an amicable parting?'

That irritated Jake. He brushed the question aside. 'Don't get involved. There's no way you're responsible.'

'I introduced you.'

Jake gave a harsh laugh. 'Don't worry about it. Rosie would have found a way to meet me one way or another. She was working on it. And Rosie Newman always gets what she works for.'

Ahmed's eyebrows flew up. 'Definitely not amicable. So you are breaking up badly.'

'Wrong tense. We broke up several weeks ago. Only the ill will is still running.'

Ahmed looked disturbed. 'I'm sorry. I didn't know that.'

Jake shrugged. 'No reason why you should. It's been folding for months. It was on its knees by Christmas. I just didn't want the world finding out too soon.' He took another swallow. 'Might have affected the share price.'

He drained his glass and went back to the drinks cabinet. He filled a glass with ice and uncapped the whisky bottle. Ahmed watched him seriously.

'Newman's share price or yours?'

Jake sent him a quizzical look over his shoulder. 'Ahmed, my friend, you're a shrewd guy. My engagement isn't worth a ha'penny on Dare's share price. Most people who hold our stock don't know whether I'm a man or a machine. They certainly don't care if I'm married.'

'Old Newman using you to underwrite his borrowing?'

16

Jake looked ironic. 'Nothing so crude. Nobody actually asked me to sign anything.'

Ahmed read anger and bitter self-mockery in his friend's face. 'But –?'

Jake poured his drink and came back.

'Oh, you know the form.' He sounded weary suddenly. 'Select dinner parties. The conversation turns on Newman's projects. I've never heard the details of any of them and I'm not interested enough to ask. But the dining table is stuffed with bankers. They know I'm the son-in-law elect. They think I'm part of the deal. Only they're much too polite to *ask*. So it all floats along on innuendo and false assumptions.' He looked down into the liquid in his glass as if it were a personal enemy. 'The last guy to find out is the poor fool taking the fall.'

Ahmed waited.

'God, I hate the English. They're so damned well-mannered and such damned liars.'

'So you got out?'

Jake shrugged. He did not say any more.

'But no one is quite sure? Is the break-up still secret? Nobody told me there was an announcement.'

Jake looked at the ceiling. His expression was the height of boredom. 'Rosie's department. She'll get round to it.'

Ahmed hesitated. 'Do you want to talk about this?'

Jake grimaced. 'What's to talk about? I made a fool of myself. Not the first. Won't be the last. At least I got away before the alimony started ticking up.'

The prince was shocked, though he tried to hide it. Jake saw it. He gave a grin. There was more than a hint of the devil in it.

'Not chivalrous enough for you, old buddy?' he mocked.

'Not chivalrous enough for you,' Ahmed corrected quietly. 'I've never seen you like this. What happened, for heaven's sake? Is this really because Rosie's father is an old fixer?'

But Jake had thrown up a hand. 'Not the subject for a gentleman to talk about. And no fun at all for a friendly evening. Let's just say I know more than I did about woman the deceiver. A good lesson well learned, as my old granpappy used to say.'

Ahmed looked even more disturbed. He started to demand further explanation. But then Marriott came in to announce dinner and the moment passed.

It was only later that Ahmed had another disturbing glimpse of the change in Jake Dare. They were discussing the possibility of a climbing holiday in the Dolomites when Jake suddenly pushed back his chair and stood up.

'Oh, it's impossible. I'm nothing like fit enough.'

'Then get fit,' said Ahmed equably.

'No time.' Jake was curt. 'Too many projects.'

Ahmed laughed. 'Delegate. You're the big boss now. That's what bosses do.'

'Only if they have the people to delegate to. My development manager has no initiative and my field manager has too much. Plus I have a PA with an IQ struggling to make it into two figures and a public relations department that spends all its time making speeches to schools.'

He sounded wry, but there was no disguising his real impatience. Ahmed, who knew him very well, saw it clearly. It was there in the tense shoulders, the snapping eyes.

'You look like a man about to lose his temper.'

Jake pushed one hand through his hair. He gave an angry sigh. 'What's the point? They all need brain transplants. I sometimes think I'm the only one who can do anything.'

'Dangerous,' murmured Ahmed.

But Jake didn't hear him. 'Take this Lawrence thing. Complete fiasco.'

'What Lawrence thing is that?' asked Ahmed obligingly.

Jake looked startled for a moment, as if he had forgotten he was talking to someone else. A rueful smile touched the corner of his mouth and his tone became more measured.

'It's a project in Oxfordshire. Nothing important. It's tiny. It should be completely trouble free. It certainly shouldn't give anyone nightmares about the responsibility. In the context of Dare Properties, it couldn't be less important. But can they handle it? Can they fly to the moon?'

His friend watched him, amused. 'So you have to take it on yourself,' interpreted Ahmed. 'Even though it's so unimportant?'

Jake's teeth flashed in a ghost of his old devil-may-care smile. 'In the context of Dare Properties it's unimportant,' he corrected. 'In the context of my ego, it's a record breaker.'

'At least you're honest,' Ahmed said drily.

Jake lifted one shoulder. 'I don't lie to myself. Whoever else I might – er – mislead. No point.'

Ahmed nodded, accepting it. That was Jake Dare as he remembered him. 'And why is your ego involved at all?'

'My company. My ego,' Jake said simply. 'Besides, the

opposition is some little old spinster lady who wants to turn the place into a cat sanctuary.'

'What?' Ahmed stared.

'You heard me. Ninety years old if she's a day and talking to the animals, God help us. Presumably she thinks out-of-town shopping malls are contrary to the law of nature.'

Ahmed flung back his head and roared with laughter. Jake spread his hands.

'You have to see my point,' he pleaded. 'I can't let Dare Properties be outmanoeuvred by some geriatric fruitcake. You've got to see that. It's not just ego. It's a matter of self-respect.'

Ahmed stopped laughing. 'And what about the self-respect of this little old lady, my friend?'

'She'll get over it. I'll give her the money to build the biggest cat sanctuary in the western world,' said Jake indifferently.

Ahmed was concerned. 'And all because of some deal which you admit is not important to you? Just because you have to win? Don't you care about anything except winning anymore, Jake?'

The smile died out of the handsome face, leaving it hard and determined.

'Can't afford to,' Jake said curtly. 'Caring is for losers.'

'Caring,' said Ash aloud. 'What a mistake.'

She was curled up in the big Queen Anne chair in the library and she was looking at her wedding photograph. She remembered the day so clearly: dressed up in stiff satin, made-up and lacquered to within an inch of her life;

20

so desperately anxious not to let anyone down; so grateful. Oh, she had cared then, all right. Cared altogether too much for Peter, her family, everyone. Cared so much that she had never even thought that she might need a little left over to look after herself.

Outside the dark was almost total. Above the trees, the moon was visible in fuzzy outline. The room was silent apart from the snores emanating from Rusty. The dog had crawled under the library table and fallen asleep, his nose on his paws. In spite of the snores, Ash was grateful for his presence. It made her feel less alone.

'Why was I such a *fool*?'

She sat very still in the pool of light cast by a small table lamp. She was holding the photograph on her lap but she was not really looking at it any more. She shivered. Her fingers were cold. They had gone numb with the pressure she was exerting on the glossy paper.

'It's not even as if he ever said he loved me.'

Not before the wedding. Not even when he asked her to marry him. And certainly not after. In spite of the public indulgence of his girl-bride, as he called her.

'Ugh,' said Ash, shifting in angry embarrassment at the memory.

Oh yes, he had told everyone what a precious creature she was. So young, of course, and hopelessly naive. According to Peter, she was helpless without a husband to take care of her. But it was, he announced, his privilege to do just that. In witness of it there had been photographs of her everywhere: in his wallet, in the London flat, in a big formal frame on his desk at the bank.

Her grandfather had been delighted. She was very

lucky, he told Ash. Not many eighteen-year olds found steady, mature chaps like Peter. Even fewer could boast a husband so utterly devoted to them.

Ash shuddered, looking down at the picture between her icy fingers. She and Peter were side by side on the church steps. She was wearing clouds of white, with her grandmother's pearl and diamond necklace pressed into service to secure the heirloom lace that was her veil.

Peter had been pleased. 'You look like a princess,' he had said.

Ash pressed the picture to her bosom suddenly, her mouth twisting. Once that photograph had stood in a silver frame on the desk in Peter's elegant study. The frame was now empty, pushed into the bottom of a drawer of spare linen. She had moved the photograph to the library. She kept it in the bookcase between *Pride and Prejudice* and *Tales of Robin Hood*. No one but Ash knew it was there.

She did not look at it often; just sometimes when she needed to remind herself. Truth, she thought, was a tricky thing. People saw what they wanted to see and in Ash they saw a young and grieving widow, bereft at the cruel end of a perfect marriage. Sometimes, after a weekend with Peter's family or a visit from particularly tactful friends, she almost believed it herself.

That was when she came to the library, took Jane Austen off the shelf and brought out this secret talisman. It reminded her better than anything of the truth of her marriage. The truth that no one else knew.

'I could be a completely different person.'

The girl in the picture was infinitely younger, not just by the ten years that separated her from her wedding but

22

by a knowledge she could not even have imagined then. Although, even then, she had known there was *something* . . .

She was almost beautiful in the photograph, Ash thought now dispassionately. She had had a professional make-up for the wedding. People said every bride did. Peter had insisted. She had not felt very comfortable but, as she always did in those days, she assumed everyone else knew best. They were always telling her they did.

So here she was, arm in arm with her handsome husband, looking at the camera with cleverly shaded eyes. It was like an eighteen-century cameo, pretty and expressionless. Only her mouth gave her away. And then only if you looked closely.

Ash put her head on one side, considering it as if the girl in the shot were a stranger. Sweetly full about the lower lip, exquisitely shaped and tinted, her mouth nevertheless seemed to tremble on the edge of expression. It was as if she had not known whether to smile or cry out in desperation. The photographer, she remembered irrelevantly, had not been pleased with his efforts.

'I don't understand it,' he had said when he brought them to her after the honeymoon. 'I'm usually better than this. I couldn't get the starch out somehow. I just couldn't find the joy.'

Ash had smiled and been polite. She could not blame him. She knew exactly why, for all his expertise and fashionable professionalism, he had not been able to find the joy. It was because, she had realized, it was not there. Already, after less than four weeks of marriage, the slow freeze had started inside her.

23

She flung the photograph away from her angrily and got up.

'Ancient history!'

Rusty stirred and lifted his nose in sleepy enquiry. Ash jumped, becoming aware of him suddenly.

'Sorry, dog.'

She put a reassuring hand down and patted the top of his head. He gave a gusty sigh and went back to sleep. She went over to the window and looked out into the shadows of the garden. How many times had she done the same thing, waiting for Peter to come from London?

'Ancient history,' she said again fiercely. 'Don't get self-pitying at this stage, for God's sake. What you need is food.'

She prowled restlessly round the kitchen, considering and rejecting everything that the fridge or the cupboards had to offer. In the end she decided to make herself a cheese sandwich, hacking off doorstep slices of crusty bread and packing them with wedges of cheese the size of chicken thighs. When it was finished, Ash looked at it critically.

'Wine,' she decided.

She hardly ever drank. But for some reason, tonight's restlessness had resolved itself into a hard determination to do whatever she damn well pleased. She investigated the cellar and came back with a prize. Putting everything on a tray she took it back to the library.

'There,' she said, curling up in her chair again with her goodies. 'No one to tell me to have a balanced meal. No one to make me sit up at table and eat properly. Bliss.'

Ash sipped the wine thoughtfully. It was delicious on

the tongue, redolent of summer herbs. It was one of Peter's prize white burgundies. He had bought it, she was fairly sure, to impress their guests. Probably her grandfather, Ash thought wryly.

Peter would be horrified if he could see her drinking it on her own, still dressed in grubby jeans, without a scrap of make-up or a single jewel. Peter had known the value of things like wine. He knew Chablis Premier Grand Cru deserved caviar and diamonds and a proper audience.

'Which has to be you,' Ash told the sleeping retriever. She raised her glass to him. 'Wonderful year, darling.'

The dog did not react. Ash gave a choke of laughter and reached for her doorstep of a sandwich.

'The trouble with you,' she told him, 'is you don't care about appearances. You just encourage me.' She stirred him with her foot. 'No point in trying to hide it. Our standards have slipped so far they're off the graph.'

She took a chomp of her giant sandwich and washed it down with the Chablis. She felt an ignoble triumph.

'Just as well there's nobody to see. Let's make sure it stays that way.'

CHAPTER 2

Three days later Ash sat in the library in the Manor with the morning's post in front of her. She was in a towering temper.

'How dare they? Oh, how dare they?'

The trouble was that it was not just temper. Dare Properties had begun to sound threatening. Their latest letter was from Chief Executive J. T. Dare. Ash had read it in disbelief. The threats were veiled, but Ash could see them clearly enough. If she did not co-operate J. T. Dare was going to make sure his corporate henchmen did everything they could to run her out of her own home.

It was nonsense, of course. The rational part of Ash knew it was nonsense. But the irrational part of her – the part that had once been a frightened child listening to her grandfather's cold tirades – remembered all too clearly what powerful men could do when they put their minds to it.

Only a few days ago, she had had that shivery feeling that she might leave the Manor. Was it prophetic? Could her sub-conscious mind possibly have picked up that it was inevitable that J. T. Dare would turn her out of her beloved home?

'Sheer superstition,' said Ash, aloud.

But she could not quite forget that restlessness, that incomprehensible sense of doom. It was an affront. She found she hated J. T. Dare. By a simple letter he had managed to churn her up to the point where she was no longer thinking clearly. What was more, he had managed to stir up a host of unwelcome feelings that Ash had thought were put to rest a long time ago.

What made it particularly offensive, thought Ash, looking at the brief letter on its heavy cream notepaper, was that he had not even bothered to sign it himself. She could just imagine the scenario: J. T. Dare stamping off to some amazingly important meeting, flinging an instruction at his secretary as he went.

'Just type these up and sign them will you, Miss Jones?'

She had heard her grandfather do it a hundred times. And Peter had been developing the same imperious manner when – Her thoughts broke off sharply.

'I *hate* big business,' she said out loud. She said it with real passion.

That was better. Anger was good. A determination to fight back would be even better. She reread the letter in gathering wrath. She was not belligerent by nature but she was quite clear that Mr J. T. Dare needed to be taught a lesson. A big lesson. Soon.

She was composing some choice ways of pointing this out to him when the library door burst open. Ash looked up. She was torn between annoyance at the interruption and a reluctant feeling that a period to cool off would be no bad thing.

If her upbringing had taught her anything, it was that it

was wiser not to start a war in a white-hot temper. Or not if you wanted to win. Particularly not if your enemy was a clever strategist. However much she disliked business-men, Ash did not make the mistake of underestimating them. If J. T. Dare was half the opponent her grandfather would have been, then she needed to think about her next move very carefully.

A domestic crisis was never welcome. But on this occasion it might provide a useful diversion, Ash thought wryly. It was just as well she was prepared to take a long view. When her housekeeper stormed into the room it was clear she was not going to go away. Ash pushed J. T. Dare's impertinent letter away from her.

'What is it?'

Em Harrison was a large woman with a large voice. 'It's got to stop.'

Ash was startled. She knew most of Em's habitual complaints and this announcement did not seem to be leading toward any of them.

'What has?' she asked, reasonably enough.

Em was not in a mood to have any truck with reason. 'Enough is enough. I've had my bellyful. Time something was done. And if you won't, I'm going to.'

Ash got up from behind the mahogany desk. It dwarfed her slight frame and she knew it. She had seldom felt less in control and this sounded serious.

'What on earth is wrong?' she demanded anxiously.

Em glared. 'Animals,' she said in tones of loathing.

That, of course, explained everything. Some of the anxiety left Ash. 'Oh.'

Ash's lips twitched. She felt a strong desire to laugh, but

she suppressed it. Em Harrison did not like animals. Or at least she strongly preferred children. It was her view, frequently expressed, that Ashley Lawrence was deliberately wasting her considerable affection on a lot of smelly, furry things, when she should be finding a nice husband and having babies.

Ash was well aware of this. She said firmly, 'Animals come with the territory.'

Em sniffed. When she had first come to work for successful young Mr and Mrs Lawrence it was in the clear expectation that before long there would be lots of little Lawrences for her to take care of. Polishing and cooking were all very well, but what she really liked was running a nursery. It was a bitter disappointment to her that no babies arrived. Then young Peter Lawrence died tragically in that terrible car accident.

Ash had been shattered, Em knew. For weeks she had walked around as if she had not known which planet she was on. Even her father had not been able to get more than a perfunctory smile out of her. For a while Em had almost despaired.

When Ash started to help out at that animal centre Em had been glad. At least she had started to look human again, even though she had lost a shocking amount of weight. It was only slowly that Em began to realize that the animal centre was not the temporary therapy she had thought it would be. The housework became even more unsatisfying. Animals walked all over her beautiful shining furniture before she had put her polishing rags away. And when she complained Ash just laughed.

All that had been three years ago. Ash was better now,

no question. The shadow was almost entirely gone from her sherry brown eyes. She no longer looked like a skeleton. But she still showed no sign of remarrying and starting the family she was so patently meant for, in Em's opinion. And, worst of all, she still filled the house with animal waifs and strays.

No, Em definitely did not like animals. When roused, as now, her contempt for them was terrible to behold.

Ash said soothingly, 'It can't be that bad. Whatever it is, I'll clear it up. Which animals and what have they done?'

'Cats,' snarled Em. 'One of those dratted kittens has been in my flour bin.'

'Oh,' said Ash. She made a gallant attempt but her voice was not entirely steady.

Em gave her a look of deepest suspicion. Not surprisingly, as Ash was having trouble maintaining her sober expression. She coughed, hoping it masked the rising laughter. From's Em expression, it did not do so well enough.

'All very well for you to laugh. Them cats are downright insanitary.'

'Yes, I know,' said Ash contritely. 'I'm sorry.'

'I'll have to throw the flour away. All of it. Great big five-pound jar,' said Em, grieving. 'It's a wicked waste.'

'I know,' Ash said again.

She did not say that with all her money she could afford any number of five-pound jars of flour for her cats to play in. It would not have occurred to her. Waste had been one of the deadly sins in her childhood. In fact it was probably the only deadly sin, apart from murder, that her grandfather had never committed. Flour, he would have said, was food and food was precious when so many people did not have enough. Ash could hear him say it. A part of her even agreed with him.

So she did not try to console Em by saying they could easily make good the kittens' depredations. Instead, she made a sympathetic noise and concentrated on keeping her face straight.

'*And* it's trodden in all over my kitchen,' Em added challengingly.

'I'll clean it. I'll clean it,' said Ash.

She looked down at the leather correspondence folder on her desk and slammed it shut. This was real. The palaces of steel and glass which, rumour said, Dare Properties wanted to build on her five-acre Hayes Wood were not. J. T. Dare and his high-handed announcement that he would call on her would just have to wait.

She refolded his letter and shoved it into the back pocket of her jeans before running after Em. J. T. Dare, she thought with a grin, would not like it if he knew his high-handed letter was less important than her housekeeper's feelings about a bunch of kittens. She thought of what her grandfather's reaction would have been. Apoplexy probably.

Maybe she could find a way to mention it in her reply. J. T. Dare deserved apoplexy. Ash laughed aloud, her temper restored.

But the moment she got into the kitchen she forgot her preoccupation. It looked as if there had been a small snowstorm. Ash stopped dead, impressed.

'See?' said Em gloomily at her shoulder.

The devastation was so complete that it banished all her

31

darker thoughts. Common sense returned. Ash found herself repressing a desire to giggle.

'I see what you mean.'

Em must have been preparing to cook pastry. It was all set out on the scrubbed kitchen table – butter, jug of water, mixing bowl, rolling pin; and of course the flour bin. It was an old-fashioned white affair, about two foot high, with FLOUR written on it in black letters and a lid like a Chinaman's hat.

The lid had been pushed sideways. An enterprising kitten had clearly clambered up the side of the bin until the container tipped over, scattering flour and kitten across the table and a fair part of the surrounding floor. There were small white paw marks where he had run for his life as the bin began to fall.

There were more paw marks where the kitten – and several of his brothers, Ash deduced – had returned to the flour. They had obviously darted in and out of the bin many times before collapsing in a white powdered heap on the rocking chair. They now lay there, three of them, wrapped around each other and deeply asleep. A faint treble purring rose from the collection of fluff and whiskers. The imprint of white-floured paws covered the kitchen.

'I'll clean it,' Ash said again hastily before Em could start to complain again. She could feel her shoulders shaking. 'I'll just get the Hoover.'

She did so. Em sat down on the bentwood chair by the Aga and watched her critically. There was much to criticize. Ash was not good with machinery.

'That's all very well. But what about my baking?' Em shouted over the noise of the machine.

'Don't worry about it,' Ash shouted back.

'But you won't have a scone or a bit of cake in the house to offer anyone.'

'That's OK. I'm not expecting anyone.'

'But what if the new man at the Gate House comes up to introduce himself?'

Ash decided that the machine had done all it could. She switched it off. From now on she was on her hands and knees with the dustpan and brush.

'Why should he?' she said absently.

Em lowered her eyes and tried to look innocent. Ash was alert suddenly.

'Why should he?' she repeated.

Em gave an elaborate shrug. 'He was in the shop on Saturday morning. Handsome chap. Nicely spoken, too.'

Ash closed her eyes. 'You told him to call,' she said on a note of mock despair.

Em looked virtuous. 'Neighbours should know each other. Only right.'

Ash opened her eyes. 'Em, you're impossible. I suppose you told him to come to tea? Did you actually put a date in the diary or is he going to come strolling up here one day when I'm up to my armpits in the compost heap?'

'I didn't tell him to do nothing,' said Em, offended. 'He was the one asking. He wanted to know who lived in the Manor. I just answered him civil.' She drew herself to her full height. 'And I'll thank you to do the same.'

'And I'll thank you to stop matchmaking,' Ash retorted.

Em sniffed, unrepentant. The rocking chair began to rock ominously as one of the kittens stretched and turned. Em turned a basilisk stare on it.

33

'Look,' said Ash hurriedly, 'there's no point in you sitting here watch me make a pig's ear of this. Why don't you go and sit outside in the sun? I'll bring you a cup of tea when I've finished.'

'You don't pay me to sit idle sunning myself,' objected Em.

'And I don't pay you to kill my cats,' Ash said candidly. 'Which is what you will do if you have to clear up this mess. Go on. It won't take me long.'

It took an hour. She went at it with a will, but she had more enthusiasm that science and it showed.

'The trouble is I wasn't trained for this,' Ash told the kitchen ruefully.

The trouble was she had been trained for nothing, she thought. Or nothing but being the wife of the next man to run Kimbell's. Neither grandfather nor Peter had ever expected her to spring clean a floury kitchen. Or do anything except look elegant, arrange flowers and organize impeccable dinner parties. She thought involuntarily: and never, ever need love.

The memory made her momentarily violent. Under the fierce slap of her brush the flour flew up in a cloud of white dust. It settled on her red curls like eighteenth-century hair powder. A kitten sneezed in its sleep. It dispelled the dark memories like sunlight. Ash laughed.

'No method,' she said sadly. 'Story of my life.'

She resumed brushing but less vigorously and in the end it was done.

When Ash took the promised tea out to the housekeeper, Em was as deeply asleep as the kittens. Unlike them, however, she snored. Grinning, Ash put the mug

34

quietly down on the wooden table beside her. It was going to make a ring stain on the wood, she saw. Ash fished in her pocket for something to stand it on.

The only thing that emerged was the letter from Dare Properties' J. T. Dare telling her he thought they had better meet.

'That's what I think of you and your letter,' Ash told him silently.

She stuffed it under the mug. And promptly forgot it.

In fact, she forgot the matter so comprehensively that it was not until she was taking the dog for a walk in the twilight that she even remembered that she had still to reply to the letter. It was no longer outside on the table. Nor, though Ash rooted around in the kitchen, was it there. But it had gone. Em must have thrown it away.

Ash considered the pedal bin for a courageous moment, then made a face.

'Not that important. If J. T. Dare wants a reply he can always write again,' she decided reasonably.

She put it out of her mind.

Jake Dare was still in the office. He was not in a good temper. He had stormed in like a whirlwind after a site visit to find his staff celebrating somebody's birthday.

'Have some wine,' said Tony Anderson. He was Jake's PA and braver than most. Besides, he had a position to maintain.

Jake declined and went to his office.

After that the party decided to move on to a West End wine bar. Promising to join them later, Tony went to his chief's room.

The desk was a chaos of notes and architects' plans but Jake was not looking at them. He was standing at the window, surveying the fine view of the park which had doubled the rent over their previous building. He had discarded jacket and tie; his hands were in his pockets. He was very still.

Tony Anderson took one look at the back of his head and decided the boss was in his most dangerous mood.

'Anything I can do?' he said from the doorway.

Jake did not look round. 'The Hayes Wood development. Nothing seems to be happening.'

'Well, Stenson is making the announcement on Thursday. After that, the formal permissions should come through in a couple of days. The planning authority has OK'd them in principle. Of course we still have to deal with Mrs Lawrence . . .'

'Yeah,' said Jake softly. He turned. 'Tony, do you know what is most likely to go wrong? Where the vulnerabilities are at this stage of a project?'

Tony looked blank. 'Vulnerabilities?'

'Opportunities for cock up,' said Jake sweetly. 'Yeah. Where are the risks?'

The PA thought about it. 'Well – I don't know – um – maybe if the planning people changed their minds?' he offered.

Jake sighed. 'Or the banks decided not to lend. Or the sub-contractors put up their prices. Or the specifications were increased so they wiped out the profit. All of those. And do you know what is the most likely reason for any of those?'

Tony decided prudently not to venture a suggestion.

'Publicity. Stinking publicity. Locals decide they don't want us and the whole thing starts to smell like burning rubber. So who do we need to keep on our side?'

That one was easy. 'The locals.'

'And what sort of contact have we had with the residents?'

Tony began to see what was coming. In swift self-defence he said, 'We've got deals with the three main people who are affected. They're not really organized.'

'Not,' said Jake grimly, 'yet. How do you think the villagers are going to feel when Mrs Lawrence totters down to the village hall and pins up that stupid letter you wrote her?'

Tony grinned. 'You wrote to her.'

'What?'

'I got Barbara to sign it on your behalf. More impressive coming from the boss. Besides,' he added honestly, 'she sent me off with a flea in my ear. Mrs Lawrence didn't like me one bit. I thought she'd be more respectful if you sent the letter.'

Jake drew a violent breath. 'It doesn't matter a damn who the letter comes from. What matters is what it says. What you've written is tantamount to a threat.'

Tony started to protest. Jake silenced him with a chopping movement of the hand.

'She's not a City player. You can't write to her as if she were.'

'But – '

'You have to handle members of the public carefully. Especially,' added Jake cynically, 'when they're lone females with a caring agenda and a bunch of extras with four feet and fur. Think of the photo opportunities. Can you imagine what the papers would make of it?'

'Oh,' said Tony. He sucked his teeth. 'What do you want me to do about it?'

'You've done enough. From now on, I'm handling Mrs Lawrence myself.' Jake shrugged himself into his Savile Row jacket as if it were cowboy's suede. 'You may be able to handle the opposition, but you've got a lot to learn about the caring, sharing movement.'

'Caring,' said Ash aloud as she made her way to the old stables the next morning through the dew wet grass, 'can be overrated.' She shivered.

The twin sons of a neighbour had found a wounded badger cub and brought it to Ash a few nights ago. The local RSPCA inspector had inspected it, shook his head dubiously over its chances of survival, and left Ash a regimen for the little creature. So far, in spite of Bob Cummings' doubts, the badger seemed to be holding his own.

This morning the badger raised a sleepy nose from his box when she went into the garage. Ash saw it with relief. At least he had weathered another night. She was feeding him when the Hall twins arrived under the escort of disapproving Em. They were accompanied by Ash's golden retriever, Rusty, returned from his morning forage along the stream.

Ash looked up, pushing the tangle of red curls back from her face. Rusty thrust his nose under her elbow and she rubbed his head as he wanted her to.

'Hello.'

'Hello,' the boys said politely.

But there was no doubt where their main interest lay. Standing up, Ash relinquished the feeding of the badger cub to his rescuers. She stepped back, watching critically. At her elbow, Em sniffed.

'Fine way to spend your time, wild animals and other people's children. What you want is some of your own,' she told Ash roundly. 'And a man, of course. You're not getting any younger,' she added with the licence of ten years' service.

'I'm twenty-eight,' Ash said evenly. 'Which makes me old enough to run my life.'

'And a fine mess you're making of it,' Em muttered.

Ash remained determinedly impassive. The flour disaster had clearly upset Em more than she had realized. Normally she confined her disapproval of Ash's solitary lifestyle to heavy hints. Except when she got together with Ash's father, of course. Sir Miles and Em were at one on the unnaturalness of a girl of her age living alone in the middle of the country.

Though their preferred solutions were different, Ash thought, biting back a sudden grin. Em's ideas ran to a white wedding on the lawn with several hundred guests. Sir Miles was much more inclined to urge his only daughter to find herself a lover and start having some fun at last. Fortunately, Em was unaware of the precise nature of this paternal advice, or their cosy chats together would have ceased abruptly.

She really cared for Ash, though. So it was gently that Ash said, 'It's a mess I've chosen and a mess I like. Not anyone's business but mine.'

Em sniffed. But she did not say anymore. Partly because she knew Ash was not going to listen, partly because they were joined by someone else. Em did not talk about Ash's affairs in front of other people, especially those she disapproved of.

Ash looked up as Rusty began to bark at the new arrival. She smiled when she saw the uniform.

Bob Cummings was a friend. He had joined the local RSPCA two years ago, so he had never known Peter. Ash found that helped in developing a spontaneous relationship. Also, sharing her interest in animals, he did not think she was seriously peculiar because of the creatures that wandered in and out of the Manor. This made a welcome change from most of her neighbours.

'Hello, Bob. You're about early.'

'Got a conference in Oxford,' he said. 'Thought I'd drop in on the way. How's the cub?'

Ash made a gesture at the box the boys were poring over.

'As you see. Alive and greedy.'

Bob looked pleased. 'Good for you. I didn't think he'd survive.'

'Nor did Alan,' said Ash ruefully. Alan was the local vet. 'But Humbug has had intensive care from the boys.'

'Humbug!' Bob shook his head. He did not approve of giving names to wild animals.

Ash laughed. 'Don't worry. The badger will go back to the wild. You have my word. Anyway, he'll get bored with the garage when he's better and want to go.'

'Ah, but will the boys get bored with the badger?' said Bob unanswerably, with a nod in their direction.

40

Neither of them looked up or seemed aware that he was there. He raised an eyebrow. Ash laughed again, shaking her head.

'You may have a point,' she admitted. 'We'll have to sort that one out when we come to it.'

Bob went across to the injured cub. The boys fell back respectfully. They did not think much of the vet, who specialized in horses, but Bob was a man who knew about birds and woodland animals and was prepared to spend time teaching them.

Em watched suspiciously. She might want Ash to marry, but she was not enthusiastic about her getting so close to a middle-aged RSPCA inspector, with two marriages and, if the village grapevine was to be believed, crippling debts behind him. But she also knew there was no point in trying to influence Ash.

'I'll make coffee,' she said, giving up.

She stomped away, leaving Ash deep in conversation with Bob about the badger. The Hall twins added their contribution freely. Rusty, tense with concentration, was just managing to sit still, watching them.

Until, that is, the retriever heard the car and began to bark. He rocked backwards and forwards with agitation as he gave tongue.

'Rusty, shut up,' Ash said automatically. She knew she sounded as if she did not expect to be obeyed. She was not. 'I'm sorry,' she said to Bob Cummings. 'He thinks he's a watchdog. It goes to his head, rather. I'd better go and see who it is.'

'Probably someone missed his way,' said Bob, watching the badger cub's attempts to move about in his straw

41

bedding. 'He'll turn round when he realizes it's a private drive.' He looked up and smiled. 'No one but the RSPCA comes calling at eight in the morning.'

Ash grinned back. The car engine grew louder. Rusty began to shake himself hoarse with excitement. Ash dropped an absent hand onto the dog's head.

'Shut *up*, Rusty.' She sighed and said to Bob, 'I'll go and get rid of whoever it is. I'm not wild about visitors.' She caught sight of the boys' anxious faces and shook her head, catching herself quickly. 'I don't count the intensive care nursing unit as visitors, guys. Don't worry.'

Rusty was now leaping up and down. His bark was deafening. Ash sighed.

'*Quiet!*' She turned to Chris Hall. 'I'll go and see who it is. Keep Rusty under control, will you?'

Bob looked down at the retriever. He was jumping his own height from a standing start, his tongue lolling in pleased expectation.

'Bites milkmen?' Bob asked, amused. He knew that Rusty was as amiable as he was noisy.

'No, but he's taken to chasing cars,' Ash said. 'I think he's jealous that they make more noise than he can.'

Bob laughed. 'You keep him under control, young Chris. I don't want to have to explain to my boss about having my bumper bitten by a retriever.'

The boy grinned and took hold of the dog's collar. Bob looked at his watch.

'I ought to be off. The little chap doesn't seem distressed, anyway. And if he's taking food, there's a chance. I'll call back tonight if you like.'

'Thank you,' said Ash with real gratitude.

42

She led the way out into the sunshine and round the side of the Jacobean mansion. The Hall twins, carefully not touching, stood watch over the little badger, as Rusty subsided under Chris' restraining hand.

'They're good boys, those two,' Bob said approvingly.

Ash grinned. 'Not if you listen to their mother. Or Em.'

Bob stopped, a hand clapped to his pocket. 'Em. I promised her Steve a tape. I'll just stop off in the kitchen with it.'

'Fine,' said Ash.

Her tone was absent and there was a faint frown between her brows, as he went. The car was not turning round and going back the way it had come. In fact, it sounded very much as if it was stopping.

She hurried round the corner of the house, oblivious of the soft scent of wallflowers or the last of the dew winking like diamonds on the lawns. But when she saw the car, Ash stopped dead, blinking.

It was even bigger and shinier than any of the rocket-engined monsters that Peter had insisted on buying, but then Peter had preferred flash to style. As it cruised to a stop, an unwelcome suspicion began to rise.

'Damn,' she said under her breath.

Agitated, Ash stood on one leg, scanning the scene. She was running one foot up the back of her other calf. She became suddenly aware of it and stopped, self-conscious. It was a nervous habit she had never been aware of until her marriage. Peter had hated it and had shouted at her whenever she did it. She had not done it for years, she thought. Not since Peter died. She bit her lip.

The gleaming black door opened. Long legs in expensive pearl-grey suiting swung out. They were followed by an equally long, powerful body and an air of effortless command. The man got out and looked about him. He had a high, haughty profile. It made him look as if he were surveying land he was about to conquer.

Ash watched, mesmerized. *Oh no*, she thought. Not this one. Not now, when I'm feeling edgy and uncertain and everyone is getting at me to change.

Her instinct told her that this was Dare Properties returning to the charge. Why, oh why, had she just dustbinned that letter? Why had she not replied by return of post? Or, better still, phoned them and told Mr J. T. Dare in person what she thought of his bullying? Now she could only watch the stranger in gathering dismay.

All she could think of was that he was entirely different from the one before. The first one had been elegant, smooth and diplomatic. This one was, if possible, even more elegant. But there was nothing smooth about him. His air of power was like a second skin. Just to look at him said that he knew what he wanted and how to get it. He would not bother with diplomacy. He would not need to.

Ash swallowed, her mouth drying. Take control, she told herself. Take control. You're being fanciful again. This man can do nothing to you. Take a good look at him. He is a man, not a force of nature.

She did. He was tall, she saw. He had broad shoulders but he was thin as a razor. His eyes were hidden by dark glasses. But nothing hid the high, haughty cheekbones and aquiline nose; or the unmistakable aura of ruthless power. The thin, almost harsh, face was without expression as he looked around him.

44

And at last that slow inspection found her. Their eyes met. In spite of the fact that the darkened lenses hid his eyes, Ash knew it. A little shock went through her body and her head jerked backwards as if at a physical impact.

The hair rose on the back of her neck. Something caught at her throat. This one's dangerous, she thought; really dangerous. For endless seconds his eyes seemed to bore into her, like a drill, exposing every quivering nerve to his uninterested gaze.

Then, with an almost visible shrug, his inspection moved on. She had been dismissed as negligible. Ash went very still. She had been dismissed as negligible before. But not for a very long time. And not when she had the weapons to fight back. No one – *no one* – was ever going to do that to her again.

Ash began to walk towards him, delicately, like a cat in unknown country. She was going to make him look at her, acknowledge her as a person, if it was the last thing she did. One look at the car, the tailoring and the air of confidence and a host of forgotten feelings began to surge inside her. And they all needed purging.

He stopped his assessing sweep of the Manor and gave her a brief, indifferent nod.

'I'd like to see Mrs Lawrence, please.'

As she would have expected the tone was pleasant but with an air of easy authority. He did not expect to be denied. All the autocrats Ash had ever known had sounded like that and she had been brought up by autocrats. For a moment she hesitated.

'Who are you?' she demanded abruptly.

The dark stranger looked at her again. His brows rose in

faint surprise. Ash deduced with satisfaction that he was used to a warmer greeting from the female sex, even from unimportant members of staff. She had not bothered to disguise her hostility and it disconcerted him. Or at least, it surprised him sufficiently to make him look at her properly, she thought. He even took off his dark glasses. It was a victory of a sort.

His eyes were green ice and as cold as the north pole. He let them travel over her. Under his slow, incredulous scrutiny Ash began to wonder if it was such a victory after all. She became conscious of the stains that the badger had left on her tee-shirt and the straw that had attached itself to various areas of her person. She knew her face was dirty, probably smudged with dust. She had just pulled her curly red mop into a rubber band at the base of her neck this morning and fronds had been escaping ever since; so her hair was all over the place. The stranger's inspection told her so. It also told her, very clearly, that she looked scruffy and belligerent and about sixteen.

He did not say anything. He did not have to.

It put her even further at a disadvantage. She felt her colour rise.

She saw the man take it in at a glance, that swift shaming blush. She saw his surprise turn to sudden and unwelcome interest. Not that it warmed his eyes up by a single degree. It made her acutely uneasy, that cold examination of a new phenomenon.

For his part, Jake Dare made a slow, thoughtful assessment of the picture before him: not as tall as her disreputable garb made her look; reed slim; the grubby face a perfect oval with the red-head's ivory skin. And the long-

46

lashed eyes were the colour of Madeira wine and would no doubt melt a heart of stone if she chose to use them properly, he thought. At the moment she was glaring.

To Ash's astonishment the stranger, having finished his leisurely inspection, gave her a charming smile. And his eyes weren't cold any more. Not cold at all.

'My name is Jake Dare. I wrote. If Mrs Lawrence . . .'

Ash almost stamped, she was so angry. She recognized the name, of course. So the foot-soldier, defeated, had called in the cavalry, she thought in fury. Well, she could deal with the cavalry too.

She lifted her chin. Stiff-backed she said curtly, 'I'm Mrs Lawrence.'

That, she saw with real satisfaction, stopped Jake Dare in his tracks. The charm flickered out. His eyes narrowed. She saw she had been wrong about the colour. They were not wholly green, there was grey in there too, no less icy than the green but somehow more menacing. Meeting them squarely she had the conviction that the news had astonished him; and, quite suddenly, made him very angry.

'*You?*'

'Ashley Lawrence,' she said crisply. 'What can I do for you?'

'The little old widow lady? Living alone with only her menagerie for company?' He sounded incredulous.

For no reason she could think of, Ash flushed. 'You seem to know more about me than I do about you,' she said, trying to sound indifferent.

He submitted her to a comprehensive survey. 'On the contrary,' he said slowly. 'I don't seem to know anything at all.'

47

It did not sound as if it were intended as a compliment. Ash glared.

From the way his mouth tilted, she saw that she had made a mistake. Jake Dare clearly found her dislike faintly amusing, even a challenge. He had probably negotiated with a lot of people who started off hating him, she thought. He had the relaxed air of a man who had seen this sort of reaction before and didn't let himself worry about it.

Then he gave her a smile of sudden, blinding, charm. 'I'm sorry. You got me off-balance there for a moment, Mrs Lawrence. I must be more jet-lagged than I thought.'

He held out his hand. Ash looked at it woodenly. Her thoughts were in turmoil. Her every instinct told her that this was a dangerous animal. If she wanted to fight him and his project she would have to do it very carefully. Be diplomatic. Be cautious.

But pride and an odd, irrational panic, urged her to order him off her land now.

She curbed the panic and looked him up and down, much as he had inspected her. At least, she thought wryly, she was not entirely without defences. She had lived with Peter quite long enough to learn the jungle tactics of big business.

Looking at his outstretched hand, she recognized this one: dazzle the poor little country girl with his international sophistication; then explain to her that the only mature and sensible thing to do was what he wanted.

She contemplated refusing to shake hands. The business jungle operated on superficial good manners, at least in the outer reaches. Blatant rudeness would give him a problem. She wondered how he would deal with it.

But then she remembered the state of her own hands, covered with dirt. Smiling grimly, she took his outstretched hand and shook it, liberally transferring debris to his own impeccable palm.

Jake Dare was too experienced to flinch. But there was no doubt that he stiffened. However, his recovery time was minimal. Reluctantly, she had to concede that. Almost at once, he was giving her another charming smile.

If possible it made her even more suspicious. She met his eyes levelly. That gave away nothing. Whatever his shock when she had announced who she was, he had regrouped his forces fast. Yes, definitely in a very different league from his predecessor.

Bob Cummings came round the corner of the house and stopped. Ash realized that her unwelcome visitor was still holding her hand. With a slight gasp, she tugged it away. She turned to Bob a little breathlessly. To her fury she knew there was unusual colour in her pale cheeks.

Bob gave her a faintly puzzled smile.

'Get lost did you? Easy to do on that road,' he said with a friendly nod in Jake Dare's direction. Without waiting for an answer he said to Ash, 'I'll be getting along then. Reckon you'll have things to do. I'll ring about the little fellow later.'

Ash felt deserted. But she was too proud to invent an excuse to keep him there until Jake Dare was gone. She sighed. 'All right, Bob. I'll do my best.'

He smiled at her. 'I'm sure. Nobody better. Good luck.'

He swung himself into his van and drove briskly off. As the noise of the van died away down the drive, Jake Dare leaned against his detestable shiny limousine and crossed his arms over his chest. He looked as if he was prepared to stay there all day, if necessary. Ash noted it from under her lashes.

Conscious of his steady gaze, she stared stubbornly at the ground. Em would no doubt think she ought to ask him in and offer him coffee or something. Ash compressed her lips and remained silent.

Eventually he sighed and said quite gently, 'Look, Mrs Lawrence, I didn't mean to get in the way. I can easily come back when it's more convenient.'

Ash resented the warm smile he gave her. The charm was almost tangible. Most women, she supposed, would have smiled in return. Most women would have been reassured by the gentle tone. Of course, most women did not have her experience of smooth businessmen to draw on. Jake Dare clearly knew a lot about women; presumably particularly if he wanted something from them. He would find Ashley Lawrence a new experience, she promised herself.

Ash shook her increasingly loosened hair back off her shoulders and said, 'If you're here to talk about buying my land to develop, no time would be convenient.'

He was clearly taken aback by the rudeness. Equally clearly he made one of those lightning decisions to ignore it. Ash watched his eyes flicker. In the blink of an eye she saw him decide that she was hardly more than a child after all and would repay patient handling. The speed of that calculation chilled her.

He said coolly, 'That's not very sensible.'

Ash's eyes flashed. 'I am not selling,' she said between her teeth.

The abominable man looked at her measuringly. 'Have I asked you to?'

It was somehow more threatening than the bullying she had braced herself for. He sounded so in control, so unconcerned. So – though she would have given all she possessed not to hear it – like Peter.

Ash began to shake. She could not have said herself whether it was due to temper or nerves. She saw his alert green eyes register her trembling. It was temper, she told herself. Pure temper and nothing else. She was not afraid of this man. He could not do anything to hurt her. He did not know her well enough to hurt her. So he was not like Peter at all.

'You don't have to,' she answered him contemptuously. 'Your errand boy made it perfectly clear. When *he* walked in without an invitation. And I told him. None of my land is for sale. At any price. Now get in your car,' she said, her voice rising, 'and go back the way you came. Before I call the papers and tell them you're harassing me.'

Jake Dare stayed where he was, still smiling. But the clever green eyes narrowed.

He said soothingly, 'Don't you think you're over-reacting?'

'No,' said Ash with unmistakable conviction. She was aware that anyone watching them would probably think she was unbalanced and decided stubbornly that she didn't care. 'I know people like you. Get out.'

His eyebrows climbed. 'My dear Mrs Lawrence . . .'

'I am not your dear anything,' Ash said furiously.

Jake Dare gave her a long, thoughtful look. Then he said equably, 'Of course, I'll go if you want me to. But I'm sure it would be better to talk.'

There was the faintest hint of challenge there. Just as there had been in his letter. Ash was sure it was quite deliberate.

She set her teeth. Her chin came up. Jake Dare met her angry eyes. He gave a lop-sided smile.

'Let me give you my card.' To her fury he did not sound angry; he sounded soothing. He brought a slim silver card case out of his breast pocket and opened it. 'Then you can call me when you've talked it over with your advisers.'

He handed her a small slip of pasteboard. Ash took it gingerly between finger and thumb, not looking at it. The gesture would, she hoped, make it perfectly plain that the small rectangle would be scrunched up in her fingers and lobbed away the moment his back was turned. And at least she had not been trapped into any more infantile petulance.

Jake Dare sighed. He did not look as if he was impressed by her gesture. He looked tired, Ash realized suddenly: not the contrived weariness of a man waiting for someone to come to her senses, but bone-deep tiredness, as if he was short of sleep and driving himself too hard.

It jolted her. It made him suddenly seem all too human. Ash twitched her shoulders impatiently. She did not want to start seeing this man as human. He was a predator and she could not afford to forget it.

But even as she was hesitating, Jake Dare lifted himself away from the car. He shrugged.

'Thank you for your time, Mrs Lawrence,' he said wryly. 'I'll be in touch.'

Ash made no attempt to answer him. For some reason the cool green gaze filled her with trepidation. In theory she had won but she had an uneasy feeling that Jake Dare was not the type to give up that easily. So she just stood there, looking, if she had but known it, young and beleaguered. The brown eyes were defensive and full of hostility.

Jake gave her an odd look. For a moment he seemed to hesitate. Ash held her breath. But then he shrugged again, quickly, and his mouth twisted as if in distaste. Without another word, he got into the car.

Ash let out a long, relieved breath.

He did not look at her again. With total concentration he engaged gear and turned the car round in a small, steady circle. Ash noted that, tired and annoyed as he undoubtedly was, he still drove with rally driver precision. The big engine made hardly a sound.

Ash saw him take a quick last look at the scene. Committing it to memory, presumably: essential information for the next battle in the war. She was not going to let him frighten her. She stood very straight, her expression implacable.

She was concentrating so hard on the man in front of her that she was not aware that Chris Hall was coming round the side of the house. Jake Dare did not notice anything either. He was staring ahead, his mouth grim. He was as startled as Ash when the air exploded into a cacophony of barking.

Ash spun round. Chris, a look of horror on his face, began to run forward. But he was a critical half-second behind Rusty. Realizing what was about to happen, Ash jumped for the dog's ruff – too late.

Jake caught only the briefest glimpse of the flying

retriever as Rusty leaped forward, aiming for the front offside wheel of the Mercedes. The look on the boy's face, however, was enough to have him hauling the wheel in the opposite direction as hard as he could go.

The tyres screamed. The big car skidded and slewed across the gravel. Dust rose like smoke from under its wheels. Only half-braced for the impact, Jake was flung violently sideways. His head connected with the offside window with an almighty crash.

In rapid reflex he turned the keys in the ignition and pulled them out as he sank, astonished, into oblivion.

CHAPTER 3

Ash was already running. Behind her, Chris was shouting. Delighted by his success, Rusty was circling the rocking vehicle, still barking. Ash forgot her dislike of Jake Dare. She even forgot that inexplicable, shaming kick of alarm when the green eyes had locked with hers. She began to wrench at the driver's door.

Jake's head had hit the window with a thump like the crack of doom. The sound momentarily turned Ash to ice. Then her practical nature reasserted itself and she ran forward.

Chris was very white. 'I'm sorry. I thought . . . I mean I didn't realize . . . Rusty . . .'

'Rusty's a naughty dog and it isn't your fault,' Ash said in an amazingly calm voice. She was shaking. But it was important that the boy did not see it. 'Can you get hold of him? He's getting in my way.'

Glad of the task, Chris began to try to round up the excited dog while Ash flung wide the driver's door and propped up Jake Dare against the back of the seat. She leaned forward, one knee braced against the upholstery, and peered into the unconscious face. He looked dreadfully white, as if there were no blood left in him but she could not see any sign of a wound.

She looked doubtfully at the window. Although the impact had sounded so dreadful the glass was still intact. Maybe he wasn't so badly injured: though of course concussion could be serious.

It seemed to Ash that his breathing was constricted. Not very dexterously, she began to fumble with the knot of his tie. It was a long time since she had taken off a man's tie. She was crazily self-conscious, even though he was out cold.

'This is ridiculous,' she muttered, setting her teeth and attacking the buttons at the neck of his shirt.

Behind her, Chris had managed to attach a hand to Rusty's collar. The dog was hauling away from him, dragging the pair of them towards the fallen enemy.

Gently, Ash pushed the constricting cloth away from Jake Dare's throat and straightened. He did not move.

'I think I'd better call a doctor,' she said, still with that calm which amazed her.

The man stirred, groaning. At once Rusty made a great surge forward, towing Chris after him and barking.

Ash pushed the dog away as best she could. 'Shut *up* Rusty.' Very gently she turned the man's face towards the air. 'Can you hear me? Can you open your eyes? *Please*,' she muttered, her calm slipping a little, 'open your eyes.'

He groaned again. He said something that sounded like 'Rosie'.

The body propped against her was unexpectedly muscular. It was also heavy and, just at the moment, helpless. For a moment, as she looked down at him, he seemed almost vulnerable. For that moment, Ash's implacable perception of him as the enemy wavered. Her hand hovered above the disarranged black hair. But then a little shudder went through him and his lashes lifted. Immediately Ash drew back, her hand falling.

His focus came and went. Even so, Jake was aware of that withdrawal even before he made out the figure bending over him so anxiously. He frowned, trying to make sense of the picture: a pale, pointed face; freckles; wide, wary eyes. Surely he knew those eyes? They seemed familiar; more than familiar: as if he had known them for ever. It was just their expression which was not right. They should not be looking at him as if their owner were afraid of him.

Mustering all his energy, he tried to smile.

'Don't look so worried, darling,' he said in a voice that was hardly a voice at all. 'I'll survive.'

Ash was, if anything, more alarmed. There was a warmth in those dazed eyes which was crazy in the circumstances. It put her even further on her guard than she had been before. Ash took good care to avoid men who looked at her with warmth in their eyes, even when they were not bullying property developers. What was even more alarming was the under note in that flagging voice. It was, she thought disturbed, almost a caress.

Her arm stiff, she pushed him back against the luxurious seat. Jake seemed unsurprised. His eyes flickered and he mimed a kiss in her general direction.

Ash jumped, looking over her shoulder in acute embarrassment. But Chris was too busy trying to restrain the dog to have noticed. Ash pressed the back of her hand to a hot cheek and looked back at the semi-conscious man, harassed.

Jake's hand wavered up as if he was going to touch her. Ash cursed inwardly and held her breath. But then he seemed to lose direction and his hand dropped like a stone. His head fell back against the headrest. He found a voice from somewhere.

'I won't . . .'

But the effort was too much for him. His voice died as he slipped heavily sideways again.

Ash caught him. For a moment his unconscious head rested against her breast. She looked down at the dark hair almost wildly.

Shaken, she pushed him upright again and said with an attempt at briskness, 'Definitely a doctor.' Her voice was breathless and higher than usual.

Chris Hall peered over her shoulder, Rusty dancing at the end of his arm.

'Do you think he's badly hurt?' he asked, worry warring with satisfaction at being present at a real emergency.

'Of course not,' Ash said robustly, though she cast an anxious look down at the unconscious, handsome face.

'You ought to feel his pulse,' Chris said helpfully.

Ash jumped. But in the face of Chris' innocent expectancy there was nothing she could do but comply. Chris was studying the shuttered face with an interest not entirely divorced from the powerful car and the man's air of city elegance. He did not notice her reluctance.

Calling on all her powers of self-discipline, Ash did her best. Jake Dare's wrist was warm; warmer than the face she had so briefly touched. There were soft hairs along the back of the forearm. Feeling them under her fingers, Ash swallowed. She set her teeth and concentrated hard.

But as soon as she found the hurrying pulse, her whole body flinched. Any moment he could wake and hit her away, her shivering body thought, although her mind told her it was nonsense. Memories swept over her like a tidal wave. Ash knew they were physical memories, as tangible as the hot metalwork of the car. They made her palms sweat – but she would not let them surface.

For a terrible moment Ash thought she could not control them; that she had no alternative but to pull away and run. Then she saw Chris Hall, the helpless man in the car, and common sense returned. She fought the memories back into their cave.

This time Chris did notice. 'You look really scared,' he told her.

He sounded rather pleased. After the first shock Chris Hall was enjoying himself.

Ash shook herself. The tidal wave of horror receded. Chris was only a boy after all and she was responsible for him. What was more, it was shocking that he was responding to this crisis more calmly than she was. She thought ruefully, I'm not much of a guardian if this is the best I can do.

She said, 'I'm concentrating.'

Chris looked dissatisfied. Before he could point out that she concentrated on animals without that look of sick horror, she gave a slightly theatrical cry of triumph. Immediately the boy leaned forward, interested. They both watched Jake Dare's eyelids quiver.

'Well, he's alive,' said Ash.

Rusty, the contra-pressure on his collar released, thrust forward and pushed a damp nose into the man's palm. Jake Dare's body jerked. His eyes opened.

Ash found herself staring into grey-green eyes a matter of inches away. There was no residual confusion in them. They were alert and perfectly unreadable. Hurriedly, she removed her knee from the seat beside him and stood up.

'A doctor *now*,' she said even more breathlessly.

The doctor, when he arrived, was a stranger to Ash. He was young and brisk and in a tearing hurry. He waved away Em's offer of coffee and looked disapproving when he found his patient had already had a cup.

But on examination, Jake Dare's injuries did not impress him. The patient himself was virtually silent throughout. He submitted to it, however, with a narrow-eyed composure that Ash found singularly worrying. From time to time he looked at her. He looked as if he were calculating something rapidly and all too accurately for her comfort.

'Rest overnight and he'll be right as rain,' the doctor said, having peered into his patient's pupils and listened to his heart. 'Bit of shock, nothing more.'

Ash frowned. 'But shouldn't he go to hospital? Have an x-ray?'

Doctor Grindlay was not impressed by Mrs Lawrence either. Too much money and time on her hands, in his view. He shrugged.

'Skull x-ray? Bit over the top.'

'He knocked himself out,' Ash said hotly.

The doctor shrugged again. 'National Health Service isn't made of money . . .'

'I'll pay for it,' Ash flashed.

Dr Grindlay did not like rich reclusive young women who did not play a proper part in the community. He drew himself up.

'If you want, of course,' he said coldly. He looked at her. 'And no doubt you'll be available tonight in case he takes a turn for the worse?' he added maliciously.

Ash jumped. 'Tonight?'

'Shock,' Dr Grindlay reminded her with pleasure. 'He shouldn't be left on his own. And of course he won't be able to drive.' He allowed himself a big smile. 'Just as well you have plenty of room here, isn't it?'

From the eighteenth-century chaise longue in the drawing room, Jake Dare watched them both with interest. Seeing Ash's stiffening at this suggestion he made a faint, courteous protest. He did not intend it to be attended to. It was not.

The doctor looked down at him now and said encouragingly, 'They'll have you x-rayed and out in no time. And then Mrs Lawrence will take care of you.'

The green eyes flickered. Jake said carefully, 'I couldn't impose . . .'

Dr Grindlay was not to be contradicted by a patient who had only recently knocked himself out. His expression said as much. His look at Ash was even more eloquent as he said, 'It was her dog that did this, wasn't it?'

That was unanswerable.

Ash felt herself chill. But she recognized the inevitable and, in considerable trepidation, bowed to it. But she was not going to let the bullying doctor see the effect his demand had on her.

She said crisply, 'You'd better give me a note for the x-ray department, hadn't you?

The doctor complied; and left.

Ash went into the kitchen.

'Em, can you keep an eye on the boys? Molly Hall will be over for them later. But I've got to take Mr Dare into the clinic in Oxford. Can you stay until I get back or Molly turns up?'

Em, cooking in the well-scrubbed kitchen, was captious. She had her daughter-in-law coming over. She had to get Steve's tea.

Ash pushed a not entirely steady hand through her hair.

'*Please*.' She bit her lip. 'I've got to try and keep him sweet. The accident was Rusty's fault.'

Em wavered.

'You should see the man,' Ash said despairingly. 'He's from the company who wants to buy the Wood. I haven't been very nice to them in the past so – Well, I think he may be quite glad to have me owing him.'

Em drew a saucepan of butter, sugar and golden syrup off the heat and tipped a plate of oats into it carefully. She did not look at Ash.

'Probably is,' she said, stirring the mixture carefully. She kept her eyes on the spatula.

'Look, Em. I'll make it up to you. Double time,' said Ash. 'Or swap today for another this week. Honestly, I do need to make sure the man has his x-ray. Something about him scares me,' she added on a rush of unmistakable honesty.

Em sent her a sharp look. 'All right,' she said suddenly. 'I'll ring Steve at work.'

Ash hugged her. 'You're a lifesaver.'

Jake Dare had recovered enough to walk unaided to the car, Ash observed sourly. He even smiled at her. He had an attractive smile. It crinkled up the corners of his eyes and made them look warmer and more grey than that icy green she had encountered earlier.

She smiled back, but perfunctorily. She didn't have to brace herself to get into a car any more. But it still took all her concentration to drive without breaking out in a cold sweat. The doctors had said that it was normal and that, like the sleeplessness and the deep sense of guilt, it would go in time. Three years later, Ash still had them all.

But she was not going to let Jake Dare see it. She knew businessmen and she knew that as long as Dare Properties wanted her Hayes Wood, Jake Dare would be pitting his wits against hers. Perhaps they would not quite be enemies. But she would need to guard against any hint of vulnerability from appearing when Jake was around.

She held the passenger door open for him. He acknowledged the courtesy with a rueful nod.

'Thank you.'

She closed the door on him and went round to her own side. Sliding behind the wheel, she sent him a quick look as she fastened her seat belt. She had thought he looked perfectly well. But now she was not so sure.

'Have you got a headache?' she asked, putting the car into gear and letting it glide gently out of the half of the garage which had not been turned into a badger run.

He tipped his dark head back against the head rest. 'I'm not sure I know.'

Ash went gently down the drive, avoiding the worst of the bumps, stopped and looked for oncoming cars, and then swung the Rover gently out onto the metalled road.

'You must know if you've got a headache or not,' she objected.

He turned his head on the head rest and gave her a faint smile. He looked, she saw out of the corner of her eye, weary all of a sudden.

'I flew in from Brazil four days ago and I haven't stopped since. I'm still so jet-lagged I'm not sure where my head is, let alone whether it's aching,' he said ruefully.

'Oh.'

Ash was briefly conscience-stricken. Her father usually took to his bed after a long flight, sometimes for several days. But then, out of the corner of her eyes, she caught sight of the muscles under the perfect tailoring. Something clenched in her stomach. She squashed her conscience. This was a young, fit man, she told herself, not to be compared with her father in any way. She found she did not want to think through the implications of that.

She drove round a steep curve with care and groped for a neutral subject of conversation. 'What were you doing in Brazil?'

'Rather more than I intended.' He was wry. 'I went to look at the possibility of building a factory. But while I was there they asked us to quote for the workers' housing complex as well. The site is riddled with volcanic rock. So it's an interesting construction problem.' He yawned hugely and then gave a small laugh. 'So interesting that I didn't get to bed the last three nights in Rio.'

Ash sniffed. She knew people like that. All the bright, competitive managers in the family bank were like that. Peter had been like it – once they saw the prospect of a deal, everything else went out of their heads, including their own well being. It had impressed her grandfather enormously, after his disappointment with his son, but it had not taken many months of marriage to chill Ash to the bone.

She said more crisply than she had intended, 'Or since you got back either, from the sound of it. Why on earth did you come down here today if you're under so much pressure?'

Jake Dare's eyebrows flew up at the undisguised censure. But he said mildly enough, 'Because negotiations for this site were supposed to be finished last month. And Tony was clearly out of his depth.'

'Tony? Is he the one I sent away?' Ash asked unwisely.

The mildness dimmed. He sent her a frosty look. 'Maybe Tony let his good manners get the better of him,' Jake said with a slight edge to his voice. 'I hear you were not polite.'

Ash shrugged. 'I told him the truth. My wood is not for sale. I didn't want him hanging around.' She sent him a quick look before slowing down for the outskirts of town. 'The same goes for you.'

Jake did not move. But something, which Ash fortunately did not see, stirred in his eyes.

'I imagined it did,' he murmured.

'Good. Well as long as we understand each other . . .'

He shifted in his seat and winced a bit. 'I wouldn't say we'd got that far, yet.'

'Oh, yes, we have,' Ash assured him. 'You want to bully me. I'm not bullyable. End of story.'

She said it with such finality that she was not entirely surprised he did not reply. When she allowed herself a quick sideways look, he was staring straight ahead, his brows drawn together in a frown. That's told him, she thought, pleased.

She did not need to watch for the signposts to the clinic. It had been there that she had waited by Peter's bedside every day for the ten days before he died. It was there that she had gone herself for the therapy the doctors had insisted on for her own mental scars. Afterwards she had endowed a new body scanner in Peter's memory. The clinic regarded her as a prize patient and a benefactor. They had even asked her to go on their Board but she had refused. If they only knew, she sometimes thought.

She parked the car under the swathe of trees that curved up to the entrance. Jake Dare got out at once, not waiting for assistance.

'Very nice,' he said. 'More like a hotel than a hospital. Definitely a rich man's playground. Costs an arm and a leg, I bet.'

Her conscience pricked again. 'I'm paying,' Ash said swiftly.

Jake gave a little unamused laugh. 'How pleasant to be able to buy your way out of trouble.'

She did not know how to answer him. They went inside. Ash introduced him to the staff who knew her well. Then she turned decisively and sat by the window. She could not have distanced herself from him more completely without actually leaving the clinic.

The silence between them remained unbroken through the receptionist's chatter and the radiographer's calm instructions. So it was a shock when the latter, showing him through the double doors to the x-ray department, turned her head and winked.

'Gor – jus,' she said, raising her eyes to heaven. 'Why don't glamorous men ever have accidents on my door-step?'

She whisked away after her patient. Ash looked after her in consternation. Glamorous? *Gorgeous*? He was an arrogant businessman who thought he could push the world around. Where was the glamour in that? Sally Jebb must be out of her mind.

And then another thought hit her. Sally Jebb was not a conspirator, like Em Harrison or her father, but she had become a friend after the accident and Ash knew she was not above a spot of gentle matchmaking. Heaven send she did not think Jake Dare was a candidate, Ash prayed, horrified at the prospect.

She got up and moved restlessly about the reception area. She knew the pictures by heart. She had waited here such hours for news of Peter. It seemed like only yesterday, too. Three years ago and she still sometimes woke up in a sweat thinking she would be late for the hospital.

Yet now, for the first time in three years, she looked at the pictures and did not feel that terrible guilty lurch of the heart. She felt anxious and wary and more than a little angry – but about Jake Dare and what was going to happen next, not about Peter and the past.

'I suppose that's an improvement of sorts,' Ash muttered at a balloon seller in rainbow chalks. She said aloud, 'I hate these bloody pictures.'

The receptionist was philosophical. 'They're supposed to be soothing.'

'They don't soothe me.' As soon as she said it, Ash wished she hadn't. I sound like a sulky child, she thought, mortified.

But the receptionist was used to dealing with anxious friends and lovers. She smiled forgivingly.

'I'm sure Mr Dare will be fine. Mr Francis will look at his x-rays. You remember Mr Francis? You needn't worry. You can take the x-rays away with you.'

Ash ground her teeth. 'I am not worrying,' she said between clenched teeth. 'The man's nothing to do with me. I don't care if his x-rays go to the National Gallery.'

She went back to her couch.

It was not long before Jake Dare reappeared, accompanied by Brian Francis with an attentive Sally carrying the x-rays in a large brown folder. Ash stood up. It was Brian Francis who was trying to persuade her to join the hospital Board. He and his wife were another couple with strong views on her reclusive lifestyle.

Now, she saw with misgiving, he was beaming.

'Good news and bad news,' Brian Francis said to her cheerfully. 'No lasting damage. I've written a note to his GP. But he wasn't in the best of condition when he got that bang on the head, so he'd better take it easy for a week or so.'

Ash looked at him suspiciously; then at Jake. Were

the two men exchanging conspiratorial looks? Or trying too hard not to look at each other at all?

Francis said airily, 'Could be some headaches. Loss of peripheral vision. Quite temporary, but he shouldn't try to drive until the risk has passed. I gather Grindlay's already suggested he stay at the Manor for a bit. Best thing you could do.'

Jake said nothing. Was he suppressing a smile? Ash could have screamed.

'Thank you,' she said frostily. 'But surely if Mr Dare is ill he should stay in hospital? It would be, of course, on my account.'

Brian Francis could not prevent himself glancing quickly at Jake Dare. Ash's eyes narrowed, suspicion hardening into cast-iron certainty.

'No need for that,' the consultant said hastily. 'Mr Dare just needs a rest, for a while. You know the sort of thing, pleasant surroundings, pleasant people.'

Jake Dare turned his head away. Ash was almost sure he was laughing. She was being set up and she knew it. She could have danced with fury.

'I am not,' she said with bite, 'a pleasant person.'

Jake's shoulders shook. Brian Francis pretended not to hear.

'No additional stress. That's what he needs. Come on, Ash. You know better than anyone how stressful being in hospital can be.'

'I see.' She gave them both a glittering smile. 'Well, in that case I'll find someone to drive Mr Dare back to London. He can rest in his own home.'

This time Brian Francis managed not to look at his

69

so-called patient, Ash noted. For some reason that fuelled her rage even more.

'London would be the worst possible place for him,' he said firmly. 'Too much noise, too much pollution, and much too easy for his subordinates to get at him. No, no. The Manor is ideal.'

'Not from my point of view.'

Brian succeeded in looking astonished.

Jake decided to take a hand. He said softly, 'But they tell me you're always taking in the weak and wounded.'

Ash looked at him with loathing. She had no doubt at whose door to lay the blame for this. Brian Francis might be giving her all these unwelcome instructions, but she was quite clear Jake Dare had taught him his part. He was not even trying very hard to hide it.

'Animals,' she said evenly. 'I take in animals. Creatures you can trust.'

Their eyes locked. Out of the corner of her eye Ash saw that Brian Francis was looking a little ashamed at that. But Jake Dare was made of sterner stuff. He was not ashamed. He was enjoying himself.

'Was that how you got that mutt that ran into me? And you *trust* him? I'd have said he was a bit of a rogue. Probably thrown out of his first home for biting.'

There was a fraught silence. Ash glared. Rusty was not a rogue; but he was excitable. She had never known him to bite a person. But it was true that he had been thrown out by the family who took him home as a Christmas present for their son after he had chewed his way through far too many of other people's Christmas presents. She wondered how he had found that out and remembered he had talked to Em when she had brought in the coffee.

In the hands of a good lawyer Rusty's history could be made to look bad. And Jake Dare would have only the best lawyers. She was being set up and there was not a damned thing she could do about it.

'Blackmailer,' she muttered.

'What?' Jake Dare was bland.

'All right,' she said, nearly spitting it out. 'A few days.' She swung round on an interested Brian Francis. 'How many is a few? Three? Four?'

'I'd be happier with ten,' he said quickly. 'Maybe even fifteen.' He saw her face. 'Well, ten should do it,' he allowed.

She did not look at Jake Dare. But Ash was certain that the hateful man was shaking with suppressed and private laughter.

'Then it seems you must enjoy the hospitality of the Manor for the next ten days,' she told Jake Dare. 'Unless you decide to go home earlier, of course.'

He looked wary all of a sudden, the hidden laughter evaporating. Ash felt an undignified satisfaction. Oh, she was going to show this man that she could not be manipulated with impunity. She wasn't sure what she was going to do yet, but it should be something that would have him fleeing back to London as fast as his Mercedes could carry him.

'Goodbye,' she said to Brian Francis, pointedly not shaking hands. She glared at an open-mouthed Sally, too. 'Come along, Mr Dare. Or do you need help to get into the car?'

'No, thank you,' he said hastily.

He said his goodbyes with a good deal more cordiality than she had done and followed her.

Ash said nothing all the way back home. She was so furious she did not dare to speak. Jake Dare had made a fool of her comprehensively. If she started on the subject while she was driving, she was likely to lose control of her temper and the car alike. So she maintained a grim silence.

Jake tried to converse once. 'So you're a hospital benefactor.'

'Yes,' Ash said curtly.

'They seem very fond of you.'

She snorted.

'They told me about your husband,' he said soberly. 'I'm sorry.'

'Thank you.'

'Had you been married long?'

'Seven years.'

He nodded slowly. 'That's a hell of a slice of your life. I can see why you might want to retreat for a while.'

Ash tensed. 'What do you mean?'

Jake sounded surprised. 'Just that you're said to prefer your own company. Is it a secret?'

There was no criticism in his tone, just a quiet amusement at the vagaries of another person. It made her feel naked, somehow. And defensive. Her simmering temper suddenly soared up, overflowing uncontrollably. She felt savage.

Ash said furiously, 'Did you spend all your time in x-ray talking about me or did you actually manage to do what you were there for?'

72

He seemed not to notice the savagery. If anything he sounded even more amused. 'We chatted . . .'

'Did you tell them you were pestering me?'

He laughed. 'Hardly pestering. A couple of letters and . . .'

'And then the invasion,' flared Ash.

'Invasion? Aren't you being a little dramatic?'

'Did I invite you?'

He was silent.

'Then it's an invasion, isn't it?' she flung at him.

Jake gave up. Ash ignored him.

When they got to the Manor, however, she found she could do so no longer. He got out of the car on his own. But instead of following her to the front door he leaned wearily against the side of the car. He looked as if he was summoning up all his strength to walk the few yards to the big studded door.

Ash bit her lip. He was a wily businessman and a blatant manipulator. She already loathed him more than she had ever loathed anyone in her life. But he really did not look well and she did not think he was feigning it.

As she watched he began to walk carefully toward her, undisguisable weariness in every movement. Instinctively, in spite of her earlier fury, Ash went to his side. She slid a hand under his elbow.

He smiled faintly. 'Even untrustworthy humans if they're weak and wounded, hmm?'

'If you collapse in my driveway you'll probably find some way to say it was my fault,' Ash said tartly.

But she guided him unobtrusively into the house. It was quiet. Both Em and the Hall twins seemed to have gone.

73

She led her unwanted guest into the library. Rusty was lying on the rug in a patch of afternoon sun. At their entrance he rose from his snooze under the leaded windows.

'Sit,' Ash said swiftly.

To her relief, Rusty obeyed for once. Jake Dare gave a soft laugh.

'Is that the appeal of animals? They do what they're told?'

She looked at him with dislike. 'If you knew Rusty better, you would know that he never does what he's told.'

'And yet you still love him? Lucky Rusty,' he murmured.

He sank into a winged tapestry chair and tipped his head back, his eyelids dropping. Rusty made a soft, disturbed sound. With his eyes closed, Jake reached down and offered the dog his fingers to smell. Rusty edged closer.

Ash stood looking down at him moodily.

'Do you want something to drink?' she asked at last.

Her reluctance was almost palpable. Jake's smile grew. He did not open his eyes.

'Maybe something warm and sweet for shock?' he murmured provocatively.

Ash refused to acknowledge a double meaning. 'Cocoa,' she said briskly. 'I'll get it.'

She made it quickly and took a tray back into the library. Jake Dare had not moved. Rusty, though, had now disposed himself on the Kilim rug with his nose on the highly polished shoes. Highly expensive, hand-made shoes too, Ash noted. She had once known a lot about such things.

Ash put the tray down carefully. She contemplated the

74

silent figure, frowning. What was she going to do? It had been three long years since she had looked after anyone and she did not want to do so again. The very thought of that enforced intimacy made her shiver to her bones.

She became aware that she was being watched. Startled she stiffened. Jake had turned his head against the tapestry chair back and was regarding her quizzically.

For no reason at all, Ash felt her colour rise. 'You're awake.'

'Put it down to the smell of cocoa,' he said amused. 'You weren't making a sound. You're a very silent lady, do you know that?'

The personal observation made her feel uncomfortable; as if he had her at a disadvantage, watching her while she was unaware of it.

She didn't answer, giving him his mug of the hot, sweet, chocolate-tasting stuff. She pushed a plate of small sandwiches close to his elbow.

'You missed lunch.'

'So did you. Don't you eat? Or is it just that you won't eat with me?'

Ash sent him a look of dislike. 'I've got to get your room ready. I'll eat when I've finished.'

'I am filled with remorse,' he said with gentle mockery.

'Somehow I doubt that.'

Ash did not wait for his reply. She marched out, shutting the door behind her with a sharp thud.

She made the room up swiftly. She was only halfway through when she became aware of being watched yet again. She straightened, flushing.

Jake Dare was propped in the doorway, his cocoa in his

hand. He was looking round the master suite with raised eyebrows. He appeared startled.

'I didn't mean to turn you out of your room.'

'You're not,' Ash said shortly.

She went back to stuffing pillows into pillow cases. Her grandfather had not only bought them the house he had had it professionally decorated. Even when she and Peter were first married, she had never liked the specially designed sheets. They were brown, embroidered with a feather motif which reflected the seventeenth-century carving on the panelled walls. The gold thread on the pillow case scratched your cheek, Ash remembered. Or at least, it did if you were tossing and turning. Jake Dare, presumably, would be too exhausted to notice.

She straightened the duvet cover and flung the gold sunburst coverlet over the bed. Jake unpropped himself and strolled forward.

'You mean there's a grander bedroom suite in the house?' he asked incredulously.

Ash bit her lip. 'No. This is the master suite. I just don't use it,' she said curtly.

The grey-green eyes were disconcertingly sharp. But after a pause, he just nodded and went over to the window seat. The ceiling was low above the window embrasure and he had to bend his tall head to look out.

Ash watched him. It was painful. The last time she had been in here with a man it was with Peter. He had had his back to her, too. He had kept his back to her while he went through the list of her deficiencies as a wife. The long list. And why, given those deficiencies, her demands were unacceptable. She swallowed.

76

Jake brushed the brown and gold curtain back. 'You moved into another room when your husband died?' he asked. It sounded idle enough.

Ash said, 'Yes,' in a tight little voice.

He was scanning the garden, golden in the afternoon sun. He said to the distant willows, 'Peter Lawrence of Kimbell's Bank. One of the young high fliers. I've even heard of him. Killed when his car hit a tree in a rainstorm three years ago, throwing the succession at Kimbell's into turmoil.'

'Yes,' she said colourlessly.

'You've stayed here on your own? Why? Because it was the home you made together?'

Ash smoothed out the coverlet, not answering him. If she concentrated hard on the extravagant embroidery, she could almost push the quiet voice out of her consciousness.

'Your friends in the clinic don't think it's healthy, you know,' he remarked after a pause. 'Three years on – you should be getting out and having fun again, not turning inwards. They say you're a virtual recluse.'

'Thank you Sally,' Ash said, recognizing the accusation. 'Don't believe her. She reads too many horror stories.'

Jake Dare swung round to face her suddenly. His face was grey with tiredness but the eyes searching her face felt like a laser.

'How old are you?' he said abruptly.

She was so startled that she answered without thinking. 'Twenty-eight.'

'I'm ten years older than that and I wouldn't want to bury myself out here,' he told her frankly. 'What do your friends say? Your family?'

77

Ash glared at him. 'Thank you for your interest in my affairs, Mr Dare, but I'm sure you've got better things to do than bother about my living arrangements.'

He was not abashed by the rebuke. 'They don't approve,' he interpreted.

Ash felt her temper go up a notch. 'Forgive me, but I don't see that it's any of your business.'

His smile was crooked. 'Know your opponent. That's the first law of business. And you're my opponent, aren't you, Mrs Lawrence?'

So they had it out in the open at last. It was a relief, after the day's fencing. She stared at him for a moment, unspeaking. Then she sighed.

'Yes,' Ash said simply.

'Mind telling me why?'

Ash was incredulous. 'I hate the idea of a shopping mall anywhere near here.'

His eyes narrowed. 'But it's not just my poor development project you hate, is it?' he said softly.

'What do you mean?' Ash's voice was high, spiked with an alarm she could not explain.

Jake looked at her thoughtfully for a long moment without answering. Under that steady gaze Ash found her alarm increasing.

To disguise it she said challengingly, 'Are you telling me we're natural enemies, Mr Dare? That we would be, even if you didn't want to fill the countryside with steel girders and glass?'

Jake Dare seemed to hesitate, she thought. Then he said slowly. 'I must be more shaken up than I realized. I don't think . . .' He broke of and sagged against the window all of a sudden.

Ash forgot her anger as if it had never been. There was an unmistakable film of sweat over his cheekbones, she saw. He needed help.

She swallowed. There was nothing else for it. She wiped her palms down the side of her old jeans and tried to pretend the faint, persistent trembling was not there. She had handled sick animals again and again. She would just have to pretend he was another animal, hurt and needing her help. She could do it as long as she did not meet those too-acute green eyes.

She said with constraint, 'You need help to get into bed, don't you?'

He answered by taking a step forward. He looked rather strange, Ash saw, watching him narrowly. He put out a hand and hung onto the curtains with a grip that almost brought them down. At once Ash darted over and put her arm round his waist.

'Thank you,' said Jake, evidently not best pleased.

'Lean on me,' said Ash, forgetting her aversion in concentration. 'Let's get you onto the bed first.'

To his chagrin, Jake found he was walking like a drunk, leaning heavily on Ash. It was clear that he didn't like it.

'I'm sorry,' he said stiffly. Or at least he tried to say it. He made an impatient sound.

Ash guided him gently. He was unsteady but he did not have to be carried. For all his muscularity, he was, she realized with a detached part of her brain, unexpectedly thin; certainly thinner than Peter had ever been. He had long, beautiful bones. The hand resting so heavily on her shoulder was well-shaped and beautifully kept but, even in his dazed state, there was no disguising the sinewy strength. It was just as well he was conscious enough to help himself.

She manoeuvred him carefully against the side of the bed and let him subside slowly. Without her supporting hands he was clearly weak as water all of a sudden.

'Delayed shock,' he said. 'Damn.'

Ash propped him against the bed head and began to undress him rapidly. Her embarrassment, her reluctance, had all gone, overwhelmed by compassion. He looked ill. And he did not look like a man who was able to handle having to ask for help.

Jake did what he could. But every movement brought him out in a sweat. The world was spinning round him. He was hardly aware of it when she stepped back and pulled the duvet over his still partly clothed form.

Later she was back. He knew it before he opened his eyes from the wafting scent of new-mown hay and sunshine. Then there was that cool, gentle touch on his forehead which had become curiously familiar. He struggled with the fog.

'Rosie,' he murmured again.

Ash watched him as he stirred himself into consciousness. She wished she knew more about human medicine.

'Rosie?' she prompted gently.

But he was too deep to hear. He was turning, his eyelids fluttering. She put down her tray of tea and the pyjamas she had dug out for him and bent to help him. Under her hands he twisted like an animal in pain. Startled, Ash held him more strongly as, with a great surge, Jake liberated himself into consciousness. He came upright before she had time to draw back.

For a heart-stopping moment Ash found herself staring directly into green eyes. They were dazed with sleep, warm and lazily entertained. Just for an instant, she froze. Then she sprang back as if the skin of his bare shoulders had burnt her.

'Why are you looking like that?' Jake said softly.

His voice sounded so normal that Ash jumped. She could feel the blood rushing into her face and was furious. She turned her head away and began to fuss with his tea, hoping he would not notice. All at once, the terrible schoolgirl embarrassment was back.

Jake saw it. Beneath her lashes she saw the way his eyes narrowed. It made her feel even worse. But all he said was, 'I'm cold.'

Gratefully, Ash stumbled into speech. 'Of course. I thought probably . . . that is, I've got you some . . . My father's pyjamas,' she finished simply.

Her eyes did not quite meet his as she extended the neatly folded purple silk. Jake, wholly awake now, looked rueful.

'Purple?'

For no reasons at all, Ash flushed again. She said with a defensiveness that infuriated her, 'Well, he doesn't come here all that often.'

Jake gave a great laugh at that. It made him wince. But he was looking more alive than at any time since Rusty had attacked his car, Ash noted. He reached out a long finger and hooked up the purple jacket on it. He held it out, head on one side.

'What is he? Emperor of China?'

Ash recovered her cool with an effort. 'He's a captain of industry,' she told him coolly – and not entirely truthfully.

Jake grinned. 'Then he'll probably sue me for wearing his property without a full takeover bid.' He let the garment slide off his finger onto the floor.

Ash looked at it. Animals, she thought, were not this much trouble. Her embarrassment began to fade in direct proportion as her irritation grew. She raised her eyes to meet his.

'*I* don't care if you catch pneumonia,' she told him sweetly. 'It's up to you.'

Jake chuckled. 'Imperial purple to keep out the cold,' he murmured as if to himself. His eyes gleamed at Ash.

She could have hit him. Instead, she bent deliberately and picked up the jacket. She draped it over the bed, where he could get it if he wanted and turned away.

'There's some tea there, if you want it. You ought to rest, I think.'

Jake pulled a pillow more comfortably behind his head and settled back as if for a long conversation. There were beads of sweat on his forehead when he had finished but the wickedness of the grin was undimmed.

'Then you'd better take away the imperial purple. It gives me a headache.'

Ash glared. The last vestige of shrinking embarrassment disappeared entirely, this time driven out by straightforward indignation. She picked up the offending pyjamas.

'Is there anything else you want?' she said between her teeth.

Jake contemplated saying she could sell him a parcel of

land and decided against it. She did not look in a humour to respond to being teased. So he just shook his head.

Immediately he wished he had not. Daggers stabbed into his left shoulder and the back of his neck. He caught his breath, wincing.

The glare died out of Ash's expression. At once she was beside him, her soft hand on his shoulder, her brown eyes concerned.

'Don't worry,' said Jake, touched. 'I'll live.'

Ash was aware of that faint breath of warning again; that deceptive warmth was dangerous. She looked down at him, torn. Surely it was ridiculous to fear him? He was obviously as weak as a kitten and in pain still from the accident. And yet . . . Still she hesitated.

In that moment Jake Dare looked down at the strong, supple little hand on his shoulder and up again quickly into her eyes. Ash's inner struggle showed.

Jake said softly, 'You're looking frightened again. What is it about me that frightens you?'

Ash froze.

Jake said, 'I don't like it.'

Giving in to a strong, inexplicable urge he put up a hand to her face and drew her down to him.

Startled, Ash gasped. Off-balance, she was not collected enough to resist the surprisingly strong movement. And Jake Dare kissed her neatly on her parted lips.

CHAPTER 4

Ash gave an outraged exclamation and fell forward onto the bed. Before she knew what he was about, Jake gave a quick twist, taking her with him. She found herself lying underneath his naked chest.

'What the hell do you think you're doing?' she yelled.

Jake grinned down at her. 'The usual.'

For a moment she did not understand him. It was so long since a man had flirted with her. Even longer since she had thought about whether she might want him to. It was like a language she had forgotten. Only with Jake Dare so wickedly close, she was beginning to remember.

Ash's throat closed. She had thought he was dangerous. She had not realized how dangerous. Inwardly she began to shiver.

She must not let him see it.

'Let me up.'

Jake was unimpressed. With a practised sweep of the hand, he pulled the pillows to cushion her. Then he laid her solicitously back among them. That solicitude was like an insult. The shivering intensified. At all costs she had to hide it. Quick and fierce as one of the kitchen cats, Ash struck out at him.

It did not move him at all. He did not even flinch. Hardly seeming to move, he caught her hands and held them. Then he was smiling down into her furious eyes. Quite as if she were the melting female he was no doubt used to, Ash thought outraged.

She thrashed wildly, her hair tangling under her. 'Let me *up*.'

Strands of red hair caught in her eyelashes. Ash blinked convulsively, her eyes watering.

'Hold still,' said Jake, his voice warm. There was a distinct suggestion that he was suppressing laughter. But when he stroked the hair back off her brow, it did not feel as if he were laughing.

Ash was disconcerted. To hide it she glared. Jake looked amused.

'Are you always this ornery?'

'I am not,' said Ash bitingly, 'given cause. Usually.'

'I can see that,' he agreed. He was infuriatingly un-repentant. He brushed the back of his hand across her cheek. 'I ask myself why.'

Something inside Ash clenched tight at the idle caress. But the implicit question was worse. She did not want Jake Dare asking himself anything about her. Still less did she want him asking her. His hold could not have been gentler but every muscle in her body screamed to be free.

She had to relax, she knew. She could not do anything while she was wound tight as a spring. She knew that from bitter experience. Concentrating hard, she made the tense muscles of her shoulders yield into the pillows' softness.

And then she forced herself to meet his eyes.

'Perhaps because I don't know anyone else who would abuse hospitality like this.'

He drew in an audible breath. 'Ouch.'

But he did not look quite so amused, Ash saw with satisfaction. She had not exactly drawn blood but at least he was not so abominably sure of himself. She surveyed him from under lowered lashes and decided to turn the knife in the wound.

'Even uninvited guests don't usually manhandle their hosts.'

But it did not have the effect she expected. He looked astounded. 'Manhandle?' Far from eliciting embarrassment, it seemed almost to disgust him. 'Oh, you English and your lies.'

'*My* lies?' Ash gasped. 'I'm not the one pretending to be a sick man.'

It was clearly not what he was expecting. Jake frowned. At once Ash saw the predator she had recognized this morning. The laughing charm had quite gone. Here was the ruthless opponent again.

Illogically, it restored her confidence. She struggled up on one elbow. It brought her face so close to his that she had to narrow her eyes to bring him back into focus. She did not care.

'If you're well enough to torment me, you're well enough to go home,' she flung at him.

That disconcerted him. He seemed to freeze. 'Torment –?' he said blankly.

Ash's head went back. Her brown eyes were defiant. 'What else would you call it?'

His brows twitched together. For a long moment he searched her face. Then, 'That's quite a hang up, you've got,' he said slowly.

'Hang up?' Ash choked in disbelief. 'Because I don't like being mauled by a man who has bullied me and lied to me? And who manipulates anyone he comes across? *Hang up*?'

'That's what it looks like from where I'm sitting,' Jake told her calmly.

Ash was so angry she thought she would explode. 'Then maybe you should sit somewhere else,' she said between her teeth.

That startled him. For a moment he stared down at her, searching her face as if she had set him some immensely challenging puzzle. Then he gave a harsh laugh and let go of her hands. It was so unexpected Ash rocked and grabbed for the nearest support. A mistake. Because it was, of course, Jake.

Already off-balance, he could not help himself. Ash fell backwards, taking him with her.

Oh God, *no*, she thought. I can't even blame him for this one. This time I've no one to blame but myself. He'll think I meant this to happen all the time. And in the split second before his mouth found hers – he'll never take me seriously again.

And then she stopped thinking at all.

She heard him give a low laugh. She was quite right. Jake was certainly giving every sign of not taking her rejection seriously now. He might have been prepared to let her go earlier. But whatever advantage she had gained was gone now.

As if he had every right, he began to brush his mouth

back and forth across her startled lips. Ash shut her eyes tight and tried to turn her head away. Jake would not let her. It felt as if he had all the time in the world – and intended to use it to the full.

Nothing like this had ever happened before. The inner shivering would not stop. But it no longer had anything to do with fear.

He touched a finger across each eyebrow, brushing back her riot of hair. It was subtle, sensuous. There was no threat there, no force. Just complete mastery. Her body seemed to turn to him of its own accord. It felt as if Jake Dare were taking possession of her.

Ash was drifting on a tide of gentle pleasure. Why have I never felt like this before? she thought. She felt warm, hazy, irresponsible. It was like heaven; as if Jake had cast a spell on her. She could drift like this forever.

A spell! Suddenly Ash realized. She was letting Jake Dare do what he wanted, take her wherever he wanted. What was she doing? Coming to her senses, she gave a long, deep shudder.

Oh, it was a spell all right. A cruel, clever spell.

She opened her eyes. 'Stop,' she said chokingly.

Jake went on tracing her features.

'Sure?' he murmured, a smile in his voice.

His touch was so light it was hardly a touch at all. It felt almost unbearably tender. Ash could feel it through every nerve. She thought: it feels like love.

She jackknifed upright. Jake fell back with an exclamation of mock alarm. Ash hardly noticed. Her face was a mask of horror.

Never felt like this in her life before? Oh, but she had,

hadn't she? She had. And it had all been a horrible illusion. Ash pressed her hands to her face.

Jake said sharply, 'What is it?'

Ash reached for common sense. The illusion was an old one; nothing to do with here and now. It was just a flurry of memory, that was all. A memory Jake Dare knew nothing about. No one knew anything about it. She steadied her breathing.

There was no *reason* for her to feel like this. She did not know Jake Dare. He did not – God be thanked – know anything about her. And he would be gone in ten days. If not before, she thought, fighting her way back to composure.

Jake said again, 'What is it?'

Ash smoothed her hair. She was not going to be terrorized by shadows. Not after she had kept them so carefully at bay for so long.

She said rather shakily, 'I told you – '

Jake Dare propped himself on one elbow and surveyed her. He gave no sign of having heard. She risked a quick look down at him. There was a curious expression on his face.

He said slowly, 'You were frightened.'

Try as she would, Ash could not suppress her instinctive flinching. 'No, of course not, I – '

'Frightened,' he said again, unheeding. He sounded as if he could hardly believe it: only believed it in spite of himself.

Ash gathered her forces. 'That's nonsense,' she said curtly.

Jake's eyes flickered. Then, suddenly, he put out a hand

and deliberately ran it down Ash's bare arm. Unprepared, she could not suppress her recoil.

'Is it?' he asked. The idea plainly intrigued him.

Ash pushed him away and struggled to her feet. 'Stop it,' she said again. 'It's not fair. I won't play games.'

He stood up too. Ash could not meet his eyes. She had never been any good at hiding her feelings. It was one of the things Peter had complained about most. She could not bear it if someone were to uncover those shadows after all this time, not now that they were safely in the past. Especially not Jake Dare. She could no longer hide her shivering.

He said softly, 'A grown woman: frightened of a touch.'

'You're imagining things.'

He ignored that also. 'Well, it's not me you're frightened of,' he argued, half to himself. 'You've been squaring up to me from the moment I arrived. So what is it? Just being touched? By anybody?'

Ash stiffened. Jake's eyes narrowed. He was watching her carefully.

'Or is it your own reaction? Was that what scared you?'

'What the hell do you mean?' Ash said furiously.

He gave a negligent shrug. 'Being mauled by the uninvited guest,' he mocked. 'You might not like it. But it turned you on, didn't it?'

Ash went cold. She forgot she could not look him in the eye. She took a hasty step forward, her gaze flaming. 'No, it did not. It takes more than a hamfisted bully to turn me on.'

Jake was smiling. He pursed his lips in a silent whistle. 'Unkind.'

'Honest.'

He laughed.

'*Unlike* you,' she said goaded. 'What's the diagnosis now? Still shocked and exhausted?

Jake's smile grew. He stretched. 'Surely am,' he drawled.

Ash regarded him with the deepest suspicion. His face became immediately solemn.

'I am. That was one hell of a bang I took.' And he pressed his palm to his brow.

Looking at the innocent face and the wickedly laughing eyes, Ash experienced a strong desire to scream. That or slap the smug look off his face. Both were utterly beneath her dignity, of course. In spite of his deplorable behaviour, she could not deny that blow on the head. It had knocked him out, after all. He could still be in pain from it.

She contented herself with an evil look. It was intended to make him thoroughly ashamed of himself. It had no noticeable effect at all. Ash could have danced with frustration.

'You're impossible,' she muttered.

'Sorry about that. Must have knocked out all my inhibitions. Shock can take you like that, I guess.'

Their eyes locked in a battle of wills. He was pale but his were laughing. In spite of his evident physical weakness, he looked somehow implacable. Hers were the first to fall.

'I would be very surprised to learn that you had any inhibitions worth the name,' Ash said tartly. 'Including normal good manners.'

He chuckled. 'You are beginning to know me,' he told her in congratulatory tones.

Ash was briefly speechless. 'I knew one day I would discover some great ambition,' she said at last with awful irony. 'That must be it.'

His look was a caress. 'Ah, you feel that way too,' he said, mock ardent.

Ash ground her teeth audibly. 'I feel,' she said with precision, 'that I am being conned. You're no more ill than I am. How much did you slip Brian Francis to say you had to stay here tonight?'

He shook his head sorrowfully. 'Bribe a doctor? You shock me, Mrs Lawrence. And it was ten days,' he added in a far less exalted tone.

Ash was reminded of his sneer at the clinic. This was the ideal opportunity to return it. 'How pleasant,' she said with satisfaction, 'to be able to buy your way out of trouble.'

His brows rose in quick surprise. Suddenly he was not laughing any more. Ash caught sight of a steely intelligence. It made her even more suspicious.

Jake said crisply, 'Whatever you think of me, you obviously know Brian Francis. Do you seriously think he would accept a bribe of any sort?'

Some of Ash's anger dissipated. Her eyes fell. 'No. No, I suppose not.'

He was still watching her with that alert attention. 'He clearly underestimated the burden, though,' Jake went on smoothly.

That brought her eyes up. 'Oh, no, he didn't.'

He looked amused. 'He didn't?'

'No, he didn't. He knows exactly how I feel about – '

She caught herself. There was something in his expression

which said she was revealing altogether too much.

'I suppose Brian Francis told you it would be good for me not to be all alone in this big house for once,' she interpreted bitterly. 'Didn't he?'

His expression stayed noncommittal. 'Something of the sort.'

Ash exhaled explosively. 'And what else did he say? That I need bringing out of myself?'

The beautiful, sensual mouth tilted. 'Not exactly,' he murmured. 'Do you?'

The last of the instinct for battle went out of her quite suddenly. Ash ran her fingers wearily through her tangled curls. 'Some people seem to think so.'

Jake Dare flung himself on the bed and leaned back among the pillows. He clasped his hands behind his dark head and surveyed her with undisguised calculation. 'And you don't agree? Why is that?'

Ash looked at him with dislike. 'Don't pretend to be disingenuous, Mr Dare. It doesn't suit you. I'm quite sure you learned all you wanted to about my lifestyle. Sally Jebb made it perfectly clear. You were grilling them all, weren't you?'

He chuckled. 'Not grilling,' he demurred.

'Well, that's what it sounded like.'

'You shouldn't leap to conclusions. Nobody needed grilling. They were all falling over themselves to talk about you.'

'What a thing it is to have friends,' Ash said bitterly.

He nodded. 'It is. They are concerned about you.' He considered her candidly. 'God knows why.'

Ash was astounded. 'What?'

93

He shrugged. 'You're not forthcoming, are you? Not exactly a committed member of the community.'

She was so startled by this perverse attack, she almost forgot to be angry. 'What do you mean?'

'Won't go on the Board at the clinic, won't help at the village fête, won't go on the old folks outing . . . Shall I go on?'

'I always contribute – ' Ash began indignantly.

He looked at her. She broke off, flushing.

'Buy your way out of civic duty as well, do you?' he said pleasantly.

She made a derisive noise. 'Civic duty. Per-lease. Do you know how pompous that sounds?'

'OK,' he said, equanimity unimpaired. 'What about: you pay your neighbours to go away?' There was a bite to it.

Ash flushed furiously. 'Don't be ridiculous.'

'What else would you call it?'

Against all her instincts, Ash found she was excusing herself. 'I'm not good in company. I like being by myself. I need my space.'

It was Jake's turn to snort. 'Need your space! Spare me the New Age platitudes.'

Ash stared at him. He was lounging on the bed, with his hands behind his head, quite as if he did not care a fig. And yet, and yet – She sensed real anger. It did something to dispel her own.

'Why are you so worked up about this?' she asked curiously. 'What does it matter to you how I run my life?'

He looked annoyed. 'It doesn't, of course.' He sat up. 'It just ticked me off, you sneering at those good people at the clinic. They do more good in one hour than you have

94

probably done in the whole of your selfish life.'

Ash blinked under the attack. Lots of people had taken her to task about her solitary habit of life. No one had said it was selfish. 'And you're a model citizen, I suppose?'

Jake gave an unamused laugh. 'Depends who you talk to. I pay my dues.'

'So you go on charabanc rides to the seaside with the over-sixties?' Ash persisted in her sweetest tone. 'Run the tombola? Things like that?'

He regarded her with hostility. 'Of course not.'

'Yet you're quite sure you pay your dues,' she marvelled. Her voice hardened. 'Now, I don't do those things either. And that's why you've got me down as a parasite. Could it possibly be because you're a man and I'm a woman?'

Jake's expression set. 'Sex discrimination, the root of all evil?'

'I didn't say that.'

'No, but that's what you meant.' She had been right. The anger was almost tangible in the air between them. 'I've heard it before.'

'I didn't – '

He swept on. 'The world according to Women's Rules. Men are villains because they're physically stronger. So we are supposed to pretend that we aren't, that men and women are the same in every way. Until a woman *wants* to be different. Then we are supposed to sit by while they empower themselves, God help us. And if a man dares to suggest that life works best if both sides pull their weight, then he's being oppressive and insensitive and it's time for divorce.'

95

Ash seized on the only part of the tirade that made sense. 'You're divorced.'

'No,' said Jake grimly. 'And I'm not going to be.' He sent her a look in which hostility still smouldered. Hostility, she inferred, to the whole of her sex. 'If you don't marry, you can't divorce.'

'Makes sense,' Ash agreed with caution.

He laughed suddenly. 'And you're wrong, you know.'

'Am – am I? What about?'

'Your friends. They're worried about you, all right. But they weren't the source. Or not the first source. I knew all about your lifestyle, as you call it, before I came down here today.'

And that was true enough, Jake thought wryly. The report had been very full on *how* she lived her life. It had just omitted to mention that she was young and crazy.

Ash stared. He raised an eyebrow. Suddenly, she had a chilling suspicion. She swallowed. 'You knew all about me?' She shook her head. 'I don't understand. Why?'

'You stand in the way of one of my major projects,' Jake Dare informed her coolly. 'I like to know everything about the enemy. My people told me you were being difficult. I was in Brazil, then. Not much I could do about it. But I told them to make up a dossier on you.'

The chill was pure ice water and it was trickling down her spine. 'A *dossier*?'

'Of course. Ten pages of it. A full break down on how you spend your days.' His eyes brooded suddenly. 'It missed out one or two other salient facts, though. I shall have to speak to Tony about that.'

'You – had – me – investigated?' Ash said. It was not

much more than a whisper. Her face had gone very white.

Jake Dare did not register the danger signals. 'Yes. And a damned unprofessional job it was,' he said, pardonably annoyed. 'These bright young graduates. They're so determined to impress with all the detail they've dug up, that they don't see the wood for the trees. They told me you were a widow living on a pension with a local reputation as a bit of a recluse. Only known emotional commitment to an animal centre. I thought you were ninety! And major fruitcake material.'

Ash was so angry she could hardly speak. 'Sue them,' she advised in a strangled voice.

'I shall certainly reconsider whether they stay on the management training programme,' he agreed.

'I should.'

The heavy irony passed him by. Ash stared at him. She was shaking like a birch tree in a high wind. With temper she assured herself. He took in her glittering eyes and his brows rose. He sighed.

'What is it now?'

'You don't get it, do you? You don't see anything wrong about setting your – your – minions to spy on me.' In her vehemence, she was nearly incoherent.

'Minions? Hey, I'm just a simple businessman.'

The tears were perilously close to falling. She dashed an angry hand across her eyes. 'You think you're entitled to do any damned thing you want as long as it's for your precious business.'

That got through at last. His mouth thinned. 'And you just think you're entitled to everything.'

'I don't,' Ash shouted. She drew a shaky breath and

97

tried to control herself. 'Just ordinary human consideration. Just not to be *spied* on.'

'Oh, I've invaded your precious space, is that it?' The
mockery was savage.

Ash refused to back down. 'Yes, yes you have,' she told
him. 'And I give you fair warning. I won't have my private
life crawled over and chopped up just to make you a big fat
profit.'

Jake was intrigued. 'You said that with feeling.'

'That,' said Ash icily, 'was because I meant it. Men like
you are despicable.'

He looked cynical. 'Men *like* me? Whose punishment
am I taking here?' He paused and then added softly,
deliberately, 'The late Mr Lawrence's?'

Ash stopped as if he had shot her. Looking into those
lazy, clever eyes she had the feeling that it was just in time.
She remembered being on a horse once which had refused
to jump a hedge at the last moment. By some miraculous
chance, Ash had managed to stay on, but she had never
forgotten the sensation of having avoided disaster by
inches. She had the same feeling now.

Jake was looking hatefully tolerant. It seemed she
amused him. Ash shook her head as if to clear it.

'I don't think I like your tactics, Mr Dare,' she said
slowly. 'I don't like them at all.'

The amusement disappeared. He shrugged. 'Tell that to
my shareholders.'

She nodded as if he had confirmed something she had
expected and already condemned. 'I'm sure you're very
successful.'

'You got something against success?'

'It depends on how it's achieved.'

His eyes flickered. 'I see. English gentlemen's rules only. Yet you're happy enough to collect your dividends, I bet. How do you think your pension is paid? From the proceeds of investment in companies like Dare. Would you be happy if I behaved like a chivalrous moron and lots of little old ladies lost their life savings?'

Ash's lip curled. 'Very impressive, Mr Dare,' she flung back at him. 'Of course you don't *like* dirty tricks. I'm sure you only employ them most reluctantly . . .'

'If you think commissioning a report on you qualifies as a dirty trick, you need a crash course in twentieth-century ethics,' Jake Dare said crisply.

'And you need a crash course in morality,' she flashed. 'Do you think I'm taken in by that high-minded nonsense about your duty to your shareholders? You like winning, Mr Dare. That's why you use dirty tricks. It's got nothing to do with little old ladies or anyone else who invests in your company. It's because you'll do any damned thing in the world to *win*!' She spat it at him. She did not even attempt to disguise her contempt.

There was a sharp silence. The green eyes narrowed to slits. Beneath the heavy lids they glowed like a light in a distant furnace. Ash felt a sudden shiver of apprehension run up her spine.

She said hurriedly, 'I shouldn't have said that. I'm sorry. I don't know anything about your business ethics.'

The steady gaze felt like a burn. He looked alert and dangerous – and angry.

'But you know about somebody's business ethics,' Jake

Dare said quietly. 'Don't you, darling? Now is it just because you read the wrong newspapers? Or have you got some personal stake in this?'

Ash paled. He saw it with satisfaction.

'It sounded very personal to me,' he said watching her.

She shrugged, looking away from him.

'Did the sainted Peter Lawrence get carved up by some slick businessman?' he probed.

For a moment she was quite still, though he saw her throat move as she swallowed. Then she rubbed her arms quickly as if she were cold. She looked sick.

Ash saw him taking note. She sought about for something to deflect him and found nothing. In the end she said desperately, 'That's none of your business.'

'I think you just made it my business.'

'No,' she said, horrified. Then, more collectedly, 'If I've been rude, I apologize. I admit I'm not too keen on big business or the people who run it. As for my reasons – read the papers. I don't need a personal vendetta. All I have to do is remember what companies like yours do to the countryside. I don't like it.'

She went to the door. Jake watched her, unspeaking. She turned.

'But then I don't have to like you, do I, Mr Dare? You'll be gone as soon as you're better. I'm sure it won't take you ten days. Shall we say three?'

He was amused again. 'Now why does that sound like a challenge?'

Ash gave him a sweet smile. 'Not a challenge, Mr Dare. A prophesy.'

She walked out, closing the door decisively behind her.

100

In the echo, she thought she heard him laughing. She fled downstairs.

On the bed, Jake stopped laughing as soon as Ash's footsteps died away. He got off the bed and went to the window. He looked out at the formal garden without seeing it, his mouth set.

Tony Anderson was not going to get another chance to mess this one up again, he resolved. From now on, Jake was taking care of this one himself.

Ash did not stop until she reached the hall. She leaned back against the wall. She was shaking, a deep cold trembling that seemed to come from her very heart.

The awful thing was, she knew that feeling. She had not felt like this for more than three years. But she still recognized it: helpless, inadequate, in the wrong.

But I held my own, she thought, bewildered. I held my own. He knew it and so did I. Why do I feel as if I've been pulverized?

She had never held her own against Peter, she reminded herself. In the end she had not even tried. There are some things you can't argue about. Eventually he only had to look at her and she felt that cold weight of defeat. But she had fought her corner with Jake Dare.

Now she closed her eyes. 'No,' said Ash. 'Oh no, not again.'

She opened her eyes. The sun struck cheerfully through the great arched window. It showed Jake Dare's big Mercedes where it had come to rest.

She gave herself a shake. That car would have to be

moved. The gravel would have to be raked back into its former smoothness, too. She did not look, as she never looked, at the tall tree by the gates. There were practical things to be done.

She went to deal with the practicalities. She slid gingerly behind the driving wheel and turned the key. The Mercedes responded like a thoroughbred. Ash slid it into the far end of the garage where Peter had always kept his car. She refused to think of that.

As she was getting out, she kicked something. She looked; bent; picked up the smashed thing. Jake Dare's mobile telephone looked way beyond repair.

She would have to tell him. She thought about it and decided that telling him could wait. She had had as much of Jake Dare as she could manage for the moment. In fact, if she was honest, probably rather more than she could manage. She would feel strong enough to face him again, of course she would. But probably not just yet.

She left him alone for several hours. In the end it was conscience which drove her back upstairs. She opened the door to his room and stood in the doorway.

'It looks like I owe you a mobile phone,' she announced.

There was no answer. She came a few quiet steps into the room. Still no words. Ash went toward the bed.

Jake was out cold. He was stretched out on the double bed, one arm flung above his head. The attitude of abandon was oddly appealing, Ash thought. As if he were lowering all barriers. She paused, taken aback by her reaction.

'Careful,' Ash admonished herself, alarmed.

'No one ever cared as much as you,' Joanne had said. It

102

was horribly true. Ash took herself to task.

Caring was fine. As long as you didn't let yourself care for people. People hurt. Caring should be confined to animals.

Ash looked down at the unconscious Jake Dare. 'You can't afford to get protective about this one,' she muttered. 'He doesn't need it. He's far too sophisticated. And way out of your league.'

The dangerous sophisticate had pushed the covers down so that they were tangled round his hips. The pillows he had pulled around her were now all over the place. Two were on the floor beside his bed. Ash trod softly to the side of the bed and picked them up. Jake did not stir.

She put them back on the bed. There was a faint sheen of sweat on his bare chest. Ash looked at it. She frowned. Then, so delicately that he would not feel it, she touched the back of her hand to his forehead. It was warm.

She bit her lip. It could be because of the heat of the summer evening, she thought. Or alternatively, he could have a slight temperature. Was there really some substance to Brian Francis' insistence that he rest? She looked down at Jake, troubled.

He stirred then. He turned a little and reached across the bed.

'Rosie,' he said for the third time, his voice slurred with sleep.

Oho, thought Ash. No divorce, no marriage but that did not mean no lady, clearly.

She was about to step away when one drowsy hand reached out waveringly. It found her wrist. Ash stood very still. It was not a strong grip. Ash could have detached herself easily. So there was no reason why she should stand there as if turned to stone while a half-unconscious man ran his thumb gently back and forth across the leaping pulse.

Then something extraordinary happened. It had nothing at all to do with their earlier battle. In fact it had nothing to do with anything she had felt since she was eighteen. But quite suddenly something wild and sweet and long-forgotten stirred in her.

Ash held her breath. It was almost like being in pain. Peter — She screwed her eyes up tight, trying not to remember. But she still stood there and let Jake Dare stroke her wrist while she remembered dreams she had not dared even to think about since she was eighteen.

'Mmm. Rosie,' he said, pleased. His eyelids twitched.

Ash jumped as if a flashlight had gone off. She whisked away from his bedside, blushing furiously. For the second time that day, she fled his room in disarray. And this time he was not even conscious.

You're out of your mind, she told herself. And worse. You can't just leave him. He might even be ill.

She looked back at the figure on the bed. He was sleeping peacefully now. Not that ill, she told her conscience. She would check on him *first thing* in the morning. Now she needed to regroup her forces.

The doorbell to the London apartment rang in the kitchen. Marriott stopped chopping parsley and picked up the handset.

'Yes.'

'Hello, Marriott.' It was a woman's voice. 'Jake in?'

Marriott's nose twitched with distaste. Nothing of his feelings showed in his voice, however, as he said, 'I am afraid not, Miss Newman.'

'Come on, Marriott, don't be stuffy. I've been waiting at the office. They said he had an appointment and must be going straight home.'

Marriott frowned in concern. He had been assuming that Jake was still at the office. There was certainly no suggestion this morning that his trip to Oxfordshire would take the whole day.

He was not going to tell Rosie Newman that, however. He said, 'I am afraid Mr Dare has gone out of town. I do not know when to expect him back.'

'All right. I'll come in and wait.'

Marriott's nose twitched even harder. But he could not refuse to let her in without specific instructions from Jake. He must make sure Jake gave him those instructions tomorrow, Marriott thought grimly. For the moment, however, as far as the newspapers were concerned at least, Jake Dare and Rosie Newman were still officially engaged. He sighed and pressed the entry button.

'Very well, Miss Newman. I will send down the lift.'

Rosie Newman had been shopping. She came out of the lift strung about with designer label carrier bags in laminated jewel colours. She was wearing a determined expression and an air of ladylike exhaustion. The latter dropped from her the moment she saw Marriott.

'Oh,' she said. 'Jake really isn't here?'

'I'm afraid not, miss.' Marriott relieved her of her burden. 'May I give you tea?'

'A large gin would be better,' she said frankly. 'I've been late-night shopping and I thought I'd catch him afterwards.'

She flung herself back on the sofa and watched Marriott pour her drink.

'He's avoiding me, isn't he?' she said abruptly.

Marriott stiffened. 'I really could not say.'

'I leave messages here. Messages with the office. I've even called his mother.'

Marriott was startled out of his professional incuriosity. 'You rang Palm Beach?'

The visitor nodded. 'For all the good it did me. He wasn't there and she doesn't know where he is. You do, though, don't you?'

Marriott said, 'I am sure Mr Dare has received your messages.'

'Don't,' she said sharply. She swung round on the couch, looking up at him in appeal. 'Look, I flung the ring back at him. I wasn't thinking. He wouldn't listen to me and it made me mad but – '

Marriott looked as if he had been stuffed. Rosie gave a small laugh, half-angry, half-embarrassed.

'I *must* talk to him. All I need is to see him. It will take ten minutes. No more, I promise.'

Marriott very much doubted that but he inclined his head. 'I will tell him so, miss.'

It was dismissal and they both knew it. Rosie lost her air of appeal. She frowned in mighty displeasure. Marriott was unmoved. Rosie was not used to that.

She banged her half-full glass down on the table and left without a word.

'Good night miss,' said Marriott as the lift doors closed. 'So fortunate Mr Dare was not here.'

He looked at the grandfather clock. Fortunate perhaps, but not reassuring. Jake was a considerate employer. If he had intended not to be back that night he would have said. Or telephoned if something came up. He must have been held up.

No need to worry, Marriott told himself. If Jake could climb some of the toughest peaks in the Rockies, he could look after himself on a day trip to the Home Counties. What was more, he was not a schoolboy to have to phone home if his schedule changed.

The idea of ringing the Dare office died as soon as it was born. Miss Newman had said he had not been back there. Besides, Jake would not be best pleased if he found his manservant had been worrying about him.

Marriott, with some reluctance, went back to his parsley.

Ash fed the animals, but when she thought of food for herself, her stomach rebelled. She felt as shaken up as ever she could remember.

'A conversation with that man is worse than going to the dentist,' she said aloud.

But there was more to it than that. She knew there was. She knew it all evening, as she walked the dog, played with the kittens, checked the badger cub. She knew it as she put a load of washing through the machine. She knew it as she started on a pile of mending untouched for months.

She knew it as she looked in one more time on her uninvited guest. He did not stir. And she did not get any closer than the doorway. Her flesh could still remember that unconscious touch, as if his fingers were still around her wrist. Ash shivered involuntarily and then looked narrowly at the sleeping figure.

Thank God he was not awake. Thank God he had not woken up then. Thank God, above all, that he had not seen the effect it had on her. It turned her blood cold to think what he would have made of that moment of – what was it, anyway? Weakness? Naive sentimentality?

Ash shook her head. She could not explain it. It must have happened because she was tired, she thought frantically. Not just tired, but over tense. The accident, driving the car, Jake's threats to Rusty: they all added up. It was not surprising if she was tense.

Going to the clinic had reminded her of Peter, too. Normally she could put the thought of those old wounds out of her mind. Today they had been thrust upon her forcibly. It was only to be expected that it would upset her. Memories and battles: no wonder she was feeling vulnerable. A good night's sleep and she would be herself again.

Ash backed out of Jake's room, closing the door softly. In the light of a new day, those feelings when he touched her wrist would recede, she assured herself. They had been a momentary aberration. They were the product of a tough day. No more than that. She would laugh at them tomorrow. The best thing she could do was to go to bed and forget all about them.

But when she closed the door of her own bedroom, she was breathing as hard as if she were in full flight from an enemy. And the enemy was not Jake Dare, she was honest enough to admit. It was herself.

CHAPTER 5

The next day was another warm wonderful day. Above the hedgerows bees buzzed lazily. For all the dense morning shadows, the air was hot and still. On the horizon, the fold of green fields seemed to shimmer. The distant church spire looked like an unsteady toy.

At six-thirty Jake Dare was sleeping deeply. Even a retriever's nose under his elbow, before Ash had time to call Rusty off, did not wake him. Girl and dog retreated to the garden.

'It will be all right,' Ash told herself, taking comfort from the view. 'It *will*.'

In London, Marriott went round the apartment drawing down blinds against the effects of morning sunlight. He had established that Jake's room had not been slept in. He was no longer pretending that he was not going to call the Dare office as soon as it opened.

The new inhabitant at the Gate House had had a wakeful night, too. He was sitting at a desk, with bills and scribbled calculations strewn all over it. The telephone rang. He seized it, extending the aerial with hurried fingers. He waited. No one spoke.

'Don't waste my time,' he said wearily.

In Jake Dare's office, his personal assistant and his secretary were looking at each other in consternation. They had just put the phone down on Marriott.

'He was going to see the Lawrence woman,' Tony Anderson said. 'He couldn't have got lost.'

The secretary had been with Jake ever since he had set up in business. Even more than Marriott and Tony Anderson she knew how uncharacteristic it was for Jake not to come back when he said he would.

'He could have had a brainstorm.'

'Oh, come on, Barbara.'

'He could. He's been driving himself too hard. I've seen it.'

'Well, I haven't.'

'When did he last have a holiday?' she challenged him.

'Well – um – his family were over at Christmas.'

Barbara's expression said very clearly what she thought of Jake Dare's mother and sister. 'That was no holiday. He was supposed to be going skiing and then he didn't.'

'Well, Miss Newman took a chalet. They weren't getting on that well. He probably thought it wouldn't be restful,' protested Tony.

'No, but he didn't do anything else instead. *And* the moment he got back from Brazil he went straight into a sixteen-hour day again. It's not right. It's not healthy.'

Tony put his hands on the corners of her desk. 'Look. If

he crashed the car, we'd have heard. He's got papers, credit cards.'

'They could all have been – destroyed,' said Barbara. She had a dramatic imagination.

'And he could have been abducted by aliens, but I'm willing to offer you good odds he wasn't. He's a fixer, Barbara. He's got out of tight corners all over the world. He can handle himself.'

'The mobile is switched off,' she said in a voice of doom.

'Maybe he doesn't want any calls.'

Barbara looked at him eloquently. 'Why?'

'Well – ' Tony could not think of a reason that convinced him, either. 'Maybe he's eloped with Rosie Newman and he's taken her off on honeymoon,' he suggested with a twinkle.

It got a faint smile out of Barbara. 'Well, he hasn't done that. I've already had madam on the phone this morning. If he turned that phone off voluntarily, it's more likely to be because he doesn't want to take any more calls from her.'

Rosalind Newman was at the breakfast table before her father for once. He came into the pretty breakfast-room, frowning.

'No good,' she said, as soon as he walked in. 'He's gone to ground. That robot who looks after him wouldn't tell me where he is.'

The frown deepened. 'That's just not good enough. Good God, Rosie, how could you have let it go on so long?'

She shrugged. 'I thought he'd come back. They usually do.'

Her father snorted. 'You're talking about the fools you normally play around with. Didn't it occur to you that Jake Dare would be different?'

'Why should it?' she said in a hard voice. 'He's still a man, isn't he?'

He gave a bark of laughter. 'One who started life in the Memphis slums. He didn't get where he is by letting someone else call the tune.' He looked at his watch and quickly helped himself to a croissant. 'You should have worked that one out.'

'Thank you for your advice,' she said with bite. 'Bit late, though.'

'Have you put a notice in the paper yet? The marriage arranged will not now take place and all that guff?'

'No,' she said shortly.

'Then it's not too late.' He swallowed the rest of his croissant, got up from the table and picked up the *Financial Times* from the dresser. 'You'll just have to work a bit harder, that's all.'

'How can I, if he won't see me?'

But her father was on his way out. 'Change your tactics,' he suggested indifferently. 'Eat humble pie. Chain yourself to his railings. Camp out in his bedroom. Hell, I don't know. That's your department.'

Rosie looked at him with acute dislike. 'Anyone would think I'm the only one involved.'

'You're the one with the most to lose,' her father pointed out. 'If I go bankrupt, the trustees will give me enough to live on. They won't give you a thing. They'll think you ought to be earning your own living. You've got more than your dress allowance riding on this. Don't forget it.'

They did not kiss goodbye.

Upstairs at the Manor the uncurtained sun woke Jake Dare with a start. For a moment he lay among tumbled sheets, wondering where the hell he was. All he could remember was that it had not been a comfortable night. His head ached. And when he struggled up into a sitting position, the landscape beyond his window was utterly unfamiliar.

'What the –?' began Jake.

But it was not just the sun that had awoken him. There was a knock on the door; clearly not the first.

'Come in.'

It opened to admit a middle-aged lady wearing a flowered overall and a speculative expression. Jake's eyes widened. He had stayed in a lot of hotels and he knew the look of hotel staff. This woman was clearly not of their number.

'Good morning,' she said, thumping a tray down on his bedside chest.

The tray was exquisitely inlaid. The mug it bore was thick, mass-produced china. Jake's brows knit, trying to make sense of these conflicting pieces of evidence. The aroma of coffee distracted him.

'Good morning, indeed,' he said, reaching for it gratefully. 'This is very kind of you, Mrs – ?'

'Harrison,' she said. She straightened his pillows. 'Ash said you wouldn't be wanting tea. You being American. Course I knew that. When Mr Lawrence was alive, we had

113

a lot of Americans staying. Official entertaining, he used to call it. They all drank coffee.'

Jake blinked, not quite sure what he was being told but certain it was more than the beverage preferences of his compatriots.

'And very good it is too,' he said, noncommittally.

Em nodded. 'She makes a good cup of coffee, Ash.' She made a business of tidying the untouched dressing table. 'She's a good girl at heart. Not had an easy life, for all she's got so much money. Have to admit, she can be a bit difficult.'

And then, suddenly, he remembered where he was.

'Ashley Lawrence,' he said slowly.

Red hair; so slim her hands felt like bird bones a man could crush; skin like magnolia under her freckles. He shifted uncomfortably. And she could be a bit difficult.

Jake was remembering more than where he was. He did not like the pictures that came into his head. The accident; baiting Ash last night. If she was being difficult this morning, well, he had given her every reason yesterday, hadn't he?

Jake shook his head, hardly believing his own memories. What on earth had got into him? He had known he was at the start of a delicate negotiation, for heaven's sake. Why had he allowed himself to be tempted into teasing her like that? She could be as difficult as she knew how and he would have only himself to blame.

He was rueful. 'She's not the only one who can be difficult. I don't think I was the ideal guest yesterday.'

Em was predisposed to like any unattached male staying in the Manor. Now Jake's smile utterly won her over.

114

'Nothing to worry about,' she said briskly. 'Shock. Whatever you did, Ash won't hold it against you.'

She marched downstairs to make sure that Ash realized her duty.

Jake settled back among his newly comfortable pillows and thought about Ashley Lawrence. He began to smile.

On the terrace below him, his reluctant hostess was attacking weeds between the paving stones with vicious concentration. Molly Hall, delivering her twins for badger duty, stopped dead at the sight that met her eyes. Her eyebrows lifted in amusement.

'You look hot,' she said.

Ash whipped round as if she were expecting an enemy. Molly Hall's brows rose even higher. She had known Ash a long time. She had never seen that look on her face before.

'Trouble?' she asked in quick concern.

Ash looked a little shamefaced. She shrugged and cast the trowel from her.

'Didn't Chris tell you about Rusty attacking someone's car yesterday?'

'Yes, but – '

'The driver knocked himself out. He's here,' Ash said succinctly.

'Here?' Molly looked up instinctively at the Jacobean walls. 'In the house? But you never have people to stay. You – ' She encountered a speaking look from Ash and realized that the window to the main bedroom suite was open. She hurriedly changed what she was going to say. 'That will be a lot of work for you. Shall I take the boys back? They've gone round to see the badger cub but I can easily . . .'

'No, don't,' said Ash swiftly. 'I'd like them to stay. It will make it feel a bit more normal.'

She flung herself down on the wooden seat and patted the place beside her. Molly looked round as if she too expected an invasion of strangers.

She lowered her voice. 'Where is he?'

'Upstairs,' Ash said. She gave a jerk of her head at the open window. 'Lolling about in my father's pyjamas pretending to be in shock.'

Molly chuckled. 'Oh,' she said enlightened. 'That must have been what Em was talking about when I brought the boys in. Tall, dark and handsome?'

Ash glared. 'That's a matter of opinion.'

'Well, that's Em's opinion. He sounds intriguing.'

Ash gave her a smouldering look. 'Em doesn't know what she's talking about. He's an executive-class dictator.' She kicked at a clump of moss between two paving stones in front of her.

Molly smiled. 'I've never met one of those. Bring him over for a drink when he's on his feet again.'

'When he's on his feet again he's out,' Ash said firmly. And loudly.

A choke of laughter drifted down to them. Ash set her jaw. Molly Hall looked up at the leaded window then back at Ash. Molly was incredulous. Ash might not like visitors but she did not insult them deliberately. Usually she discouraged them by being gently vague. This rudeness was utterly new in Molly's experience.

'There?' she mouthed at Ash silently.

Ash nodded. A faint colour mounted into her cheeks. This time she lowered her voice. 'I'm so used to being on my own,' she muttered. 'I didn't realise he was listening. Damn. I suppose he heard every word.'

'I shouldn't think any of it was much of a surprise,' said Molly drily, preparing to leave. 'Is it all right if I pick the boys up about six?'

'Fine,' Ash said absently, looking up at the window.

There was no figure in purple pyjamas lurking behind the glass. Perhaps she had imagined that laughter. Perhaps he was still asleep, after all. Either way, it was too late to do anything about it. She shrugged and saw Molly to her car.

Then, because she could not put it off any longer, she took him his breakfast. Em had flatly refused to, on the grounds that at her age she could not be expected to keep running up and down stairs all day and she had already taken him a cup of coffee when Ash was too hard-hearted even to put her head round the door and see how the poor man was. There was no answer to that. Bowing to the inevitable, Ash meekly picked up the beautiful breakfast tray Em had prepared and went.

Jake Dare was sitting up in bed, a thin sheet moulding his long legs, his chest bare. It was a very tanned chest, decorated with curling hair that was as black as that on his head. Ash averted her eyes from it but not quickly enough to hide her shock. Jake grinned.

'You look like a pirate,' she said, annoyed.

'An executive-class pirate, I hope?' He was bland.

So he had heard. Ash winced. She put the tray down on the bedside chest. He had somehow pulled the telephone awry in the night. She pushed it gently back into place with the corner of the tray.

'Eavesdroppers never hear any good of themselves,' she said.

It was no more than he deserved. But remembering what else she had said, she still flushed.

He laughed. 'How true.' He turned and took in the soft colour in her face. 'Hey. Don't look so miserable,' he said, touched. He flicked his fingers briefly against her hot cheek. 'You've already said worse to my face.'

Ash jumped away from his touch as if she had been stung. 'Yes, I did, didn't I?' she said in a constrained voice. 'Does that make it any better?'

Jake reached for toast. He shrugged. 'On the whole I prefer it. Most people don't have the guts to call you names to your face. So they do it behind your back.' Was there a hint of bitterness in his voice? 'Your way at least we all know where we stand.'

Ash poured coffee. 'Not much doubt of that. You said it yourself. You and I were born to be enemies.'

He plumped up his pillows and then sprawled back against them, laughing at her. 'Did I say that?' he drawled. 'Must have been the crack on the head. I'm not usually a pessimist.'

One look at the gleam in his eye and Ash decided against demanding an explanation. She pushed his coffee towards the corner of the tray nearest his hand.

'Not pessimistic. Sensible,' she said. 'I dislike everything you stand for.'

He was not noticeably downcast. 'You don't know everything I stand for,' he said tranquilly.

118

'Most, I think.' She was dry.

'You haven't even scratched the surface, honey.' He was even drier.

Ash glared at him. 'Don't call me honey. It sounds as if we are friends. We are not. And believe me, Mr Dare, we aren't going to be.'

He chuckled. 'I'll make a bargain with you. You don't call me Mr Dare. I don't call you honey. How's that?'

She looked at him with dislike. 'Do you turn everything into a bargain?'

Jake smiled at her slowly. 'Most things,' he drawled.

Ash retreated from the deliberate innuendo like Rusty from a hedgehog. 'Well, I don't,' she said sharply. 'And I don't intend to let you get under my skin, either. So you can stop trying.'

For a moment there was a hint of deep, deep anger on the dark face. Ash saw it with satisfaction. But in a second it seemed she had imagined it and he was laughing again.

'I wouldn't dream of it,' he assured her. He leaned back, lathering his toast with creamy butter and Em's home-made marmalade. He was enjoying himself. 'In fact I don't want to be any more of problem to you than I can help.' He met her eyes limpidly. 'So if you'll just get my mobile, I will call my assistant and ask him to come down and help out.'

'Your mobile's broken,' Ash told him, flatly.

He frowned. 'Then I shall have to use yours temporarily.'

'Feel free.' Her irony was heavy.

Jake ignored it. 'I was sure you wouldn't mind.'

'Oh, were you?' She looked at him evilly. 'If you want

your assistant here, you must be feeling well enough to work.'

Jake's lips twitched. He controlled them. Instead he gave Ash a faint brave smile.

'I still have my responsibilities,' he said nobly. And evasively.

Ash said, 'If you're going to work – '

'Not work.' He was reproachful. 'Not properly. As long as I take everything else very easy, I can manage to make the one or two key decisions. I'll have to delegate everything else to Tony Anderson.'

Everything, he thought with private amusement, except the subjugation of Ashley Lawrence. That clearly needed a master's hand. Tony had already proved unequal to the task. Now it was the turn of the professional.

Jake lay back and sipped his coffee. He did not believe she would buy his story for a moment, but the beauty of it was that there was not a thing she could do about it. Not unless she wanted to risk his lodging a complaint about that over-excitable dog of hers. Enjoying himself, Jake lowered his lids and watched her work it out for herself. First blood to the professional, he thought, pleased.

'I see,' Ash said.

And she did. The man had decided to move in on the Manor and, unless she was willing to put poor old Rusty at risk, all she could do was accept it gracefully.

'I thought you would,' he murmured.

She glinted a look down at him which, if he had been watching her, would have put him on his guard. But Jake, secure in his victory, was reaching for another piece of toast.

She handed him the telephone. 'Make your call.'

He did.

'And now I must do all I can to make sure you do get that rest,' Ash said dulcetly. 'Until your assistant gets here.'

She bent and with a swift tug pulled the telephone connection out of the socket. Jake shot out a hand in protest. But it was too late. She had gathered up the telephone and was leaving the room.

'You won't want to be disturbed by phone calls.'

Their eyes met in a silent duel. Jake sat bolt upright, astonished. Then he gave her a faint, respectful nod. The respect was some consolation to Ash, but not much.

He said softly, 'Without a means of communication, I could get awfully depressed up here on my own.'

Ash just looked at him.

'Shock can bring on severe depression.'

She frowned. 'You mean rest isn't enough? You think you'll need stimulus as well?' She tried hard to sound uneasy.

It seemed she managed it. Jake sank back among his pillows and clasped his hands behind his head. He even smiled.

'Definitely.'

That was when Ash smiled back. Her sherry brown eyes suddenly came alive with mirth. Even as he sat up, concerned, she gave him a wide grin.

'Then I shall arrange it, of course,' she said.

She left before he could say any more. She ran down the stairs and into the kitchen.

'Well, you've got a bit of colour in your cheeks at last,'

Em said pleased. 'Nice to have someone your own age for a bit of company for once.'

Ash paid no attention. 'Where are the boys?'

'Throwing sticks for Rusty the last time I saw them,' said Em, surprised. Ash pretty much let the Hall twins have the run of the place when they were on holiday. She didn't usually check up on them. 'Why?'

'I've got a job for them,' Ash said, a beatific smile on her face. 'Playing with Rusty, eh? Maybe Rusty too, then.'

She went into the garden. Em stared after her as if she were mad.

Chris and Martin were kind children. They made no demur about coming indoors on a beautiful day. They were only too willing to cheer up the invalid. His dramatic arrival had caught their imagination and the powerful car garaged behind the badger's run had clinched it.

Ash left them alone to get on with it for an hour or so. Then she went upstairs, the picture of solicitude.

The sight that met her eyes was one which might well have turned any hostess' blood to water. The duvet was on the floor with a large dog-shaped mound scuffling about under it. One Hall twin was standing on the window seat shouting encouragement while the other swatted at the mound with a cushion.

Jake Dare, in purple silk pyjama trousers and bare chest, was standing by the bed giving instructions – without noticeable effect, Ash was glad to see. The remains of his tea cup, smashed beyond repair, were scattered across the Chinese silk rug.

'Oh dear,' said Ash, not even trying to sound regretful.

Jake slewed round and glared at her.

'There you are. What the hell . . . That is,' he said recalling himself, 'could you persuade your children to play elsewhere? They,' he added with something of a snap, 'take no notice of me.'

Ash did not correct his error in respect of the provenance of the Hall twins. Partly because she liked Jake Dare believing false information. It made her feel safer somehow, when he did not know all the facts. Partly it was due to Martin. The boy gave her no time, saying to Jake reproachfully, 'We're cheering you *up*.'

'A kind thought,' said Jake 'but . . .'

'It was Ash's idea,' said Chris. He was a conscientious boy.

Jake gave her a speaking look. 'I'm not at all surprised,' he muttered. 'But . . .' He stopped as Rusty wriggled out from under the duvet and flung himself on a delighted Chris. 'You seem to have no control over that dog whatsoever,' he snapped at her. 'After yesterday, I'd have expected you to have shut him up.'

Ash caught hold of Rusty by the scruff of his neck and calmed all three excited participants. The look she gave Jake Dare was cool. 'Oh? Why?'

'He's dangerous.'

'Because he chased your car? Don't be ridiculous.' Ash gave a mocking laugh. 'It's bigger than he is.'

Jake regarded the panting dog with disfavour. 'The creature looks highly untrustworthy.'

'Animals,' said Ash softly, 'are a lot more trustworthy than people. Rusty didn't attack you. You're just annoyed with him because your reactions weren't fast enough.'

Jake surveyed the dog. Rusty panted at him in a friendly way.

123

'It's not even ashamed of itself.'

'Why should he be? Even if he remembered, which he doesn't, what did he do wrong? He had a lot of fun chasing a car and no one got hurt. So I wasn't angry with him. Satisfaction all round.'

'*I* got hurt,' said Jake, outraged.

Ash waved a dismissive hand. 'Maybe.'

He sat down on the side of the bed and looked at her. 'I'm surprised you haven't rewarded him,' he said after a pause.

Ash narrowed her eyes at him. 'For bringing you into the house?' she asked incredulously.

There was a short, dangerous pause. For a moment Jake Dare looked furious. Ash found she was reminding herself that he could not do her any harm. Hence she was not afraid of him. Of course she wasn't.

Then suddenly Jake laughed and flung up his hand in a defeated dueller's gesture. 'I surrender. I surrender entirely. Only *please* just take the livestock away. I've been entertained enough.'

'Of course, if you're going to rest . . .' Ash said dulcetly.

Jake sighed. He stood up, picked up the crumpled duvet and threw it over the bed. Then he climbed back into the bed and drew the cover up to his chin.

Satisfied, Ash gathered up broken crockery, dog and children and left him to the contemplation of his sins. But that moment's glimpse of what his anger could be like had shaken her.

When the assistant arrived, she went out to meet him as soon as she heard his car. She did not bother to remind him of their previous barbed encounter. Tony Anderson was presumably the man who had gathered the information in her dossier but she did not bother to take that up with him, either. She was just too glad to hand over dealing with Jake Dare to somebody else.

'Mr Dare is upstairs,' she said, taking him into the house after the briefest of greetings. 'Turn right at the top of the stairs. Second door. Here,' she shoved the phone she had confiscated earlier into his hands. 'You might need this.'

Accepting it, Tony looked at her warily. Her clipped tones were not friendly. She shifted a sleepy kitten in her arms, draping it over her shoulder and waved a hand in the direction of the stairs.

'You're very good,' Tony said politely. 'This must be an awful nuisance for you.'

'Awful,' she agreed with unmistakable feeling.

Then she relented. It was hardly Tony Anderson's fault. Anyway, she needed him on her side. She gave him a reasonable attempt at a smile. 'By the way, the doctor says Mr Dare shouldn't get too agitated about work problems.'

Tony blinked. Ashley Lawrence had not smiled at him before.

He went to see Jake with a troubled expression. 'How are you feeling?'

Jake grinned, but he was looking preoccupied. He also had the curbed excitement that Tony sometimes saw when Jake was at the planning stage of one of his ground-breaking projects.

'That's a complicated subject.'

Tony stared at him. 'I don't understand.'

'Well, on balance and all things considered, I'm fighting fit,' Jake said. 'But for the purposes of the delectable Mrs Lawrence, I'm on my last legs. I've got everything from a ruptured liver to a wind crater between the ears. Probably a broken heart as well,' he added thoughtfully.

Tony goggled. He had seen Jake in a dangerous mood before. He had never seen him like this. He began to wonder exactly what had happened in that accident.

'You're not trying to do too much too quickly, are you, Jake?'

Jake gave a private smile. 'On the contrary. I'm trying to do just enough. And it may be a little too late.'

Suddenly the answer came to Tony. 'It's the Hayes Wood project. You've thought of a way. You're going to get that wood off her,' he said on a note of discovery.

Jake looked at Tony with faintly mocking approval.

'But how . . .?'

'Trojan horse, my friend,' said Jake blandly.

Tony began to feel a sense of foreboding. He liked and admired his boss, but there was no denying that sometimes Jake's reckless streak took them into some difficult situations.

'I'm not snooping round the house pinching deeds,' he said, with the frankness of a close association. 'And neither will you, if you've got any sense.'

Jake shook his head, disappointed. 'I'm not crude,' he protested. 'Devious, yes. Crude, no. Neither you nor I are going to go rifling Ash Lawrence's deed box at dead of night, my friend.' He shuddered. 'She'd probably set the hound of the Baskervilles on us if we tried it.'

'Then what . . .'

'I,' said Jake sweetly, 'am going to blind her with my charm.'

'*What*?'

'What that woman needs is some love and appreciation.'

Tony murmured a faint protest. Jake ignored him ruthlessly.

'It was all there in your own report,' he said, warming to his theme. 'You just didn't see it. When I read it, I thought she was some elderly eccentric. But she isn't thirty yet. Why didn't you mention that?'

'I didn't see it was relevant. I still – '

'Think about it, Tony. Here she is, a complete solitary. Never goes out. Guards her privacy like a film star. No close friends. No lovers. Spends all her time grubbing about with animals. Well, you can see it, look at her. Is that normal at twenty-eight? I ask you. It's time she had a little fling.'

Tony groaned.

'I'll be doing the world a service.'

'You can't treat the woman like that. It's not fair,' Tony protested.

Jake gave his predatory grin. 'Love and war, Tony. Love and war.'

'She doesn't have the weapons to fight your sort of war,' said Tony Anderson with feeling. 'Look, Jake, I know you don't think much of women, but they're not all like Rosalind. You can't treat every one of them as if they were out to cheat you.'

Jake looked momentarily startled. 'I won't hurt her.'

'I've met her twice,' Tony said. 'She's got her head in the clouds. Probably never been in love in her life.'

'She's been married. She's even got a couple of damned badly behaved children to prove it.'

'That doesn't mean she's been in love,' said Tony unanswerably. 'Not the way you play the game, anyway. If you make her fall for you, you won't be able to help hurting her.'

For a moment Jake stared at him. He seemed to be debating inwardly. Then, slowly, he shook his head. 'I'll just have to risk it.'

At the Gate House the new resident was talking to his client.

'I don't know what's going on. Someone is giving me the silent phone-call treatment. I think it's supposed to scare me off. Then again, it could just be kids fooling around.'

A question came from the other end of the line. The new resident gave a hard laugh.

'Jake Dare doesn't scare easily. Nor do I.'

From the moment Tony Anderson disappeared upstairs, Em's campaign began. Ash ought to offer him a coffee, a meal, a bed for the night. Ash ought to go up and see if that poor man was still all right. Ash ought to *talk* to him.

In the end it was easier to stop arguing.

'I'll offer them coffee,' Ash agreed wearily.

She made for the stairs.

'Aren't you going to change first?' said Em, shocked.

Ash was wearing her usual jeans and tee-shirt and a day's gardening and gravel raking had done their worst. She grinned.

'He'll just have to get used to it.'

But her smile died as she tramped upstairs. Em was quite besotted by the man. Change, indeed. Probably Jake had suggested it. That had been a muddy handshake she had given him yesterday, she thought with a gleam of satisfaction.

No doubt Em's idea that Tony Anderson should be invited to move in had come from the same source. Well, this was the prize opportunity to snub Jake Dare and snub him hard in front of his assistant.

Ash marched into the room. 'Coffee?' she said, preparing herself to tell him in set terms that he had won all the concessions from her that he was going to.

But he took the wind out of her sails with a single sentence. 'Tony will be off soon,' he said firmly, with his most innocent smile. 'We don't want to trespass on your hospitality to excess.'

Ash stopped dead. She was almost certain that he had read her mind. Wrong-footing her, she thought, would be a bonus for Jake in an otherwise boring day. It infuriated her, but there was not a thing she could do about it. She just about stopped herself from grinding her teeth. But it was an effort.

Jake's smile widened and got, if possible, even more innocent. He tapped his subordinate's briefcase with a rolled gold pen. From the way Tony Anderson jumped, it was clearly a command.

'No time to sit around over coffee.'

Tony Anderson, she realized, was looking deeply apprehensive. To her surprise, Ash was aware of a wry fellow-feeling. If anyone had told her a week ago that one day she would be feeling sympathy for the smooth young man who had offered to buy her house so convincingly, she would have laughed them to scorn. But after a few hours of Jake Dare, Ash was beginning to take her support where she could find it. And looking at Tony's wary expression she found herself thinking, Jake Dare does that to me, too.

So in spite of all her resolutions, she said now, 'There's plenty of room here if Mr Anderson would like to stay.'

For some reason that did not please Jake at all. He said in a steely tone, 'Out of the question. He's got work to do. I shall do better on my own.'

Although he was smiling, his eyes were suddenly implacable. Ash saw it. For some reason that made her even more uneasy. She looked quickly at Tony Anderson. He was looking worried. Almost, thought Ash suddenly, as if his conscience was troubling him.

But he murmured obediently, 'It's very kind of you, Mrs Lawrence, but Jake is right. You'll have your hands quite full enough looking after the invalid.'

There was something in his tone that Ash could not interpret. She looked swiftly at Jake and saw that he plainly had no trouble in interpreting it and, equally plainly, that the implication did not please him. Her brows rose. So Tony sometimes dared to criticize the boss.

That was interesting. In her experience, the boss was next door to God and a good deal more unforgiving. She tried to remember if she had ever heard a subordinate criticize her grandfather. Just the thought was enough to make her wince. Even Peter had not dared to, she thought painfully, and her grandfather had owed Peter. After all,

Peter had married Ash, hadn't he? Thereby making sure that both the bank and the family name were in safe hands, as her grandfather had planned. But even so, Peter had not dared to disagree with the old tyrant.

She came back from the past with a little jump to find both men staring at her.

'I don't beat them,' Jake said softly.

Ash was startled. 'I'm sorry?'

'Guys who work for me,' he explained. 'They're employed to do a job. Not run my fan club.'

There was a taut silence. Tony Anderson shifted uncomfortably. Ash's eyes narrowed.

'Are you reading my mind?'

Jake grinned. 'Ain't hard.'

Ash sought for something crushing to say. She did not find it. Clearly entertained, Jake leaned back among the pillows, clasping his hands behind his head. He looked so at ease it was a positive insult.

She said between her teeth, 'You think you're very clever, don't you?'

His smile grew. 'Yup.'

Tony said hastily, 'Mrs Lawrence, I think we ought – '

'Don't interrupt, Tony,' Jake said lazily. 'Mrs Lawrence was about to tell me why I ain't as clever as I think I am. Here comes the character assessment.'

The other man looked on the edge of panic.

Ash said with cold fury, 'I don't give a damn about your character.'

He surveyed her placidly. 'Ah, but you do. Wasn't that why you came up here in the first place? You haven't come offering coffee before.'

Ash stared. He was smiling, but there was a horrible steely confidence about him that she recognized. It was exactly how her grandfather had looked when he dealt with staff who showed signs of mutiny. Or recalcitrant granddaughters. She tried to think of an answer and could not.

Jake said softly, 'Didn't you want to tell me I'd run my length? In front of a witness?'

Tony Robinson shifted uncomfortably. Ash jumped. She had almost forgotten he was there.

'What do you mean?'

Jake settled himself comfortably into the pillows. His eyes gleamed. 'Lay it on the line for the man. Not another millimetre into your life,' he explained coolly. 'Isn't that the message?'

Their eyes locked with a clash that was almost audible. Ash felt as if she had walked round an innocent corner into mayhem. She became aware of her heart beating quick and hard.

For a moment there was absolute silence in the sun-filled room. Tony looked from one intent face to the other and took several steps backwards. Neither of them noticed.

Jake stretched insolently and lay back, waiting. His whole demeanour said he expected Ash to rush into battle; and that he was looking forward to it. One amused eyebrow rose.

Ash saw it. She pulled herself together. If Jake Dare wanted a confrontation, he could have it, she thought. But she was not making a fool of herself for his entertainment.

So she opened her eyes very wide and said dulcetly, 'You took the words right out of my mouth.'

Tony Anderson gasped. He turned it quickly into a cough but there was no disguising his shock. Ash did not look at him but she felt a distinct triumph at his reaction. Presumably people did not normally talk to Jake Dare like that.

Jake himself was singularly unshocked, however. If anything he looked pleased. 'I thought I might,' he said affably.

Ash could have hit him. She opened her mouth to answer him. Then met his eyes and closed it. There was more than steel behind those smiling eyes. There was a bright curiosity that made her feel suddenly as if she were under a spotlight. It chilled her. She swallowed.

'I –'

'Don't get me wrong. I understand. I understand completely.'

And the awful thing was, thought Ash, as a little shiver went up her spine, that she had the feeling that he did indeed understand a great deal. That it included a whole trunkful of feelings that she had slammed the lid on a long time ago. She tore her eyes away and pulled the tatters of her dignity about her.

'Then no doubt we'll get along beautifully from now on,' she said at last.

The look of steel disappeared. Jake's eyes danced. 'Now that I really look forward to.'

I will not blush, Ash thought. I will *not*.

She turned on her heel without another word.

CHAPTER 6

Tony Anderson rushed to open the door for her. Ash swept through with a nod of thanks. She ignored Jake.

She wished she could ignore the feeling of his eyes on the back of her neck. Or the soft, appreciative laugh that echoed in her ears long after she had stamped off to her room.

There she plumped down in front of the mirror and glared at her reflection. The pointed chin was quivering with tension. Her eyes burned and there was a flush along her normally pale cheekbones. She looked like an angry cat, thought Ash, critically. He would have seen that. What was more he would have seen that there was more than anger involved.

She leaned her elbows on the dressing table and propped her chin on her hands. Slowly she let the anger leach out of her. There was no reason to let Jake Dare get to her. In a few days he would be gone. In a month she would not even be able to remember what he looked like.

Well, maybe what he looked like. Not the way he looked at her, Ash assured herself fervently.

Except that no one had ever looked at her like that before. Just thinking of it set up a small, shameful tremor. Ash looked down at her unsteady and slightly grubby fingers in disgust.

'You've got no backbone,' she told her reflection furiously. 'All you had to do was tell that man – '

A piece of twig fell out of her tangled curls and lay among the untouched jars of cosmetics on her dressing table. Ash looked down at it. For a moment she could have picked up one of the exquisite little crystal jars her father had given her over the years and flung it, hard.

But the habit of common sense was too strong for her. She looked at the inoffensive, unused Christmas presents and her lips began to twitch. Then the full ridiculousness of the situation swept over her. Ash began to laugh.

'All right. All right. I don't suppose many people tell him things he doesn't want to hear,' she admitted to her image. 'But you could have made a better attempt at trying.'

Ash would have been astonished if she could have heard Tony Anderson at that moment.

'Charm her?' he was saying. He did not quite hoot with laughter but there was a strong impression that it was only professional respect for his chief that stopped him. 'Charm *her*?'

Jake was unmoved. 'Yup.'

Tony shook his head in disbelief. 'You'll never swing it.'

Jake swung his legs briskly out of bed and stood up. 'You're an expert on women?' he asked over his shoulder.

'I don't have to be. I've never seen a woman less susceptible to charm in my life,' Tony said frankly. 'Especially yours.' He shook his head. 'She is seriously not a fan.'

Jake sat at the dressing table and pushed the brushes and combs aside.

'She is still a woman,' he said indifferently. He held out a hand. 'Contracts, Tony.'

Tony was frowning. 'But –

Jake snapped his fingers. 'Concentrate. Contracts. Get the things dealt with and you can get going.'

Tony put the required papers in front of him. Jake bent his head, as he ran swiftly through the contracts. The technical wording gave him no problems but once he crossed something out in heavy black ink and once he slashed through the best part of a page.

He gave a short laugh and said, 'Nice try. Forget it.'

'What?'

'Just a little additional clause Stenson thought he'd put in after we agreed the draft contract.'

Tony was mortified. 'I should have noticed that.'

'Yes,' Jake agreed. But his tone was absent. He finished reading the rest of the paper with undiminished attention. Then he looked up, recapping his pen.

'You're too honest, Tony. Nobody ever got rich underestimating the opposition.'

'But Stenson isn't the opposition. Stenson's your partner in this.'

'Same difference.'

Tony took the papers slowly. 'You don't even trust your partner?'

Jake surveyed him cynically. 'God, you've got a lot to learn.'

'But – '

'You particularly don't trust your partner.'

'That's – unpleasant.'

Jake shrugged. 'That's business. Your smart degree didn't teach you much if it left that out.'

136

Tony looked disturbed. 'Do you trust anyone, Jake?'

Jake swung round. His teeth flashed in a smile that was almost savage. 'First law of the jungle, Tony. Trust no one but yourself, and keep an eye on your back.'

His assistant was not impressed. 'Sounds like two laws to me,' he muttered.

'Two aspects of the same one, maybe. The point is,' Jake emphasized the point by stabbing the air with his rolled gold fountain pen, 'people look out for themselves. Only a fool forgets that.'

Tony looked uneasy. 'Yes, but some people are better at looking after themselves than others.'

Jake laughed. It had a harsh sound. 'Second law of the jungle.'

Tony's uneasiness increased noticeably. He hesitated, clearly wrestling with a private problem. But then he seemed as if he could not keep it in any longer. 'Does that apply to Mrs Lawrence as well?' he burst out at last.

Jake's eyes narrowed. 'Why not?'

Tony flung his hands out helplessly. 'She's not a – a business rival. She's not – ' he gave up.

'A worthy opponent?' suggested Jake mockingly. 'You underestimate her.'

The telephone by the bed shrilled, cutting the conversation short. Jake reached out to answer it but the bell had already stopped. He paused. Then, while his assistant watched him in horrified disbelief, he picked the telephone up. The care with which he did it made it obvious that this was not the first time he had eavesdropped on someone else's telephone call.

'You can't – ' began Tony

But Jake hushed him with a look.

'Hello?' said Ash.

She had always hated telephones in the bedroom and hardly ever used the instrument beside her bed. But when they had moved in, Peter had insisted he needed one and so would her grandfather when he came to stay in their best spare room. She had just never got round to having them removed. And on this occasion, she admitted, it was useful not to have to tumble downstairs to the hall or the library. Still there was an odd echo on the line.

'Hello?' she said again uncertainly.

'Ashley? Tim. Tim Padgett. How are you?'

'Fine,' said Ash cautiously. 'You?'

Tim was a local barrister. She liked him well enough but he had been Peter's friend rather than hers. She never felt entirely comfortable with him on her own. She had no idea why, and was slightly ashamed of her reservations. But, ashamed or not, she stayed cautious. Tim had a nasty habit of roping people in to sit on committees.

He said now, 'Ace, thanks. What's this I hear about your kidnapping Conan the Destroyer?'

There was an odd bubbling sound on the line. Ash held the telephone away from her ear.

'What?'

'Your cleaning lady told my cleaning lady,' Tim explained. 'Isn't it true?'

Ash said coldly, 'If you mean have the barbarians got past the gates, the answer's yes. But kidnapping, no. The last thing I want is that man here.'

Tim laughed. 'It's true then? You've got Jake Dare in the attic?'

'In a manner of speaking,' Ash admitted. 'And the sooner he's out the better.'

Tim laughed but his tone was serious when he said, 'Do you think you can hang on to him for a bit? It might be useful. Give us a chance to put our case, that sort of thing.'

Ash was not deceived. 'Us? You mean you want to come over and harangue him, don't you?'

'Not good policy to harangue a man like that,' Tim said thoughtfully. 'But if I could put a few facts to him . . .'

'As long as you don't want *me* to convert him, you can do whatever you like,' Ash said with fervour. 'I just don't have the powers of persuasion required.'

Tim laughed indulgently. But he did not contradict her, she noticed. 'Fine. You do the tea and sympathy, I'll do the business,' he said. 'Friday all right?'

Ash's heart sank at the thought that Jake Dare would still be there the end of the week. 'Yes,' she said. Her depression must have shown in her voice.

'Relax,' said Tim bracingly. 'I'm not asking you to do a Mata Hari. Just make him comfortable and leave the rest to the professional advocate.'

He rang off. There was that queer, outer space echo on the line again.

'Blast,' said Ash with real feeling. She slammed the phone down.

She caught sight of herself in the mirror and stopped, shocked. She looked like a witch, her eyes blazing and annoyed spots of colour in her pale cheeks. Then she laughed.

'Just as well you're not on Mata Hari duty,' she told her reflection ruefully.

She leaned forward, inspecting herself. The thin ribbon she used to confine her hair had been reduced to a convoluted knot. As she turned her head a torn end of ribbon straggled over her shoulder. Ash sighed. That was not a knot that would ever be undone. She fished scissors out of a priceless porcelain vase – a gift from her grandfather, that one – and hacked the offending ribbon in two.

For several energetic moments Ash brushed her hair ruthlessly. She had the obscure feeling that if she was at least tidy, she might stand a better chance in a battle of wills with Jake Dare. There was no doubt at all in her mind that the next meeting she had with him would be a battle of wills. And the next. And the next. And the man was under her roof for an indefinite period.

'Blast,' she said again. 'Oh well, no point in putting it off. The sooner I get the next round out of the way, the better.'

She pulled off her grubby top and replaced it with a rather more elegant shirt bearing an appliqué motif in her favourite olive green. Then she changed into dark green jeans, found matching low-heeled shoes and turned back to the mirror. Well it was better but – she put her head on one side.

There was no doubt. With her hair round her shoulders in a cloud of red curls, she looked much too young and vulnerable. She did not want to look vulnerable while Jake Dare was in the house, Ash thought grimly. She could not afford it.

So she hauled her hair so hard it made her eyes water and confined it with a neat velvet bow in the nape of her neck. She surveyed herself anew. Better, but not much. The vulnerability still showed.

Rusty emerged from under the bed and stuffed his nose into her hand. It was comforting.

'Yes, I know,' Ash said with a sigh. 'It's never going to be impressive, is it?' She rubbed her hand over his silky head. 'Still at least now I'm clean.'

Rusty huffed in agreement and looked up at her with doggy devotion. Ash grinned suddenly.

'Not that you care, you mucky hound. You love me as I am, don't you? Unlike any man I've ever known,' she added wryly. 'Come on, then. Let's go and find you a biscuit before I have to face Mr Dare again.'

They were on their way downstairs when Ash thought she heard Jake Dare call out to her. She stiffened. There was something in the dark timbre of his voice which brought all her defences onto red alert. She was telling herself she was a fool, that he was a guest and not a strong one at the moment, when she realized Jake had not been addressing her at all. He was still talking to his assistant.

Ash was just on the point of relaxing when she realized why she had made the mistake in the first place. Jake Dare was not talking to her. He was talking about her.

'You don't want to be sorry for Ashley Lawrence,' Jake Dare was saying. 'Don't let her deceive you. She might look like a prepubescent scarecrow but she has the bite of a piranha fish.'

He sounded cheerful; even appreciative. But hard, Ash thought. Hard and utterly, utterly indifferent. It pierced her to the core, that indifference.

Ash was so startled she nearly missed her footing. She grabbed hold of the banisters and a handful of Rusty's coat.

141

'Don't underestimate her.'

Rusty gave a soft warning growl. Ash recovered herself. She ruffled his coat reassuringly. She tried hard to reassure herself as well.

The slighting reference to her looks was hurtful but – well, hadn't she just been thinking something very similar herself? As for the rest of his character sketch – Ash told herself she was rather pleased. Nobody had ever thought it possible to underestimate her before.

An honourable woman would at that stage either have moved out of earshot or else marched into Jake Dare's room and tell him he had been overheard. She knew that perfectly well. Ash had never previously thought of herself as dishonourable, but she did not hesitate. She put a hand on Rusty's head to keep him quiet and propped herself up against the banisters to hear what other gems of insight Jake Dare had achieved into her character.

'That's nonsense,' Tony Anderson was protesting.

'Is it? You didn't get very far negotiating with her,' Jake pointed out with odious smugness. 'A useful lesson for you. There's more to business negotiation than a Harvard MBA will teach you.'

If she were Tony Anderson, Ash thought wistfully, she'd walk right out of the room. Her feelings of sympathy increased to positive warmth.

'Now I,' Jake went on, 'am going to teach you about the real world. Making deals is a real world game. You are going to go back to London. And there you're going to start digging into what makes the unusual Mrs Lawrence tick. And this time,' his voice was no less pleasant but there was steel in it suddenly, 'do it properly.'

'What sort of digging?' Tony sounded suffocated.

'Everything,' Jake said. 'I want to know every damned thing about her. Hobbies, weaknesses, family, friends, lovers.' He sounded as if he was ticking them off on his long fingers, Ash thought furiously.

She stuffed the back of her hand into her mouth and bit down hard on the knuckles in sheer temper. It was a poor substitute for scratching his eyes out, but if she wanted to hear the rest she had to keep quiet. And she did, very much, want to hear the rest. It sounded very much as if Jake Dare was plotting her downfall.

'*Lovers?*'

Even from the staircase, Ash could hear Tony goggling. Jake Dare, she thought savagely, was atrocious.

'Lovers?' Tony said again. Ash could hear the horror in his voice. 'I can't trawl through London looking for men who have been to bed with Ashley Lawrence.'

It wouldn't take him long, she thought. Or, if you looked at it another way, it would take him forever. Since the people he was looking for didn't exist, he would never come to the end of the task Jake had set him. It made her feel better. She grinned, this time without effort.

'Unlikely, I agree,' Jake said lightly.

Abruptly Ash stopped grinning.

'But never overlook any possibility. There could be a boyfriend who persuaded her to keep hold of the land so he can run it for her. Or develop it himself.' Jake sounded deeply cynical.

Tony Anderson said cautiously, 'If you think she's a frustrated widow . . .'

Jake Dare laughed aloud at that. Outside on the stairs,

Ash's hands clenched slowly into tight, tight fists. If Tony had come out of Jake's room at that moment, her face would have shocked him.

'Frustrated?' Jake mocked. 'She wouldn't know the meaning of the word. I've never met a woman less sexually aware in my life. God knows how she ever managed to have those children. She dresses like a schoolgirl. She behaves like a schoolgirl. And she runs away if a man so much as breathes on her.'

Tony made a small protesting sound. Ash could imagine Jake waving the protest aside.

'I want to know why,' Jake said. 'I don't know what is going on in her mind and I need to. It could even be something as banal as a bad conscience.'

Ash went very still. She was conscious of a slight ringing in her ears. She could not hear what Tony Anderson said in reply. She could not hear anything except the shocked beat of her own pulse. She felt sick.

By the time she had control of herself again, Jake was speaking. He sounded ironic.

'Not that I know much about attacks of conscience. But I hear they can have weird effects. Maybe even make you lock yourself up in the middle of nowhere and turn down good money.'

Tony Anderson laughed.

Abruptly Ash sat down. Her breathing hurt. It was as if she had been struck. She knew there were beads of sweat on her temples. She knew she ought to move. But she felt as if she had lost all power of movement. She sagged against the banisters and felt her bones shake.

He knew. He could not possibly know, but he did. Jake

144

Dare was a pirate and a stranger but he had only had to look at her and he had seen . . . Unconsciously, she pushed her fists against her trembling mouth. One look at her and Jake Dare *knew*.

Everything was swept away in an overwhelming wave of remembered anguish. Jake's words had sent her out of the here and now and back to a time when there had been no Rusty, no wry self-mockery, no defence at all. When there had been only loneliness and failure after failure and then –

She could not think about it again. She *could* not. Ash drew a ragged breath. But Jake's words had opened Pandora's box and now she could not banish the cold, cruel memories he had unleashed.

Rusty pushed his shoulder against her anxiously. Ash came to herself slowly. She rubbed his head with a cold hand. She was still, she registered remotely, trembling.

All of that was over, she told herself. *Over*. Nothing could put it right. But nothing could bring it back again, either. The bad time was over. Nothing Jake Dare said could make any difference to that.

She hauled herself up and leaned heavily against the banisters. If Tony Anderson had come out of the room then he would have been more than shocked. She was moving like an old woman.

Ash felt faint and oddly frightened. For a wild moment she wondered if Jake Dare was some sort of Nemesis. It was a crazy superstitious thing to think, but she could not help herself. She had been waiting to pay for her sins, Ash thought, for a long time. Maybe Jake Dare was the man who would collect.

She became aware that they were still talking but were clearly coming to the end of their discussion.

Tony said doubtfully, 'Well, I can try I suppose.' There were sounds of paper being packing up. 'But I wish you'd find someone else. Or better still think of some other way – '

Jake laughed.

Ash promptly forgot all weakness and fled down the stairs so fast she nearly killed Rusty. Or was killed by him as he plunged between her feet. Neither girl nor dog stopped until they were outside.

Ash headed determinedly away from the house.

'Ridiculous,' she muttered. 'Sheer bad luck. The man just happened to say something that triggered bad memories. That's all. Chance. He doesn't *know* anything. If he did he wouldn't be sending his sidekick to dig into my past, after all.'

And that was a nasty thought, too.

'Be sensible,' she adjured herself, striding down to the river and not looking behind her, as if there were a chance that Jake Dare himself might already be in pursuit.

Rusty brought her a stick and danced around her hopefully. Ash threw it. Her own agitation was no reason for taking it out on the dog, after all.

'Especially as you're making a fuss about nothing,' she scolded herself. 'Tony Anderson isn't going to find anything out if he digs from now to Doomsday. There's nothing to find out. No dark secrets in the closet.'

The dog ran a long loop over the meadow and round to the field beside the main drive. Following him, Ash could see the great tree that overhung the gates in the distance. She shuddered

Well, maybe there was a secret of sorts. But only she and Peter had ever known it. It had bound them together in an unacknowledged conspiracy of silence, not admitting it even to themselves, still less to each other. Until in the end it had been resolved in the most brutal way. And now the only person left knowing that terrible truth was Ash.

She had never spoken of it to anyone. She would not now. She knew that. If the years had taught her nothing else, they had taught her that some truths could hurt more than weapons. The only way to deal with them was to keep them safely locked away so no one else could suspect they even existed. That is what she had done. The truth, the cruelest truth, was buried long ago.

No, there was nothing for Tony Anderson to find. Or Jake Dare either, for that matter. So why did she still shudder at the thought of those too-knowing green eyes?

'Pure nonsense. Pull yourself together. He's hardly come equipped with a truth drug. You're not going to blurt anything out to *him*.'

Unless her bad conscience drove her to it, said a small voice inside her. Jake Dare seemed to know something about the effects of bad conscience.

She shook her head violently. This was bordering on the perverse. 'I haven't got a bad conscience,' she said out loud.

Of course she had not. The secret was safe. But even if it had not been, it was not something which ought to give her a guilty conscience. Ash was rational enough to recognize that. Or so she told herself forcefully.

'So there's nothing to worry about,' she told Rusty.

Delighted, he chased the stick she threw again for him.

Then he went off after several squirrels, half of them imaginary. He dived in and out of clumps of meadow flowers, bright with the red papery petals of poppies. Ash traced his peregrinations by the plumey tail waving above the grasses. Slowly, she regained her equilibrium.

Jake Dare did not represent any danger to her. All the menace was in her head. All she had to do was stay calm and not let him get to her.

By the time she whistled to Rusty to return to the house, Ash had succeeded in banishing the dark memories back to the cellar where they belonged. She was herself again. Once more she was the Ashley Lawrence she knew – self-possessed, knowing what she wanted out of life, however unusual that might be, delighting in the pleasures of the natural world – who did not permit herself a single wish that depended on someone else to satisfy.

Except, thought Ash startled, that she was aware of a new and intense desire to see Jake Dare roasted slowly over boiling oil. And the fact that he had kissed her somehow made the desire about twenty times as fierce as it would otherwise have been.

Ash found herself working hard not to think about that outrageous kiss. Not with a great deal of success. The crazy thing was that she had felt, just for a moment, that she had caught a glimpse of what being in love might have been like. Only a glimpse, and it was pure fantasy, of course. The conversation she had overheard proved that all right. Besides, she was half afraid of the man, for heaven's sake. But still . . .

Had Peter ever kissed her like that? Before they were engaged, when she thought he was in love with her, perhaps? With a little sigh at the frustrations of memory, Ash shook her head. She did not think so. She did not think anyone had ever kissed her like that. Or was it so long since she had been kissed that she had forgotten? The thought made her smile ruefully.

Ash whistled to Rusty and began to make her way back to the house.

One thing was sure, she thought wryly. It certainly wasn't long at all since Jake Dare had been kissed. And their kiss did not seem to have made much of an impression on him. Not if he was calling her a prepubescent schoolgirl.

But with the bite of a piranha fish, Ash reminded herself. It made her feel better. At least Jake Dare did not think she was negligible.

She had to remind herself of that when she heard steps in the hall outside the kitchen. At once she stiffened. But, when the door opened, it was not Jake Dare, venturing out of bed against his obliging doctor's orders. It was Tony Anderson.

He was looking distinctly less than the cool executive she had met before. Ash saw it with dawning amusement. For the first time since she had overheard Jake Dare's assessment of her character, she smiled.

'Er – ' Tony Anderson said. He looked deeply uncomfortable.

'Mr Dare all right?' Ash asked blandly.

'Yes. Fine.' He caught himself. 'Well – '

'As well as can be expected,' Ash supplied.

He looked even more uncomfortable. 'I don't think it's anything serious,' he said uneasily.

He did not manage to meet her eyes. Instead he plunged into an explanation that sounded dangerously close to an excuse. 'I suppose this doctor must have seen that Jake was exhausted before the accident. He went straight from the debâcle of the Newman's merger to this project in Brazil. He's been working sixteen hours a day without a break for over a year now. And of course the business with Rosalind didn't help . . .' He broke off, embarrassed.

It was not, thought Ash, watching with interest, that he had suddenly realized she would not have the faintest idea of what he was talking about. It was because he thought he had told her too much. Told her something private about what drove Jake Dare. Maybe even been disloyal to Jake in doing so. Ash wondered who Rosalind was. And told herself at once that she didn't care.

She certainly did not permit any glimmer of interest to appear on her face. Still less was she going to ask. Tony looked relieved. He also looked a little puzzled. Clearly most people would have asked.

'Jake really needs a break,' he concluded lamely.

'Very possibly,' said Ash in a discouraging tone. 'I fail to see why he has to take it in my home, though. Why doesn't he go to the South of France?'

At that Tony smiled. 'He probably would have done if your dog hadn't run him down,' he said gently.

There was a pregnant pause. Ash glared at him. 'Tell me, Mr Anderson,' she said with poisonous cordiality, 'does your company always do business by blackmail? Or is that Jake Dare's personal speciality?'

He laughed, comfortable again now that he was back negotiating. 'He's very grateful to you,' he said smoothly.

'We all are. He's a terrific guy, really. A bit of a genius. A really great guy to work for. But he can be – '

'Bloody?' Ash suggested sweetly.

'Demanding,' Tony corrected. He looked at his expensive watch, 'I've got to go. He's given me a list as long as my arm of errands. All to be done by yesterday, of course.'

'I heard,' muttered Ash.

But Tony Anderson did not hear her. Which was probably just as well, she admitted to herself. In the doorway he turned.

'Try and get him to rest, if you can, Mrs Lawrence. We'd all appreciate it. He really does need it.'

Ash made a noncommittal reply and saw him to his car. She was not having anyone think they could turn her into Jake Dare's temporary nurse. But there was no point in telling them.

Suddenly it occurred to her that, if she left Jake alone and fed him a ruthlessly invalid diet, she might be able to drive him out with sheer boredom. She pondered. It was worth trying. She was not telling anyone that either.

She said an absent goodbye to Tony Anderson and made her way back round the house. She debated between beef consommé and chicken soup – both equally digestible, nourishing and boring. A mischievous smile tilted her mouth. There were times when cooking became a positively pernicious pleasure.

In the end she decided on chicken soup. It looked the more disgusting. She took it up to Jake on a tray with the thinnest slices of bread and butter she had ever cut in her life.

Jake looked at the tray speechlessly. 'What – is – that?'

Ash told him. She watched his expression with enjoyment.

'Take it away and bring me steak. Blue.'

'I'm afraid,' said Ash with pleasure, 'that there is no steak in the house. This is not an hotel.' She added with spurious concern, 'Perhaps you would be more comfortable in an hotel?'

Green eyes locked with brown.

Jake said quite gently, 'And perhaps you would prefer to be sued?'

Ash was genuinely taken aback. '*Sued*?'

'It was your dog that got me into this mess,' he reminded her, still in that deceptively gentle voice. He made a gesture that could have been directed at the chicken soup but equally could have included the whole situation. 'Injury,' he mused. 'Damage to the car. Loss of earnings.'

Ash sucked in her breath. She was almost sure he was bluffing. Almost. Jake met her eyes limpidly.

'I'll talk to my solicitor,' Ash said coolly. 'Thank you for warning me. But you still eat the soup. Or, I'm afraid, you starve.'

She walked out of the room, head high.

Her solicitor thought it was hilarious.

'Jake *Dare*?' he repeated, after she had given him a crisp account of the previous day's activities. 'You've got a tiger by the tail there, my sweet. His loss of earnings bill would make a hole in even your income.'

'Thank you,' said Ash. 'You're a great comfort. What I want to know is, can he do it? The thing was a pure accident.'

David Colwell chuckled. '*I* believe you, Ash. Of course,

152

if you continue to sound so murderous I don't know whether the Court will . . .'

'Stop giggling,' Ash told him. 'This is serious.'

'Well, it was on your land. So you might be able to counter-claim for trespass. My professional judgement is it sounds like there's a chance of going either way. My personal advice – as an old and valued friend – is talk him out of legal action any which way you can.'

'Thanks. How?' snapped Ash.

He chuckled. 'Feminine wiles, my love. You must have heard of them. Bat the old eyelashes a bit. That's what other women would do. Try it. You might even enjoy it.'

Ash could imagine his grinning, bony face. She had known him since they were children.

'If you were here I'd throw a flower pot at you,' she said wistfully. She had done exactly that as a five-year old. 'I wanted your advice; not your silly jokes.'

Colwell said, 'My advice is to entertain him royally and agree abjectly to whatever he suggests. As long as you don't sign anything, of course.'

'Thank you,' said Ash with restraint. 'I'll remember that.'

She put the phone down with his laughter ringing in her ears.

She went into the kitchen.

'Now what's put you in a temper?' Em asked, looking up from her inventory of the store cupboard.

'I am not in a temper,' said Ash furiously.

She scooped a kitten off the work surface and absent-mindedly dusted the traces of sugar off its whiskers and into its fur. The kitten closed its eyes and purred.

153

'Didn't Mr Dare like his soup then?' asked Em, not deceived.

'Not so's you'd notice. He said he'd sue me,' Ash said between her teeth.

Em took that in her stride. 'Better keep him sweet then,' she advised. 'He's been calling for you. I heard him when you were on the phone.'

Ash smiled, not pleasantly. 'I didn't. And if one more person tells me to be nice to Jake Dare, I shall run away to sea.'

Em looked startled. 'Hadn't you better go and see what he wants?'

'I know what he wants. Steak. He can't have it. And I've got tomatoes to water,' Ash said with dignity.

She looped the kitten over her shoulder and went to engage the hose to the outside tap. She would give the tomato plants a thorough soaking. She hauled the long hose down the path of the kitchen garden and pointed it like a weapon. The tomatoes bent under the stream of water, like palm trees in a gale. Ash and her passenger were thoroughly splashed by the impact. The kitten gave a squeal of protest and leapt for cover.

Conscience-stricken, Ash moderated the force of the water. It was not her tomatoes she wanted to assault, after all.

She was finishing the exercise more soberly when there came a sudden shout from the house. Ash was lost in her thoughts, but the unexpected sound shocked her out of her reverie. She jumped and swung round. The hose sent a wide arc of water across the kitchen garden and down Ash herself.

'Damn,' said Ash.

The kitten fled.

The shout came again. It came from the first floor. Her justified annoyance with Jake Dare was suddenly replaced by alarm. She ran toward the house. She managed to remember to drop the hose but not to turn it off, so she got another soaking. Impatiently she went back, turned off the gushing water, and pelted for the house.

Em's bicycle was no longer outside the kitchen she saw. So the housekeeper had gone. Which meant that Jake Dare was alone in the house. Perhaps he really was in trouble.

Ash tore up the stairs and flung open the door to the master bedroom.

Jake was reclining on the bed. There was no visible sign of injury. He was wrapped in a sober navy blue robe. It made him look like a commander resting after battle at sea. Or before battle, perhaps. She concluded that Tony had brought it on instructions.

Ash leaned against the door jamb and tried to get her breath back. She put a hand to her side where she was aware of an incipient stitch. She regarded him without charity.

'I thought you were hurt.'

Jake was watching her, the green eyes intent and, just for a moment, unsmiling. Ash was startled. Instantly she was on her guard. But at once he seemed to shake himself. The remoteness fell away from him like a discarded cloak. He relaxed against the pillows that he had pulled into a comfortable tumble about him and gave Ash a melting smile.

'You're only going to talk to me when I'm hurt?'

'*Are* you?' asked Ash, unmelted.

155

Jake managed to look noble and pathetic. 'Nothing to make a fuss about,' he said bravely.

Ash snorted. His smile grew. She curbed her instinct to smack that smiling face. Really, it was extraordinary, she noted dispassionately, that in that incisive face he had the long, curling eyelashes of an eighteenth-century beauty. It did not endear him to her.

She pushed her hands into the pockets of her jeans and straightened, banishing her treacherous appreciation of that handsome face. 'What was that cry of anguish, then?' she demanded.

He looked pleased. 'Was that what brought you up here so fast?'

'It sounded as if you were dying.'

'I fell over your dog when I went to the bathroom.'

'Rusty is here?' Ash was startled. Rusty was normally a one-woman dog.

Jake's smile was bland. 'Not any more.'

At once she was alarmed – and angry. 'If you've hurt him . . .'

'Would I? We've all got to get along in this world,' Jake said piously. The green eyes gleamed under down-dropped lashes. 'I just put him outside. I wouldn't want you to think any worse of me than you do already.'

Ash stared at him in deepest suspicion. He met her look with a dazzling smile. But there was a twitch of genuine amusement about the sculpted lips. Ash did not like it at all. She searched his face.

'Digging in for a long stay?' she interpreted at last.

If possible Jake became even more melting. 'As long as it takes,' he said ambiguously.

Ash refused to acknowledge the seductive note in the low voice. She was, after all, the least sexually aware woman he had ever met, she reminded herself. For a moment she was tempted to remind Jake Dare also. But then she decided against it. It was too good a weapon to waste on a tiff, no matter how annoying. There could well come a time when she would be very glad to throw that piece of overheard slander in his face.

So she flicked her gaze away from him and said nothing. His eyebrows rose. Jake was puzzled by her lack of reaction, she saw. It was like winning a skirmish. The rush of pleasure surprised her. Perhaps she had one or two weapons to use against him after all.

Not only puzzled, she thought, but also slightly annoyed. Presumably he was not used to women ignoring that playfully seductive tone. Suddenly Ash began to feel a lot better.

She said with spurious anxiety, addressing the feather motif on a pillow beside his head, 'Of course, we're very isolated here. If you were to need emergency attention . . . I wouldn't want the responsibility . . .'

'I will take full responsibility,' Jake assured her softly.

Their eyes met. His were very steady. He was not talking about his health, and they both knew it. In spite of herself, Ash gave an involuntary shiver. She bit her lip.

'How long?' she said abruptly, abandoning the duel.

There was a pause. The bed creaked. Startled, her eyes flew back to him. But Jake was only settling himself more comfortably, locking his fingers behind his head.

'As long as it takes,' he said again.

Ash looked away quickly. 'And if I object?'

The small private smile grew. 'I'm sure you are much too smart to fight battles you don't need to,' he said smoothly.

Ash could not resist any longer. Her mouth thinned. 'On the contrary, Mr Dare, I understood you thought I was too much of a *schoolgirl*,' she told him dulcetly.

His eyebrows hit his hairline. Too late Ash realized she had given herself away. Furious with herself, she flung away from him. Jake watched unsympathetically.

'Well, well. Snooping were you? Listening outside doors. And me tied to my bed of sickness.' There was no doubt at all. The private smile had turned into outright laughter. But he still managed to sound reproachful. 'Not very polite in the circumstances.'

She turned on him. 'Then that makes two of us,' she flashed.

It should have been a crushing snub. Jake Dare, however, was unrepentant. Smugly he quoted her own words back at her. 'You should have remembered that eavesdroppers never hear well of themselves.'

Too late Ash gathered her dignity about her. 'I didn't set out to eavesdrop. You were neither of you exactly whispering. Frankly, I didn't expect to find myself discussed in those terms by a guest in my house.'

Jake winced theatrically. 'OK. I apologize. I shouldn't have discussed you. No gentleman would.' The preposterous eyelashes drooped and the sculpted, sensuous mouth laughed silently. 'But then you already knew I wasn't a gentleman, didn't you, Ash?'

She drew a deep, indignant breath. Under the drooping lids, his eyes glinted with laughter.

'It had occurred to me,' she agreed with restraint. 'Everything you have done so far seems to point in that direction.'

He laughed out loud at that. 'Poor Ash. And you've been a great hostess. Tony thinks you're very sweet, you know. He said you'd warned him not to agitate me.'

Ash flashed him a look of pure dislike.

'I don't care if he agitates you into spontaneous combustion,' she told him.

Jake gave her another of his melting looks. 'You don't mean that.'

Ash said coolly, 'Provided you don't do it in my house, you can self-destruct with my good will.'

Jake took that without a flicker of an eyelid. A wicked smile began to curl the corner of his mouth.

'In that case,' he said softly, 'you shouldn't wear that blouse when you're going to get wet and then come in here and bully me. It's the sort of thing that can give a man a heart attack. Especially a convalescent like me.'

For a moment Ash stared at him, uncomprehending. She did not like that knowing smile. He clasped his hands round his knees, not taking his eyes off her. His smile grew.

Following his glance, Ash looked down at herself. She realized, with something approaching horror, that the damned, unmanageable hose had soaked her. Her sodden shirt now outlined her breasts and long waist in explicit detail. And Jake had lain there enjoying it without saying a word throughout the whole conversation.

Her feelings for Jake Dare rose to hatred.

CHAPTER 7

Ash walked out. It was that or scream at him like a fishwife. She was shaking. Angry tears filled her eyes. She brushed them away furiously.

Ash heard him call her name. He sounded startled, perhaps even remorseful. But nothing would have induced her to walk back into that room.

Jake Dare had humiliated her enough, lying there laughing at her while he stripped her with his eyes. He had *known* she was unaware of what the hose had done to her shirt. He had enjoyed her being unaware.

Well, she was not unaware now and she never would be again. She would watch Jake Dare like a prison guard. Oh, she would make him sorry, Ash raged to herself. She would make him sorry he had ever set foot in Hayes Manor.

He called after her again, an urgent note in his voice. She ignored it. He was not deceiving her again. No more rushing into his room because she thought he was hurt, she vowed savagely. From now on if he fell out of bed he could call the fire brigade. She was not going into that room again.

Meanwhile, in Jake's office Tony's announcement was received with disbelief.

160

'He's doing *what*?' said the Finance Director.

'Taking a holiday,' said Jake's secretary faintly.

She received a withering look. 'Oh, come *on*. If he's in some sort of trouble you can tell me, Barbara.'

But she shook her neat head helplessly. 'A holiday. That's what Tony Anderson said. He's calling Marriott now to tell him what to pack.'

They stared at each other. 'He must be ill,' said the Finance Director at last.

'Well, I wondered,' admitted the loyal secretary. 'Either that or in love.' She fiddled with her several diaries, lining them up neatly. 'What do you think?'

The Finance Director thought about it. He was not a romantic man and he knew Jake Dare very well.

'Rosalind back, do you think?' he said at last doubtfully.

'He wouldn't cancel a week of appointments for Rosalind Newman,' said Barbara with something of a snap. She had been with Jake a long time and took a tolerant attitude to his love life, but she had not cared for Rosalind.

'Well, he wouldn't let any of his bimbos interfere with work,' exclaimed the Finance Director. He, too, had been with Jake a long time.

Barbara folded her lips together in disapproval. Whatever her personal views on Jake's private life she did not encourage other people to comment on it.

'Sorry,' the Finance Director said, remembering too late.

Barbara relented. 'Tony says this is work in a way,' she volunteered. 'Something to do with that out-of-town shopping centre.'

The Finance Director grimaced. 'I thought he was

161

going to walk away from that one. I told Jake the figures didn't add up.'

Barbara looked worried. 'I thought so, too.'

They stared at each other, frustrated. Then the Finance Director laughed.

'Same old Jake.'

'No doubt he knows what he's doing,' agreed Barbara.

'And he'll let us know when he's good and ready.' The Finance Director stuffed his document case under his arm and prepared to leave. He looked back over his shoulder. 'Just as long as he leaves me time to go liquid if he needs to start buying. But he will, won't he?'

'He'll let us know when he starts to win,' said Barbara shrewdly.

The Finance Director gave a snort of amusement. It was tempered with alarm, though. 'You know us all too well, Barbara,' he said, going.

She smiled. But when he had gone her smile died. Tony Anderson's account had been sufficiently discreet for an experienced secretary to detect that something was going on. From the moment that Tony had admitted that Jake had thought that Mrs Lawrence was a little old lady – and was furious when it turned out that he was wrong – Barbara's intuition had been alert. She knew in her bones that this uncharacteristic change of plan was something to do with the deceptive Ashley Lawrence.

'Oh, Jake, be careful,' she said under her breath.

She would have been intrigued to know that Marriott's sentiments were identical. Not that anyone would know. He received Tony's instructions on what to pack with no more

162

than a nod. But when the suitcase was ready, the professional mask dissolved into worry. When the door bell rang he was not quite quick enough to slip back into character.

'Your Highness!'

'Hello, Mariott. Just dropping off a map I promised Jake.' Ahmed looked narrowly at the manservant. 'Something wrong?'

'Not at all.' Marriott drew himself up to his full height and held out his hand for the fat envelope. 'Mr Dare is away at present ut – '

'Away?' Ahmed stared. 'He didn't mention it.'

Marriott's elegant profile twitched. 'It is somewhat unexpected,' he admitted.

Ahmed's curiosity was thoroughly roused. 'And you don't approve? What's he got himself into?'

Normally Marriott would not have discussed his employer with anyone. But the Prince was probably Jake's oldest friend. Jake had never done anything so totally out of character in all the years that he had worked for him. Marriott was worried. He gave Ahmed an account of the story as he had heard it from Tony.

When he finished, the Prince looked thoughtful. 'Odd,' he agreed. 'Are you joining him?'

Marriott looked shocked. 'He has not asked for me – ' He gestured to the suitcase by the door, 'He does, however, want his clothes. Mr Anderson will collect them later.'

'Ah,' Ahmed looked thoughtful. 'He'll be alright you know, Marriott. Anderson said the hospital checked him over. They would not have let him out if he was walking around with a fractured skull.'

Marriott winced. He had not been admitting it to himself but that was undoubtedly the fear lurking at the back of his mind. 'No, sir,' he said woodenly.

Ahmed had an idea. 'Tell you what, I'll deliver the bag for you. I've got to go down to Oxford before I leave. The Foundation has given my old college a manuscript. There's a ceremonial lunch. Why don't I drop in on Jake on the way? Have you got the address and telephone number?'

Marriott produced the required information. Ahmed turned over the paper in his hand, musing.

'Hayes Manor? Sounds familiar.' He searched his memory. 'I must have seen the name when I was last in Oxford.' He raised a hand in farewell. 'Don't worry, Marriott. Jake can take care of himself in the Brazilian jungle. Rural Oxfordshire isn't going to give him any problems.'

'I am sure you are right, sir.'

In rural Oxfordshire Tim Padgett was zipping along through the lanes in his brand new BMW to the sounds of mediaeval plain song. As was his wont, he was not listening to the music. He was talking to his passenger.

'Bit of luck that,' he shouted over the Spanish monks' voices. 'We'd never get an opportunity like that otherwise. Ash didn't sound too pleased, though.'

His passenger, the new arrival at the Gate House, did not know Mrs Lawrence nearly as well as he would like. He said so.

'Shy little thing. Always was,' Tim said. 'Devastated when her husband died, of course.'

'I thought it was me she didn't like,' said Roger Ruffin.

He was a tall, broad-shouldered man with a perpetually irritable expression. At present, having found his car out of commission just when he was ready to set off for his afternoon's appointment, Tim had to admit he had some justification. Tim, an amiable man, tried to forget that the summons to his neighbour's assistance had been distinctly peremptory.

'Lord, no. Like that with everyone.' Tim chuckled. 'Should think she's giving poor old Dare a dusty welcome. By the time I get to him on Friday, he'll be delighted to see a friendly face. Believe me.'

Ruffin gave a slightly absent-minded smile. 'Let's hope so.'

'No doubt. Ash can make herself pretty plain when she wants to.'

Ruffin looked out at the summer fields, drowsy in the afternoon's heat. 'Going on your own on Friday?' he asked casually.

Tim was taken aback. 'I suppose so. Hadn't thought about it. Why?'

'Dare might be more impressed by a delegation.'

Tim snorted. 'Where am I going to get a delegation at that sort of notice? Nobody round here wants to get involved until you show them how it's going to affect their own front door step.'

Ruffin said, 'I don't mind getting involved.'

'Really?' Tim took his eyes of the road to survey the dark, discontented face. 'Do you mean it?'

'Of course.'

'Then I may well call on you,' Tim said, surprised and

grateful. 'I'll give you a ring. Now, where do you want me to drop you?'

'The garage will be fine. I can hire a car for a couple of days and they can send someone out to the Gate House to pick up the Land Rover.'

'Nuisance when that happens,' said Tim. 'Accident?'

Ruffin's voice hardened. 'Nothing of the kind. Someone poured sugar in the petrol tank, if I'm any judge. Pure vandalism. I'm being pestered by local kids, I think!'

Tim was shocked. 'Never heard of that happening round here before. Hope it doesn't start a trend.'

Ruffin grunted. But they were in sight of the garage. Tim pulled up on the forecourt and his passenger got out with a curt word of thanks. At the last moment he turned and bent down to the window. He said, 'Call me on Friday. I'll be ready.'

Unaware of the impending descent on her visitor, Ash had fled his company. She was dashing about the kitchen where circling animals encouraged her to open tins of food. It did not quite take her mind off the iniquities of Jake Dare but it helped. Even so, she was still muttering direfully when there was a knock on the kitchen door. Bob Cummings put his head round it.

'Coast clear?' he asked.

'Conan the Destroyer is still in bed, if that's what you mean,' Ash said putting down the last saucer of food for the kittens and running her hands under the tap.

Bob looked startled. 'I was thinking of Mrs Harrison.' He came in, closing the door behind him. 'For some reason she doesn't approve of me.'

166

Ash shrugged. 'Nor me. Don't let it worry you.'

'She's a fierce lady,' he said with feeling. 'How does what did you call him? Conan the Destroyer? How does he get on with her?'

'So far, suspiciously well. He's seen to that. Though Em can be temperamental.' Ash grinned as a thought struck her. 'He'd better keep on the right side of her. Or he won't get anything to eat.'

Bob's eyebrows climbed.

'I'm not cooking for him. I've done all the waiting on him I'm going to,' she said roundly. 'I don't believe there's a thing wrong with him. He's insufferable.' She meant to keep it light but her voice broke on the last word.

And to Bob's consternation as much as her own, she began to cry.

'Hey,' he said, patting her shoulder awkwardly. 'It can't be that bad.'

Ash blew her nose. 'No, of course not,' she said waterily. 'He just – got to me.'

'Delayed shock,' Bob said comfortably. 'You must have had a nasty moment when Rusty went for that car. You need time to get over it as much as he does.'

Ash gave a small choke of laughter. 'Oh, I do. I do.'

'There you are, then.' He gave her back a last relieved pat and stepped back. 'A good cry and it's all over. Now what about a cup of coffee for a tired working man?'

She laughed again, blowing her nose on a scrap of kitchen paper. 'You're a nice man, Bob Cummings. Coffee it is.'

She put it on to brew. Bob sat down at the scrubbed table, scratched Rusty politely between the ears and opened his briefcase. Rusty went back to his food bowl.

'I brought the stuff we're preparing for the Planning Committee,' he said. 'Tim Padgett drafted it. He's not going to charge, of course.'

Ash was at the old-fashioned range. 'Planning Committee?' she said absently. 'Come on, Bob. You know I don't have anything to do with committees. What's more, so does Tim.' She looked over her shoulder at him and gave a very good impression of her normal, rueful smile. 'I'm no good with bureaucracy.'

He shook his head at her. 'Don't think you can wriggle out of this one,' he said good-humouredly. 'It's on your doorstep. They've got Hayes Wood in the plans as part of the second stage of development. You're going to have to tell the Committee you've no intention of selling. I assume you haven't changed your mind?' he added on a sudden alarmed note. 'With the Great Man staying here and all. He hasn't talked you into supporting it?'

The coffee began to bubble. Ash looked at it.

'Jake Dare,' she said coldly, 'couldn't talk me into a weekend in paradise.'

Bob's mouth fell open. 'Good Lord.' He leaned forward and took her hand. 'But – '

His eyes slid past Ash and he stopped as if he had run out of petrol.

Ash felt the hairs on the back of her neck lift. She turned round from the range very slowly. She had heard nothing but the coffee percolating quietly. The animals, still busy at their bowls, had not twitched a tail or a whisker. But there was no doubt who it was.

'I thought I smelt coffee,' Jake Dare said in self-congratulatory tones.

168

He closed the hall door gently behind him and strolled into the kitchen. He was wearing trousers in some light material, impeccably tailored, and a cream shirt with the sleeves pushed up to reveal tanned forearms. She supposed he must have had the outfit delivered by Tony Anderson. He looked cool, elegant and about as far from an invalid as you could get, Ash thought, oddly breathless.

Bob removed his hand from Ash's. Seeing it, Jake flicked up one eyebrow as he sank gracefully onto the kitchen bench at the head of the table. Ash would not look at him, but her down-bent head smouldered. Jake smiled blandly.

Bob was looking at her in silent surprise. Ash might be shy but she usually had beautiful manners. She could feel the silent reproach. It was too much for her.

'Jake Dare,' she said reluctantly. She still did not look at him. 'Bob Cummings.'

Bob nodded. 'Nice to meet you. We were just talking about you,' he said.

Jake's eyes narrowed. 'I guess I needn't ask what about. Are you a fellow conservationist?'

Bob was bewildered. 'You're interested in conservation, too? But I thought – '

Jake eyes swept over Ash in a way that could only be described as caressing. 'I could be – converted.'

Ash turned her shoulder, transferring her attention sharply back to the range. She began fussing with the coffee. Bob looked slightly startled. She brought three mugs and a milk jug back to the table. Jake took his mug and shook his head at milk and a large bowl of brown sugar that she pushed towards him. She avoided his eyes but she could sense him watching her bent head.

'You ought to know how I take my coffee by now,' he told her softly.

There was a taut silence. Ash did not know what to say. All the things that occurred to her would only make it sound as if she and the wretched man were indeed as intimate as he was trying to imply. She seethed. But she could not think of a way out of the impasse. Jake Dare, she noted for future reference, was a highly successful manipulator.

So successful that beside her she felt Bob stiffen. He sipped his coffee and watched Jake over the top of his mug.

'Feeling better? Getting over the accident?'

'Slowly,' Jake allowed.

'Must be good to be back on your feet.'

Jake smiled. 'Ash certainly wanted me – back on my feet,' he murmured.

The innuendo was blatant. Ash was so indignant that she forgot that she was not looking at Jake Dare. At once he captured her eyes, a laughing challenge in his own.

'Isn't that what you said?'

Ash kept her face impassive and said coolly, 'Em and I will certainly be glad not to have to keep running up and down the stairs after you.'

Jake laughed. 'Florence Nightingale, you're not. Not much of a nurse, are you, my lovely?'

In spite of her resolution, Ash felt her hold on her temper slipping. 'You're not much of a patient,' she flashed.

Bob looked from one to the other and pushed his chair back. 'I'd better be going. I've got another early start tomorrow.' Casually he gathered up the papers before Jake

170

could look at them. He tucked them under his arm. 'Come and see me off, Ash.'

She went with him. Outside in the dying light Bob looked down at her, hesitating.

'I think I'm beginning to see what you mean. Is he making a nuisance of himself?'

Ash gave a harsh laugh. 'In spades.'

'Tell him to go.'

Ash bit her lip. 'I – my solicitor told me to placate him,' she said. 'In case he sues me. Or Rusty.'

Bob looked astonished. 'Would it help if I – er – had a word?' he asked delicately.

Ash shook her head. 'My fight, Bob.'

He gave her a curious look. 'I never thought of you as a fighter.'

She shivered suddenly. 'Nor did I. But I think I've come to the point in my life where I have to fight or – ' She broke off.

'Or?' Bob prompted gently.

She stopped dead. It was a question she had avoided asking herself. But all of a sudden the answer was there: or lose, finally and forever, the battle to keep some sort of self-respect. Ash was startled with the intensity of the thought. She wriggled her shoulders.

'Oh, or he'll turn half the county into a shopping mall with ice rink attached,' she said lightly, after a pause. She held out her hand. 'Leave me the papers, Bob. I'll do my homework.'

He passed them across. 'Give me a ring when you've read them. We're counting on your support this time.'

'Just as long as you don't make me go to committee

meetings, you'll have it,' she promised. 'I told you. I'm already braced for a fight.'

As she walked back to the house she realized how accurate her words had been. A fight was definitely on the horizon.

Ash shuddered. She hated confrontation, hated polite voices, only just masking the leashed anger. Above all she hated the cold, vicious insults that were the culmination of every battle. She had learned how to defend herself from Peter's anger. But she was not sure she had the armour to withstand Jake Dare if he chose to be cruel. She swallowed, her throat drying at the thought.

'I am not afraid of him,' she told herself fiercely. 'There's nothing he can do to me. I am *not* afraid.'

In the kitchen Jake had helped himself to more coffee and stretched out in the rocking chair beside the range. Rusty was lying in front of his chair, nose on his paws, eyes watchful. One of the kittens, less experienced and more trusting, had hauled itself up that long length of leg and tucked itself into the curve of his neck. Jake let it stay there.

As she walked in, the kitten raised its head, purring. Ash stopped dead and looked at the tableau. The contrast with her imaginings could not have been greater. Her lips twitched suddenly. It was certainly not a picture to be afraid of unless you were seriously paranoid, she thought.

'Boyfriend gone?' he asked. His tone was amiable enough but there was an edge to his tone.

Ash ignored it, along with the implied question.

'Making yourself at home?' she countered on a challenging note.

172

Jake gave her his sunniest smile. 'It's not difficult. I like this kitchen. It smells of all the right things.'

'I know,' Ash said drily. 'Principally Colombian coffee.'

Jake grinned. 'One of the great perfumes,' he agreed. He stretched. 'But not quite what I expected.'

'Oh?' Ash raised her brows.

'I was thinking along the lines of baked beans. Or fish fingers. The sort of things growing boys like,' he said softly, watching her from under his lashes.

'Oh?' said Ash again, her expression wooden.

He laughed suddenly. 'Come on. Tell the truth. Whoever those monsters were, they're not your sons. Are they?'

Ash shrugged, looking away. 'I never said they were.'

'But you didn't correct me when I assumed they were.' He was thoughtful. 'The interesting thing is why.'

She picked up Bob's used mug, not answering him. She was conscious of his eyes on her all the time, though.

'It could be my own strategy, of course,' he said in a musing voice. 'Confuse the enemy. The more inaccurate information he has about you, the less likely he is to make a hit.' He paused. 'Is that it, Ash? You think I'm your enemy?'

She twitched her shoulders, her back to him. 'I don't think about you at all,' she said, not entirely truthfully.

He chuckled. 'And I couldn't talk you into a weekend in paradise? Very wounding. I'm going to remember that, you know.'

Goaded, Ash swung round on him. 'You don't look wounded.'

'Ah, but I'm very good at disguising my feelings,' he

173

told her with a great air of frankness. 'The financial press has always said it is my greatest asset when I do business in this country.'

'Well, it won't do you any good with me,' she said between her teeth. 'I'm not doing business with you.'

He bit back a smile. She saw him do it.

'So certain,' he said marvelling.

She glared. He met her eyes, his own amused, and something else that she was not sure about – determined, perhaps. He laughed suddenly.

'Why don't you come and sit down before you break out into flames? I seem to have the knack of making you mad. I wish I knew why.'

Ash expelled a long breath and subsided into Bob's vacated chair. 'I've never met a man who rubs me up the wrong way the way you do,' she admitted. 'And it's deliberate, isn't it? I just don't understand it. If you want to buy my land, you ought to be buttering me up. Or at least, that's what I'd have thought. Just what do you think you're doing?' she asked in rising exasperation.

There was a pause. Jake looked at her watchfully. The kitchen was very quiet, too quiet. The warm coffee-scented air could have been the precursor to an electric storm. Ash felt a cold curl of tension in her stomach.

Then Jake said calmly, 'Trying and failing to disarm you.'

Ash stared. She could not tell whether he was telling the truth or whether this was another of his elaborate strategies.

Jake's mouth tilted ironically. 'I'm telling you the truth,' he said, as if he could read her mind. 'I find it's simpler, usually. You can trust me on that, at least.'

174

Her eyes narrowed to slits. 'Somehow I find that hard to believe.'

He shook his head. 'Wounding. Try me. Ask me anything you want and I will tell you the truth.'

Ash wished she had had the time to read Bob's papers. Then she could have asked him something crucial about the project – and would have had a reasonable chance of judging whether his reply was the truth or not.

Instead, to her astonishment, she heard herself say, 'Who is Rosie?'

One eyebrow rose. It made him look like a pirate, Ash thought. Tough and amused and quite unscrupulous. And horribly attractive.

'So you know about Rosie, do you? How did you come by that? I didn't think you were the kind to gossip.'

'You said her name a couple of times,' Ash said curtly, hoping she wasn't blushing as deeply as she felt she was.

His look of amusement intensified. 'Not when we were kissing, I hope?'

Ash was so angry, she did not even think about blushing. 'When you kissed me,' she pointed out. 'There's a difference.'

'There is indeed,' he agreed suavely. 'Though I'm surprised you do.' He went on without a pause. 'So what do you want to know about my love life?'

Ash's chin rose. 'Not a thing. I just wondered who she was, that was all. And,' she added cattily, 'if there was a lady figuring in your life, why it was down to me to look after you on your bed of sickness.'

Jake pulled a face. 'Fair point,' he said, surprising her. 'Rosalind Newman was my fiancée,' he said deliberately.

Ash found she was surprised. He did not look like a man

on the edge of marriage. Or even close to it. She looked at him searchingly. 'Was?'

'She threw back the ring when I decided not to go ahead in a merger with her father's company.' His mouth thinned. In a level voice, he went on, 'She explained that was the only reason she had agreed to marry me in the first place.'

Ash winced. It struck echoes she would rather not have heard. Would Peter ever have married her if her grandfather hadn't promised him a seat on the Board of Kimbell's?

To push the memories away she asked, 'Did you love her very much?'

His smile was unreadable. For a moment she thought he was not going to answer. Then he gave a quick shrug. 'Love? Define your terms.'

Which, of course, was exactly what she could not do, not with her history. She said with difficulty, 'Oh, affection, I suppose.'

He was looking at her strangely. Oh God, how many clues had she unwittingly given him now?

'And respect,' Ash added hurriedly. 'Serious affection and respect.'

Jake's mouth turned down in what looked horribly like a sneer. Ash winced again. And after she had vowed she would not make a fool of herself in front of him again! Why could she not remember that the only way to deal with this man was not to react; not to his questions, not to his mockery. She put a hand to her head. The tension at her temples was all too familiar, though since Peter's death she had felt it rarely.

She became aware that Jake was answering her.

'The only serious thing about love is not to let it get

serious. It's a game to take lightly.' He tilted his chair back, his eyes narrowing at the memories he had called up. 'Rosalind doesn't play games.'

Ash suppressed a shiver. Neither do I, she wanted to say. She refrained. Everything she knew about Jake Dare told her that he would interpret it as an invitation. Or choose to pretend that was how he interpreted it. So it would be the height of folly to encourage Jake Dare to enter into a debate on the nature of love; especially if it led him to think he could convert her to the sort of games that seemed to amuse him.

Instead she said, 'So why did you get engaged if you weren't in love?'

He gave her an incredulous look. 'The usual reasons. She wanted the good life and her father was running out of money. I wanted her. She made it very clear that marriage was the price. I'm thirty-eight. I figured it was probably time I settled down. So – we agreed.' His voice hardened. 'What I hadn't realized was that I was supposed to provide the good life for a burned-out company as well. When I found out what a mess Newmans was in, I dropped the bid. And Rosie gave me the ring back.'

Ash said curiously, 'You don't sound broken-hearted.'

He looked really startled. 'Broken-hearted? About a failed merger? Heck, it's only money.'

'I was thinking about your engagement,' Ash said drily.

'Oh, that.' He shrugged, dismissing it as supremely irrelevant. 'I wasn't. I was bloody mad for a bit, I admit. If Rosie had been straight with me from the start, I'd never have asked her to marry me. Still, you live and learn. It won't happen again.'

177

It was Ash's turn to raise mocking eyebrows. 'No more engagements?'

He laughed. 'No more engagements,' he agreed. 'If I marry, I marry, but I'm not going through that again.' He shuddered reminiscently. 'Endless dinners and teas and Hunt balls with people I have nothing in common with. God, why do the English do it? Every woman I met was bent on telling me every damned clever remark Rosie made from the age of four. No, never again. The next one is going to be an orphan. No siblings. No godparents. No old girlfriends from the Pony Club.'

In spite of herself, Ash laughed. 'I remember,' she said with feeling.

His eyebrows rose. 'Lawrence was a teenage gymkhana champion?' He made no attempt to disguise his astonishment.

She gave a choke of laughter. 'Peter? No.' For the first time in what felt like a lifetime she had said his name without an inner wince. She realized it after a heartbeat. She stopped dead in what she was going to say. She was incredulous.

'What is it?' demanded Jake, seeing her expression.

But she always wanted to curl up into a tight, tight ball and wait for the hurt to go away whenever she thought of Peter. Always. Yet now she had said his name as if she thought about him all the time without pain. What was happening to her?

Jake said softly, 'Come back.'

'What?' Ash came back into the present with a jump. 'What?'

Jake's look was shrewd. But all he said was, 'If

Lawrence wasn't the Pony Club groupie, who was?'

'Me.'

Yes, she could not only speak about him, she could think about him without that agony of guilt and regret. In her relief Ash gave Jake a blinding smile. He went very still.

Ash did not notice. She was too busy remembering the engagement. It sobered her. Did she, even in those first happy days, already have an inkling of how difficult her marriage was going to be? She had not acknowledged it, of course, not even to herself. She had not even recognized it. But she had known something was wrong. Hadn't she?

It felt as if she was discovering it for the first time. She said slowly, 'His family and I had nothing in common. They were diplomats and academics. Terribly brilliant and competitive. A family meal was like one of those word games on the radio. They'd all sit round and cap each other's clever remarks. I just wasn't quick enough. Or well read enough, I suppose. His friends from university were the same. I used to sit there sometimes and think – what am I doing here?'

She shook her head ruefully at the vulnerability of her younger self. Jake looked at her oddly.

'So what were you doing there?'

Their eyes locked. Ash felt an odd little frisson run up her spine. 'Oh, following the man I loved,' she said lightly.

'And he?'

She bit her lip. It was as eloquent as if she had shouted aloud that Peter Lawrence did not love her; had never loved her. She did not need to answer.

'I see,' Jake said slowly.

179

She saw that he did. It was a shock. And then she thought, well, why not? Peter never made much of a secret of it and neither did Grandfather. It was only me who thought it was a fairy tale match. Maybe this is where you tell someone else the truth for once. Or some of the truth, anyway.

'So why did he marry you?'

Ash said quickly in a hard little voice, 'Dynastic reasons. Like your Rosalind, he saw marriage as part of a package deal. House, status, future career and a wife thrown in.'

She was shocked at how bitter she sounded. She turned away, not wanting him to see the naked pain in her eyes.

What was there about Jake Dare that made her remember these old agonies? She had put them behind her, built a new life for herself. Yet ever since he had crossed the threshold she had been remembering the disaster that had been her marriage at every turn.

If he had seen the pain, he did not refer to it. Instead he said consideringly, 'Dynastic marriage. So you must be a Kimbell.'

Ash swallowed the razor sharp lump in her throat. 'The last of them. That was why Grandfather was – '

She stopped. Too late. Jake was too clever not to see that she had been on the brink of a confidence and too determined not to pursue his advantage.

'Was – what? Angry at having only a girl to inherit? I know these crazy English upper-classes. Only a boy will do to carry the flag. Or didn't he care about that? Did he want you in the business?'

The idea was so far from the truth that Ash smiled, albeit briefly. She made a little helpless gesture. 'He was anxious to see me settled,' she said carefully.

She encountered an ironic look. 'Settled? Or used as bait to hook a suitable heir apparent?'

Ash winced. She said in a low voice, 'I loved my grandfather very much. He knew he was dying. He'd brought me up, but he'd always wanted a boy to follow him in the bank. Peter was his protégé. My father was a frightful disappointment and so was I, for different reasons. I suppose I thought I owed him. But I had a crush on Peter, too. Grandfather knew that. I would never have married him if I hadn't thought I was in love.'

Jake said with a distinct edge to his voice, 'Very convenient.' He scowled at the table top.

'Everyone thought so,' Ash agreed steadily.

When Jake looked up and met her eyes across the room he was no longer laughing.

'Something else that damned report failed to tell me,' he said harshly. 'No wonder you don't need the money for the damned wood. So Ambrose Kimbell talked you into a marriage of convenience.'

He tipped the kitten gently onto the floor and leaned forward. He put his elbows on his knees and propped his chin on his locked fingers. Over them, he considered her sombrely.

'You must be a rich woman, Ashley Lawrence. I assume this house and all that goes with it was your reward for falling in with his plans.'

Ash swallowed. 'No,' she said quietly. 'I didn't need a reward. I was in love. I was very young and stupid but – I was in love.'

Jake's eyes narrowed. 'You were in love? Just you? Not Lawrence?'

Ash closed her eyes briefly. He was going to make her say it out loud. Even her father had not challenged her as bluntly as that. Or used that harsh, accusing tone when he did so. In that moment of supreme trial, she did not even think about telling Jake to mind his own business. This was something she had to admit to herself. It was almost an irrelevance whether Jake Dare was there to hear it or not.

'Just me,' she agreed.

There. It was said. She could say it. Ash was aware of an overwhelming sense of relief.

Jake, however, seemed furious. '*Why?*'

She opened her eyes, bewildered. What was there to anger him in her past follies? 'I don't know,' she said at last in a low voice.

'You – '

Suddenly she was angry too. 'Look, I don't know why I thought I was in love with him, but I did. Everyone warned me; my godmother, my best friend. Everyone – oh, except my grandfather, of course. Even my father took me on one side at the wedding rehearsal and said there was still time to reconsider. I didn't listen. I thought I was sure.'

Jake looked at her gravely. 'How old were you?'

Ash almost jumped. 'Why?' she asked suspiciously.

He hesitated. 'I don't want to offend you.'

She gave a sharp laugh. 'Oh, go on, why not? You haven't let that hold you back so far.'

He shrugged, his expression cynical. 'OK, then. It doesn't sound to me like the sort of feeling you build a marriage on. It sounds like a crush. First love, if you will.'

Then on a spurt of anger, 'You know, the adolescent sickness we all get before we develop immunity.'

Ash flinched. 'It didn't feel adolescent at the time.'

'Does it ever?' Jake sounded weary suddenly. 'That's what hindsight is for. Maybe you just don't remember what it was like.'

Ash looked away from him. Now that she had started, she was remembering, all too clearly. Almost to herself, she said, 'Peter seemed so – grown up. Stable. Responsible. As if everything he did or thought was – well – normal.'

Jake snorted. Ash flashed him a look.

'When you've had the sort of childhood I had you value things like that. I thought our children would have the most wonderful father. He wouldn't always be going off to French casinos or Indian Ocean islands and forgetting the end of term or my birthday or – '

Jake moved sharply. It recalled Ash to the present.

'I can see now that it was stupid,' she said, defensively. 'I am well aware that there ought to be more to a marriage than that. But he seemed to take such *care* of me. I suppose I'd never had that much attention before.'

Jake looked blank. 'Never had much attention?' he echoed. 'The Kimbell heiress?'

Ash was wry. 'Girls didn't get attention from my grandfather. And my father was never around. When Peter started paying me compliments and taking notice of me, I could have sworn we would be happy for the rest of our lives. I was – dazzled.'

Jake was very still. 'When did you stop being dazzled?' he asked at last.

183

Ash shook her head. She had told him all she was going to. And that was more than she had openly admitted to anyone else. For some unfathomable reason, Jake Dare seemed to have the knack of getting the unvarnished truth out of her. And the unvarnished truth was painful.

He saw her resistance.

'You'll tell me one day.' His voice was very quiet but there was a note in it which made Ash look at him in sudden trepidation. He sounded very sure, Ash thought with foreboding.

She said with an effort, 'Maybe.'

'No. For sure.' He stood up. 'But I can see you've gone as far as you want to. For the moment. I can live with that,' he said tranquilly.

There was a pause. It was fraught with tension. Then, to her own astonishment Ash gave a spurt of laughter. 'That's big of you.'

'No.' His eyes glinted. 'Just good strategy. So I'll back off gracefully if you show me round.'

Ash stared. 'Round? Round the house?'

'Or the garden, if you'd feel safer outside.' His voice had a faint edge to it.

Ash prudently refrained from saying that she did not feel safe anywhere with him. Instead she said, 'It's late.'

'Not that late. There's still twilight out there.'

But Ash did not want to walk round the gardens drenched in evening sun and the scent of old roses with this man.

She said hurriedly, 'Maybe tomorrow. If I have the time.'

He laughed. 'Between attending to stinging nettles and children and small animals?'

Ash bristled. 'It's my life and . . .'

'My dear girl, I'm not criticizing,' Jake told her. 'I admire you. You're a rich woman, after all. You could spend your time playing bridge. Or going to coffee mornings and looking beautiful.'

There was more than an edge to that, too. Ash wondered, in a flash of comprehension, who was the rich lady who inspired that bitterness. Rosalind Newman? And yet he had not seemed bitter about her.

She was not going to ask, though. She did not want to know anything more about Jake Dare, she told herself firmly.

So she shrugged. 'I'm no good at bridge,' she answered flippantly. 'Too much coffee makes me twitch. And I don't have the raw material to look beautiful. Not without major surgery, anyway. Hence the gardening.'

There was an odd silence. Then Jake said slowly. 'You mean that.'

Ash was startled. 'Of course.'

Jake surveyed her. Ash thought uneasily that she had no clue as to what was going on in that handsome head.

'Take your hair down,' he said at last, very softly.

Ash's head reared back as if a twenty-foot demon had suddenly leaped out of the old-fashioned larder and towered over her.

'*What*?'

He did not repeat himself. Instead, before she knew what he was about, he took a swift step toward her and took her chin in his hand. For a disbelieving minute Ash felt his fingers in her hair. Then it was falling, tumbling against her neck, swinging against her hot cheeks in a curly tangle.

185

She backed away. 'What do you think you're doing?'

'You were saying something about raw material?' he drawled. 'Looks reasonably promising to me.'

Ash winced. That hurt. She had learned a long time ago to live with her lack of attraction – for Peter and the rest of the world – but that did not mean it had been easy. Or that she wanted this daunting stranger to remind her of it.

She said in a constrained voice, 'You're not kind.'

His eyes flared. 'Kind?' He sounded contemptuous. 'Good God, of course I'm not.' He reached out and slid his hand round the back of her neck, fanning her hair with his fingers. 'With material like this, who needs kindness?'

Ash stood as if she had been turned to stone. She hardly heard what he said. The blood was drumming in her ears at that casual, confident touch. Something was happening to her body, something new. Even Peter, even when she was still desperately in love with him, had not made her feel like this – melting, unfolding, *yearning* . . .

The shock of it slammed through her. It was starting again, she thought, shocked. Oh, she knew it so well, that terrible need for the tenderness of a touch, a caress, for the closeness that Peter had said was out of the question. Her eyes creased tight shut at the awful memories.

She could not bear to remember. But she could not afford to forget. She said it to herself deliberately: that terrible, shameful craving for love.

With a little sob she tore herself away. 'Don't touch me,' she said in a ragged whisper.

She opened her eyes. Jake was staring at her. He was a little pale. But apart from that, his expression was un-readable. Ash thought suddenly, though she did not know

186

why, He is shocked. I have shocked him.

She flinched. First Peter, now Jake Dare. She gritted her teeth, waiting for his contempt to hit her.

But he said with unexpected formality, 'I apologize.' A muscle worked in his cheek. 'I should not have done that. It was stupid. I'm – sorry.'

For some reason it was almost worse. Peter had detached her clinging arms and walked away, but at least he had not used that deadly politeness.

Shaken, Ash said in a voice she did not recognize, 'Don't ever touch me again.'

The green eyes lifted, bored into hers like a laser. Under their intensity, she took a step back, clutching Bob's papers to her breast like a shield.

He said, 'I can't promise that.'

She felt all the humiliation rise up in her throat like bile. 'Touch me again and I'll have you out of this house with a Court Injunction not to molest me,' Ash flung at him.

She was talking wildly. She had no idea whether she had the grounds to do any such thing. In a way she didn't care. It was threaten him or flee ignominiously. And she was not going to start running away from a man in her own house.

'You may think you've had bad publicity before, but believe me, if you lay a hand on me again, you'll find you ain't seen nothing yet.'

Jake looked at her for a long moment, his face a handsome mask. 'I believe you.'

Ash had the impression of a clever brain working at lightning speed behind that impassive expression. And not liking the answers it came up with. She shivered involuntarily.

'I wish I knew what was in that report about me,' she said on a flash of instinct. It astonished her. She had not realized how much the existence of that report bothered her.

'It wouldn't tell you anything you don't know,' Jake said drily.

Ash shivered again. 'It's different if it's written down though, isn't it?'

She fell silent, brooding.

'Is it?' He looked at her oddly. His voice gentled suddenly, as if she were a nervous animal that needed reassurance, she thought. 'The facts may be accurate but they're not the whole story, you know, Ash. A person is a lot more than the sum of her circumstances.'

She did not understand him. Her expression said so.

His voice warmed into laughter. 'For instance, whenever I thought about how to approach the reclusive Mrs Lawrence, it never occurred to me she'd be a professional hedger and ditcher.'

There was a long, complicated pause in which his eyes seemed to be giving her a message she could not decode. Then a reluctant laugh was drawn out of Ash. It was not, after all, so far from the truth. He must have seen her hauling at weeds in the kitchen garden from the vantage point of his window. And, of course, the state of her clothes would tell their own tale.

'That's fair enough,' she admitted with a little sigh.

Jake surveyed her from under down-dropped lids. 'Am I allowed to ask why?' he drawled. 'Surely the heir to Kimbell's could find some less grubby way to pass her time?'

Ash shrugged again. 'We all like to do what we're good at. I'm sure you're good at developing properties. I'm good with hedges and ditches,' she told him sweetly.

One wicked eyebrow flicked up. 'And other people's children?' he countered with equal sweetness.

Ash stiffened. She did not like his expression at all. She said suspiciously, 'So?'

'Shouldn't you be thinking in terms of children of your own?' His tone was idle, but the grey-green eyes were acute.

So her suspicion was justified. Ash went rigid. 'That's not likely,' she said curtly.

He searched her face. 'No room for children in your career of hedging and ditching?' he mocked.

Ash looked at him with dislike. 'You misunderstand me. I think children should be part of a family. I am not.'

He nodded as if it was what he was expecting. 'No husband – for the moment, anyway. So why not? You're young enough. You've been a widow for three years. Isn't it time to rejoin the human race? You can't mourn forever.'

Dislike deepened into downright loathing.

'Unmarried women are still members of the human race,' Ash said arctically. 'Haven't you heard? Women don't need a man to define their existence any more.'

'I've heard,' Jake said tranquilly. 'Don't mean to say I buy it. Especially with some people.'

'*Oh*!'

Ash paled. So he did feel contempt, she thought hazily. It cut cruelly, just when she was thinking she did not have to brace herself after all. The pain of it literally took her breath away, as if at a physical blow.

Jake saw her reaction, of course. Momentarily he looked startled. 'Now what have I said?' He was impatient. 'Did you think going into mourning for the rest of your life was part of the marriage deal? What are you doing? Putting your feelings into cold storage forever?'

Ash backed away. She made a helpless gesture. She could not master her voice.

'Were you still so in love, then?' He sounded odd. 'Even when he died? Even after all this time?'

Ash flinched. She did not answer but something about her face must have led him to another of those lightning deductions. His eyes narrowed to slits. He said, as he had said to Tony Anderson, 'Or is it a bad conscience?'

She gasped. She could not help herself. His eyes flared; locked on hers. They stood staring at each other across the kitchen like a pair of swordsmen about to embark on a duel to the death. And she knew she was outmatched.

Despairing, all but voiceless, Ash said, 'You just don't give a damn, do you? Is there one single thing you won't do to get that land?'

For a moment he looked blank, as if she had reminded him of something he had completely wiped out of his mind. It was almost, she thought, with that part of her brain that was still working, as if he had forgotten why he was engaged in this battle at all. Then he turned away, shrugging.

'All's fair in love and property deals.'

Ash said huskily, 'I hate you.'

CHAPTER 8

It was a tough evening for Ash. Having decided to get dressed and appear in company, Jake Dare would not go away and leave her alone. He honoured his promise not to dig into her deepest feelings any more. But he clearly did not feel that included her daily life. He wanted to know all about it. And, it became apparent, he was quite determined to join in.

He went with Ash to the garage to feed the badger cub. He accompanied her when she watered the flower beds. He offered helpful comments on her preparations for dinner, until Ash handed him the knife and tomatoes and suggested that he take over.

'No, no. I'm sure you're a great cook. I wouldn't want to interfere,' he assured her solemnly.

Ash sucked hard on her teeth and bit back an acid retort. She did not want to get into another argument with him. He had made her admit aloud things about her life with Peter that she had hardly allowed herself to entertain, even as a hypothesis. It had left her feeling shaky. She was certainly not ready to risk another exchange which could turn intimate.

But when Jake announced his intention of going with her when she took Rusty for his evening walk before dinner, Ash had had enough.

'If you're well enough to walk the estate, you're well enough to go home,' she told him. She managed to sound exasperated. Given how vulnerable she still felt inside, that was a triumph all on its own.

Jake shook his head sadly. 'I thought women were supposed to be caring and nurturing.'

Ash snorted. 'They may be. They also don't like being exploited.'

There was a lurking smile in his eyes. 'It would take a brave man to exploit you, Ashley Lawrence.'

But he gave in. He went indoors, announcing his intention of reading. Ash directed him to the study and took Rusty off for his walk, fast, before Jake could change his mind. She shot out of the garden and on to the bridle path with a startled dog finding himself dragged past some of his favourite smells.

'Phew,' said Ash.

She had a sense of being let out of a Turkish bath she had been in for too long. As she ran Rusty's lead through her fingers she noticed that her hands were trembling. She frowned. Before she went back to the house she was going to have to stop that trembling.

Shaking out her hair, she strode on. Rusty rushed ahead, chasing imaginary rabbits. Ash was grateful for the dog's company. It made her fell slightly less shaky.

What on earth had possessed her? Of all the men to confide in, Jake Dare was the last she would have chosen. He was a stranger, a foreigner, a member of that species she had learned to avoid, a businessman. Quite apart from all that, he made no secret of the fact that he was trying to influence her to sell her land when she had told him she did not want to do so.

She could not have distrusted him more; and with reason. So *why*?

Ash shook her head. It was a long time since she had talked about herself to anyone. Perhaps too long. Perhaps Jake Dare had identified that. And taken advantage of it.

'What you need,' she told herself, 'is a good long session with an old friend. Then you won't be tempted to confide in a passing pirate. How long is it since you spent any time with Joanne? Or Sue? Or anyone else, for that matter? Call them.'

The long evening shadows lengthened.

'Yes, that's what I'll do,' thought Ash. 'I'll ring Joanne. I'll do it tonight.'

Slowly, slowly, she felt the tension within her begin to unwind.

At last she came to a stop. The bridle path had brought her to the top of a hill. At her feet the ground fell away steeply to a small valley. The hill sides folded gently down to the little river that ran through it. On one side, a flock of sheep drowsed in the evening sun. Their black faces turned towards her incuriously as their lambs scrambled and pranced about the field.

Ash whistled to Rusty. He was a country-bred dog and knew he had to leave sheep alone but, she reasoned, it was still wiser to put him on a lead when they came across a flock. Especially with Jake Dare's threat of legal action hanging over their heads.

Rusty came obediently and Ash clipped the lead on to his collar. Then she started off downhill to the stream. As she went, she frowned.

How serious was Jake Dare's threat? All her main instincts told her that it was just a strategic ploy on his part, that he had no real intention of putting it into practice. But she was not – quite – sure. Other, and it seemed to her deeper, instincts told her that Jake Dare would go to any lengths to get his own way. In her life, she had known at least two men like that, Ash thought with a shiver.

But, then again, she had never known anyone like Jake Dare. He seemed to treat everything as a joke. Even when he kissed her.

Particularly when he kissed me, thought Ash, wincing.

It hurt, but Ash was honest enough to acknowledge it. Jake's kiss had been enough to throw all her careful self-containment off-balance and into free fall. She still felt dizzy, remembering it. Even at this distance of time and out of the disturbing presence of Jake Dare, the thought of that kiss still set her trembling, however slightly. But he had made it plain, thought Ash, that for him it had been a moment's amusement, nothing more.

She had stood there, shaken to her core, and he had *laughed*. So he could not take her or her affairs at all seriously, could he? In which case she really need not worry about the gravity of any threat he pretended to pose to her. In all likelihood, he was just amusing himself again.

Or was he?

'Which brings me right back to square one,' muttered Ash. She swished irritably at the hedgerow. 'Blast the man. The sooner he leaves the better.'

The shadow of the hill had been creeping slowly over the ground as she walked. She now noticed, with a slight shock, that it had completely obliterated the last pool of sunlight. In the greying sky the first stars were beginning to appear. A breath of a breeze had sprung up.

'Time we were turning back,' decided Ash.

She looked about her. With a start she recognized that she had come further than she intended. Soon it would be too dark to see her way. If she was not to go stumbling in rabbit holes in the dark, she would have to walk back along the road. She hated walking along road. Another thing to put down to Jake Dare's account.

She had been walking along the metalled lane for ten minutes, however, when a van pulled up beside her.

'Need a lift?' asked a vaguely familiar voice.

Ash peered into the car. It was Brian Francis.

'Good heavens, don't often see you round here,' she said.

He chuckled. 'Dining with the squirearchy. My wife insisted. I got held up, so she went on. Lift?'

Ash looked doubtfully at Rusty. Even in a dry summer he managed to find some mud to roll in. Brian Francis saw her glance.

'Don't worry about the dog. We've two of our own, not to mention the kids. The back seat is permanently covered in rubber sheeting. Stuff him in there.'

Ash laughed and surrendered gratefully.

'You're very kind,' she said, getting in.

'My pleasure.' He set the car in motion. 'I'm disappointed. To be honest I'd hoped you'd be there tonight. Leaven the lump. Tim Padgett's a good fellow, but he was born ninety and there's a limit to the number of lawyers I can take in one dose.'

Ash smiled guiltily. She had been to Tim's dinner parties too, though she had managed to avoid most of them since Peter had died.

'Tim can be a bit pompous,' she agreed. 'But I'm on his side at the moment.'

'The Conservation Society?' said Brian, negotiating a steep bend with concentration. 'I hear they're fighting the Hayes Wood development.'

'Mmm. He called Jake Dare Conan the Destroyer,' Ash remembered pleasurably.

That startled Brian so much that the next bend took him by surprise. 'Good heavens,' he said, pulling the car back to the left and straightening it. He sent her a quick look. 'How did Jake Dare take that?'

'Not to his face,' Ash had to admit. 'But Tim's coming round on Friday, so I have hopes.'

Brian's eyebrows rose. 'Do I infer you're not getting on with the patient?'

'*Patient*!' Ash snorted. 'He's more like a full-scale invasion force. Every time I turn round, there he is. He's had his assistant marching in and out of the house at will,' she added with pardonable exaggeration, 'I can't call my house my own.'

'Ah,' said Brian. He frowned at the road in his head-lights.

'In fact, that's why you found me on the road. Jake Dare got me in so much of a temper that I forgot to pick up a torch. So when I went further than I meant, I had to come back along the road.'

Brian's eyebrows rose even higher. 'Temper? You?'

Ash was rueful. 'Don't rub it in. I never knew I was such a nasty person. I always thought I was pretty calm. But with Jake Dare – well – he just seems to rub my fur up the wrong way.'

'Ah,' Brian Francis said again.

Her eyes narrowed on the silver ribbon of road in the car's headlights. 'I've got this feeling that he's got some *plan*. I don't know what. Or why, for that matter. I know he was very angry that I wouldn't sell my land to him, but there's nothing he can do about that. And anyway, this doesn't feel like business, somehow. It feels like – oh, I don't know.' She pushed her tangled hair back, frowning out into the night. 'I've never felt like this before, so jumpy.' She turned to Brian. 'I know it sounds stupid but it feels as if I've got a foreign agent stalking me.' Her voice shook.

Rusty growled at her tone. Ash swung round and put a comforting hand on the silky coat. She shook her head.

'No one's ever done that before.' She did not know how bewildered she sounded.

Brian said uneasily, 'New experiences are good for us.'

'Character-forming, you mean?' Ash said drily. 'I'm not sure how keen I am on the bits that seem to be forming under Jake Dare's influence.'

Brian laughed. But when he had swept round the Manor to the kitchen door and dropped Ash off, his expression was sober. It was an abstracted consultant who sat through Tim Padgett's dinner party.

'What's wrong?' his wife demanded as they left the table and made for the drawing-room and coffee.

'I'm having second thoughts about a decision,' Brian said absently. 'It seemed a good idea at the time but – I'm not sure I took everything into account that I should have.'

His wife was concerned. 'A patient?'

But Brian gave a jump and came back into the present. 'No. Nothing like that. Don't take any notice of me.' He took her arm. 'Let's go and listen to Tim holding forth on rural property values.'

Ash went into the kitchen warily. The light was on above the Aga, but apart from that the room was undisturbed. No sign of Jake Dare. She let out a breath she had not known she was holding.

She drew some water for Rusty and rinsed mud and leaf mould off her hands. Though she was reluctant to admit it, her conscience was telling her that she ought to tell him dinner was ready. However much she might want him elsewhere, Jake Dare was still a guest under her roof.

A quick glance at her watch. Past ten o'clock. It got dark so late these long summer evenings. Perhaps he had decided not to wait for supper. Perhaps he had already gone back to bed, she thought hopefully. Straightening her shoulders, she went to see.

Of course he had not. There was a light under the study door and he was listening to music. As she got closer, Ash could hear the sounds of a single violin and some wood-wind instrument in dreamy conversation with each other. With a slight shock, she recognized it. It was one of her favourite pieces, an eighteenth-century clarinet concerto, orderly and heartbreaking.

She was filled with sudden, inexplicable outrage. How

dare Jake Dare? Oh, how *dare* he? He moved into *her* house, thoroughly upset her domestic arrangements and now helped himself to the music centre as if he were welcome in her house. No, worse than that, as if he were *familiar*.

The door banged rudely back on its hinges as Ash marched in. The sight that met her eyes stopped her dead in her tracks.

Jake Dare was sprawled in one of the high-backed eighteenth-century chairs that her grandfather had given them as a wedding present. They had been in the family a long time and were among her grandfather's favourites. It was almost the only sentimental gesture Ash ever knew him to make. At the time she had been touched almost to tears. Later, of course, she had realized that it was a measure of her grandfather's determination to do everything he could to get the marriage off to a good start.

Peter had said the chairs were uncomfortable. He insisted that they be put in the study he had ordained for his own use. But he never sat in one unless her grandfather was visiting.

Ash always liked to curl up in them, even as a child. She would tuck herself right back into the security of the brocade wing and read her favourite books. While she was coiled up in their protection she felt nothing could get at her to hurt her. Sometimes, when Peter was away, she would venture into his study and tuck herself up in one of the old chairs, trying to recall that childish comfort.

Once or twice she had been there when Peter arrived back unexpectedly from London in the small hours. It provoked him unbearably. It was one of the many things towards the end of their marriage that did provoke him. He never said anything, but Ash knew all the same. In the end she had stopped going into the study at all.

Now, seeing someone else doing much the same as she had been prevented from doing, Ash felt as if she had received a blow directly on to her heart. She put a hand to her side. For a horrible instant she felt literally as if she could not breathe.

Then he turned his head idly and her breathing came back to normal.

He was not tucked up, of course. His legs were too long. He had stretched them out to rest on another family heirloom.

Ash said freezingly, 'My grandmother embroidered that stool.'

Any decently mannered man would have removed his feet at once, she thought. Jake just grinned.

'And a first-rate job she made of it. This is one comfortable footstool.'

Ash glared. Her tone became marginally more arctic. 'I'm sure she would have been flattered.'

Jake laughed aloud at that. But he brought his feet down to the floor with a crash.

'Thank you.'

'You call the shots,' he said lazily.

That was so obviously untrue that it was all Ash could do not to grind her teeth and throw things. Jake stretched, watching her from under steeply dropped eyelids.

'Do you mind me being in this room?'

'No, no,' Ash began. Courtesy to a stranger was a reflex action to someone of her upbringing. She caught herself in disgust. Jake Dare was rapidly becoming less of a stranger by the minute. And he had certainly done nothing so far that deserved courtesy. 'Yes,' she finished, lifting her chin with resolution.

He looked surprised. 'Do you?' He looked round. 'Are you saying this is your den?' He sounded incredulous.

For some reason that annoyed her even more. 'Why not?' she demanded with wholly uncharacteristic belligerence.

He grimaced. 'No reason.'

Ash took a hasty step forward. 'You don't say anything without a reason. Since you landed yourself on me, I've come to learn some things about you at least.'

One eyebrow rose. For a moment Jake looked disconcerted; even annoyed. Then he shrugged. 'OK. If you really want to know.'

'I do.'

'Then since you ask, it's not like anybody's den. In fact, if you ask me, it's the most anonymous room I've been in since the last time I stayed in a Holiday Inn,' he said dispassionately. 'Even the books look as if they were bought by the yard.'

Ash's temper flared to new heights. 'How dare you?'

He shrugged again. 'You asked me.'

'I didn't ask you to insult me.'

He considered her. 'Insult? What insult?'

Ash floundered. 'Saying the study is . . . has . . . that you . . .'

'That I've seen more character in a film set,' Jake supplied helpfully. 'That's not an insult. It's a statement of fact.'

Ash took hold of her temper. 'It's an expression of opinion,' she corrected. 'Your opinion. Or do you think your opinion amounts to a matter of fact, Mr Dare?'

His eyebrows flew up. 'Touché,' he said. He sounded surprised; and not at all pleased.

Ash strode across to the CD player and switched off the disk. In the ensuing silence she swung back to face him.

'Dinner in the breakfast-room in ten minutes. If you want it.'

She did not wait for his answer. As she banged out of the room she heard him call out something. She ignored it.

But later, over pasta with a sauce of home grown tomatoes and basil, he said, 'Did you listen to your messages?'

Ash looked up from her plate. 'What?'

'Telephone messages. While you were out. I let the machine pick them up.'

Ash stared.

'I didn't like to answer them,' he explained innocently. 'I thought it might embarrass you to have a strange man take your calls.'

She assimilated that. The answering machine was in the study. He would have heard every word.

'You mean you sat in there and listened to people leaving messages for me?' she said in gathering wrath. 'Private messages.'

He pursed his lips. 'Nothing sounded that private to me. A disappointing selection from that point of view.' He put his elbows on the table and leaned forward. 'Tell me, do you have any private life at all?'

Ash strained back in her chair as if there were no

202

polished table between them and he could reach out and touch her whenever the whim took him.

'You mean, do I have a sex life?' she interpreted with disdain.

He did not bother to deny it. 'OK. Do you?'

That was not a question Ash was going to answer. She dismissed it with a scornful gesture.

'I thought not,' said Jake in a satisfied voice.

Ash was not going to be trapped into losing her temper again. She pressed her lips firmly together and stood up, reaching for his plate. He stopped her by the simple means of putting his hand round her wrist. Ash froze.

Their eyes met; locked. Ash felt something begin to slither up her spine. She kept her expression wooden. But she could not repress that tell-tale trembling in her finger tips. For a moment they stayed like that, immobile as waiting enemies.

Slowly, Jake smiled. It was not a kind smile. It was speculative, provocative, amused. But not kind.

The trembling increased. Ash found she was holding her breath.

Then his lashes flicked down over that equivocal expression and he said in a matter-of-fact voice, 'Let me do that. You go and listen to your messages.'

He let her go. Without thinking, Ash rubbed the place where his fingers had closed on her wrist. She felt oddly shaken.

The green eyes were watchful. 'Did I hurt you?'

'What?' Ash realized what she was doing. Her hand fell rapidly to her side. 'No. No, of course not.' She turned away. 'I'll be in the study.'

The messages were unexciting. Ash patched through them quickly, made notes of things she had to answer and then sat back. She had promised herself she would call Joanne. She looked at her watch. It would not be late by Joanne's standards. Joanne was a party girl. Ash began to dial.

'Hallo?'

There was loud music on the other end of the telephone. It was not Mozart.

Ash raised her voice. 'Joanne?'

'Speaking. Who is – ' Awareness cut in. '*Ash*? Ash? Is that you?'

'Yes. I know it's only been a few days – ' Ash began hesitantly, but was cut off.

'Hang on.' The music was abruptly silenced. 'Ash darling how good to hear from you again so soon. I hope you're calling to tell me you're coming up to London at last?'

Dear Joanne. She did not change, Ash thought. Hearing her old friend's cheerful tones, her throat was unexpectedly tight.

She said, 'I'll come up some time. But I can't at the moment.'

Joanne's low husky voice was amused. 'Don't tell me. Rural obligations. The sheep are calving or something.'

Ash laughed. 'Not at this season.'

'Well, then, come and stay. We'll hit the town running.'

'I wish I could,' said Ash with real feeling.

'You're your own mistress. With an indecent income, to boot. What's the problem, if the sheep are OK?'

'The problem is human,' said Ash gloomily.

Instantly Joanne was serious. 'Oh, no. What's happened?'

Ash explained. There was a moment's silence.

Then Joanne said incredulously, 'My God, I thought someone had died. You mean you've got gorgeous Jake Dare all alone with you in that damn great house and you're *complaining*?'

This was not quite the sympathy Ash had hoped for. She said stiffly, 'I didn't invite him.'

'Some people just get lucky,' said Joanne with a chuckle.

'Lucky!'

'What else would you call it? He's rich, he's handsome and he's total charm. Hell, he's even available. The rumour is that he's returned Rosie Newman to store. Half the women in London would kill to be in your place.'

'They'd be welcome.'

'Oh, Ash,' sighed her friend. 'You don't change, do you?' She gave a despairing laugh.

It annoyed Ash. 'Do you?' she said.

The bubbling laugh was cut off abruptly. There was a sharp little silence.

'Ouch,' said Joanne at last. 'If that's a way of asking about Rufus, he moved on.'

Ash was conscience stricken. It was a mean dig at someone she knew as well as she knew Joanne. Ash knew more about Joanne's chaotic emotional life than anyone.

Ten years ago, their smart summer weddings had been held within weeks of each other. Within a month Joanne's marriage had been in trouble. By Christmas it was over. After that she had disappeared for a year. When she emerged it was to announce that from now on she was going to have the brightest career in London.

At the time Ash had been horrified, convinced that it would be the end of their friendship. It had not turned out like that. Joanne had certainly gone on to do what she wanted. But over the years, hearing Joanne's struggles and self-doubt, Ash had gradually become reconciled. These days, though she was glad for her ambitious friend's success, she was no longer intimidated by it. She knew the price she paid for it.

Repentant, she said now, 'What went wrong? Working too hard again?'

'Among other things.' Ash could almost see Joanne's shrug. She sounded bored, but the weariness underneath was plain to her old friend. 'I suppose I just don't have your talent for taking care of a man.'

Ash was startled into a chuckle. 'That's not what Jake Dare thinks. He says I'm no Florence Nightingale.'

'Does he?' Joanne's voice lightened, became curious. 'What on earth have you been doing? Poisoning his feed?'

Ash snorted. 'Merely pointing out that he's no more ill than I am.'

'Good grief.' Joanne was hugely entertained. 'No wonder.'

'He's playing some game of his own,' said Ash darkly.

'It sounds like it.' Joanne was bubbling again. 'Do you need reinforcements?'

It was, of course, exactly what Ash had hoped for. Now it was on offer she had another of those inconvenient attacks of conscience. 'But aren't you very busy?'

'I've got a mobile, a laptop and a weekend,' Joanne said practically.

'But – '

'And I'd pay good money to see you putting any man in his place, let alone dashing Jake Dare.'

'What?'

'You're the worst case of dutiful female I've ever seen,' Joanne said frankly. 'You'd think the whole of the second half of the twentieth century hadn't happened. Dutiful granddaughter, dutiful wife. Hell, you even obeyed the rules at school. If you've started biting back at last, I want to come along and cheer from the sidelines.'

'Thank you,' said Ash without noticeable gratitude in her voice.

Joanne was airy. 'Think nothing of it. I'll see you on Friday. Can I bring anything?'

'You mean in addition to the mobile phone and the laptop computer?' Ash mocked.

'I mean to eat.'

'I usually do salady things in this hot weather. Most of that is home grown.'

'Wonderful. All right then, what about a pud?'

Ash was surprised. Her figure was a cause of perpetual anxiety to Joanne. 'Are you eating puds these days?'

Joanne sighed. 'I've given up on the calorie front until I've won the war at work. One battle at a time.'

'Sounds sensible. Then bring a pud by all means. Jake Dare will be glad to see it.'

'You *are* putting poison in his feed,' crowed Joanne. 'I knew it. I shall win him away from you with my rival delicacies.'

'Please,' said Ash with feeling.

'This weekend,' said Joanne, 'is going to be fun. Friday. Don't let him go till I get there.'

When she rang off she was still laughing.

Ash went out of the study and hesitated. She had no desire to see Jake Dare again, but good manners demanded that she at least say good night to him. If she did not he was quite capable of following her to her own room, she thought.

A strong smell of coffee made up her mind for her. It wafted out of the kitchen like a warm west wind. Jake Dare was making himself at home again.

He looked up when she came in. The old-fashioned percolator was bubbling on the Aga. He had found two earthenware mugs.

'Nearly ready,' he said. 'Milk? Sugar?'

'Neither,' snapped Ash.

Jake's eyes crinkled at the corners. 'Thank you,' he suggested.

'Thank you,' said Ash with restraint. She added with spurious solicitude, 'Should you be drinking coffee at this time of night? You being so frail, after all. Convalescents need their sleep, I believe. Coffee will only keep you awake.'

He took the percolator off the heat, closed the lid to the Aga ring and poured the dark liquid into the waiting mugs. He put down the percolator and brought one across to her.

'Only one thing keeps me awake,' Jake said. 'And it isn't coffee.'

Ash nearly dropped her mug.

He gave her one of those speculative smiles again. 'What about you?'

'Wh-what about me?' Ash asked warily.

'What keeps you awake?'

He was laughing at her. It did not take a genius to recognize that. But, though he was enjoying himself laughing at her expense, there was more to it than simple mockery. There was a real challenge there.

Ash's jaw clenched with the effort of not reacting to it. She said sweetly, 'Oh, coffee does it for me.'

He raised his eyebrows as if she had surprised him. Did he think she was going to dissolve in a schoolgirl puddle of embarrassment at his feet? Ash thought savagely.

She took a sip of her coffee. 'For instance, I've got a lecture I need to watch on television tonight. This will help.'

He was even more surprised. 'Lecture?'

Ash was pleased. 'I'm doing an Open University course. The programmes are often pretty late.'

There was a pause. Then Jake shook his head. 'You are – astonishing.'

'Oh. Why?'

He hesitated. 'I've never met anyone who was less like the advance publicity,' he said at last. 'I keep revising my information and I still keep getting it wrong.'

Ash was even more pleased. 'That will teach you not to waste your money on private detectives.'

Jake's expression was wry. 'You could be right.'

'Snooping never did anyone any good,' she went on virtuously.

'Not unless it gets the right answers, certainly.'

Ash frowned.

Jake said hastily, 'Time I was in bed. I'll get out of your

hair before I reveal any more of the weaknesses in my research department. Good night.'

He went, leaving Ash curiously unsatisfied. In theory she had won that round. Hadn't she? Well, if so, why didn't she feel triumphant?

She banged off to the small sitting-room where she kept her television. She had been looking forward to this evening's presentation, but for once she had real difficulty in concentrating. A helpful professor drew charts of winds and tide flow but Ash kept finding her thoughts drifting away.

What was it that Jake Dare saw when he looked at her? What did he really want from her? Was it just the sale of Hayes Wood? Above all, what was Ash going to do about it?

In the end she put her notebook away and turned off the set and set the video. Her notes did not make sense and she had been watching so intermittently that she could not reconstruct them from memory. She'd record the programmes in future and watch them when Jake Dare had left.

'The sooner that man gets out of my house the better,' muttered Ash.

But at the same time she would have been almost disappointed if he just packed his bags and left. Ash acknowledged it with more than a hint of shame. It was not very creditable, she thought. But she could not help it. She wanted to be the one to throw him out. Jake Dare had laughed at her too much, manoeuvred her too much. For her own self-respect, she needed to get the better of the man. The only problem was, she had not the slightest idea how to do it.

It did not make for a peaceful night.

She was still pondering the problem the next morning when Molly Hall rang.

'Ash, could you possibly have the boys for the day again?' she asked, without preamble. She sounded strained. 'I know that's twice in as many days but – '

'Yes, of course,' said Ash startled. 'What's wrong?'

There was a strange choking sound. 'Thanks. I'll be round as soon as I get them loaded into the car.'

Molly arrived in fifteen minutes. The impression Ash had received from the telephone call was not belied by her appearance. Molly's normally neat hair was all over the place, as if she not brushed it this morning and her eyes darted here and there like a cornered squirrel's.

Ash sent the boys off to look at the badger and urged Molly onto a garden seat in the sun.

'Sit and bask,' she said. 'You look as if you need it.'

'Oh, Ash,' said Molly. Her voice had a distinct break in it. 'Don't I just.'

She subsided onto the wooden seat and rubbed her eyes vigorously. Ash looked tactfully in the opposite direction until she was in command of herself again.

Molly gave a long sigh. 'Sorry about the dramatics. I thought if I had to spend one more minute listening to that woman tell me how my children were running wild, I'd kill.'

'Ah.' This did not need interpreting. Ash knew Molly Hall and her family very well. 'Mrs Hall?'

'Mrs Hall,' Molly agreed. 'That female serpent in best cashmere. The one who lays waste the countryside and devours a virgin every full moon. Or at least a small boy

211

from the grammar school,' she added with a return to reason.

'She's been getting at the boys?'

'The boys. Me. Mike. Whoever's in reach. Last night it was some kid, friend of Chris's. The boy came over to show Chris a new computer game he'd got and my beloved mother-in-law gave him a lecture on manners in the days of the Raj.'

'*What*?' said Ash, laughing.

'You can laugh,' said Molly gloomily. 'First she told him it was rude to go calling in tennis shoes.'

'Why on earth – ?'

'He was wearing trainers. Then she told him he should stand up when she came into the room. As she was making herself a cocktail, she was popping in and out of the sitting-room all the time. Reasonably enough, you may think, Chris pointed this out.'

'I see. That's why he's running wild?'

'That's not the only reason. In the end she went and plonked herself down in the sitting-room with them and complained because they were playing a computer game instead of talking to her.'

'Oh, Lord.'

'They should have kicked the old bat out,' said Molly passionately. 'It's Chris's home. He can invite whoever he wants back. They can play computer games all night if they choose. They've got their rights.'

'If you said that to Mrs Hall, she must think you're running wild, too.'

'She probably does. I don't care. If she weren't so damned nosey she would have left the boys alone. She just can't bear not to know what everybody's doing all the time. And Mike won't either stop her or make her go home. I tell you, Ash, I'm at the end of my tether.'

Ash could see that. Molly's nice brown eyes were filling up again.

'Come and see the roses,' she said hastily.

Molly sniffed and rummaged for her handkerchief. 'I'm sorry. I didn't mean to make a fuss,' she said getting up obediently. 'It's just that I don't know how much longer it's going on. Or how soon somebody's going to crack and tell her what an interfering old witch she is. Probably,' she added fairly, 'me.'

'Well, you see most of her,' said Ash comfortingly. 'She doesn't usually stay this long, does she?'

'No, but her boiler exploded and she's had to have it replaced. Then they found some rising damp and the builders said they'd take the opportunity of her being away to get it all fixed. That was six weeks ago and they still show no signs of finishing. And Mike says I can't get her to hurry them up because it looks as if we don't want her.'

Ash said nothing but her eyes were brimful of mischief. Molly met her look and smiled reluctantly.

'All right, all right. We haven't actually *told* her she's unwelcome.'

'Do you need to?'

'Oh don't, Ash. You're making me feel like a toad.'

Ash shook her head. 'Don't. I've got no right to lecture. I've got a visitor, too. And I am not even pretending to make him welcome.'

Molly was sufficiently intrigued to stop sniffing and let

213

her handkerchief fall. 'Tall, dark and handsome! I'd forgotten he'd still be here.'

Ash showed her teeth. 'Yes.'

'Why are you worried?' demanded Molly.

'If I knew that, I'd be a lot less jumpy than I am.'

'He's fallen in love with you. He is going to rescue you and carry you off to his castle in the mountains,' said Molly rapturously. In between working on the Hall's small farm, bringing up two inventive boys and teaching at a primary school two days a week, Molly read a lot of romantic fiction.

'There's nothing to rescue me from,' Ash pointed out. 'You're the one with the dragon in residence.'

Reminded, Molly pulled a face. 'You're right, of course. I suppose he wouldn't like to come and rescue me instead?'

'Stick around. You can ask him.'

Molly was startled. 'Ask – You mean meet him? Here? But I thought – Isn't he ill?'

'His state,' said Ash carefully, 'is best described as convalescent.'

Molly looked a question.

'He is perfectly capable of doing anything he wants to and much too ill to do anything he doesn't,' Ash interpreted.

Molly cheered up perceptibly. 'And he doesn't want to leave the Manor?'

'Not so as you'd notice, no.'

'Then he has to be in love with you.'

Ash stiffened. 'I don't follow.'

'Well, what else is there to do here?' Molly asked sensibly. 'Especially for some glamorous townie. No,

214

don't try to convince me otherwise. I need some romance in my life with Mrs Hall lashing her tail about the place. Love at first sight, that's what it was.'

'Don't talk nonsense,' said Ash, her sense of humour deserting her all of a sudden.

Molly did not notice. 'Do you good,' she said robustly. 'About time you had a follower.'

Ash marched quickly ahead and busied herself with a trailing branch of a greeny white rose. 'This Virgo is getting completely out of hand. I'll get some secateurs. Then I can deal with it now, while I think of it.'

She fled back to the house.

It was one of Em's late days, so the kitchen should have been empty. It was not.

'Good morning,' said Jake Dare pleasantly.

He had helped himself to coffee again, Ash saw. But there the similarity to last night ended. He was frowning, so that deep indentations appeared running from mouth to nose. It made him look an altogether more formidable character than the teasing pirate she was used to. More formidable, thought Ash involuntarily, but not less attractive.

The reflection shocked her so much that she nearly dropped the secateurs she had located, for some reason, in the cutlery drawer.

'Good morning,' she said breathlessly, quite forgetting that she resented him helping himself to coffee. 'I'm – er – outside. With a friend. Take whatever you want for breakfast. It's all in the larder.' She waved her hand at the door in the corner of the kitchen and backed out.

Not less attractive. Not less *attractive*? What was she

215

thinking about? She didn't find Jake Dare attractive. That was Joanne. Joanne was turned on by men like that. Ash had known the type all her life and she knew she wasn't attracted to them.

She did not get as far as the rose garden. Molly was strolling to meet her. 'Is that coffee I smell?'

Hell, thought Ash. I don't want her meeting Jake Dare. She'll be friendly and curious and then he'll think he has even more right to behave as if he owns the place.

But the habit of good manners was too strong for her. 'Yes. The lodger's breakfast. Have a cup.'

Molly followed her back into the kitchen. Jake was standing by the scrubbed pine table, flicking impatiently through the business pages of the newspaper Ash had not yet read. It looked, thought Ash, as if he were looking for some particular item. He did not seem to be finding it.

Jake looked up as they came in. Just for a second his frown deepened. He looked almost savage. Then he straightened, and the frown disappeared as if it had never been. It was chilling, thought Ash, watching him set out to charm Molly, how quickly, how *totally* he had wiped away his true expression.

He must be very use to hiding his feelings. It came to her in a blinding flash of illumination. It shook Ash. Although it was her instant reaction – and she had learned to be cautious about her instant reactions – it felt like truth. Used to hiding his feelings and quite without conscience in the mask he donned to cover them.

Ash withdrew to the corner by the stove. She made great play of brewing more coffee, but she watched the interchange between Jake and Molly all the time. Molly, she saw, had not a single suspicion that Jake was not as cheerfully charming as he seemed.

She was already confiding the day's domestic difficulties. Jake gave every appearance of being interested. He laughed, he sympathized, he even offered suggestions.

'It's quite hopeless,' Molly assured him. Under the charm of the man she had lost her weariness, Ash saw. She sounded positively sunny now. 'Mrs Hall has never made it into the twentieth century.'

Jake grinned. 'Oh, you English.'

'It isn't only the English who have problems with mother-in-laws,' objected Molly. 'Do you get along with yours?'

Jake greeted this unsubtle ploy with amusement. 'None on the books at present.'

'Ah.' Molly sent Ash a pleased look.

Ash refused to acknowledge it, but the blood rose in her cheeks as she saw Jake take in the byplay.

Jake said easily, 'I wasn't talking about in-laws. I was talking about this passion for the past.'

Molly was rueful. 'How right you are. Ancient monuments coast to coast and too many of them still drinking three pink gins before dinner.'

Jake was entertained. 'That's what your mother-in-law does?'

'*And* smokes like a chimney. I just can't get the smell out of the curtains.' She turned to Ash. 'I didn't tell you. The final straw last night was when she took the boys to task for not lighting her cigarette for her. Chris's friend gave her a snap run down on the carcinogenic properties of tobacco. Then he told her that if she wanted to kill herself

217

she was welcome to but she was polluting the air for everyone else as well. He said if she was so keen on people having consideration for others she might try it some time. And then he stamped off.'

'He didn't,' said Ash, awed.

Jake let out a great bellow of laughter.

'He did. I thought she was going to explode.'

Ash said thoughtfully, 'You have to admire him. At least he had the courage of his convictions.'

'Courage is right. She terrifies *me*.'

'So what did you do?' demanded Ash.

Molly shrugged. 'What could I do? Sent Chris after the boy with enough money to buy them both a cinema ticket. Poured the rest of the gin bottle into Mrs Hall. Apologised to everyone. Waited for the storm to blow over.'

'I know the feeling,' Ash said with sympathy.

Quite suddenly Jake stopped laughing. His green eyes narrowed. For a moment the massive frown was almost back.

'What do you mean, you know the feeling?' he asked.

The attack was so sudden that Ash did not know what to say. Her chin went up. Molly looked from one to the other, her mouth open.

Jake's voice sank. 'You don't wait for storms to blow over,' he told Ash harshly. 'You set them loose. And I hope to hell that you've got the courage of your convictions because you're going to need them.'

218

CHAPTER 9

Jake walked out. Molly stared at Ash.

'What was that about?'

'I haven't the slightest idea,' said Ash with asperity.

Molly shivered. 'I thought he was so nice. Then all of a sudden – that.'

'Successful businessmen. They do that,' agreed Ash in a neutral voice. 'It goes with the one-track mind and the multi-million bank account. And the belief that they're entitled to any damn thing they happen to fancy.'

Molly looked abashed. 'I suppose you'd know about that. I've never met a millionaire before.'

'You haven't missed much. I wouldn't worry about it.'

Molly made a face. 'I think I'd almost rather have Mrs Hall. At least I know when she's going to bite my head off. How much longer is he staying?'

'I wish I knew.'

'But surely – '

'Brian Ferris said ten days. I suggested three, but Conan the Destroyer seems to have conveniently forgotten that. The theory is that he stays here until he's recovered from the shock of knocking himself out on his own dashboard.'

Ash jerked her head at the door through which Jake had left. 'Shocked, would you say?'

If there was one subject on which Molly Hall was an expert, it was that of unwanted guests digging themselves into her home and refusing to budge. She looked sympathetic. 'So it really is just a pretext?'

'And a pretty thin one.'

'But *why*?'

'You were suggesting he had fallen madly in love with me, as I recall,' Ash reminded her drily.

'Ah,' said Molly. 'Yes. So I was. Well, I was obviously way off beam. Cancel the idea. I withdraw it absolutely. I didn't know what I was talking about. He *may* be capable of falling in love, but it certainly won't be with you.'

Ash pushed her hair back off her face. 'Told you so,' she said with a gleam of mischief.

But it was a double-edged triumph. She had convinced Molly. But just for a moment and shamefully, Ash almost wished it had been the other way round.

Meanwhile Jake was annoyed with himself. Why had he let the girl provoke him like that? It was not even as if it was for the first time. It seemed as if he got within her orbit and he lost his head. He was famous for his cool. He could not remember a time when he had not been in command of himself, no matter how sanctimonious the opposition might be. Until now.

Out of earshot, Jake permitted himself a loud snort of derision.

The trouble was, he should never have let his reactions show in the kitchen. Never show your feelings, especially if you're angry or disappointed. That was one of the first rules he had developed for himself, and not just in business. You could not afford to let the people who you were negotiating with see into your heart, or they would be able to pre-empt your next move.

He went into the study and flung himself into the chair behind the desk. It looked out across sun-filled lawns. The serene prospect gave him no pleasure.

Was Ashley Lawrence clever enough to read him? If so, did she have the influence or the contacts to forestall his next move? Or, most galling of all, had she already done so?

The newspaper this morning had been a shock. Jake could not think of any reason why the announcement had not been made. It should have been. Eric Stenson had assured him it would be. He had even shown Jake copies of the tombstone advertisement. It should have been published today at the latest.

Unless, somehow, one of the banks involved had decided to back out at the last minute. And Ashley Lawrence was a Kimbell. Did she still have that sort of influence over her grandfather's bank, even though Ambrose Kimbell had died five years ago? And if she did, had she used it?

Jake picked up the phone and punched out the number of his PA's private line. He should have known that Stenson would change his mind about advertising the new acquisition. If he had known and not told Jake he was in hot water. If he had not known, the water was boiling, Jake thought grimly. Tony Anderson had some explaining to do.

It was clear from the way he answered the telephone that Tony had come to the same conclusion.

'What happened?' demanded Jake without preamble.

'I'm trying to find out. They were still on course the day before yesterday. I can't think what's gone wrong.'

'Can't you? Then do some digging. Speaking of which, how are your researches on Mrs Lawrence progressing?'

Tony allowed his impatience to show. 'It's in hand.'

'So you haven't actually got any further?'

'Jake, you're obsessed about the woman. I have done as much digging as I could without attracting attention. Eric Stenson seems just to have told his people to put everything on hold. Ash Lawrence can't have anything to do with that.'

'So you haven't found out who her grandfather was?' said Jake amiably.

'Her grandfather?' Suddenly Tony Anderson was alert. 'You mean there's someone involved with her who *counts*?'

'Are you a male chauvinist?' Jake mocked.

'No, I'm not,' snapped Tony. 'It's obvious that Ash has no interest in business . . .'

'I shouldn't be so sure of that. The late husband was Kimbell's great white hope.'

'Peter Lawrence?' Tony sounded stunned. 'She's that Lawrence?'

'She's not only that Lawrence. She's that Kimbell. Old Ambrose brought her up.'

There was a silence at the end of the line.

'I've really cocked up, haven't I?' Tony said at last miserably. 'I should have found out.'

'Yup.'

222

'What shall I do?'

'What I told you to do in the first place.' Jake was cool. 'Find out all you can about this woman.'

'But what about the Hayes acquisition? Do you want me to find out what's happening? If it is postponed indefinitely?'

Jake's voice was hard. 'I'll deal with Eric Stenson.'

Tony reflected that he did not envy the entrepreneur.

'OK. I'll get back to Ash Lawrence's file,' he said with reluctance. 'I've called up press cuttings back ten years. Will that do?'

'It's a start.'

'A *start*?' Tony did not attempt to disguise his dismay.

'A lot of old press cuttings aren't going to tell you the things I want to know.'

'I remember,' said Tony gloomily. 'Hobbies, weaknesses, family, friends, lovers. I just hoped you were joking.'

'I never joke about business.'

'Why didn't I remember that?' asked Tony sarcastically.

Jake was unmoved. 'Yes, that's right. Why didn't you?'

'And I suppose you want the full run down by yesterday?'

'Twenty-four hours,' said Jake. His voice was mild, but Tony felt a cold wind brush the back of his neck. 'Or I come back to London and do it myself.'

He put the phone down on his assistant's protests. His face was thoughtful. Ash Lawrence was proving to be more of a conundrum that he had bargained for. He had told Tony not to underestimate her. Now he was beginning to have a nasty suspicion that he had done exactly that himself.

Was she a sharp-tongued tomboy with no idea of what she was doing? Or was she a powerful woman who just chose to disguise the extent of her power and work behind the scenes? He had no idea. And the trouble was, until he made up his mind, he had no idea how to deal with her.

Jake frowned ferociously at the daisy-studded lawn. He did not like not knowing how to deal with people, friend or foe. Usually he knew exactly. It ensured that he stayed in control.

Now he felt unsure. For the first time in years, he was not sure that he was going to be able to keep control of this particular situation. And it was all the fault of Ashley Lawrence. He was aware of a cold anger.

It was yet another item to be set down to her account. She would pay for it, Jake promised himself. If she thought she could make a fool of Jake Dare she was going to learn very differently. Oh yes, before she was finished, Ash Lawrence was going to make restitution in full.

Fortunately unaware of the fate awaiting her, Ash said goodbye to Molly and went to check that the twins were not mistreating the little badger. She need not have worried.

Chris was hanging over the edge of the box, nose to nose with the interested cub. Martin was making notes in the notebook suspended from a nail. Ash had taught them that they must make notes on everything that happened when an animal was ill so they could tell the vet which symptoms occurred when.

224

She stopped in the doorway of the garage, surveying them. For a moment, she felt touched and oddly proud. They almost felt as if they were her own sons. It startled her.

Then Martin looked up and the feeling went.

'Hi, Ash. He's moving around more.'

'He's still limping on the right front paw,' reported Chris. He immediately undermined his professional manner by whiffling at the badger in a conversational way. 'Aren't you, Humbug?'

Ash went into the garage. 'Has he eaten? He wasn't very interested yesterday evening.'

Chris looked into the box. 'Nothing left.'

'Well, that's a good sign.'

'And he's awake. Really awake,' added Martin. 'He got up and came to the edge of the box as soon as we came in.'

'More alert,' mused Ash. 'Have you written it down?'

Martin nodded. Chris replaced the water and carried the bowl carefully back.

'Can we stay?' he said longingly.

Ash looked at the badger. Martin was right. He was a lot more alert than he had been since the boys had brought him in.

'He could probably do with the company,' she agreed. 'Don't let him run around on that leg, though. And when he's tired, write it in the book, with the time, and come and find me. I'll either be outside or in the library.'

They settled down happily to badger watching. Ash went back to the house.

There was no sign of Jake. The post had been left on the kitchen table. She riffled through it, dumped the circulars unopened in the kitchen waste bin, and went through to the library. The sound of a deep voice coming from the study made her hesitate for a moment. Then she realized – Jake was on the phone. How easily he had moved into the study and made it his own. Just like Peter had.

For some reason the thought made her feel chilly. She clasped her arms across her body. Well, Jake was welcome to it for as long as he stayed here, she told herself firmly. She hardly ever went in there normally, except to listen to the answer phone. Still, when Jake left she would not have to move rooms to get away from his memory.

Ash pressed her lips together, startled. She was annoyed with herself. What on earth was she thinking of? When Jake Dare left her house she would let off fireworks to celebrate.

She went on to the library. It faced south, towards a wide bed of cottage flowers, with the apple orchard behind. In the distance you could just make out the trees of Hayes Wood.

Ash opened its french windows. At once birdsong came floating in. The smell of lilac filled the room. Ash breathed deeply, closing her eyes. Life was good if you stopped to notice.

She sank onto the chaise longue in a patch of sunlight and stretched out her jean-clad legs in front of her. Idly she began opening the post. It was the usual: a bill, a round robin letter from a charity she supported, a report from her stockbroker, an invitation to a wine tasting in Oxford from a company Peter had bought his wine from. Ash did not drink much. The cellar was still full of his purchases. She tore it up and tossed it with the envelopes into the waste paper basket.

'Dull,' she said, sighing.

The last letter, however, was different. It was typewritten, but not very expertly. And it had her bouncing up from the chaise longue in excitement.

Em had arrived. This was what she called her polishing day. She was plodding round the kitchen assembling the materials she considered necessary for polishing the antique furniture. She looked up with disapproval as Ash came dashing in.

'Roses in the hall are dropping,' she announced.

Ash was impatient. 'I'll deal with them later. Have you seen my camera?'

'Dead flowers are bad luck.'

'I'll risk it.' Ash pout her head on one side. She swung her glance round the kitchen, searching. 'I thought it was behind the cupboard door.'

Em denied all knowledge of the camera. She was rummaging through the cleaning cupboard. 'You moved my natural beeswax?'

'No, of course not,' said Ash, trying to remember when she had last used the camera and where she might have put it.

Em sniffed. 'No, of course. Never touch it. All them lovely things and you never take so much as a rag to dust them.'

Ash shifted her shoulders. She felt guilty. Em was quite right. Ash loved the garden and would work in it until the moon rose, but furniture did not inspire her imagination.

'I know. I don't deserve them.'

Em's silence was eloquent agreement.

'I would never have bought them for myself,' Ash said defensively.

Em disappeared completely into the cupboard without deigning to answer.

A distinctly pleading note entered Ash's voice. 'They were Peter's. Or presents.'

Em found her polish and emerged. Having made Ash feel suitably inadequate she was prepared to assist.

'Camera is it? Seems to me you had it when you was taking photographs of the dratted dog.'

'For the fête,' said Ash, enlightened. She hugged Em. 'Right. Then I finished the film and took it to be developed and – ' She began stalking across the kitchen, retracing her steps. 'I came back. I put the shopping down,' she patted the kitchen table, 'here. The phone rang. I went into the hall.'

She opened the door. Em followed and stood in the doorway, surveying her progress with tolerance.

'And I needed to write down an address. So I got out some paper – ' She opened a drawer in the gleaming refectory table. 'And pushed the camera into the drawer out of the way.'

She wrenched it out by its leather strap. The table trembled. Another rush of rose petals fell onto the table. Em's tolerance disappeared like magic.

'Watch that,' she snapped.

She gathered up the fallen petals. The vibration was too much for the rose bowl. Two other roses reduced themselves to a skeleton in seconds. Em clicked her tongue.

'All right, all right. I'll do another bowl,' said Ash, reading Em's expression with the accuracy of long practice. 'Just not *now*.'

Before Em could protest, she hooked the camera over

her shoulder and bundled out of the house, laughing.

Hearing her step, Rusty emerged from the garage. He gambolled across to her, barking a greeting. Martin put his head out round the door. Ash waved. He gave her the thumbs up sign. So the little badger was still awake and playing.

'Another plus to chalk up to the day,' said Ash. Rusty pranced beside her. She rubbed his head. 'Who cares about Jake Dare? I've got sunshine. Birdsong. The smell of lilac. And the badger cub is getting better. And now – ' she broke into a little dancing run ' – I'm going to get my otters.'

She spent a happy morning photographing the river from every vantage point she could think of. Rusty raced in and out of the water, soaking them both in the process. Ash threw sticks for him, holding the camera up high out of his way as he leaped for them. By the time she made her way back to the house she was feeling happier than she had done since Jake Dare had knocked himself out in her driveway.

Em was wheeling her bicycle down the path.

'People been ringing. I left the messages on the hall table. When I got there,' she added darkly.

Ash shrugged. 'If it's important, they'll ring back.'

'I didn't mean they rang off. I meant that American chap answered before I could get to the phone.'

Ash bit back a smile. Em liked to know what was going on. Even when she and Ash were together, Em raced to the phone to find out who the caller was. If Jake Dare had been beating her, no wonder he had been demoted to 'that American chap'.

229

But all she said was, 'Thanks for the warning.'

Em muttered something which might have been about ingratitude and the modern way of going on. Ash did not ask her to repeat it. She reflected, however, that Jake Dare was going to find he had lost his most ardent local supporter. She could have hugged herself.

In the kitchen she found Em had left a shopping list of cleaning materials. It was not a very subtle hint, but it was slightly less blunt than the empty rose bowl, stood in the middle of the kitchen table, flanked by the secateurs. Ash took one look and burst out laughing.

She was sitting at the table making a list of her own when the door opened and Jake Dare stormed in.

'What the hell – '

He saw her and stopped dead.

'Oh I – ' He did not quite apologize, but he did have the grace to look slightly uncomfortable. 'I was looking for that woman.'

So Em was not the only one who had fallen out of love, Ash thought gleefully. She controlled her expression, however. 'Em?'

'Mrs Harrison. Em, do you call her?'

'That's the one. My housekeeper. What has she done?'

'Not done,' corrected Jake grimly. 'I was expecting an urgent call. I mean urgent.'

'Ah,' said Ash, understanding. 'And Em took a message and forgot to give it to you?'

'Too right. If I hadn't gone through those scraps of paper on the hall table I still wouldn't know that he'd called.'

Ash raised her brows. She was enjoying herself. 'Oh,

you've gone through my messages have you, Mr Dare? My *private* messages,' she added with point.

His discomfort did not increase noticeably. 'Just as well I did. Or your dog could have major loss of earnings added to the ticket.'

All desire to laugh left Ash abruptly. 'Don't be ridiculous. You couldn't possibly sue.'

Jake narrowed his eyes at her. 'Don't take any bets on it.'

'Oh, *how* I loathe you,' Ash said involuntarily.

There was a pause. Just for a moment she thought he was taken aback. But then he shrugged and she knew she was wrong.

'Surprise me,' he said, bored.

She got up, moving agitatedly about the kitchen. 'Well, I don't know why you're in here roaring about poor old Em,' she said with spirit. 'Why don't you return your beastly phone call, if it's so damned important?'

'I have,' he said; then added coolly, 'And now I need a ride into Oxford.'

She stared at him in incredulity. He could not possible mean that she should drive him. Could he?

'Are you by any chance trying to imply that I ought to get the car out and take you into Oxford?' Ash asked levelly.

Jake was supremely unaware of her outrage. 'Unless Mrs Harrison has wheels,' he agreed.

Ash thought of Em's normal form of transport. In spite of her annoyance her lips twitched. 'How long since you've ridden on the cross bar?'

He looked blank.

'She has a bicycle.'

'Ah,' he said enlightened. 'Then there's your answer. You drive.'

But in spite of his high-handed order, he did not like being her passenger. Ash noted it with a good deal of amusement. She had reluctantly fallen in with his demands, although it went against the grain, because she knew she had to go shopping anyway. So it was some compensation that he shifted restlessly in the passenger seat beside her.

'Don't like being driven by a woman, Mr Dare?' she asked sweetly.

'Don't like being driven,' was the short answer.

She glanced at him mockingly. 'So you've never had a chauffeur?'

He sent her a look of dislike. 'Don't you watch the road in Europe?'

Ash ignored that. In spite of her fears, she was a good driver and she was careful. She knew it. This was one area in which Jake Dare was not going to get a rise out of her.

She gave a small chuckle. 'Never? Important man like you?'

'I've been driven, yeah. From time to time. I can live without it.'

'So what makes today different?' asked Ash, negotiating her way round a bend with exaggerated caution.

Jake was blank. 'What?'

'You here. Me driving.'

'Oh that.' He recovered himself quickly. 'Until I've got a clean bill of health, it wouldn't be right to take the wheel,' he said virtuously.

Ash could have hit him. Her hands tightened on the wheel with the effort not to let it show.

After a moment she said in a thoughtful tone, 'I suppose we're talking about control.'

She could feel him watching her.

'Oh?'

'Driving a car means a person is in control. Normally. On the other hand, making someone drive you who doesn't want to is also being in control. Probably even more so.' She shot him another look. The challenge was not quite disguised. 'What do you think?'

Jake stretched out his legs in front of him and locked his hands behind his head. He turned his head on the head rest and smiled at her lazily. 'Could I be in the hands of a feminist, here?'

It was Ash's turn to look blank.

'The dreaded word,' he explained.

'What?'

'Control.'

Ash was still puzzled. 'I don't understand.'

'No?' He shrugged. 'If you say so.' But his tone said that he did not believe her.

Ash scented an insult. 'What are you talking about?' she demanded.

'Obviously nothing.'

He clearly meant to be irritating. Ash ground her teeth.

'You can't sit there sneering at me and not tell me why,' she said hotly.

'Sneering? Me?'

'Yes, sneering. And what's more you want me to know it.' Ash drew a long breath, calming herself. 'All I'm doing

233

is asking you why,' she said in her most reasonable voice.

For a moment she could feel him hesitate. Then he shrugged again, quickly, as if he was annoyed with himself.

Jake said in a hard voice, 'I guess I'm not wild about people who choose the rules they play by according to what suits them best at the time.'

Ash was totally taken aback. 'What?'

He did not answer. He was looking out of the window at the golden fields. Ash had the impression he regretted having said so much. Her own anger had evaporated in sheer curiosity.

'I don't think you can have known a very high class of feminist,' she said at last drily.

'You could be right.' It was curt, dismissing the subject.

Ash was tempted to ask exactly which feminist had given him his jaundiced view. But then she reminded herself she did not want to know. She didn't want to know anything more about Jake Dare than she absolutely had to. It was altogether too dangerous to her peace of mind.

And that thought made her so furious that she was silent all the rest of the way.

Roger Ruffin was reporting to his client.

'The Hayes Wood is the key to the project. If they can't get Ashley Lawrence to part with that, there is a great big hole in the middle of the site. It would wipe out the profit.'

The client nodded. 'Does she know?'

Ruffin shrugged. 'Most likely not. She's got good advisers, if she remembers to use them, but she's not the sort of woman to be suspicious. She probably hasn't asked too many questions.'

'You're sure she won't sell?'

Ruffin looked at his computer screen. He made careful notes. He had been making them since he had moved into the Gate House.

'Only two reasons I could think of why she should.'

His client waited.

'She could be charmed into it. Dare is staying there. Not by chance, from the sound of it.'

'Ah,' said the client. 'He's a very charming fellow, Jake Dare. Do you think that's what he's doing?'

'I'm going over there tonight,' Ruffin said. 'I'll be able to answer that better afterwards.'

The client nodded. 'And the other possibility? You said you could think of two reasons she might sell. What's the other one?'

Ruffin looked back at his screen. The discontented face was angry.

'If she's scared into it,' he said.

Ash pulled into the car park and stopped. 'Park and ride,' she said with pleasure. She wondered how long it had been since Jake Dare had travelled on a humble bus.

But he showed neither surprise nor dismay. In fact, he seemed hardly to notice what she was saying. Throughout the journey he had been sunk in thought. Now he seemed to be totally preoccupied.

Ash sighed. 'How long do you expect to be?'

He was frowning and did not hear. She repeated the question in a tone of barely controlled exasperation.

'I'm not sure,' he said slowly.

He did not, she noticed, ask how long her shopping normally took her.

She said briskly, 'I'll be ready to go back by two, I should think. I'll wait until two-thirty. If you can't be here by then you'll have to take a cab back. There's a rank outside the station.'

He nodded, clearly still distracted. Ash thought there was a very good chance he had not taken that in, either. She shrugged. His problem.

The bus took them into the centre of town. He hardly spoke on the journey and his goodbye was perfunctory. But as soon as they got off the bus, he set off purposefully. So he was no stranger to the city. She need not have told him where to find the taxi rank. Ash was inexplicably annoyed.

She banged through her shopping at a furious rate.

Jake made directly for the Town Hall. A brief conversation with a helpful lady who took him for a graduate student, more enthusiastic than knowledgeable, and he was looking at a map bearing a bewildering number of coloured lines and notes.

'I guess you get to know what this all means,' he said, with an attractive air of diffidence which would have startled Tony Anderson.

The kind lady bent over the map and explained. Jake frowned.

'So this is what they have already agreed? And this – ' he pointed to a line of dots and slashes ' – is what they are discussing now?'

'Yes, broadly speaking. In England,' said the kind lady,

'we give what we call outline planning permission. After a time that lapses, if the buildings don't get put up.'

'What happens if it lapses?'

'If you want to put up the same building you just re-apply.'

'But it must be difficult to get planning permission reinstated?'

She smiled. 'No. Usually easier than starting from scratch.'

He looked back at the map. 'Complicated, isn't it? I suppose you don't have any notes to this?'

She produced in quick succession guidelines from Central Government, the local Council and eventually, as the poor man was clearly still puzzled, the minutes of the Planning Committee.

'But aren't they secret?' asked Jake, all shining integrity.

She smiled. 'The meetings of the sub-committees are secret. Business confidentiality, you know. But the main Committee has to publish its decisions. Matter of public interest.'

'Thank you,' said Jake gratefully.

She brought him a large leatherbound book and he settled down to take notes. What he read caused him first to frown and then to scribble keenly. It also took a long time.

Jake looked at the clock once, shrugged, and went back to his task. Ash would have to go back without him. This was too important to put on hold, even for the pleasure of continuing his campaign against her opinion of him. This was a revelation.

* * *

Ash was not surprised to find Jake was not waiting for her. Nor was she really surprised when he did not appear at the end of the half-hour she had promised she would wait for him. It did not surprise her, but it made her refreshingly angry.

'He can come back when he likes, see if I care,' she announced, marching into the kitchen and flinging three of her many shopping bags onto the kitchen table. 'If I'm lucky, he'll never come back at all.'

Em had already left. There was a note in the middle of the mantelpiece above the Aga.

'Mrs Lambert's secretary rang. She will be here about four. Mr Vane called about otters. He said you would know.' Then, further down, her writing getting smaller. 'Mr Anderson called for Mr Dare. And Tim Padgett.' Here the paper was full and Em's writing had given up the ghost entirely. She had scribbled something that looked like 'Prince Charming' across the bottom left-hand corner.

Ash snorted. Em had clearly spent much of her time while they were out in answering the telephone. She would not be pleased. Jake Dare was going to need more than the intervention of Prince Charming if he was going to get back into Em's good books. That was good news. Anything that prevented a resumption of the Em Harrison – Jake Dare alliance was welcome. She turned the paper over.

'And change them roses,' Em had scrawled.

Ash laughed. She unpacked her purchases and laid out the preparations for dinner. Then she went out into the garden to pick flowers for the house. She was wandering through the rose garden wondering which blooms she could bear to sacrifice when she heard a car on the gravel.

Ash stiffened. No doubt it was Jake Dare's taxi. She was *not* going to leave her flowers to go and meet him. She was not going to pretend that he was a guest or even half-way welcome in her house. She snipped viciously at a full blown Ena Harkness that she would normally have left on the tree. She was not going to do anything that she would not normally do, she told herself. He had wished himself on her. He would have to fit in. She was not going to change her routine by a whisker. He could accept it or he could take himself back to London where he belonged.

She was still fulminating when steps came round the side of the house. Ash's shoulders tensed. She did not turn round.

A light, surprised voice said, 'Am I early? Shall I go away and come back when you're ready?'

Ash spun round. 'Jo.' She dropped the trug of roses and ran forward to hug her friend. 'Oh, *Jo*. I'm so glad to see you, you wouldn't believe.'

'Well, that's a relief. I thought you were mad at me.' Joanne held her away and surveyed her. 'You look mad,' she said candidly.

Ash pushed back her hair. 'I was. I am. But not with you. I thought you were that terrible man.'

Joanne chuckled. 'Which terrible man would that be?'

'Jake Dare.'

'Aha. The cowboy who wants to buy your wood. The one who crunched himself outside your house and then moved in?'

'That's the one.'

'And he sneaks up on you when you're doing your gardening?'

'He doesn't sneak,' said Ash bitterly. 'He marches up as if he owns the place. And it doesn't matter what I'm doing: gardening, talking to someone else, dealing with my private papers. Jake Dare thinks I ought to drop everything and jump when he claps his hands.'

Joanne was not impressed. 'Don't they all?'

'Not like this one. He – ' Ash sought for words to explain her unease and could not find any that satisfied her. She could hardly say, sometimes he sounds like Peter. What she did say was, 'He doesn't seem to care what anybody thinks: he just does exactly what he wants and the hell with anyone else.'

'By which I presume you mean yourself?'

'Oh, he doesn't care what I think, that's for sure.'

Joanne looked at her narrowly. 'Certain of that, are you?'

'Positive,' said Ash bitterly. 'People only count with Jake Dare if they're involved with business. He's noticed me because I've got in his way. Once I'm out of it, he'll forget me.'

Joanne was intrigued. 'I thought you wanted him to forget you?'

'Yes. No. I don't know.'

'Admirably clear.'

Ash laughed reluctantly. 'It isn't what you think.'

Joanne raised exquisitely shaped brows. 'And what do I think?'

Ash sighed. 'That I'm attracted and won't admit it.'

'Ah.'

'You're wrong, you know. Even if I were back in the

market for a – ' She could not find the right word.

'A dance round the maypole,' Joanne supplied helpfully.

Ash gave a choke of laugher. 'All right. A dance round the maypole. Even if I wanted something like that, Jake Dare is the last person I'd chose to do it with. I never know what he's thinking.'

Except that – once or twice – it had been disastrously clear. Ash remembered that too late. Her face flamed.

Joanne observed it with interest. She was too tactful to point it out, however. Instead she said, 'Do you want to know what he's thinking?'

'I want to know what he knows,' Ash said with sudden intensity.

Joanne was astonished and showed it.

Ash tried to explain. 'All the time – it's like he's laughing at me. Like he knows something I don't.'

'Be fair. He probably knows quite a lot that you don't. I looked him up. He's been around, has Jake Dare.'

'That's no reason to treat me as if I'm negligible,' exploded Ash.

Joanne's eyebrows hit her hair-line. 'Wow. He has got under your skin.'

Ash recollected herself. She was shamefaced. 'No. No, he hasn't. Not really. I suppose I'm just not used to it.'

'No used to what exactly?' Joanne was curious.

But Ash was not going to be drawn any further. 'Oh, male chauvinist piggery in its finest flower.'

Joanne laughed. 'You surprise me. With your upbringing, I would have thought it was the one thing you were used to.'

Ash smiled but it was an effort. Not just my upbringing, she thought. She said, 'I must have forgotten.'

'You must really have worked at it, then. Your grandfather was mediaeval,' Joanne said frankly. 'I remember the way he bought this house. Never asked you and Peter if it was what you wanted. Even took on the staff. By the way, you've still got Em, I see.'

Ash nodded. 'She lives in hopes I'll turn over a new leaf and start having babies.'

Jopanne was entertained. 'Has she a father in mind?'

'A short list, I suspect,' said Ash gravely. 'She was thinking of adding Jake's name to it. But then he started beating her to the telephone and she crossed him off.' She clicked her fingers. 'That reminds me.'

'What?'

'There were a whole load of telphone messages for him.' She chuckled, remembering. 'Including something about Prince Charming. I can't make up my mind if it's an insult or an after shave.'

'Probably a code. Fly at once, all is discovered!'

Ash sighed. 'I only wish he would.' She picked up the roses. 'Oh well, come on. You unpack and I'll do the flowers and we'll both tell Em that I put a vase in your room before you arrived.'

'Done.' Joanne slid a hand through Ash's free arm. 'Jake Dare sounds a lot more exciting than I thought. Come and help me unpack and tell me all about him.'

Ash did not quite tell her all there was to tell. But she told more than she would have expected. She would have been surprised to know how much Joanne deduced in addition to what Ash did tell her. So much, in fact, that when Joanne was finally introduced to Jake Dare she was very cool indeed.

Jake did not notice. He had just come into the kitchen, after an uncomfortable cab journey, and was frowning over Em's messages.

'Hi,' he said, acknowledging the introduction. Then, to Ash, 'I don't know any Tim Padgett. Do you know who he is?'

Ash was not disposed to be informative. 'A local resident.'

She was putting the final touches to the salmon she was intending to bake for supper. Carefully, she began to wrap it in foil.

Jake looked at her narrowly. 'So? What does he want?'

Ash finished her parcel and checked that each end was folded tight enough to prevent the juices escaping.

'I expect he wants to call you a vandal and a despoiler.'

Jake was not offended, but a faint look of annoyance crossed his face. 'Does he have to do it in person?'

Joanne laughed quickly; then equally quickly turned it into a cough. Neither of the combatants looked at her.

'Don't like facing the unpleasant truth?' Ash mocked.

'Don't like wasting my time,' he corrected.

'Then it's a shame you aren't back in London where you could get on with your work,' Ash said sympathetically. 'Tim wouldn't be able to track you down there.'

Their eyes clashed. The kitchen, thought the unheeded Joanne, might as well have been crackling with electricity. Then Jake gave a soft laugh.

'You have a point. I may even think about it.' He hefted an unwieldy armful of photocopies from one hip to the other. 'But now I've got work to do. Call me when he arrives. I can spare him twenty minutes.'

He went out of the kitchen. Ash glared at the door he left swinging behind him.

'Yes, sir,' she said malevolently. She looked at Joanne. 'See what I mean?'

Her friend came forward and sat down at the table. 'Well, it was pretty clear what he was thinking, at least.'

Ash put the silver parcel on a baking tray and began to tidy the work surfaces. 'Was it?'

Joanne was puzzled. 'Yes. He was annoyed by your local protesters, that was all. Wasn't it?'

Ash was attacking the kitchen table with abrasive cleaner, as if it were the man himself.

'He didn't have any papers at all when I left him. He's picked then up in town somewhere. And he's very pleased with himself for doing it.'

There was a pause. Then Joanne said, 'You do – watch him closely, don't you?'

'So would you in my place.'

Joanne picked up the twig of bay that Ash had left behind after using all the leaves she had wanted in the fish. She turned it over and over in her fingers, an absent look on her face. When she spoke it was with apparent irrelevance.

'Ash – do you ever think about getting married again?'

Ash looked up from her cleaning, startled. 'You know me, Jo. Chemical allergy to marriage.'

Joanne smiled, but it was perfunctory. 'I don't mean now. I know our four-footed friends do you very nicely for the moment. I mean ever. Some time in the future.

244

Company round the fireside in the old age. That sort of thing.'

'You calling me eighty-eight again?' Ash said suspiciously.

Joanne shook her head. 'I'm serious.'

'Oh.' Ash sat down, her hands stilling. 'What's brought this up? Feeling broody, Jo?'

'No, but – well, let's be honest. My marriage was a disaster from day one and should never have happened. But you were different.'

'Was I?' said Ash quietly.

Joanne was bent on trying to untangle the knot she had set herself and did not hear her. 'The last thing I want is a rerun. Some people are just not meant for marriage, I think. That's me. But you were.'

Ash did not say anything. She studied her ringless fingers, a faint frown between her brows. Joanne spread her hands.

'Look at you this evening. You *like* domesticity. Not just cooking – the garden, everything. I'd go up the wall if I had two guests, one turning up early, one late. And the late one intending to hold court in my house – even for only twenty minutes,' she added drily. 'But you take it all in your stride.'

Ash's head reared up. 'I was furious.'

Joanne smiled. 'Jake Dare winds you up. That's not the same thing. You can take the unpredictable visitors in your stride.'

'And that makes me a natural marriage partner?' Ash said drily.

'Well, it helps.'

'Does it?'

'That's how I remember it.'

Ash did not answer. She stood up. Joanne looked at her curiously. Ash went over to the kitchen cupboard and started to set a tray with glasses and a dish of Em's melting cheese straws.

'Let's take the wine out into the garden. It's so beautiful at the moment. The weather is just too good to miss.'

Joanne knew when she was being told to keep out. She nodded. But, when she followed Ash into the evening sun, her face was sober.

Tim Padgett, accompanied by Roger Ruffin, turned up at the appointed hour. Jake commandeered the study and Ash did not feel inclined to argue about it. She was more annoyed when Jake waved aside her offer of refreshment before either Tim or Roger had the chance to open their mouths. But then she remembered that Tim was quite capable of engineering an invitation to dinner if she gave him any encouragement. So she allowed all three to go off into the house with no more than a cool smile.

Joanne had watched the scene with considerable amusement. When they had gone about their business, she stretched her legs in front of her and turned her face up to the sun, laughing.

'I do see what you mean. High-handed, isn't he?'

'I hope Tim makes mincemeant of him,' Ash said vengefully.

'Tim? Oh, the little fat barrister. Not a chance,' said Joanne, not opening her eyes.

'What do you mean?'

246

'Know the type, darling.'

Ash laughed but she was put out. 'You can't possibly know a thing about him. He wasn't here more than five minutes. You exchanged two sentences. How can you make any sort of judgement in that time?'

'Long experience.'

'Of market research?' asked Ash acidly.

'Of men, darling. Of men.'

'Oh, well, there you have the advantage of me,' Ash allowed.

Joanne opened her eyes. 'Miaow,' she said amiably. 'If you mean I know what I'm talking about, you are not wrong. I've been using men like your little Tim for years and I know the ingredients.'

Ash wrinkled her nose in distaste. 'Using?'

'Utterly mutual, I assure you.' Joanne sat up and clasped her hands round her knees, warming to her subject. 'I can tell you exactly what he's like. Good citizen. *Lots* of friends. Sits on committees. Goes to charity balls.' She cocked an eyebrow at Ash. 'How am I doing?'

'Spot on so far,' Ash had to admit, trying not to laugh.

'Plays bridge. Sponsors local arts. Social engagement every night of the week. Takes a different lady to each. True?'

'Sounds right. Though I don't have any evidence about the last. All I can say is he's never taken me to anything.'

'Bet he's asked,' said Joanne shrewdly.

'We-ell – '

'Of course he has. I told you I know the type. The more the merrier.'

'You make poor Tim sound like a complete Don Juan.'

Joanne was shocked. 'By no means. Can you see it? Your Jake Dare maybe. Not Tim Padgett. Get real.'

Ash tensed at the mention of Jake. But she said evenly, 'Then why should he bother?'

Joanne primmed her mouth. 'There's more to life than sex.'

'*What*?'

'As long as Tim Padgett is spreading himself around the grateful spinsters of the parish, no one of them is going to get any funny ideas about marrying him. I bet he's a great supporter of independent women, too.'

Ash was fascinated. 'Why should he be?'

'If a woman claims to be independent she can't then turn round and blame you if you walk out on her,' explained Joanne.

Ash was suddenly not amused any more. 'Experience again, Jo?'

Joanne shrugged. But her eyes were shadowed. Ash sighed.

'We're not much of an advertisement for the modern woman, are we?'

'Modern woman, modern man, there's not much to choose between them,' Joanne said harshly. She thought. 'Your Jake Dare may be a Neanderthal, but at least he has the courage of his convictions. He isn't playing cowardly games to hide what he really wants.'

'Not cowardly, perhaps but – '

Ash stopped. The now familiar sound of tyres on loose gravel came round the house. Joanne sat up. Surprise turned to amusement.

'And I thought you were a solitary! I apologize unreservedly. This house is like Piccadilly Circus. Who is it this time?'

Ash laughed. She ticked off the possibilities on her fingers. 'Molly Hall bringing the twins to check the badger cub before they go to choir practice. Bob Cummings, as above. Molly Hall running away from her mother-in-law. Some member of Jake Dare's personal staff.'

But the man in exquisitely tailored grey who came round the side of the house did not answer any of these descriptions. He was slim and tanned with a commanding profile and eyelashes to melt the hardest heart. Ash blinked.

'Coo,' muttered Joanne. 'Have I been missing the movies recently? He looks like a film star.'

Ash stood up. 'Can I help you?'

He came towards them and smiled, revealing perfect teeth.

'This is Hayes Manor?'

'Yes,' said Ash puzzled.

'You are, perhaps, Mrs Harrison? I spoke to you earlier. My friend Jake Dare is staying with you, I believe.'

Ash was remembering the final scrawl on Em's note. A horrible suspicion was beginning to form. She looked down at Joanne in wild alarm. It was clear that Joanne was beginning to think the same.

The visitor looked disconcerted. He was obviously not used to having to explain himself at this length. Or, presumably, to two women who stared at him in blank horror.

His voice was chillier when he said, 'I am Ahmed al Saraq. Perhaps you will be good enough to tell Mr Dare I am here?'

'Oh no,' said Ash on a groan. She flashed a look at Joanne which said, as clearly as words, *help*.

Joanne lounged to her feet. She was laughing.

'Come on, Ash. You can handle this. You're the world's leading experts on unexpected guests. This, I take it, is Prince Charming.'

CHAPTER 10

He did not like it. You could see that from the way he stiffened, although he did not actually say anything. Ash sent Joanne a startled look and surged forward, her hand out.

'I'm so sorry, Mr Al Saraq. I'm Ashley Lawrence. I was out this afternoon and my housekeeper left a rather garbled message.'

'Mrs Lawrence?' His eyebrows rose but he shook hands courteously. 'I hope my call is not inconvenient.'

'Er – ' said Ash.

Joanne chuckled, 'You'll have to form an orderly queue. Your mate the tycoon is already holding court somewhere indoors.' She waved a hand at the house behind them, edged with gold in the evening sun.

Ahmed's thaw stopped abruptly. He turned. 'And you are?'

Hurriedly Ash made the introductions. Ahmed acknowledged the information with a small inclination of the head.

'Do you also live in this beautiful house, Miss Lambert?'

'Mrs Lambert,' Joanne corrected him lazily. 'No, I'm just another visitor. Though Ash did know *I* was coming,' she added with a grin.

Ahmed was not pleased. But he was too well-mannered to rise to this kindergarten baiting. 'And where is your home, *Mrs* Lambert?'

For some reason Joanne did not like him. Ash saw it with a sinking heart.

Joanne shrugged. 'Oh, home. I work in London. I've got a flat south of the river, somewhere. But if you're asking where I live, I have to say in the office.'

Ahmed's lip curled. 'A career woman?'

'With enthusiasm.'

The dislike was mutual and all too evident. Joanne looked cheerful enough, but there was a distinctly challenging look in her eye. Even Ahmed's good manners were under strain in the silent clash. Ash looked from one to the other and rushed into speech.

'Can I offer you a drink?'

'Thank you, but I would not want my unexpected arrival to put you out. If I may wait for Jake somewhere convenient – ?'

Joanne snorted. 'Who knows how long the tycoon will take? Sit down and have a drink.' She waved a hand at the bottle on the table. 'No need to be pompous.'

Ahmed was rigid. 'You are very kind but – '

'Tea,' said Ash swiftly. 'If you've been driving for long, perhaps you would rather have tea? It's more refreshing.'

'No, thank you,' said Ahmed, arctic.

Ash gave up. 'I'll go and see how long Mr Dare will be,' she said.

She went. Joanne sank back onto the rustic seat and poured herself more wine. It was an ordinary enough thing to do. She had done it thousands of times before. So why did she feel this time that it was a gesture of deliberate insolence? She lifted her eyes and met his.

'If you won't drink with us, will you at least sit down?'

Ahmed sent her a look of utter dislike and sat in the ironwork chair furthest away from Joanne. She drank a mouthful of wine slowly, savouring it. Neither of them spoke.

She put her glass down and looked into the wine. She began to think about Ash. She had never seen her friend like this. Was it Dare Properties' assault on Hayes Wood? Or something altogether more personal?

Her defiance died as she pondered Ash's behaviour. There was a long silence.

In the end, Ahmed said politely, 'And what sort of career do you pursue?' And when she did not answer, 'Mrs Lambert?'

Joanne was frowning in preoccupation. She jumped. 'What? Oh, I'm in market research.'

'Ah. Interesting.' His tone said the exact reverse.

Joanne was stung. She stirred herself to resume battle. 'Have you any idea what market research involves, Mr Al Saraq?'

'Of course,' he said serenely. 'You are one of those girls with clip boards who mug people at railway stations. I am often intercepted by them.'

Battle indeed. Joanne curbed her indignation. She was not going to lose her cool, she vowed. No doubt his rudeness was intended to make her do just that. He was too polished a man to be rude by accident.

So she said equably, 'Stations are bit old hat. These days it's usually shopping precincts.'

'Shopping precincts?' he asked distastefully.

Joanne smiled. 'Where the masses go to shop,' she explained with a great air of helpfulness.

Ahmed knew he was being wound up. His mouth compressed. 'I do not think I am familiar with one.'

'No? It's hardly a new concept. In fact,' said Joanne, beginning to enjoy herself, 'your friend the tycoon is about to build one. Over there,' she said waving her arm at the tree-strewn horizon. 'Where you see that beautiful wood.'

Ahmed looked furious. 'I have no information on Jake Dare's business affairs.'

'Surprise me.'

He swept on as if she had not spoken. 'And I am afraid I have not personally shopped in a – precinct.'

Joanne gave a chuckle. 'Then I'm afraid you're statistically insignificant.'

Ahmed was astounded. Joanne saw it, pleased. She did not think anyone could ever have told him that he was insignificant before. It gave her enormous satisfaction.

Ash came out of the house. 'I've told him you're here,' she said. 'He didn't seem to know how much longer they'd be. When Tim gets talking he can go on a bit. Would you like to stay for dinner?'

But Ahmed had had enough. He stood up. 'It is kind of you but I am afraid I cannot. I have to attend a reception in Oxford. If you would be kind enough to give the suitcase I have brought to Jake? Then I can leave you to enjoy your wine.' He sketched an ironic bow at Joanne. 'And your wood. Good evening, ladies.'

He stalked away.

'Good evening,' said Ash to his back.

'What suitcase?' said Joanne.

But that was answered soon enough. A uniformed chauffeur came round the side of the house bearing it.

'His Highness said I was to put this where you told me.'

Ash looked at him distractedly.

'His Highness,' snorted Joanne. 'King of the nineteenth century.'

Neither Ash nor the chauffeur felt equal to answering that. Ash took the man into the kitchen and directed him to Jake Dare's room. From the study came the sound of raised voices. Jake did not sound at all pleased.

'Oh dear,' said Ash.

Joanne trailed into the kitchen after them. She raised her brows at the noise. 'Tears before bedtime,' she remarked without much interest.

The chauffeur reappeared. 'Prince Ahmed said that he would call Mr Dare tomorrow morning,' he said.

Ash nodded. 'I'll tell him.'

He went out.

'The man is treating you like a blasted dogsbody.'

'I know. But he could be unpleasant about Rusty – ' Ash broke off. Joanne was staring.

'Not Jake Dare. His Loftiness out there.' She jerked her head in the direction of the drive. A deep mechanical purring announced the departure of an expensive car.

'Oh,' said Ash. For no reason at all she flushed.

'Don't you think about anyone else?' asked Joanne, amused.

'Well, it's hard when he's under your roof,' Ash excused herself. 'He sort of takes over.'

'So completely you don't even notice you're being ordered around by someone else?'

Ash smiled. 'I was brought up to carry messages to men in conference. It doesn't feel like being ordered around. Not in comparison with – ' She stopped abruptly, her colour deepening.

'Not in comparison with Jake,' Joanne interpreted. She looked thoughtful. 'He really has got to you, hasn't he?'

'No,' said Ash sharply. 'No, he hasn't. Nobody gets to me like that. I'm not eighteen any more. Nobody ever will.'

Ash decided to leave a note for Jake when he emerged from his rowdy discussion. She whistled up Rusty and set out with Joanne for a walk over her small estate. It was a perfect evening. Even Joanne, a town girl to her fingertips, admired the sweep of the landscape. She sniffed appreciatively at the tumble of roses and honeysuckle forming an aromatic tunnel through which they walked to the end of the formal gardens. And the silver birches at the gate into the meadow moved her to speak.

'Lovely. They really are heavenly trees, aren't they? So graceful.'

Ash nodded. 'They're supposed to be girls who are turned into trees after dancing with the Elf Lords,' she informed her chattily.

Joanne was speechless. She looked at her. Ash burst out laughing.

'I just said that it was a local legend. I didn't say I believed it.'

'Well, thank God for that at least.' It was heartfelt. 'You know, the resident fur and whiskers are all very well. Quite fun in their way. But I do sometimes wonder if you aren't going a bit batty down here on your own,' Joanne told her frankly. 'Elves! Girls turning into trees!'

'You have no poetry in your soul.'

'I have statistics where my soul ought to be,' Joanne agreed without rancour. 'And, believe me, remarks like that take you dangerously close to the barmy sector.'

'All right. No more elves,' Ash said chuckling. 'How do you feel about otters?'

'Otters?' Joanne looked round, disconcerted. 'Here? I thought they lived in Scotland, or somewhere. The real wild.'

'They do now. That's because we've polluted the land so much and destroyed their food supply. But if we reduce intensive farming there's a chance of reintroducing them. We've had several farmers cutting out chemicals round here. And now with land set aside, we're getting more real meadowland coming back. There's a chance – '

'You're going to reintroduce otters,' Joanne said, understanding.

Ash crossed her fingers. 'I hope so. It will take time and a lot of effort but – well, it's everything I ever hoped for. From the moment we came to live here, really.'

They walked on in silence for a moment. Joanne was deep in thought.

'You're really serious?'

'Completely. That's what I want to do for the foreseeable future. Maybe the rest of my life.'

Joanne was shaken. 'You've wanted it that long?'

'Oh, yes,' said Ash with unmistakable fervour.

'I didn't realize,' Joanne said slowly.

Ash gave a deprecating laugh. 'Peter thought I was as barmy as you do. He didn't like me to talk about it. But I would have done it in the end.'

'As you will now?'

'If it's feasible. I've got someone from the Reintroduction Programme coming to look at the river next week. At least – '

Joanne nodded. 'Difficult if Jake Dare is still here?'

'If he talks about his beastly development, yes. That would wipe out the chance. People pollute as much as insecticide,' said Ash bitterly.

Joanne thought about it. 'How likely is he to carry out this development, then?'

Ash thought about her clashes with Jake Dare. In retrospect, she could not recall that they had talked much about the project. She shrugged, frowning.

'Then you'll just have to get rid of him,' said Joanne decisively.

'Thank you. Brilliant solution. Now, why didn't I think of that?'

'Sarcasm,' said Joanne unmoved, 'is pointless. What you ought to be doing is working out a plan.'

Ash sighed. 'Do you think I haven't tried? Over and over again. I can't wait to get him out, but he just laughs when I say so.'

'Too thick-skinned to notice.'

'Oh, he notices, all right.' Ash was bitter. 'He thinks it's hilarious. He really enjoys winding me up. And that's not all – ' She broke off, wondering whether to confide her suspicions to Joanne. Or whether they would sound like paranoia; or, worse, plain unjustified vanity.

Her friend cocked an eyebrow. 'Likes to get a reaction, does he?'

Ash nodded. No, she could not put it into words. It sounded silly, even inside her head. There was no reason why a smooth sophisticated man like Jake Dare should want to make a conquest of someone like her. It would not do his project any good in the long run and he must have the intelligence to realize that. No, that nasty feeling she had had when he kissed her – that he was undertaking some secret strategy of his own and that it did not bode her any good – had to be an illusion.

She linked her arm through Joanne's. 'I think you must be right,' she said at last. 'I've been on my own so long I've lost my sense of proportion.'

Her friend's gaze was shrewd. 'Or you've forgotten the way the game is played,' she said.

But Ash did not hear her. Rusty came racing up with a stick and Ash danced off after him, playing that she was trying to wrest it away. Rusty growled happily and Ash laughed. Joanne watched them and wondered uneasily what it was that Ash could not bring herself to say about Jake Dare's presence in her house.

Was she in love with him? It seemed unlikely from all that Joanne knew of Ash and had managed to find out about Jake. Was he trying to seduce her? That seemed much more likely. A man like that could find a woman's indifference a challenge.

Ever since Peter had died, thought Joanne, they did not come more indifferent than Ash. In which case she was going to need every ounce of help her friends could supply now. No one wanted her to come out of that self-imposed mourning more than Joanne. A love affair, in Joanne's eyes, was exactly the route back to normality. But a gentle, entertaining love affair, with someone civilized.

On those criteria, everything that Joanne had learned about Jake Dare made him sound like a non-starter. In fact, she thought now, watching Ash and Rusty tugging at the stick, he sounded as wild and difficult and untameable as any of Ash's beloved animals. And several times more dangerous. If he was really after her, Ash was going to need some experienced tactical planning; at least, if she was to get away unscathed.

Joanne began to review possible tactics.

The shadows lengthened. Joanne and Ash walked back over springy grass. The air was full of the scent of warm herbs. Ash talked about her animals, her days at the animal centre, her father. Everything, thought Joanne shrewdly, but Jake Dare.

As they went back through the gate from the birch wood, Ash narrowed her eyes at the courtyard at the front of the house.

'Looks like Tim's car is still here.'

'So what happens? We ask them to dinner?'

Ash made a face. 'I don't want to ruin a lovely evening by talking business.'

Joanne nodded. Knowing Ash since they were at school,

she knew that business was the only conversation at every meal in the Kimbell household. Peter Lawrence, it occurred to her now, must have been quite similar to Ash's grandfather in that aspect. Perhaps talking business was now a cruel reminder to Ash of her lost idyll.

Ash was unaware of her friend's reflections. 'Maybe they can eat with Jake Dare and you and I have a picnic on the terrace,' she said, cheering up at the thought.

But neither Tim nor Roger Ruffin wanted to stay. Tim was in a towering temper. He could hardly bring himself to be civil to Jake Dare as he said goodbye. Roger Ruffin was more self-contained. Watching him, Ash was not sure whether he was quite as indignant as Tim. Or, indeed, whether he was indignant at all. He was looking thoughtful, rather than outraged. She saw them both off the premises.

Tim kissed her on both cheeks. 'The man's not going to move an inch. He's a wrecker. If he talks about Hayes Wood – if he says one single word – you telephone me.' Ash could feel him trembling.

She pressed his hand, grateful. 'I'll do that.'

Tim slammed his car door and drove them off with a set face.

'Dramatic,' said Jake, who had come round the front of the house to watch them go.

Ash looked at him with dislike. 'Why did you let them come if you were only going to shout at them?'

He was amused. 'Wasn't me shouting.'

'That makes it worse. You knew you weren't going to negotiate. Why did you let them think you might? Why give them hope if it was all for nothing?'

261

'I wanted to hear what they have to say.'

Ash turned away, her face darkening. 'Men like you make me sick.'

He caught her by the elbow and turned her back to face him. 'You don't know any men like me,' he told her evenly.

Ash tossed back her hair. 'Don't you believe it. The world is full of people like you. Some bits of the world don't have any other kind.'

'Bits like Kimbell's Bank?'

Ash tensed. The arm under his fingers felt like iron all of a sudden. Very carefully she plucked his fingers from her flesh and returned his hand to him.

'Are you ready for supper?'

He let her go without resistance.

'Now why don't you like talking about Kimbell's? Loyalty to Ambrose? Or something to do with your husband?'

'Try ignorance,' she said on a flash of unguarded feeling.

'Ah.'

She walked away from him, round the house to the terrace. He caught her.

'Not interested in the source of your income, Mrs Lawrence?'

Ash did not look at him. 'It's salmon. I hope you like fish.' Her tone said she did not give a damn.

He gave a soft laugh. 'Love it. Sorry!'

She still did not look at him. 'I must cut a lettuce for the salad. Joanne is on the terrace. Get her to give you a drink.'

She strode away from him. Jake looked after her

thoughtfully. Touched a nerve there. He wondered why. It bore further investigating, that. Perhaps the girlhood friend would prove a good source.

He went slowly round to join Joanne.

He found it was easier to get Joanne Lambert to open up than Ash. He was just beginning to congratulate himself when he realized that Joanne, charming and friendly as she was proving, was telling him exactly what she wanted him to know.

She picked up one of the kittens and tickled its nose with a sliver of Em's cheese straws. The kitten dabbed at it, cross-eyed with concentration.

'Of course, Ash can be deceptive,' Joanne said, concentrating equally hard.

'Really?'

She flicked the pastry round the kitten's whiskers. 'She looks as soggy an article as ever took a teddy bear to bed, doesn't she?'

Jake was amused in spite of himself. 'Maybe.'

'And in some ways she is. If you were a cat, for example, you could rely on her absolutely. If you were hungry, she would feed you. If you hurt yourself, she would heal you.'

'That seems to cover what she is doing for me anyway, even though I'm only a man,' he said drily.

Joanne allowed the kitten to catch the cheese straw. She looked up, with the little animal draped over her wrist, crunching blissfully. 'Under duress.'

For a moment he was taken aback. 'What?'

'Did you think she wouldn't tell me? You've blackmailed her,' Joanne said.

Jake was annoyed. Ash had no right to tell this woman.

What went on between her and himself was private, he thought. Ash should know that. What was more, she ought to stand up and fight her own battles without whining to outsiders.

He said crisply, 'She had a choice.'

Joanne decided she disliked him almost as much as his titled friend. 'Oh, sure. I just bet that's what you told her, too.'

Her indignation soothed his annoyance somewhat. He shrugged. 'She's a free agent.'

Joanne removed the kitten and leaned forward. 'Listen,' she said intensely, 'Ash isn't the fool you think she is. You threatened her. So she'll do what she thinks she has to do to get you off her back. But she won't forget. She's good at that, too.'

Jake's eyes flickered. 'Holds grudges, does she?'

'Learns by experience. Like we all do.'

He nodded. 'That's what I thought. Must be quite some experience.'

It was Joanne's turn to be taken aback. 'What?'

'Wouldn't you say? When they told me, I thought she had to be ninety. House the size of a museum; in the middle of nowhere; all on her own. Why do you think she does it?'

But Joanne had given him all the information she wanted to. She left him to work that one out for himself.

It was not a comfortable evening.

The next morning the telephone began to ring at eight. It was for Jake. Ash knocked on his door and informed him without venturing into his bedroom. If Jake was mobile,

264

she was no longer obliged to run in and out with trays and messages, she reasoned. And if she was not morally obliged, she was not going to risk it.

Jake had a shrewd suspicion of her feelings. They did not displease him. He thanked her mildly and picked up the call.

'Ninety years old!' said Ahmed without preamble. 'What are you doing, you madman?'

'And a good morning to you, too,' said Jake affably. 'Thank you for the delivery. I was getting tired of having to send out for new stuff every time I wanted to change my shirt.'

'What are you *doing*?'

'You've seen her. What do you think?'

'I think she is a long way from ninety years old. And not even your type. You need your head examined,' his friend told him frankly.

Jake laughed.

'This isn't like you.'

'Oh, but it is. How do you think I got my reputation? I want something, I go after it.'

Sounding shocked, Ahmed said, 'You don't want a minor development contract that much, surely?'

'I don't want to be beaten. I don't want that an awful lot.'

Ahmed heard steel in the laughing voice and gave up. He had known Jake a long time.

Downstairs a bleary eyed Joanne was surveying the sunlit garden with hostility.

'Is it always this bright?'

265

Ash pushed black coffee towards her. 'Hangover,' she said matter-of-factly.

Joanne groaned. 'I didn't notice how much I was drinking. I don't normally. When you have to drive yourself home it's easier to go without.'

Ash sliced bread for toast. 'No man to drive you?'

Joanne laughed. 'The feminists would have a field day with you. Women are allowed to drive, you know. In long distant days when I still had a partner, we took it in turns. Didn't you and Peter?'

It caught Ash unawares. She winced, stricken to silence. Just for a moment she remembered Peter's face as he stormed off into the rainy night. It was almost the last time she had seen him alive. There had been a harsh little light above the dashboard. It had illuminated the expression on his face as he turned to look back at her. He had looked as if he hated her. As if she had driven him to the end of his endurance. As she probably had.

'Peter liked to do the driving,' she said at last in a suffocated voice.

Joanne was too preoccupied with her hangover to notice. But Jake Dare, pausing in the kitchen doorway, was not. His eyes narrowed. Ash did not realize he was there.

'Well, you were lucky,' Joanne informed her, experimenting with a tea cloth over her eyes.

'Was I?'

Joanne thought Ash sounded odd. She discarded the tea cloth and turned to demand an explanation. She saw Jake.

'Well, well, look who's among us.'

Ash jumped violently and sawed the bread knife into her

266

thumb. Jake strode forward and seized her hand, holding it up while he pulled a handkerchief out of his trouser pocket.

'Wh-what are you doing?' stammered Ash, disconcerted.

'Making sure I don't get any unwanted protein on my toast,' he told her coolly. 'Ahmed got my things here just in time, it seems.'

He stopped the bleeding by pressure. Then he wound spotless linen round the injured thumb with swift efficiency. He returned her hand to her.

'There.'

'Th-thank you.'

He ran a finger down the side of her cheek. 'My pleasure. You're looking very pale. Don't like the sight of blood?'

Ash shook her head. She could hardly say that it was his impersonal touch that had sent her into shock. Especially as the look in his eyes was far from impersonal.

Joanne forgot her headache and interposed herself between them. She put her arm round her friend. Jake stepped back perforce.

'Does anyone?' she said sensibly. 'Sit down, Ash. I'll finish breakfast.'

She did. They were interrupted three times by the telephone. On each occasion it was for Jake. He did not apologize, Ash noticed. She also noticed that each call left him looking more and more grim. In the end Joanne lost patience.

'Come on, Ash. I could do with some peace,' she said with bite. 'Let's go for a walk.'

It was like that for the rest of the weekend. In the end, it was almost a relief to Ash when Joanne went back to London.

'Didn't work, did it?' said Jake, as Joanne's tail lights disappeared down the twilit drive.

Ash pretended she had not heard him. He turned her toward him forcibly.

'I don't know what you're talking about,' Ash said between her teeth.

'Calling up reinforcements.'

He touched her face again. It was all she could do not to shiver with pleasure. What is happening to me? thought Ash shaken.

'Joanne is an old friend.' She was defensive.

'Sure she is, or you wouldn't have sent her the SOS. It still won't work.'

'What won't?'

'Hiding behind someone else.'

She pulled herself sharply out of his arms. 'You're imagining things.'

'I surely am,' he said, a laugh in his voice.

Ash flushed to the roots of her hair. She shouldered past him. Furious with herself, she called Rusty and set off down the drive. Jake kept up with her.

'Face it. Admitting what you feel won't kill you.'

Ash lengthened her steps. He stayed at her side without difficulty.

'Do you think it's disloyal or something?'

They were in sight of the gate. Ash stopped dead. It was a soft summer evening, with birds calling and pale butterflies riding the warm air. But she could smell the rain, remember the dark, hear the crash of metal into the old stone pillar and ironwork.

And that was not all she could hear. There were words too, the cruel words that had caused Peter to fling himself into the car when she knew he was too tired and too overwrought to drive. Her cruel words. Ash shut her eyes, shocked.

Jake came round and stood in front of her.

'That's it, isn't it? You think you're betraying him if you fancy anyone else.'

She opened her eyes and steadied her breathing. It was a long time ago. She had not meant to drive Peter to his death. She had to bear her share of the blame and she knew it, but it was a long time ago and she never meant to hurt anyone. She looked at Jake, her eyes empty.

'That's hardly any of your business.'

He took hold of her with energy. 'It is if it means you're shutting the door on what there is between us.'

Ash was not even angry. 'There is nothing between us,' she said tiredly.

His mouth thinned into a straight line. For a moment she had the impression that she had angered him as no one had ever angered him before. That it almost surprised him. Then his lids dropped and she could not read his expression any more.

He said very softly, 'Then there is nothing to shut the door on, is there?'

He took her face between his hands and kissed it. His lips were warm, without pressure, as fleeting as the butterflies dancing in the summer air about them. He took a long, long time and he never went near her mouth.

By the time he lifted his head, Ash's eyes were no longer empty. They were blazing.

'What – ' She choked and began again. 'Why did you do that?'

He did not answer directly. 'Still say there's nothing there?'

'Oh, there's something there all right. Your ego and – '

'Yes?'

'My humiliation,' she spat.

Jake shook his head sadly. 'You're not humiliated. You're interested.'

Ash pulled herself together. She put several feet between them. 'I hardly think you're an authority on my feelings. Any feelings, for that matter. For a man who admits his engagement was a financial deal, you're way out of your depth.'

'Well remembered,' Jake congratulated her. He gave a soundless laugh. 'Do you remember everything I've ever said to you?'

Ash remembered his contemptuous conversation with Tony Anderson. She smiled.

'As well as quite a lot that you've said to other people.'

Jake was suddenly uneasy. 'And what does that mean?'

'It means nice try, Mr Dare. But no thanks.'

She whistled to Rusty and left.

Jake stayed where he was, staring after the slim retreating figure with hard eyes. If she had looked back, Ash would not have had much trouble in reading his expression now. Jake Dare was as mad as a hornet.

'Right,' he said under his breath. 'You've asked for it, Ashley Lawrence.'

CHAPTER 11

Ash slept badly. It was not the first time she had tossed and turned restlessly. It always happened after she had remembered too vividly that last confrontation with Peter. It was wretched but it was hardly unprecedented. What was unprecedented – and what she would have denied if she could – was that there was a new shadow stalking through the dark woods of her dreams. Jake Dare, invading with impunity.

'Damn,' said Ash, tossing and turning again until she ended almost in tears. 'I'll just bet that man is sound asleep.'

She was right. Along the hall Jake slept in the quiet content of a man who has made up his mind. For the last few days he had been wavering, waiting for Tony Anderson's report on Ash. If he was honest – and Jake was invariably honest with himself, if with no one else – he had been waiting for something else as well. A sign of some sort, an instinctive recognition that the time was ripe to move in on Ash. Jake put great trust in his instincts.

But after his encounter with Ash that evening, he was

271

biding his time no longer. Whether the time was ripe or not, Jake no longer cared. Ash had finally challenged him to the point where his pride could not tolerate it.

'Tomorrow,' said Jake, composing himself to sleep. 'I make my move tomorrow.'

But when he came down to the kitchen in the morning, he found that the move would have to be circumspect in the extreme. After her disturbed night, Ash was tired and snappish. What was worse, she was late.

'Em will get your breakfast,' she said, flying past him with Rusty at her heels.

Jake raised his brows and set about proving that he was not a man who needed his breakfast got for him. By the time Em Harrison arrived the kitchen was full of the smell of toast and coffee. She was sufficiently impressed to accept a cup. It was contrary to her principles to take it outside into the sun but she compromised by sitting down at the kitchen table. Jake disposed himself in the chair opposite and took the first step in his campaign.

'Where? Oh, that animal centre, I expect.'

Jake did a very good show of surprise. '*Animal* centre? but I thought the clinic . . .?' He left it artistically unfinished.

'Hardly ever goes near the place. Pumps money into it, won't even go to their Christmas party,' said Em with disapproval and more knowledge of Ash's affairs than Jake had expected. 'Mind you, can't blame her, I suppose.' She sent Jake a quick look. 'That's where they took Peter after the accident. Can't be a happy place for her.'

He nodded, looking wonderfully sympathetic. 'The accident?'

272

Em jerked her head towards the front of the house. 'Why here, right between the gates. Hit that big tree. Brought half the branches down.'

Jake made encouraging noises.

'Terrible night it was. Rain was like a sheet, you couldn't see your hand in front of you. He'd driven down from London. They said he must have been tired, not made out the drive properly, what with the rain and the puddles and the headlights. Hit the tree head on.' Em's face was sober, remembering.

'Who found him?'

She jumped, returning to the present. 'Wasn't a case of finding him. She was waiting for him, wasn't she? She heard the car hit the tree and ran out.'

Jake thought of the drive: it was nearly a mile long. He thought of Ash running down it in the dark and the rain, not knowing what she would find at the end of it. For a moment the bright kitchen seemed cold.

'Must have been coming up the road at a terrible lick. They said at the garage that sports car of his had swung right round. Pointing the other way, it was, like he was going back to London.'

Jake found Em was watching him quite as closely as he had observed her. It occurred to him that he was not the only one with a point to make here.

'How did she take it?'

Em was scornful. 'How do you think? Damn near killed her, if you ask me.'

That startled Jake. 'They were so in love?'

'They'd been married seven years,' said Em obliquely. 'She was on her own that night. Took over an hour to get

273

the ambulance out here, bad night like that and her having to run back to the house to call them.' She paused, then added heavily, 'She wouldn't get it out of her head that it was her fault.'

'I – see.'

Em rose. She had passed on the necessary information. What Jake Dare did with it was his own business. She did not know whether it would be for good or ill and by now she did not greatly care. Whatever it was, it would blast Ash out of this bunker she had built for herself. In Em's book, anything – and anyone – who did that was to be encouraged.

Jake went into the study. He was thoughtful. So Ash Lawrence was not just a misanthropist with a nasty turn of phrase. Guilt, now; that was interesting. Was it just because she had failed to contact the ambulance service by telepathy and her husband had had to wait for rescue? Or was there something else there? There was an obvious way to find out.

He rang the office.

'Oh, yes, Jake.' Tony Anderson sounded nervous. 'The press announcement. Eric Stenson is holding back because of us.'

This was so unexpected that Jake was momentarily deflected from his purpose

'What?' Jake said, outraged.

'Stenson said that when he agreed to do business with us, he was told that we were definitely merging with Newman's.'

'I never told him that.'

'Quite. Then somehow he got hold of the story that we

274

weren't. He's been chasing Newman for a week, according to his private office.'

'And the old fox has gone to ground. Don't tell me.'

'Newman hasn't been easy to contact,' Tony Anderson agreed diplomatically. 'So Stenson rang you. I fielded the call this morning.'

'What did you tell him?' Jake asked interested.

'I didn't. I listened.'

'You're learning.'

'Thank you.'

'And what did you find out?'

'Stenson is backing out. He will go into the project if Dare's are in there as well, as co-developers. He won't go in if we're just employed to do the work and aren't taking any of the risk.'

Jake was unmoved. He stretched his long legs out and rested them on the disputed footstool. His eyes narrowed against the sun streaming in from the brilliant garden.

'Did he say why?'

Tony stopped trying to be diplomatic. 'He said if it was your scheme, you'd make sure it was straight. If it was Newman's it was crooked, more likely than not, and he didn't need that sort of garbage at his time of life.'

Jake tapped his teeth with his pen. 'And that's all?'

'Why shouldn't it be?'

'Because,' said Jake shrewdly, 'unless I'm very much mistaken there's someone down here who has more than an innocent interest in the Hayes Wood development. And if he's not on our pay roll and he's investigating Desmond Newman, my bet is he is reporting to good old Eric Stenson.'

275

'I'll set up a meeting,' said Tony at once.

'Do that.'

'When?'

Jake considered. Beyond the windows the garden gleamed like a jewel. The sun striking rainbows off the grass. Roses clustered like drifts of scented silks. The air hummed with bees. If you wanted a romantic atmosphere, Jake thought cynically, Hayes Manor did the business. He smiled. It was perfect. Perfect for pleasure, perfect for seduction and particularly perfect for what he had in mind, especially when the summer twilight fell.

He stretched. 'When? Oh, tomorrow. Afternoon or early evening. My apartment.'

Tony wrote it down. 'Will you – er – be going back to the Manor afterwards? Or have you done the business?'

'Not yet,' Jake said softly. 'But I will. I won't need to come back.'

Ash was retrieving an excited hamster from a magazine rack when Bob Cummings walked into the centre.

'Nice to see you back,' he said. 'Things back to normal?'

'Getting there.' She cupped the little creature against her neck and stood up.

'How's the badger?'

'On the mend.'

The hamster made a spirited attempt to climb into her hair. She plucked it back.

'How soon do you think you can release it, then?'

Ash restored the hamster to its cage and clipped the door firmly shut.

'I don't know. The trouble is, I'm not even sure where

to release it. It was found on the road, but I have no idea which set it came from.'

'There used to be a set on the edge of Hayes Wood,' Bob said. 'Abandoned some time ago, but badgers can recolonize. They could have come back.'

'I'll go up and have a look,' she promised.

'If there are more badgers there, you'll have to be careful.'

Ash shuddered. 'The baiters? How can anyone do things like that for sport?'

'Not just the baiters. Badgers are a protected species. It's not easy to get rid of them legally. If a farmer wants them off his land the easiest thing is to hire a hit squad in secret.'

'Hayes Wood is my land,' Ash pointed out. She thought of Jake Dare and gave a smile of pure satisfaction. 'And, whatever anyone thinks, it's going to stay that way. If there are badgers up there, they will be safe.'

Jake reconnoitred the garden as carefully as a general surveying a battlefield. He patrolled the rose garden, the orchard, the walled garden with its tall acanthus and headily scented wallflowers, the woodland garden where iris grew in profusion by the small rivulet, the neat symmetry of the Dutch garden. And still he could not make up his mind. It had to be far enough from the house so that they could not be disturbed by the telephone. Yet not so far that she had time for second thoughts as they returned . . .

He heard his name. It sounded as if the caller had been shouting for some time and was getting impatient. He turned back. Em was on the terrace outside the kitchen door and her temper was not good.

'Phone,' she said briefly. 'Miss Newman. Didn't want to call back. Said she'd hang on.'

Jake took one look at Em's expression and sprinted into the house.

'Darling,' said Rosie, without a word of complaint for the delay. 'I just heard. How *are* you?'

Rosie was no longer among his intimates. Jake was not going to tell her that he was pretending stress as a ploy to infiltrate Ash Lawrence's life. On the other hand, he was certainly not going to allow her to think that he was less than fit.

He said carefully, 'Oh, just spending a few days in the country. You?'

'I've been looking for you. I think we should talk.'

Jake was wary. 'Oh?'

Rosie gave a little laugh. 'Darling, don't sound so suspicious. We're engaged. Of course we should talk.'

'We are not engaged.'

'We published a notice and we had a party – '

'And I broke it off,' Jake said levelly.

'Yes, I know, you were annoyed but – '

'Rosalind, I was much more than annoyed. There is no but.'

Her voice hardened. 'I've still got your ring.'

Jake laughed. 'That's because I played the gentleman for once and didn't pick it up when you chucked it back at me. I could change my mind. Don't ever think I can't revert to type.'

'What?'

'Give me a hard time and you'll get a letter from my solicitor demanding it back.'

Rosie gasped. 'You can't be serious.'

'Try me.'

'You'd never hold your head up again. People would cut you dead.'

'Not people who want to do business with me,' Jake said cynically. 'The rest, I can live without.'

Rosie was about to scream at him when she remembered her father's injunction. She curbed her temper and tried another tack. 'Aren't you overreacting? I know we both said things we shouldn't. I'm willing to apologize . . .'

'For the way you are?'

'What?' She was disconcerted.

'How can you apologize for what you feel?' Suddenly Jake was weary. 'I didn't break it off because of anything you said. I broke it off because of what you were willing to do.'

'I don't understand,' Rosie stammered.

'Look, Rosalind, I know you think I'm a bit of a wild man. I didn't go to the right schools. I don't play polo. I haven't read every book on the bestseller list. That doesn't mean I can't read people. Or I thought I could.'

Jake waited, but there was a silence at the other end. 'I never asked you to pretend,' he said at last.

Rosie said in a harsh whisper, 'Are you saying you were in love with me?'

For no reason at all Jake thought of Ash and her dead love.

'*No*,' he said with inexplicable anger. 'No, that was never part of the deal. I liked you. I respected you. I thought it was mutual.'

279

'It was. It was.'

'No, it wasn't. I turned you on. And I was useful. That's all. Neither is much of a basis for marriage. Or for anything.'

'So why did you ask me?' Rosie asked shrewdly. 'Didn't I turn you on? Wasn't I useful? Aren't all your women useful, one way or another?' She was spiteful suddenly.

Jake felt as if he had been hit in the stomach. He stared at the telephone and could not find an answer.

'You just don't like your own medicine, that's your trouble.'

'You may be right.' His voice was hard. 'But at least I don't pick people up and play games with them because I like the taste of danger and then run home when it gets too hot. What I start I stick to.'

'You didn't stick to me, you bastard,' Rosie screamed at him.

'No of course, Rosalind. We had a deal. You cheated.'

There was a longer silence. Then she said slowly, 'You know about Sandy. Somebody told you – '

Jake sat on the edge of the hall table. He began to run his finger round the inside of the empty rose bowl. He followed the pattern with absorption. He had been so angry, so *humiliated*. Now, to his astonishment, he felt nothing. Boredom, maybe.

'Nobody told me.'

'Then – '

'I saw you. It was quite obvious.'

'Saw us? You can't have done,' she said positively.

She did not realize she had already admitted it, thought Jake wryly. She might be sophisticated and self-willed but she was no challenge at all. Now Ash Lawrence would have kept on denying, bluffed it out, dared him to prove it . . .

Startled, Jake broke off the train of thought as soon as it was born. He said rapidly, 'It was in some dark little restaurant in Covent Garden. I suppose you thought no one you knew would go there.'

'Oh.'

'It's a very bad deal to love one man and marry another.'

As if that explained everything, Rosie said, 'But Sandy has no money.'

'Neither did I once.' He paused but she said nothing. 'Has it occurred to you that I might lose it? What would you do then, if that was the only thing binding the marriage together?'

'You wouldn't.' She sounded as if he were a child who had just threatened her with bad behaviour.

Jake laughed. 'Not deliberately, no. But things happen you can't control. I might lose the lot. Anyone might.'

The silence at the other end was stubbornly unconvinced.

He added unkindly, 'Your father did.'

Rosie was indignant. 'This isn't about us, is it? It's about poor old Daddy.'

'Well, that's your agenda,' Jake told her. 'Would you have looked at me twice if your father hadn't been in deep trouble?'

'Of course I – '

'Oh, you'd have gone to bed with me,' he told her brutally. 'Wild men are exciting for nicely brought up ladies, aren't they? But marriage? Get real.'

Rosie said in a suffocated voice, 'I think you're hateful.'

Again Jake thought of Ash. 'Join the club.'

'You're just going to walk away from us, aren't you? After all Daddy did for you. You're just going to walk away.'

'Your father,' said Jake evenly, 'took me to dinner with a lot of guys who thought I was Newman's white knight. It's going to take a hell of an effort to untangle myself from that one. I don't owe him one damn thing. If anything, he owes me.'

'You – '

He did not wait to hear what she would call him.

'Now, I'll tell you what you're going to do. You're going to call your mates on the gossip columns and tell them you've changed your mind about me. Then you're going to put a formal notice in *The Times*.' He softened briefly. 'You're not your father's keeper. Give yourself a chance with your Sandy.' Then, brisk again, 'Or not as you choose. Whichever, get out of my life. And stay there.'

When Ash got home, Em had gone. She had left a huge notice in the middle of the kitchen table saying, 'FLOW-ERS'. Right at the bottom was added, 'Mr Dare working in study, do not disturb.'

Oh great, thought Ash. Now I can't even move around freely in my own house. But she was glad enough to leave to him the possession of the dark interior. The sun was just too enticing.

The Hall twins walked over with their mother. They went off to the garage to play with the badger. Molly Hall refused tea, but stayed briefly to watch Ash cut fronds of honeysuckle and just the fewest possible roses.

'This is such a peaceful place.'

'Usually. It will be better when the last tycoon pushes off,' Ash said, drawing out a long tendril that was showing signs of suffocating itself and could therefore well be spared for indoors.

Molly pulled a face. 'Things no better, then?'

Ash said, 'I must be the only woman in the world who doesn't fall at his feet and purr. Em'll be eating out of his hand before long. But I – '

Molly looked idly across the grass. 'You're out of practice,' she said comfortably.

'That's what he says,' said Ash unwarily. At once she regretted it. She turned back to the honeysuckle, biting her lip.

'Does he?' Molly was hugely amused. 'Maybe you should believe him.'

She went, still chuckling. Unsettled, Ash took her flowers indoors and filled the bowl in the hall. She did not venture past the study door. She did not quite know why. That unsettled her even more.

The weeds were growing apace. She took tools and a large trug and went to attack the ground elder that was threatening to stifle the old-fashioned pinks. They were called sops in wine and Ash had planted them specially last year in a bed she was hoping to fill with plants that were common in the Middle Ages.

She was red faced with tugging at a particularly stubborn root when she heard Jake's step behind her. *Damn*, she thought. She did not turn round. She could feel him standing behind her watching her for a long moment before he spoke.

'The boys who aren't yours are in the kitchen demanding badger food.'

Ash gave a fair imitation of surprise. She straightened, looking at her watch.

'It's a bit early but I suppose it's all right.' She put down her fork and turned toward the house, putting a hand to the small of her back.

'Stiff?' he sounded curious rather than sympathetic, she thought. 'Don't you have someone in to help do the hedging and ditching?'

She pulled her hand quickly away from her back. 'That's the fun of it. Why would I want anyone else to do it?'

His eyes crinkled at the corners when he was concentrating, she saw. She should not observe him so closely. She set off for the house at a rapid pace. He stayed with her.

'You do it yourself? All of it?'

'I like it.' Ash tried not to sound defensive and was only partly successful.

'Plants and animals,' he mused.

'They're rewarding.'

'You mean they don't talk back.'

Ash stopped dead and swung round on him. 'I can handle people who talk back,' she told him tensely.

His eyes flickered and then went completely blank. She flung back her head.

'Can't I?' she flung at him in challenge.

'You mean you can handle me.'

Ash glared. 'Do you think I can't?'

The handsome face was unreadable. 'I think it's – an interesting proposition.'

Ash was startled. All of a sudden she had the impression of a fury perilously close to explosion. She retreated a pace, alarmed in spite of herself. She found she was shaking and was furious. Jake could hardly annihilate her.

He said softly, 'You're wasted as a hedger and ditcher you know.'

He did not take his eyes off her face. Something in his expression made her feel as if the smooth lawn had abruptly tilted to forty-five degrees. If she wasn't careful she was going to slide helplessly across it into his arms, she thought in a flash of sudden panic.

Ash tilted backwards, bracing herself. She drew a ragged breath. 'You've got no right – '

His smile was slow, deliberate. His eyes slid to her mouth and stayed there. 'I don't agree,' he said lazily. 'Any man has the right to protest at a gross waste like that.'

The sense that something was about to precipitate her into his arms increased. *Why?* Ash crossed her arms across her dirty tee-shirt. Her arms were shaking with tension.

'You don't know a thing about it.'

He put his head on one side. 'I've got a report,' he said provocatively.

Ash's temper flared up. 'I'm surprised you're not ashamed to admit it.'

Jake grinned. 'If I'm not ashamed to do it, I'm not ashamed to admit it.'

He sounded bored. He was concentrating all his attention on Ash. He did not move a muscle, but Ash felt as if he had reached out and swept an immobilizing ray over her. Her head went back so far her jaw hurt.

'In contrast to you,' he said thoughtfully. 'You're

ashamed to admit things you *don't* do. Now that is a new one on me.'

Their eyes locked. She could not read what he was thinking. She could not even begin to make a guess, she thought. Her trembling increased. She was not going to admit it, even to herself. She was certainly not going to let Jake Dare see it.

She said with dignity, 'I am glad to have extended your experience.'

Jake was looking at her intently. Had he picked up that treacherous trembling, then? Ash saw his eyes narrow to slits.

'Oh, you've done that, all right.'

With an enormous effort Ash broke the eye contact. She did not want to allow him any sort of victory, but her shakes were getting worse. She bolted for the house. If there was more than a hint of flight in her departure, she was beyond caring.

She gave the boys the badger's evening meal and saw them off, back to the garage. The kittens were fossicking about the terrace ready for a game. Normally Ash would have found it irresistible, but on this occasion she did not want to be anywhere where Jake Dare could track her down.

She fled the kitchen into the farthest regions of the garden where some heavy clumps of nettles needed to be removed. Jake Dare could look all the rest of the day and not find her there, she thought. And Ash could forget him in back-breaking digging. She pulled on heavy gardening gloves and set to work with a will.

But her peace only lasted until the light began to die, when Molly Hall, arriving to collect the twins, encountered the full glare of Jake's charm over the kitchen range. She was enchanted all over again. So she lost no time in tracking down Ash and telling her so.

Ash did not stop work. She was polite but noncommittal. It annoyed her friend.

'But he's gorgeous,' Molly expostulated.

Ash shrugged, hauling at a particularly stubborn clump of nettles. Three feet away another clump, connected by the yellow snake roots, shook with the force of it.

'He is.' Molly was impatient. 'Come on, Ash. You can't be that much of a cold fish.'

'Oh, yes, I can,' Ash said grimly.

Molly grinned. 'You won't be able to stick to it,' she said with confidence. 'That man is powerful magic. Bring him over for drinks or tea or an orgy or something.'

Ash straightened and stripped off her gardening gloves. 'I can't do that,' she said repressively. 'He's supposed to be convalescing.'

Molly snorted. 'If he's ill, I'm Cleopatra.'

Ash raised her eyes to heaven. 'That's what I've been telling you. And you want me to bring him over to drinks?' she said incredulously.

'He said you were out of practice with people,' Molly reminded her. 'I'm sure he's fallen madly for you and this is the only way he can think of to get close. I think it's very sensible of him to move in on you.'

'If he's fallen madly, it's not for me,' muttered Ash. 'Try Hayes Wood and you'd be closer.'

Molly chose to ignore that. Probably because she suspected it was true, thought Ash. Instead she returned to the familiar point of contention.

'Face it, Ash. How is anyone going to get to know you if you lock yourself away here all the time?'

'Perhaps I don't want anyone getting to know me.'

Molly ignored that, too. Her eyes were serious when she said, 'Peter wouldn't have wanted you to go into purdah.'

Ash swung round as if she had been stung. 'You've been talking about me. To Jake Dare.'

Molly was startled and just a little guilty. 'I – '

'How could you, Molly? How could you? He's a stranger. And you know what he wants to do to the countryside. How could you go gossiping to him about me? Do you know he's already had a private eye's report done?'

Molly's mouth fell open. 'Private eye's report? You mean on you? *You*?'

Ash shook her hair back angrily. 'Me. Yes. Still think he's gorgeous?'

'Must have been the shortest report Jake Dare ever read,' said Molly, not noticeably repentant.

Ash could have danced with fury. 'Don't you see? The man's not – straightforward. He's devious, underhand, manipulative. You can't trust a word he says . . .'

Molly grinned. 'Just the type to get your teeth into. I've told him you're to bring him to our barbecue.'

Ash said with rancour, 'I thought you had him lined up for an orgy.'

'Maybe next week.' Molly peered at her. 'You are coming, aren't you? I asked you weeks ago.'

'I'm not sure – '

'There you go again. Keeping your options open, then not turning up at the last moment.'

Ash bit her lip. Molly did not sound accusing, but she had the right to be. When Molly asked her, Ash always meant to accept her invitations, but in the end she just could not face it. Sometimes she even got as far as the main gates. But when she drove past the tree and thought of that last night . . . Ash shuddered.

Molly sighed. 'I said to Mike, I bet Ash won't come in the end.'

Ash was even more uncomfortable. There was too much truth in that. 'It slipped my mind,' she said. 'I mean of course I'll come.'

'Good. You can give Jake a lift,' Molly said briskly.

Ash opened her mouth to protest but Molly got there first.

'He already accepted. Didn't I say?'

'No,' said Ash with restraint. 'No, you didn't mention it.'

Molly grinned. 'With charm like that, I didn't want him getting away. Do you want this stuff all taken back to the house?'

'Thank you,' said Ash. Her tone was cool.

Molly gathered up the fork and rake and Ash took charge of the loaded wheelbarrow. On the way back, Molly talked about her sons, the mother-in-law and the logistical problems both provided. Ash said little, but Molly did not seem to notice.

The boys were already by Molly's car. As soon as they saw their mother, they climbed in. Ash deposited the wheelbarrow by the compost heap and went to see them off.

Molly swung into the car and wound down the driver's window.

'Thanks for having the monsters. I'll see you at my party.'

Ash's agreement was resigned. Molly chuckled, unoffended.

'Put your glad rags on and have some fun. About time, if you ask me.'

'I'll bear that in mind,' Ash said pleasantly. 'Any more instructions?'

Molly looked naughty. 'You could try spending the day in the beauty parlour. He won't be here forever,' she advised.

Ash did not need to ask who her friend was referring to. She set her teeth. 'It already feels like forever.'

Molly's eyes twinkled. 'If you feel like that, go for it,' she said. 'Don't let him get away.'

She let in the clutch and drove off before Ash could think of a suitably crushing retort. She clutched her hair and cursed all interfering friends with her best interests at heart.

It was almost a relief to come face to face with Jake Dare, who cared for nobody's interests but his own. He was sitting on the terrace in the evening sun. In fact, he was not so much sitting as reclining on the teak bench as if he owned it. As Ash approached he looked up. He smiled.

Molly was right, Ash thought, shaken. The charm in that smile was almost palpable. It reached out like the sunshine. Ash fought hard to remember her wrongs; not to smile back. She lost.

'Wonderful,' he said softly, his eyes sweeping over her and coming to rest on her mouth.

Ash tensed. She looked at him suspiciously. 'What is?'

He raised his eyebrows. 'Why the garden, of course.' The dancing green eyes mocked her gently. 'What else? I didn't realize there were gardens like this outside fairy tales.'

He stretched his arms along the back of the garden seat and let his eyes travel round the prospect.

'It must take some keeping up,' he said idly. 'How many gardeners?'

Ash laughed. At least this was a neutral subject, she thought. He wasn't offering to buy her garden, after all.

'I told you. Me. It was designed to be worked easily. Em's brother comes in one day a week, mainly to cut the lawns.'

That startled him. He looked incredulous. 'You mean you do the rest? I don't believe it. A little slip of a thing like you.'

Ash grinned. 'It's my substitute for a career,' she said smugly. 'Years ago it was what I wanted to do as a profession, but my grandfather thought gardening wasn't right for a girl. When we moved here, I just started as an amateur.' She laughed at his look of disbelief. 'You don't have to be hugely strong. You can hire all sorts of mechanical diggers if you want to do something big, like make a pond. The rest is just a matter of doing things at the right time. And keeping at it.'

Jake narrowed his eyes at her. 'And you're the type to stick at something once you've made your mind up,' he said eventually. His tone was wry. 'I guess it runs in the family.'

Ash tensed. 'You know my family?'

'Name me a businessman who doesn't.'

291

She relaxed. She would have said the slackening of tension was imperceptible, but Jake saw it. He looked intrigued.

'What have you got against your family?'

'Nothing. I suppose I'm just not a natural at business,' Ash said carefully.

He looked at her narrowly, but he did not pursue it. Ash was relieved. She had the impression that anything Jake Dare wanted to know, he found out eventually.

He said at last, 'That's true enough. Or you'd have taken my first offer.' He grinned suddenly. 'Well, maybe my second.'

Ash found herself grinning back. It was disconcerting. She looked at him. He looked dauntingly handsome in the last golden rays of the sun. His black hair was springy and just a little too long, judged by her grandfather's standards. With the high cheek bones and proud, sensual mouth it made him look like one of those Renaissance merchant princes whose portraits her grandfather had collected: powerful and secret.

And utterly out of her league; even further out of her league than Peter had been.

She shivered. Oh God, these days she seemed to be thinking about Peter all the time. About Peter and what, in the end, she had done to him. She said hurriedly, 'Molly says you're going to their barbecue. Why on earth did you agree?'

The glint of amusement died. Their eyes locked. They were combatants again.

'Don't even think of trying to turn me down,' he said softly.

Ash remembered all his threats. Her appreciation of his charm dwindled sharply.

'Does anyone ever?' she mocked.

He dismissed that with an impatient hand. 'We are not talking about anyone else. Only you.'

There was something in the way he said that that brought her up short. Ash searched his face. Jake looked up at her, his eyes almost silver in the low evening sunlight. He held out a hand in silent invitation. Ash stood as if turned to stone.

'Only you,' he said again softly.

Her hands clenched by her sides. 'Stop it,' she choked out. 'I know you think it's funny. Well, I don't. Stop it. Now.'

His hand fell. A muscle in his cheek began to throb. 'Ash – '

She cut him short. 'I must check on the badger cub.'

He muttered something under his breath. It sounded like a curse. Ash ignored it.

He stood up. 'I'll come with you.'

She could not stop him, of course. But she could and did ignore him as he strode beside her. And in the garage he was admirably quiet and slow moving in order not to startle the little animal.

She spent twenty minutes playing with the little badger. He was beginning to scramble up in his box at the sight of her. Even his games with the boys had not tired him today. She put him back in his box with a sigh.

'Going to let him go soon, aren't you?' Jake said perceptively, as they walked back to the house.

Ash thought about her conversation with Bob Cummings. She nodded, sighing.

'The boys won't like that.'

Ash sensed criticism. 'They knew from the start that if he survived we would have to release him eventually,' Ash said defensively. 'I told them.'

'I'm sure you did. But they will have forgotten it by now. The nature of humanity,' Jake said in deeply cynical tones, 'is to forget what it doesn't want to remember.' He sent her a considering look. 'And hope for miracles to change the unchangeable.'

Ash looked steadfastly ahead. She was conscious that his eyes never left her face. 'I'm sure you've never hoped for anything so unrealistic,' she said sweetly.

He made an impatient noise. 'You'd be surprised. I'm as much of a romantic as the next man.'

That did get her to look at him. She stopped dead in sheer astonishment. 'Romantic? *You*?'

'You're not flattering.' He sounded faintly annoyed.

She spread her hands. 'Do you *want* to be thought romantic? It hardly goes with the image.'

He looked down at her for a long moment. 'You think I'm real hard boiled, don't you, Ash?'

This was dangerous territory. Ash backed off it fast. 'I don't think anything about you at all,' she said stoutly and untruthfully.

'But then I hear you haven't got that much experience,' he went on as if she had not spoken. 'I don't think I should let it put me off.'

There were a number of answers she could have made to that. Ash debated most of them. But, seeing the glint in his eyes as he slanted a mischievous look down at her, she decided against them all.

Instead she changed the subject decisively.

'You can see Hayes Wood from here.' She raised her hand and pointed across the drowsing fields. In the twilight, the church spire stood out as sharp as a needle. The hedgerows were black splashes of shadow and the willows, bending gracefully over the stream, were lit to gold by the slowly setting sun. It was a perfect evening.

Jake looked startled. 'So close?'

'On the skyline,' Ash said.

'I didn't realize,' he said half to himself.

'We can walk down to the river if you like. You'll get a better view from there,' Ash said.

Jake debated. He looked at her, then at the fairy-tale landscape. He shrugged.

'Thank you.' His dry tone of voice said that he was not deceived by her sudden offer of companionship.

Ash did not challenge him on his own motives either. She called Rusty and he came bounding up from the kitchen garden, bearing a stick. Ash threw it for him. He flew after it, ears streaming, while Jake and Ash walked slowly across the lawns. Rusty tore back and forth and round them with his stick. Neither spoke.

It was odd, thought Ash. He infuriated her, he challenged her at every turn, he insulted her and all too often alarmed her. But walking with him in the scented evening she felt as if she had done it before a thousand times. It was crazy. She reminded herself that Peter had taken no interest in the garden, except when they were having parties. Ash had never walked with him to the river. So why this sense of familiarity? More, of completeness. Ash looked at Jake under her lashes and got no answer.

The sun sank below the horizon but the soft air was still warm. The sky turned the colour of gunmetal. A few fuzzy stars glimmered against the near blackness. The sun became a smear of apricot at the horizon. In silence they walked through the garden, assailed by the scents of Ash's flowers: old cabbage roses that seemed to lose their petals before their perfume; wallflowers under the open windows, wafting a scent into the house that had not changed in three centuries; jasmine that trailed among the other climbing plants hardly detectable except by its scent; pinks and secret clumps of night-scented stock.

Ash sighed unconsciously.

Jake looked down at her. 'What is it?'

'Oh. It's nothing.' Her eyes were dreaming.

He did not comment. But the way in which he did it demanded an answer.

In the end Ash admitted huskily, 'It's just so beautiful it almost makes me sad. I love this time of day.'

Jake said in an odd voice, 'I think I've found another closet romantic.'

Ash did not answer. But she suddenly felt breathless. She turned her shoulder. 'Nonsense. I'm a hedger and ditcher. Highly practical,' she said in a high, unnatural voice. 'Come with me. I want to show you something.'

She took him to the edge of the formal garden and over a stile into Home Meadow. Out here the smell was quite different: grass that had baked dry through the heat of the summer's day and the herbs among the grasses. It was a harsh, wild smell. For no reason at all, it always put Ash in mind of danger.

Rusty kicked up his heels and went racing off across the field, scenting the same wildness.

'Muddy,' Jake said ruefully. He stopped and brushed at his trousers.

Ash looked back at him. She was scornful. 'Don't you like getting your clothes dirty?'

Her scorn went wide of the mark. Jake chuckled.

'There was a time I was never clean. I was born in Memphis. You heard of Mississipi mud? My first job was shifting it.'

Ash stared. Then she began to laugh. 'No one would believe it. Look at the pair of us now,' she gestured down at her grass-stained work clothes; his immaculate sports shirt. 'Which one of us would you think started life as a mudlark? How did it happen?'

His eyes were on the horizon, remembering.

'When I was fourteen they started a big urban clearance programme. We were dirt poor. There was money to be made on the building sites. So I skipped school and got me my first job. My Mom didn't want to know. Then, anyway. So I slept down and out. I learned to appreciate a good shower when I could get it. And to live without it when I couldn't.'

Ash digested that. But before she could ask more about his childhood, they reached the brow of the hill. Jake looked round. He turned to her, a good deal of comprehension in his eyes.

'My company doesn't want to put skyscrapers as far as the eye can see, you know,' he told her gently, surveying the view.

Ash gave a sharp sigh. 'But don't you see, you stupid

man, what you *do* want to do will change this place just as much?'

In the dying light her pale, oval face was alight with passion. She pushed the tangle of red curls back in a characteristic gesture, leaving tendrils lying against the vulnerable softness beneath her ear. She did not see Jake's arrested expression. Her feelings were running high and she had stopped trying to suppress them.

'Do you know what is down there? A river,' she flung at him. 'For years before I – we – came here, it used to flood. It was so overgrown, you see. The fields would turn into marsh every winter. Then I cleared it. Built up the banks. Planted them properly. Stopped the blanket factory dumping its waste in the river.' There was a film of tears over her eyes. 'There are fish in there now. And water rats in the bank. It's a proper river again. And you want to spoil it.'

Jake stared at her. 'Why on earth should I? I'm not building a blanket factory.'

Ash could have screamed. 'Don't you *see*? You're changing the whole ecological balance.'

'What else did you do?' he said swiftly. He sounded angry. 'With your bank clearing and your busy bodying. You're just trying to put the clock back.'

Ash stopped dead as if he had punched her. 'You sound just like Peter,' she said involuntarily.

Jake did not like that. 'It's a question of resources.' He sounded hard. 'The best use of them. People have to have somewhere to live. People,' he added with heavy sarcasm, 'are more important than water rats in my scheme of things.'

Ash looked away. She was almost sure that a tear had

stolen from the corner of her eye down one hot cheek. If it had, she would not thank him for mentioning it. She bent her bright head.

'People destroy,' she said, in a muffled voice.

'And water rats don't? Come on.'

Ash said despairingly, 'Water rats don't wipe out whole species.' She hesitated, then went on as if she could not help herself. 'Do you know how long it is since there have been otters in that river? Or most of the rivers in England, come to that.'

Jake relaxed. He said, 'Otters are a protected species.'

Ash swung round at that, eyes blazing. 'You can't protect what isn't *there*.'

There was a small silence. She found he was staring at her intently.

Jake said on a note of discovery, 'You were going to reintroduce them.'

Ash stiffened. She started to make a gesture of denial, caught his eye and decided against it.

He took a step towards her. 'I'm right, aren't I?' He sounded fascinated. 'That's why you got so worked up about the development project, isn't it? You don't want shops and people using your precious river.'

Ash dashed a hand angrily over her brimming eyes. She shrugged. If she answered him she was likely to betray altogether too much.

Jake said idly, 'Can you go introducing new species just because you happen to be fond of them?'

Ash was not taken in by the idle tone. She said, 'It has to be a properly managed project.'

He looked down at her. 'Why otters?'

299

Ash swallowed. This was private. But somehow she felt compelled to tell him the truth. 'Because they're beautiful and free. Because they need help.'

There was silence. Then Jake laughed softly.

'Nothing that needs help is free,' he said cynically.

Ash winced. 'It would give them a chance,' she said. She sounded desolate, she thought, startled. In fact she sounded as if she had already said goodbye to her pet project. She stopped dead, her eyes shocked.

Jake put a hand on her shoulder and turned her toward him. He touched a finger to the corner of her eye and received the tear drop onto it. He showed it to her gently.

'You care.' He was sounding fascinated again. He shook his head in disbelief. 'You live in determined isolation. Never go near your own kind. Then you weep over fish-eating mammals.'

'Animals are nicer than my own kind,' Ash said thickly. She knuckled her nose inelegantly.

'Oh, Ash.' The laughing voice was full of mock despair. 'What am I going to do with you?'

The hand on her shoulder tightened. Startled, Ash looked up. With his other hand Jake took hold of her chin and tilted her face to his.

He was still laughing when he kissed her. Ash could feel it in the warm breath that invaded her shocked mouth. Not that it was a light kiss. It was a long, sensuous exploration which set her head reeling. He was totally in control.

She gave a small, shocked sound, like one of her animals coming on an unexpected obstacle, and wrenched her shoulder out of his grasp.

'What do you think you're *doing*?' she said furiously.

She rubbed her lips with the back of her hand. Her legs were shaking. That made her even more furious.

He said, quite gently, 'If you don't know, why don't I show you?'

It was not quite what he had planned. But Jake was nothing if not flexible. If an ideal opportunity presented itself, he was not the man to insist on sticking to his original scheme.

He caught her hand and pulled her toward him. She was so tense it was easy to get her off-balance. She lay against him, as if he had shot her. To his surprise he found she was trembling right through.

Jake pushed her hair back from her face, his long fingers gentle against the rigidity of her jaw. Ash's eyes closed. Her lashes were darker than her hair, he saw. She was desperately pale. Her lashes looked like bruises against her magnolia skin. She did not move. She hardly seemed to be breathing, like one of her own little woodland animals, trapped and trying to play dead. He was aware of un-expected tenderness. He bent and brushed his mouth against the tightly shut eyelids. They quivered. The tenderness squeezed at his heart like a pain.

Suddenly Jake was furious with her. He shook her. She still did not open her eyes, though he was so close he saw her lips part on a soundless gasp.

'Right,' he said.

And before she knew what he was doing, he lifted her bodily and deposited her under a willow. Ash gasped and grabbed at him as the world swung wildly. Her eyes flew open.

'That's better,' said Jake with satisfaction.

Her worn work clothes were no barrier to him at all. It seemed that he only had to touch the tee-shirt and it tore from hole to hole. Her flesh started in the cool evening air. Jake gave a soft laugh and bent over her. The warmth of his body was like fire to Ash's frozen senses. Her other clothes followed the tee-shirt. She made no attempt to stop him. She even helped him, her hands clumsier on the fastening than his in her urgency. Hardly knowing what she did Ash fell back. She writhed where he touched her. She was making soft little whimpering sounds of shock and delight.

'Well,' said Jake, pausing. He was breathing hard.

He looked down at her for a moment. Slowly Ash focused on the dark face so close to her own. She could not interpret his expression. She did not know why he had stopped. She pulled at his shoulders, her hands impatient, her mouth lifted to his, seeking . . .

And then her brain caught up with her senses and she really focused. She went cold. Her hands fell away. Jake's expression was not so hard to read after all. It was one she was used to, Ash thought numbly. She had seen it often enough on Peter Lawrence's face. It was the one she had seen just before he pushed her away and stamped out into the rain.

She closed her eyes in pain so deep she could hardly believe she could survive it.

'Oh no,' she said in a soundless whisper. 'Oh *no*.'

CHAPTER 12

When Tony Anderson arrived at work the next morning, he found the door to the Managing Director's office open. A tall figure was sitting at the desk, flinging his way impatiently through papers his efficient secretary had not yet had time to sort. Tony put his head round the door.

'Back early? How did it go?'

He encountered a look that startled him. For the first time since he had come to work for him three years ago, Jake did not smile or greet him.

'Where's that report?' he barked.

Tony was flustered. 'Report?'

'On Ashley Lawrence.' Jake showed his teeth. 'The *full* report.'

Tony swallowed. He had not expected this. 'Well, it's not really complete. I haven't put it on the computer yet.'

Jake waved a hand. 'Get it.'

In the outer office Barbara was just coming in. Tony met her surprised look with a grimace as he scampered past.

'He's back. And fighting mad.'

Barbara's surprise dissolved into amusement. 'Mrs Lawrence must be putting up quite a fight.'

Jake, however, was showing no signs at all of his customary lazy amusement. When Tony got back with his folder, Jake was glaring out of the window, hands in his pockets.

'What have you found out?'

Tony riffled through the folder. 'There's not much. Reasonable school record. Teachers wanted her to go to university but her grandfather sent her off to Florence to some sort of finishing school and then married her off to the heir apparent.'

Jake nodded. 'How old?'

Tony consulted a news clipping. 'Peter Lawrence was thirty four. She was – ' he screwed up his eyes to read the yellowing print ' – eighteen.'

'Christ,' muttered Jake.

'What?' Tony was startled.

'Nothing. Go on.'

'That's it. They lived happily ever after until Lawrence was killed in a car crash. It was a freak storm. Lot of accidents that night. Nothing unusual there. She was devastated by all accounts.'

'Hmm.' The dark face was dissatisfied. 'Why no children? Couldn't she? Couldn't he? Did she try and lose them?'

Tony was shocked. 'I could hardly get hold of her medical records.'

Jake looked impatient. 'You can get hold of anything if you want it badly enough.'

Tony omitted to point out the legalities. Instead he went straight to what Jake would think was the point. 'But – do we? I mean – Hayes Wood. You said yourself, it's peanuts.'

For a moment Jake was taken aback. Then he made an odd, angry gesture. 'Think about that later. What else have you got?'

Tony sighed. 'Well not much that wasn't in the original report. She still doesn't need the money. She's still next stop to a recluse. She isn't ninety. She just behaves like it.'

Jake said something savage under his breath. Tony blinked.

'A very well-advised recluse,' Jake said curtly. 'What about Kimbell's?'

Tony consulted his folder. 'Her shares are about five per cent. Administered by trustees. She takes no interest. Doesn't go to the AGM.' He added thoughtfully, 'Didn't even take an interest when her husband was alive. He used to keep a flat in town, went to most of the functions on his own.'

Jake's eyes narrowed. 'What?'

'She stayed playing house in the country, by all accounts. People in the bank seem to have been rather sorry for Peter Lawrence.'

There was a pause while Jake considered this new information. 'Interesting,' he said slowly. 'Was there anyone else?'

'Lovers, you mean.' Tony shifted his weight to the other foot. This was the part of an unattractive assignment that he had liked least. But he was conscientious. 'It doesn't look like it. Not for either of them. Lawrence was clearly a workaholic. In the bank all hours when he wasn't travelling on business. Mrs Lawrence – well you've met her. The jewellery stays in the bank. She doesn't go out.'

Jake said sharply, 'A woman doesn't have to go out dripping with diamonds to have a lover.'

'No, but she has to show some interest. You said yourself, she looked like a schoolgirl. She's nice enough, Ash Lawrence, but she isn't going to turn a man on, is she?'

Jake turned away abruptly and stood staring out of the window. His brows were knotted in a black frown.

'What about family? Friends?'

Tony went back to his folder with resignation. 'Only family is her dad. Sir Miles. He's got five per cent of the bank, too and takes about the same amount of interest. Not for the same reasons. He's a bit of a playboy.'

Jake did not turn round. 'Estranged?' he said over his shoulder.

'I don't think so.'

Jake nodded. 'What about the men in the area? There's a guy called Cummings. And a couple of others. Said they were neighbours.'

Tony did not have to look at the file. He knew the answer to that one. 'Cummings is an RSPCA Inspector. She works with him. Tim Padgett's a local toff. Last of an important family, barrister, local councillor. The housekeeper thought he might have been after Ash's money at one point but nothing came of it. Nearest neighbour is new. Roger Ruffin, rented the house for three months. Bit of a mystery man. She hardly knows him.'

Jake's mouth compressed in a thin line. 'And that's it?'

'Jake, the girl looks like a scarecrow, married her first boyfriend, never sets foot outside her own door if she can help it. What are you looking for?'

Jake's expression was bleak. 'A *reason* – ' He broke off. 'No, maybe not.' He seemed to shake himself. 'Anything else?'

'Well, we knew she had looked at some scheme for establishing otters. I thought she'd decided against it but I checked. According to a girl at the centre, she spent a couple of years clearing the river and doing something to the banks to improve the habitat. Someone is going down this week to look over what she's done. If it's OK, she's going to apply to join the programme. Little Helen said she'd let me know.' He chuckled. 'I promised Dare's would make a contribution to the charity. The cheque's with Barbara.'

Jake turned round. Tony saw a faint glimmer of a smile. It was a relief.

'Money well spent,' Jake assured him.

Another bad night. A very bad night. She could not remember a worse one. Ash kept coming awake sharply, thinking she was not alone. But she had never slept with Peter in that room, that bed. And it was not Peter's round figure she dreamt was moving beside her. It was a taller, darker, altogether more dangerous figure.

'Bad conscience,' Ash said to herself with grim humour.

Not that there was much to laugh at. She had thought she had already plumbed the depths of humiliation. She had been wrong; wrong by a million miles. Absolutely nothing compared with finding herself naked in the arms of a reluctant stranger. And it was all her own fault, too.

By the morning, she was heavy-eyed with sleeplessness

and the horror of meeting Jake Dare again. She came downstairs in her newest jeans and a long-sleeved shirt buttoned right up to the neck. But her caution was unnecessary. He was nowhere to be seen.

She took the papers on otter habitat into the library and shut the door with a bang. She studied, or tried to study, them for several hours. All the time her ears were stretched for sounds of Jake's presence. She heard Em come, the Hall twins, the postman. But not a sound from Jake.

'This is ridiculous,' said Ash, pouring herself her fourth cup of coffee. Three barely touched predecessors sat on her desk.

Well, Jake had not attempted to invade the library. She should be grateful after yesterday's appalling scene, Ash told herself. Especially as he did not usually show this respect for her privacy. Perversely, it irritated her to screaming point.

She hung around in the kitchen until Em came down with her polish and dusters. 'Jake awake yet?'

Em looked dour. 'He's gone.'

'*What?*'

Ash ran upstairs without waiting for the answer. She pushed open the door to the main suite. It did not take the stripped bed or the emptied drawers to tell her that its occupant had left. It smelled empty. It had smelled like that before.

Ash crossed her arms over her breast.

'Don't let me remember,' she prayed. 'I should never have said all that, never accused him. Never said I wanted a divorce. If I'd known what would happen, I wouldn't

308

have done it. I never meant to hurt anyone. *Please* don't let it all come back again. Not after all this time.'

But there was another memory to do the torturing now.

Eric Stenson did not know what to make of Jake Dare. He expected a harsh, fast-talking businessman with a ruthless determination to cut off anyone who got in his way. What he found was a cool, contained man who seemed almost *distrait*.

'Let's put our cards on the table,' Eric said. 'I was surprised when Newman came to me in the first place. By my standards it's a big project. It will stretch me. I won't be able to do anything else at the same time. That's against my principles.'

Jake nodded. 'Diversify and survive,' he agreed, amused.

'You're a man after my own heart. Well, I wondered if that's why he picked me instead of one of the big companies. So he could get me locked in. So I couldn't afford to back out if there turned out to be something going on I didn't like.'

Jake sat up, suddenly alert. 'Was there?'

'Not sure yet.'

'But you're looking into it?'

Stenson was scornful. 'Of course.' He paused then added deliberately, 'I wouldn't have worried if Dare's had been in there, too. He told me you would be. He said you were joining the family.'

'He was mistaken,' Jake said without expression.

'He's a dangerous man.'

Jake raised his brows.

'Well, a desperate one,' Stenson amended. 'If he doesn't come up with some better forecasts for the mid-term results, the company is dead.'

Jake's eyes were hooded. 'You and I were supposed to be the better forecasts.'

'Looks like it.'

'What are you going to do?'

Stenson was uncomfortable. 'I pulled back from making a public announcement just in time. But lots of people still know we were going into the development together. Including the local authority. And my bank. I can't just wash my hands of it and walk away. I've got my reputation to think of.'

'But you want to?'

Stenson smashed his fist into his open hand. 'I've been in business a long time. I've never got involved with anything crooked. Never. And this – it smells. I'm damned if I know why, but it smells.'

'I agree,' said Jake suddenly. 'Look, I'll make you a deal. I'm doing some digging. So, I think, are you. We pool our results, we find a way out together.'

Eric Stenson had obviously heard about the engagement. He looked dubious.

Jake said harshly, 'He'll find himself another son-in-law. Read the papers tomorrow.'

Stenson appeared convinced. He stood up. 'All right. It's a deal.' He held out his hand and shook Jake's. 'I'll be in touch.'

The days got longer and sweeter. Ash, not sleeping at night, went through them in a sort of daze. She tried to keep busy. She also did her best to hide her distraction. On the whole she succeeded.

The badger cub was well enough to be let out into the garden. It snuffled its way as far as the birch trees, watched by Rusty, ignored by the kittens and policed by the Hall twins. Bob Cummings took them all up to see the site of the badger set and the boys began to accustom themselves to the idea of Humbug being released up there eventually. They were both very quiet on the way back, though.

'He'll be happier in his own place,' Ash assured Chris, sitting silently beside her.

She looked in the driving mirror. She could see that in the back seat Martin was hugging Rusty's copper head into his neck. She felt helpless.

'Really. We are all happier at home, aren't we?'

'But he hasn't got any family,' said Chris.

'I expect the badgers in Hayes Wood are related to him, one way or another.'

'What if they don't like him?' said Martin, uncharacteristically babyish all of a sudden.

What indeed? What happened if a man started to make love to you and then found he did not like you after all? Ash flinched.

But she said steadily, 'I expect they will.'

'But what if he misses us?'

'Then he'll come back and see us. It's not so far. And Bob said he thought there were badger tracks as far as the river gate already. He'll find his way. And you can come over at night and watch for him with me. That will be fun, won't it?'

They were unconvinced. Ash did not blame them. She hardly sounded convincing.

'I just don't know how to talk to children,' she said, returning them to their mother.

Molly was unimpressed. 'Of course you do. You're the twins' best friend, outside school. The trouble with you,' she added, because she was one who had not been deceived by Ash's gallant pretence this last week, 'is that you think nobody else makes mistakes. We all do. And then we learn not to do it again and go on. But you think every mistake is a disaster. And every disaster is the end of the world.'

'Thank you for the character analysis,' said Ash ruefully. She did not deny it, though.

Molly hugged her. 'Learn to be a bit less hard on yourself. Everyone else does.' She took her to the car to see her off. 'Don't worry about the boys. They'll adjust.' And as Ash put the car in gear, 'Don't forget the party.'

'Well – I'm not sure . . .'

'Come on,' said Molly. 'Give yourself a break. Spend the day in the beauty parlour and then knock 'em dead.'

In spite of herself, Ash laughed. 'That will be the day.'

'Want a bet?' Molly rubbed an imaginary stain off the windscreen. 'Sorry gorgeous Jake has gone,' she said casually before she stepped back. 'But we're counting on you.'

Ash did not answer.

Ahmed said, 'You're out of your mind.'

Jake laughed for the first time that evening. 'Maybe.'

'Newman is a very respected man.' Ahmed was struggling with old loyalties. 'He wouldn't stoop to plotting like that.'

Jake sighed. 'Ahmed, my friend, you've never been

312

desperate. You don't know what he would do if he was at the end of his credit. Which I think he is.'

'You're asking me to deceive a man I've known all my life.'

'I'm asking you to help me find out the truth.'

Ahmed said shrewdly, 'You wouldn't care so much about the truth if weren't for that scruffy girl.'

Jake did not answer that one.

Eventually Ahmed sighed. 'Oh, all right. I'll do what I can. But if you're wrong, I want your word that you won't use anything I find out.'

'You've got it.'

Ahmed pressed. 'Not even to help Ashley Lawrence?'

Jake shrugged. 'No mileage in that. Ash Lawrence and I are on different sides.'

Ahmed eyed him with affectionate scorn. 'You really expect me to believe that?'

'Believe it or not, it's the truth.'

'Oh yes? Jake you've spent so long fighting your way to the top, you can't see when you're in the wrong war.'

Ash did not exactly expect Jake Dare to send her a bread-and-butter letter thanking her for a nice time but she was taken aback to find that he made no attempt at all to get in touch with her again.

'Out of sight, out of mind,' said Em with gloomy satisfaction.

'I devoutly hope so,' snapped Ash.

She flung herself into the affairs of the animal centre, working long hours to compensate for the time she had not been there the previous week. And then came the day of the barbecue. For a while Ash toyed with the idea of backing out. But in the end she decided against it. She had given her word and Ash kept her promises, even when she desperately did not want to.

'What is wrong with you?' Ash demanded of her reflection. 'At least That Man isn't going to be there underfoot all the time.'

It was a consolation. It had to be a consolation. It was nonsense to think that it would be quite nice to go to a party under the masterful escort of Jake Dare.

'Think of the last time you were together,' Ash urged. 'Don't push it away, no matter how much you want to. That is the truth, not any of your fantasies.'

She winced.

She had not been able to look at him. She had asked – no, begged – him to leave her alone. He had not liked it but, after protest, in the end he had done what she had asked. At least she had that to be grateful for, Ash thought. She had not had to face him and see distaste in his eyes.

Even after his footsteps had died away she had lain there until Rusty put his nose on her shoulder. The dog whimpered, clearly disturbed. Ash had sniffed, rubbed his head, and moved at last. She scrambled into such clothes as she could find. She had been shivering uncontrollably in spite of the warm evening.

It felt to Ash, sitting at her uncluttered dressing table on the morning of the barbecue, that she had not stopped shivering inside ever since.

Jake was still shaving when the doorbell rang. Marriott, expecting the postman, went to admit the early morning visitor. His professional calm was as nearly shaken as it had ever been by the sight of the visitor. He went into Jake's suite and knocked on the bathroom door.

'Excuse me, sir. A young lady has brought a package. She says you are expecting it. She – er – would prefer to give it to you in person.'

Jake stuck his head round the door. He was grinning.

'Dark young lady? Lots of moons and stars on chains? Eye make up by Queen Nefertiti?'

Marriott relaxed slightly. He had not been quite certain that he was right to let the girl in. 'That is the one, sir.'

Jake laughed aloud. 'Tell her I'll be right out.' Then, seeing Marriott's expression, he added soothingly, 'Don't worry, I haven't taken to witchcraft. Well, not within the meaning of the Act.'

Marriott drew himself up to his full height. It was beneath him to question his employer. 'Very good sir,' he said crushingly.

He withdrew, dignity unimpaired.

Ash spent the day in the garden, trying to forget the evening's obligation. Weeding, clipping and spraying, she made a good job of it until the kittens started climbing in and out of the wheelbarrow, indicating that it was time for their evening meal.

Ash straightened and surveyed a lavish tapestry of roses. 'Not a blackfly in sight,' she said with satisfaction. She sucked a place on her thumb from which she had extracted the last of several thorns. 'Well worth it.'

A kitten dived into the clippings and emerged with a

trail of ivy across its nose, eyes crossed in bewilderment. Ash laughed.

'All right,' she said, gently removing the ivy. 'Supper. And then I suppose I'll have to get ready.'

She fed all the animals, including the badger cub. His lively antics added another couple of scratches to her scarred hands. Ash looked at them ruefully. Molly's advice to spend the day in the beauty parlour had not been so wide of the mark after all, she thought. It was going to be a struggle getting herself to look half-way presentable for a party. Maybe –

'No,' Ash said to herself firmly. 'You promised.'

She went back to the kitchen. And stopped dead with shock. It looked like a UN declared disaster area. The kittens had lost interest in their supper. When she had fetched the tins from the cupboard, Ash must have forgotten to shut the door properly. The kittens had got at Em's stores again.

Ash gave a squeak of pure frustration and flung herself into tidying up as if she were on rocket fuel. She was fishing one of the kittens off its precarious perch on the memory board when the door opened. Caught unawares, Ash looked up straight into amused green eyes. The kitchen floor lurched.

Ash felt as if someone had thrown ice water over her. She put out a hand blindly to steady herself. She found a bentwood chair and hung onto it. She felt as if she would collapse if someone took it away.

'Wh-what –?' she stammered.

The kitten took the opportunity to wriggle out of her grasp and set off round the back of her neck. She leaned forward perforce and the chair rocked.

316

'Stop it,' Ash shrieked, momentarily distracted.

She bent further, trying without effect to remove the little animal. The kitten, sensing the opportunity for play, hooked its small claws into the fronds on Ash's neck and dragged at them, growling. It began to back down her spine, alternately purring and growling. Ash bent double so that it would not fall. And swore.

'Get off,' she yelled.

The kitten tugged at her hair, dancing over her shoulders, utterly out of reach of either hand. She felt around the back of her neck for her attacker. The kitten, delighted, bit her fingers.

'Put me down, you monster,' Ash shouted in frustration. 'Get your claws out of my hair.'

'I think you could use a little help here,' Jake Dare remarked.

The kitten, all four sets of claws out like steel-tipped pincers, was plucked off her. Ash straightened slowly, her fingers going to probe her new scars. She winced. Jake strode to the door and put the small struggling ball of fur and claws firmly onto the terrace outside. Then he turned, grinning.

'What was it you said? Animals are nicer than people?'

The kitchen floor returned to the horizontal. Ash's blood temperature came back to normal. She looked at Jake Dare.

He was different, she thought at once. Still amused, still lazy, still utterly in control. But different. There was an alert look about the deep-set eyes that made him look almost devilish. Devilish and irresistible.

Her heart missed a beat. Ash glared. She let go of the

317

chair and ran her fingers through her hair. It was even more disastrously tangled than ever.

'Only some animals.' There was an edge to her voice. 'Some of the time.'

'So sometimes people can be nicer?' He was laughing: 'Is this heresy? Or progress?'

'What are you doing here?'

He raised his eyebrows, the devil look very evident. 'We have a date.'

'*What*?'

'You're not very flattering,' he said reproachfully. 'I'm taking you to the Halls' barbecue.' His eyes swept up and down her grass-stained person and his smile grew. 'Or were you thinking of ducking out?'

She crossed her arms and subjected him to an equally comprehensive survey. Unlike herself, he was already dressed for the barbecue. Jake Dare's casual clothes consisted of impeccably creased fawn trousers and an ivory shirt that looked as if it had just come out of its tailor's wrappings, she saw. Her lip curled.

Yet, she to admit privately, that for all the urban elegance, he still looked very much a man of action. It was something to do with the muscles under the soft shirt. Something to do with the hard angle of his jaw. But mostly the look of determined purpose in the grey-green eyes.

Which at the moment were not only purposeful but brimming over with laughter. He strolled back to her.

'Are you scarred?' Jake asked solicitously.

'Only my pride.' Ash rubbed her neck.

'Let me look.'

Before she realized what he was about, he had lifted the

tangle of red curls away from her nape. Her heartbeat took off. His hand brushed hers. Ash jumped as if she had been burned and her hand fell. She stood as still as a mouse.

He inspected her neck closely. Ash fixed her gaze hard on the Welsh dresser and concentrated on not trembling. She knew she was holding her breath. She could not do a damned thing about it. After what had happened just a few days ago, it was almost unbearable.

Did he not know what his touch was doing to her? Didn't he care? Why was it taking him so long?

'Yes, I think you'll live,' he agreed.

Ash let out her breath in relief. But he did not let go of her hair; or step away from her. Disbelieving, she felt those long cool fingers brush against her exposed nape. The touch had to be deliberate. For a moment it almost felt like a caress.

Ash swallowed. She could not move away. Jake held her hair lightly enough, bunched in his hand, but it would hurt if she pulled away from him. Or that's what she told herself.

'Do you know you've got three freckles on the back of your neck, like a triangle?' Jake asked musingly.

'Yes,' said Ash.

Her voice sounded strangled, even to her own ears. This was crazy. What was he *doing* to her? No man had ever affected her like this. But then no man had ever stood so close beside her, letting his leisurely gaze wander over her bent head and exposed neck and shoulders. She could feel his eyes on her skin, even when the cool fingers were withdrawn.

'Cute,' Jake said in lazy appreciation.

Ash felt suddenly hot.

'Please let me go,' she said, the constraint back like a straightjacket.

'I don't think so.'

And suddenly his whole hand was cupping her neck. Ash jumped. She could feel the blood jumping at the pressure points behind her ears which he had found with his fingertips. And under his palm her skin was not hot. It was burning.

'*Please* let me go.' No attempt to sound calm now.

'Why?' He sounded faintly puzzled.

Forgetting the risk of having her hair severely pulled, Ash turned to look up at him, an indignant protest on her lips. It died the moment she met his eyes. So that was the purpose he had in mind, she thought confusedly. He lowered his head.

It was a very gentle kiss. No more than a brush of his lips across her startled mouth. There was nothing in it which accounted for the way her eyes closed. Or the way her body swayed against him. Surrendering, Ash gave a barely audible sigh, as if she had come home.

'Is that why?' he asked gently.

Ash opened her eyes, shocked. That tell-tale sigh lingering in the still air. It appalled her. Home? *Come home?* With this urban sophisticate and his heartless teasing? And his not so secret plan to get her land by fair means or foul? She must never forget, Ash reminded herself, that there was a *reason* for all this. And she was responding. She must be out of her mind.

Instinctively she put up a hand and twitched the red curls out of his hand. She stepped away.

'I don't know what you're talking about.'

'Yes, you do.' Jake sounded very certain.

He made no attempt to take hold of her again. He had no need to. His eyes held her. The way he looked at her, Ash thought in rising alarm, was a more potent caress than anything she had ever experienced in her life. And, damn him, he was *smiling*.

'I don't,' Ash insisted, her voice rising.

He shook his head sorrowfully. 'So young, so beautiful and such a liar,' he mourned.

'I – ' She stopped herself on the brink of another protest that he would not believe. She drew a long breath and removed herself to a safer distance by the Welsh dresser. 'Look, I don't know what you're doing here but I can tell you here and now there's no point. I wouldn't sell you any of my land if I were starving. If you're still after Hayes Wood, you can forget it.'

His eyes laughed at her. 'And what if I'm after something else?'

'What else?' Ash demanded scornfully.

He shook his head. 'So suspicious. I'll have to do something about that.'

'No!' It came out like a pistol shot.

'Don't look so alarmed. Not here and now, certainly.'

'Not ever,' said Ash with more firmness that she was feeling.

'Don't be so sure. You don't know what I'm offering in return.'

Their eyes locked. He was laughing all right. But there was something stronger and deeper there. Ash felt as if she had walked out from behind a nice comfortable retaining wall into the full force of a gale. She shook her head, trying to pull her thoughts into some sort of order.

'Oh, yes I do,' she told him, holding his eyes. 'Trouble. I don't want it.'

Jake was not impressed. 'Goes with the human condition. Deal yourself out of trouble, deal yourself out of life. At least in my experience.'

'And your experience is wide, of course,' Ash said sweetly.

His mouth tilted. 'Getting wider every hour, honey,' he told her. He looked her up and down and pursed his lips. 'And about to be widened further. I've never taken a scarecrow to a party before.'

Ash flickered a nasty smile at him. 'You're not taking me to this party. I was invited ages before you were.'

'OK,' he said peaceably. 'I've never been taken to a party by a scarecrow.'

Ash looked at him broodingly. 'You're the rudest man I've ever met.'

His shoulders shook. 'Merely because I'm honest.' His tone was reproachful. 'Surely your other escorts have complained about the dirty fingernails? Even if they didn't mind the blood and grass stains.'

Ash jumped and looked guiltily down at her scruffy working clothes. They had never been smart and were now liberally daubed with evidence of her day's activities. Once again, the infuriating man had a point.

'I will, of course, change before I go to the barbecue,' she said.

'Surprising but welcome,' Jake murmured.

'In fact I shall go and do so now.'

He permitted himself a small nod, nothing too triumphant. 'Fine. But first – a gesture of good will.'

He produced a small package wrapped in elegant plum-coloured paper. Ash looked at it with suspicion.

'What's that?'

'A token to express my appreciation for your hospitality,' Jake said fluently. He met her smouldering eyes and laughed. 'Indulge me, Ash.'

It was bath oil. The bottle itself was a work of art, with a dragonfly in flight etched onto its curves. Its fluted stopper was held in place by a silver seal.

Jake said softly, 'They say it's made up from primroses and jasmine. It's supposed to match your personality.'

Ash was startled. 'Thank you,' she said with constraint.

'I mean *your* personality. I described you in detail. It took several consultations.' He chuckled suddenly. 'My domestic staff thinks I'm employing witchcraft.'

'Your domestic staff sound as if they know you pretty well,' said Ash. There was an edge to her voice.

Jake decided to ignore the implied insult. 'Organization is my forte,' he agreed modestly.

Ash stopped dead, suddenly realizing what he had said. 'They made it up?' she echoed. 'Are you telling me this is – I don't know what you call designer perfume – an original?'

He turned the bottle in her hands so that the little seal was facing her. It had a tiny card attached which Ash had overlooked. She glanced up at him, then took the little slip between her grubby finger and thumb and read the inscription.

'Ashley' it said in italic script.

'Oh,' she said blankly.

Jake was watching her with an odd, slanting smile. 'An original perfume for an original lady.'

Inwardly Ash winced. She knew exactly how original he thought she was. He had justification. She lifted her chin. 'I know,' she said coolly. 'This is what the sophisticated scarecrow wears to a party, I take it?'

His eyes flickered but he did not rise to the bait. All he said was, 'I hope so.' He made her a little mock bow. 'I hope it lives up to the advance publicity. Go and have your bath and we'll see.'

'You're expecting a transformation?'

'I look forward to it.'

Ash smiled but her lips felt stiff. She did not need Jake Dare to remind her that she was unfeminine, she thought. By now it must be branded on her brow. Only when Peter has said it, she had somehow not cared. These days it hurt.

She said colourlessly, 'I hope you won't be disappointed.'

Jake's eyebrows flew up. 'I hope *you* won't. It's your perfume. Not mine. It's supposed to make you feel you've embarked on a magical evening of discovery.' He added solemnly 'If it doesn't, I'll sue.'

In spite of herself, Ash smiled. 'Then I'm sure it will.' She looked at her watch. 'Oh hell, we're going to be so *late*.'

'Barbecues are designed for being late. Go soak.'

She did.

As Jake had promised, the bath oil smelled delicately of evening jasmine and other fugitive scents of a summer garden. Ash found she loved it. She even began to play

324

with the fantasy that she was an ordinary girl, getting ready to go out on an ordinary date. She stretched with pleasure, lifting her arms above her head.

Well, why not? It was more than ten years since she had been on an ordinary date, but she had not forgotten what to do. Or what it felt like. And Jake Dare seemed willing enough to go along with it.

Just for tonight she would pretend that she had never known Peter Lawrence, never married him; never learned slowly and painfully that she was only the shell of a woman. Never – she said it deliberately – flung him out into the storm that killed him.

Tonight she would pretend that she was going to a party with a man who was attracted to her and wanted only to please her. She would forget Jake's ulterior motives. She would ignore her own deep reservations. She would forget, even, the disaster by the river. Tonight was for fun.

Her wardrobe still had the designer clothes Peter had insisted she buy. She had lost weight and most of them hung on her these days. But there was a pair of lichen green corduroy trousers and jacket that made her hair look like a bonfire against its expensive tailoring. Ash dug through the back of the drawer and found a hand-embroidered cream silk shirt she had inherited from her grandmother. It made her skin look magnolia pure. She brushed out her hair and let it fall in loose curling waves about her face.

'That's the best I can do,' Ash said aloud.

She looked at herself in the mirror. It could have been a different girl, staring back at her. Even without make-up, her eyes looked larger, wide and amber and excited. And just a little apprehensive. Ash gave a little shiver, part apprehension, part glee.

She went downstairs.

Jake's eyes widened when he saw her. For a moment she thought he was almost shocked. She stopped at the foot of the stairs, disconcerted by what she thought she saw in his face. But at once he was smiling again, casual, indifferent.

'No jewellery?' he asked. 'Sensible. 'You don't want it to fall into the fire.'

Ash shook her head. 'I don't ever wear jewellery.'

She had had it all; the rose diamonds, the smart ruby collar, the pearl and sapphire set that had been made for a Russian princess. All bought by her grandfather to reward her for marrying the right man. Or by Peter for her to display when they had dinner with business contacts. She had come to hate them.

Jake looked curious. 'Allergy?'

He opened the door for her and they went out into the softly scented evening.

'In a way. I don't like jewels.'

He looked even more curious. But all he said was, 'You should meet my mother and sister. They wouldn't believe it.'

He helped her into his Mercedes. Jake swung himself in beside her and started the engine.

'Jewellery is an addiction for them. They discovered it after I hit the big time,' he said drily.

Ash was taken aback. 'The big time?'

'My first million. Probably my first thousand, for that matter.' He did not sound as if he cared very much. 'It was classic. Poor boy makes good. Family makes hay.'

326

Ash found she was shocked. All the more so because he did not seem to be bitter about it.

'You're very – philosophical.'

Jake shrugged. 'People are what they are. My mother was never so fond of me as when I opened an account at Aspreys. No point in beating my brains out fighting the inevitable. Some things you can't change. You accept it and go on.'

Ash was silenced.

It was only later, as they were pulling up outside the Hall's house, that she realized she had passed the tree at the gates without noticing it. For the first time, she had driven right by it without thinking, Peter died here and it was all my fault. Maybe she was catching some of Jake Dare's philosophy. Maybe she was not going to have to pay for that half-hour's temper for the rest of her life, after all.

Molly had assembled nearly fifty people in her tangly garden. Every single one of them was astonished to see Ash. Jake kept his arm firmly round her waist the entire time and looked down at her mockingly each time another astounded neighbour said hello.

In the still air the barbecue smoke rose vertically. Jake looked round and gave a sigh of pleasure.

'I could get used to a life like this,' he said. 'Mostly I don't understand the people who belt out of London on Friday night, just to belt back on Sunday night. But I can see that there might be some sense to it on evenings like this.'

'You like parties?' Ash asked.

'Real parties for friends, yes.' He pulled a face. 'Not the cocktail parties that go with signing contracts.'

Ash lowered her lashes. 'What about before the contracts are signed?' she asked carefully.

How Peter had raged at her over those business dinners. She had tried so hard, but she had never understood what was going on and she had hated them. Peter said it showed; that it was her fault; that Kimbell's lost contracts because of it.

Jake looked down at her with a good deal of comprehension, she thought.

'A necessary evil. They oil the wheels of commerce. I keep them out of my home life.' He paused. Then added with odd deliberation, 'No wife of my mine would be asked to give dinner parties to set up business deals.'

Ash looked away. 'Then she'd be very lucky.'

He put a hand under her chin and turned her face back towards him. He smiled straight into her eyes. 'I hope so.'

Ash went very still.

Stop it, she told herself after a moment. He can't possibly mean what you think he means. He's much too cynical. He is winding you up, that's all.

But there was still something in the way he was looking at her that made her heart beat fast and light somewhere at the base of her throat. Ridiculous, she told herself. But the intent look in his eyes seemed to give the lie to all her determined good sense. She searched his face, not knowing what she was looking for, trying to read his expression.

Jake's smile died. He said urgently, 'Ash – '

Molly Hall appeared at his elbow. She was carrying two glass mugs of golden liquid topped off with a nosegay of garden mint and borage.

'Pimms,' she said. 'Food will be a while, unless I can

persuade the chef to use the grill in the house. But the boys like their barbecues authentic.'

Jake returned a laughing answer. He accepted the drinks for both of them. Momentarily incapable of speech, Ash could only admire his powers of recovery. Of course, if there had been nothing serious there in the first place, he did not have much to recover from, she reminded herself.

She sipped her drink. It tasted of walnuts and lemonade, fruits – orange and berries of some sort, she thought – and the herbs that trailed across the surface.

'Exotic,' she said lightly as Jake turned back to her.

He frowned. 'Ash – '

'There's Bob,' she interrupted. Suddenly, urgently, she needed to get away from his side. 'And Tim. How nice. I really ought to have a word.' She smiled at Molly and Jake impartially. 'Will you excuse me?'

For a moment his expression darkened. Ash almost thought he was going to bar her passage. But then he shrugged and let her go. Out of the corner of her eyes she saw Molly Hall put a hand on his arm.

She hurried over to Bob and Tim and began to talk at random about the planning application for Jake's development. Bob excused himself after a few minutes but Tim Padgett responded readily enough. In fact, he fetched her another glass of Pimms and asked about the badger set in the wood.

Ash had difficulty concentrating. Once she was unwise enough to look toward Jake too openly. He sent her a smiling glance across the smoky garden. It was almost a kiss. Ash turned away, her heart beating dangerously. She was acutely conscious of interested eyes. That charm was almost visible, she thought; and as heady as the Pimms.

Eventually Jake strolled across to her side. He slipped his arm round her waist again. It felt as if it belonged there. Her traitorous heart lurched and settled down to a hasty pattering. She was terrified he would hear it. Her face went wooden.

Jake smiled down at her teasingly. This was how people on real dates treated each other, Ash reminded herself. Go with it. Live a little. She flung her head back and smiled right back at him.

Jake looked startled. Then something leaped into his eyes, and stayed there, flickering like little flames. Ash felt exhilarated suddenly. She held his gaze, still smiling.

'Er – lovely party but I ought to be going,' said Tim Padgett. 'Lots to do. Life is one damned thing after another these days.'

'What? Oh – er – I suppose so.' Jake sounded distracted.

Ash's smile grew. The arm round her tightened painfully. Tim backed away.

'You've driven him off,' she said, reproachful.

'About time, too.'

Jake pushed her hair back with a negligent hand, stroking her cheek as he did so. 'Pompous idiot,' he said. 'He can't expect to corner the most gorgeous redhead on site for the sole purpose of boosting his ego.'

Ash giggled. 'He didn't mention his ego. I was telling him about my badger.'

'Good,' said Jake with satisfaction. 'I hope it bored him to extinction.'

And he stroked her cheek again. Ash gave a long, sweet shiver.

He bent his head toward her, murmuring, 'Are you hungry?'

All of a sudden Ash felt lightheaded. 'No. Are you?'

She could feel him laughing, soundlessly.

'Depends. Why don't we discuss it at home?'

Her mouth was suddenly dry. She looked anywhere but at him. 'Leave now, you mean?'

The arm tightened until she felt her waist would crack in the vice of it. But she did not try to remove herself.

I don't trust him, she thought. He's too clever. And much, much too attractive. And he knows it. I've already made a horrible, hopeless fool of myself over him. All he wants is Hayes Wood.

Then she thought: he said he might want something else. He brought me perfume that he had made only for me, not any other woman. And he's seen the worst of me and still come back. Whatever happens, there's nothing left to hide.

She bent her head and leaned against him. She was too shy to look at him. The hold on her waist became convulsive. Jake said something under his breath which she did not catch.

Ash looked up. His eyes were very dark.

'Time to go, I think,' he said huskily.

CHAPTER 13

It was still not quite dark. They walked back to the car under shadowed trees. Jake took hold of her hand and did not let go.

Ash did not know what was happening to her. She felt as if she had somehow become precious suddenly. It was an odd sensation. It made her feel even shyer. She had never felt precious before. She wondered if it felt as strange to Jake as it did to her. Or if it only felt like that because it was part of his clever strategy. Perhaps an ulterior motive would make its appearance any moment.

She would have asked him. Only, in the car, he took her hand again and held it all the way home. Ash found she did not care if it was part of his strategy. This evening was for more than fun, she thought. It was something to treasure in the future, when he had gone back to his millionaire's pursuits and she was walking dogs and minding badgers on her own again.

They did not speak in the car. Jake drove home fast. Ash watched his long, strong fingers on the wheel dreamily. When they pulled up in front of the Manor he killed the lights and turned to her.

'You really didn't know most of those people at all, did you? Even though you're neighbours and you've been here for years.'

Ash was not sure if it was a criticism. She looked down at her hands. 'You must have guessed. After all, they haven't been flocking to my door while you've been staying.'

'It's different when you see it in action.' He sounded pensive. 'I ask myself why.'

In spite of the lovely fantasy of the evening, Ash tensed. 'I like my privacy.'

'So do I. That doesn't mean my neighbours look at me as if I'm a visitor from outer space when I bump into them,' Jake told her frankly.

He drummed his fingers on the steering wheel.

'Molly thinks you blame yourself for the accident,' he said at last, in a neutral tone. 'That you're doing some sort of penance. Is that true?'

Ash swallowed. 'It's a long time ago.'

'And that doesn't answer my question.' He looked at her speculatively.

'Survivors often feel guilty when someone dies. Especially if they die young,' Ash said. 'I've had counselling. I know the jargon.'

'And yet you're still living in the middle of nowhere keeping nice people at arm's length? Like the sleeping beauty in the middle of her thorn forest,' he said drily.

Ash bit her lip. 'It's not as bad as that.'

'It's worse. At least according to your neighbours.'

She was surprised and a little offended. 'Why would they talk to you about me?'

His teeth flashed in the darkness. 'They could see I was – interested. Unlike you, apparently.'

Ash's mouth was suddenly dry. This was bringing the evening out of the realms of fantasy and dangerously close to real life. The sort of real life she could not begin to deal with. Time for retreat, she thought.

'I think we should go in. It's getting cold.' She put her hand on the door handle.

'It's locked.' Jake was tranquil. 'Useful things, central locking systems.'

She was outraged. 'You've locked me in?'

'I've locked us in,' he corrected gently.

'That makes all the difference, of course.' Ash was sarcastic.

He gave that husky laugh. 'I hoped it would.'

He reached out a long, lazy arm and scooped her up against him. He did not attempt to kiss her, just held her there, warm against his side.

'You're as taut as a bowstring,' he said, astonished. 'What's wrong?'

'I would have thought it was obvious.' Ash was shaking. With temper she assured herself.

'Not to me.'

'Then you're even more arrogant than I thought. I don't appreciate coercion. I want to get out of this car,' Ash said in a level voice. 'And I want to get out now.'

'So you can hide in the garage with the badger?' His tone was teasing but there was a detectable edge to it.

Ash refused to rise to it. 'If I want.'

'And what about what I want?'

The ulterior motive appearing at last. She felt a slight

shock and castigated herself. After all, she had known the magic was only temporary.

'I know what you want,' she said with spirit. 'You're not getting my wood. You can keep me locked in here until the milkman comes tomorrow morning and I'll still be saying the same thing.'

In the shadowed car his eyes glinted at her. 'I'm almost tempted,' he murmured. He shook his head. 'You don't trust anyone, do you?'

Ash snorted. 'We are not discussing anyone else. Are you implying that I should trust *you*?'

There was a little silence. Then he said in a queer, flat tone, 'You could do worse.'

Ash held onto her indignation. Justified indignation, she assured herself, in the light of that locked door.

'Hard to see how.'

For a second his mouth tightened. She saw it in the moonlight that filtered through the trees and into the car. For a moment she could almost believe he was hurt. But then she realized that had to be ridiculous. It must be anger that made him look like that. Well, he had no right to be angry with her. She had never pretended. Pride reasserted itself.

She said with spirit, 'Get it into your head. I'm not selling that wood. Bullying didn't work. And if you were thinking of giving me a thousand megawatt blast of the old Dare charm, let me warn you here and now that won't work either.'

He ignored that. 'You trust those animals of yours,' he said musingly. If he was angry he had it on a tight leash. 'Even when they scratch you to bits.'

335

'They don't – '

Quick as a snake he reached out and seized her hand. Before she could stop herself Ash gave a soft exclamation as his fingers closed round the place where the cub had left three long scratches. He went very still. Even without being able to see his face, Ash had no difficulty in reading the message.

'They don't –?' he prompted mockingly.

Ash tugged her hand out of his grasp. 'In general the animals don't turn on me. Or anyone who behaves decently to them. This was different. The cub didn't mean it. He didn't understand. It's just that he's getting better and he feels frustrated being cooped up.'

Jake's smile widened. She saw the flash of his teeth again. She also saw that he looked at her mouth.

'That makes two of us. And I haven't marked you.'

A picture of herself, vulnerable and rejected with her clothes strewn about the river bank, presented itself. Ash flushed. 'That's a matter of opinion,' she flung at him.

Jake's eyes flickered. Suddenly his body was tense; taut and silent and waiting, Ash thought. She shrank back, her heart beginning to race.

'You're saying I've made a dent in that guarded little heart of yours?' he asked at last. He was very quiet; very polite. 'In spite of it being a protected area reserved for livestock only?'

Ash swallowed and mastered her voice with an effort. 'Don't be ridiculous.'

'I'm only telling the truth.'

'No, you aren't,' said Ash furiously. 'And you haven't made the slightest dent in my heart.'

Jake laughed softly. 'No, that's what I thought,' he agreed. 'Not unless certified by the Wildlife Trust or the Cats' Protection League.'

He leaned towards her. It brought his body into fractional contact with hers. Ash backed up against the leather seat away from that electrifying touch until her spine ached. But she could not quite break it. Through layers of silk and corduroy and whatever that immaculate shirt was made of, she could feel his body heat. It felt as if she were standing too close to a fire.

'You know, you're seriously hidebound,' he said conversationally. 'Man is in there with the rest of creation, after all.'

He was undoing the buttons on that beautiful shirt. Ash stared at him, disbelieving.

He said softly, 'I'm an animal too, Ash. We both are. Feel.'

And he took her hand and slipped it inside his opened shirt. For a horrified moment, Ash did not move. She could not. She sat there, pressed into the leather until her body imprint must be there for all eternity, conscious only of dazzling, quizzical eyes which she could not meet, and the strong rising and falling of his chest under her shrinking fingers.

Only they weren't shrinking any more. They were spreading instinctively across the warm beating heart. Not too close to the fire, Ash thought, her head ringing. In the middle of the fire. She did not even try to remove her hand. She lay back against the seat where he had manoeuvred her, quiescent. In the darkness she raised reluctant, drugged eyes to his.

For a moment he looked down at her, searching her face. He seemed almost to hesitate, Ash thought. Then suddenly his mouth tilted savagely and he jerked her towards him in a hard embrace. It banished every thought from her head but trying to breathe.

She felt his hands on her back under the jacket, then under the cool silk. He tipped her back until she was wholly balanced against his powerful bracing fingers. She felt his hand splayed across her spine. Her skin tingled. She felt totally under his control, totally overwhelmed.

She thought, I don't believe this is happening.

She thought, He must think I know a lot more than I do.

His hands moved. He was murmuring into her mouth. Ash felt hot and cold at the same time.

She thought, I have never felt like this before in my life.

They did not go to the master suite where he had stayed. Ash took him to her own bedroom. It was a corner room, plain in contrast to the other. In the summer's heat, Ash generally left both sets of windows open. The room was cool enough now. It smelled of the scents of the day: lavender, jasmine, the old-fashioned roses that twined up the wall beyond the casement and, from the distance, mown grass.

It was a smell she was used to. It met her every night in the summer. Yet, when she entered the dark room with Jake Dare, she stopped dead as if she had never smelled it before.

Her mouth still throbbed from that consuming kiss. She put her fingers to her lower lip. It did not feel like her own lip at all. Nothing about her felt like herself. A floorboard creaked as they stood still. Ash swallowed, trying to absorb the strangeness of it. She shivered. The hard arm round her shoulders tightened.

'Ghosts?' Jake asked softly.

Ash bit her lip. 'No. This is – ' If it had not been dark she could not have said it. Even so, it was hard. 'I've always slept alone here.' They were alone in the house but she was whispering, too.

Jake was very still. Then he turned her toward him in the circle of his arm. She could feel him scanning her face in the dark. She hoped he could not see how her lips trembled.

'Sure?' he asked.

'I'm sure.' She thought no one but herself would be able to detect the deep, deep self-doubt there.

But it seemed Jake could. 'Oh Ash, what am I going to do with you?' He pulled her against his chest and held her, quite loosely. 'I suppose it's no use my saying I'll never hurt you?'

'No,' Ash said. 'How can you tell if you'll hurt me?'

He sighed sharply. 'You could try giving me a clue,' he suggested.

Ash was silent.

'You're so certain I will hurt you?'

There was no answer to that one either. Jake Dare was out of her league and they both knew it. He was altogether too practised; too much in control. Ash knew that by contrast she was not in any league at all. She could not control herself let alone anyone else.

She'd always known he had an ulterior motive for staying with her. Why he might as well have had the blueprint of the development and the contract of sale for

Hayes Wood laid out on the pillow in front of them, Ash thought. Knowing what she did, there was absolutely no excuse for her getting into this situation. Her only excuse was that she wanted something, even if it was only one night, even if it was pretence. She was aware of a surge of anger at herself. It did not change anything. She still wanted him.

Jake sighed again. 'Where are the lights?'

At once Ash tensed. 'No lights.'

He held her a little away from him and looked down at her. 'Insurance? Do you think you can pretend that this didn't happen if we stay in the dark tonight?'

Ash was so angry at the accusation that for a moment she forgot her sense of unreality. 'I don't pretend,' she said.

And that was true. The pretence here was Jake's. What was it he had said? Some things you can't change. You accept it and go on. He was what he was. Ash had no right to try to change him. But she could still tell him the truth, even if he did not want to recognize it.

'I don't pretend,' she repeated sadly.

'You'd better not,' Jake said.

He slid the jacket off her shoulders with practised ease. Ash should have been expecting it but she wasn't. She jumped. 'What are you doing?'

He tossed the jacket aside and laughed. 'Preparing to abuse your hospitality. What do you think?'

She gave a reluctant laugh. There were goose bumps on her arms. Not because the shadowed room was cold.

'That's one way of putting it,' she agreed. She tried to laugh but it came out too high, too nervous.

340

As if he sensed her uneasiness, Jake dropped his arms and stepped back. On a reflex movement she fled to the open window and turned her back on him. Outside the stars were brilliant and the night air still. Not a leaf moved, not a bird called.

He said quietly, 'Ash, you don't have to be afraid of me.'

Oh, but she did. She did. Not of rape, or sexual betrayal. Perhaps not even of embarrassment; Jake was an experienced man, after all. But of something much worse, of that indifference that said love was a teenager's fantasy and turned its face against all warmth. Oh, Peter had taught her exactly what she had to be afraid of, Ash thought.

She huddled her arms round herself. 'You don't understand,' she said into the blackness. Her voice was very quiet.

So was his. 'Don't I? Are you sure? What do you want, Ash?'

If she knew that, she thought bitterly, she would have taken charge of her own life years ago. She would not have married Peter. She would certainly not have stayed with him after it became obvious that he hardly wanted her at all.

Jake came up behind her and put his arms loosely round her. Ash flinched but she did not pull away. She felt him drop his face against the top of her head, caressing her hair with his cheek. He held her very gently, carefully almost, without urgency. But, tipped back against his body, Ash had no doubt that he wanted her

She stilled. *He wanted her*. It was a wholly new sensation. It filled her with wonder. She felt as if she were a new person suddenly, someone she did not quite know. She felt her hair move under the gentle caress; his breath against her heated skin.

As if he felt the change in her Jake very gently began to move one hand along her shoulder. He looped her hair behind her ear. He bent forward and his lips brushed her temple. Ash's eyelids quivered at the contact but she did not move away.

'Ash trust me.' It was hardly more than a breath.

She was so still she was hardly breathing. Something was beginning to move in her blood, warm and languid. She felt like one of the cats uncurling in a patch of sunshine, she thought. Another bit of Ash that she had not known about until Jake Dare had started to uncover her.

Jake was stroking the side of her throat with his forefinger, very gently. Ash felt her heart slow, begin to beat to the rhythm of that sensuous touch. She moved under his hand, suddenly restless. The gentle touch was a delight but it stirred rather than soothed. The rhythm in her blood beat stronger, harder; she wanted more.

Her breath came short and shallow. Inside her a great need began to spiral. And he knew. Ash did not quite know how, but she knew that Jake felt her every sensation as intensely as she did herself. It was almost frightening.

Yet still he did no more than stroke her skin; hold her gently back against him; murmur kisses down her half-averted face. It was as if he was waiting for something. Ash was helpless, and yet he still waited . . .

Suddenly something seemed to clench inside her. It was almost like a pain. She gave a gasp. She swung herself round on pure instinct, almost violently. Of their own accord her hands went out to reach up, draw that tantalizing mouth down to her.

At last the kiss was mutual. They took fire.

The last vestiges of pride blasted away. '*Please*,' said Ash.

The moment she said it, Ash froze. Oh God, not again, she thought frantically. Not *again*. Hardly knowing what she was doing, she beat herself away from him.

Jake said her name in a shaken undertone.

'No,' said Ash, her voice high. 'I can't bear it.'

He would turn away. Any moment now he would turn away from her, leaving her bereft. If she let it happen again she would lose all hope of self-respect for the rest of her life. It was a question of survival. She hauled against his hold, panicking.

Just for a moment it seemed that Jake was as startled as she was. But then he mastered himself.

'Ash – '

She couldn't look at him, tearing her hands out of his grasp, her hair swinging wildly.

'*No!*'

'Stop the ravished virgin act.' His voice was harsh. 'Just stop it.'

That shocked her into meeting his eyes. As he no doubt intended.

His voice gentled. 'Ash, I don't know what happened just then. If it was something I did, tell me.'

She did not say anything. Her breath was coming quick and shallow.

'For God's sake, Ash. You've got to trust me.'

Her laugh grated. 'Trust you?'

His head went back as if she had slapped him. Ash took courage. She stepped forward, her fists clenching at her sides.

'You intended this to happen all along, didn't you? You thought if you softened me up, I'd sell you my land. Didn't you?'

Jake's eyes flickered. 'I – '

'Don't bother to deny it. I'm not a fool,' Ash said bitterly. 'It's been done before.'

And after he'd made his deal, Peter had regretted it deeply. In the end he had not been able to bring himself even to pretend that he wanted her. And Peter had got Kimbell's as part of the package, not just a few overgrown acres.

Jake went completely still. 'What the hell do you mean?'

Twisting the knife in the old wound, Ash flung at him, 'Why else would you bother with a scarecrow?'

'*What*?'

Suddenly he was furious. Ash could see it. She shook her hair back defiantly.

'I told you, I'm not a fool.'

'That,' said Jake grimly, 'is open to debate.'

He took hold of her hard and held her away from him. Furious, Ash writhed against his grip. He hardly seemed to notice.

'Someone has done a real number on you, hasn't he?' He didn't sound sympathetic. 'Who was it?'

'No one. You're talking nonsense. Let me go,' said Ash, plucking at the fingers on her shoulder.

In vain.

'You might as well tell me. I'll find out, you know.'

She winced at that, too. She would not let him see her reaction.

'Another private investigator?' she mocked.

His fingers tightened to a vice. It was a point of pride not to cry out, but Ash could not suppress her shocked indrawn breath.

Jake released her at once. But he did not look remorseful. He looked icily, dangerously angry. Ash backed away. He was pale round the mouth and his eyes were like chips of green marble.

'You can be real hell fire, can't you, Mrs Lawrence?' His voice was level. 'No, not a private investigator. This time, I do my own investigating.'

Ash knew what he was going to do before he reached her. She could perfectly well have got away. She did not. She did not even try.

With an ease that was almost insulting, Jake swung her off her feet and onto the bed. Ash stared up at him, half-formed thoughts chasing round and round in her head and getting nowhere. Faintly, at the back of her memory, there was the echo of that humiliating 'Please'. She shut her eyes.

Jake put a hand on either side of her head and leaned over her. 'Look at me, Ash.'

She shook her head on the pillow, eyes screwed tight. Her hair dragged where a few strands had caught under his palm. She said, like a four-year old, 'You're hurting me.'

He was unimpressed. 'I'm not touching you.'

She peered at him under her lashes. 'My hair,' she protested.

He looked down; then impatiently released the hair and spread it out on the pillow behind her with ostentatious care. 'There. OK?'

'Let me up,' muttered Ash, eyes shut again.

'When you've told me what I want to know.'

Her mouth dried at the thought. 'How can I tell what you want to know?' she parried.

'Don't play games with me, Ash. You can tell.'

Her eyes flew open in indignation. 'I don't. I – '

She fell silent. Far from lowering over her threateningly, Jake was engaged in spreading her hair out on the pillow, thread by thread. He looked absorbed. Perhaps he felt her astonishment, because his eyes slid sideways, meeting her own. For a moment he looked like a schoolboy caught out writing on the blackboard. Then his mouth tilted crookedly. 'Not much point in pretending, is there? For either of us.'

Ash stared and stared, unable to make sense of what he was saying.

'I don't give a damn about the other men, whoever they were. Or are,' he said roughly.

Other men? What was he talking about?

'I know someone's hurt you. Maybe more than one. You don't have to tell me anything you don't want to. Only – ' Suddenly his voice was urgent, strained. 'Just don't judge me by them, Ash. Not the ones who hurt you. Trust me a little. Trust me tonight at least.'

Almost tentatively he touched a finger along her lower lip. Ash tried to hold onto the memory of his devious plans; his detective's report. Or, failing that, the nightmare times with Peter. Jake deserved better than to be used as a magic potion to wipe out the hurt Peter and she had dealt each other.

He did not understand the ghosts that haunted her. He saw remembered pain all right. But he had not managed to detect the guilt that consumed her every time she walked through her own front gates. Jake looked at her and never saw the darkness that fell on everything she touched. Ash shivered superstitiously. He might be a rogue and a con man but he did not deserve that. It was too great a hazard, even for him.

But it was no use. Even as she was telling herself that she had to tell him to go, Ash realized it with a sense of inevitability. None of it mattered. Not Jake's motives; not her own. For this one night she needed to be held, loved. Even if it was pretence she wanted to know, just once, what love should have been like.

Ash moved sharply. She began to haul at her clothes with determination, though her hands shook. Jake looked thunderstruck.

'Ash – '

'Not a word.'

She tugged at his shirt, her fingers clumsy. He put his hands over hers, stilling them.

'Ash, darling.'

'I want to,' Ash said, panting.

Her eyes were fever bright. Jake's grip tightened. He shook their joined hands gently.

'Hey, Ash. It's not a race. Slow down a minute.'

She tore her hands free and flung off the last of her clothes. Her eyes were glittering in challenge. 'You said you wanted me.'

Jake looked disturbed. 'Yeah, I do. I don't want to try for a marathon record at the same time,' he said drily. 'There's no hurry.'

Oh, he did not understand at all. She was shaking with tension.

'Yes, there is,' said Ash fiercely.

He laughed but he still looked worried. Almost reluctantly, he hauled the half-opened shirt over his head. He dropped it on the floor among the tangle of her own. Ash kissed his bared chest quickly, daringly. His breathing quickened.

'Perhaps you're right.' His voice was not entirely steady.

He discarded the rest of his clothes. Then he was beside her, kissing the pale planes of her shoulders. Ash trembled violently.

'My sweet,' he said.

His touch was slow; slow and infinitely exciting. Ash strained against him. She gave a harsh moan that she barely recognized as her own voice. She reached for him, shaking with need.

He knelt over her, cupping the pale pointed face between both his hands. He was looking as if he had never seen her before. Even in the darkness, Ash sensed it. As if something had shaken him, shocked him even.

She did not care. She loved him. She knew it as suddenly and certainly as if it were being written in wizard runes on the wall behind him. Oh my God, thought Ash, *love*. She groaned.

He pushed her hair off her face. 'My darling, I promise – '

She put her fingers over his mouth to silence him. 'No promises.'

He kissed her fingers. 'But – '

'No promises,' she insisted, her voice fierce.

He began to kiss her open palm, using his tongue against the vulnerable flesh. She quivered.

'We'll see about that – ' He was still laughing.

But when Ash moved, running her hands over the long, beautiful bones, he caught his breath in a sudden harsh sound.

'Tomorrow,' he finished raggedly.

After that neither of them spoke. They did not need to. Later, Ash thought she would have been astonished if anyone had told her how absolutely she would respond to his every tiniest movement. In the end it felt as if she were responding to his *thoughts*.

Only once was their harmony disturbed. It was when Jake, lying on his side and surveying her through half-closed lids, swept his hand down from breast to thigh in assured possession. In spite of herself, Ash stiffened. Her muscles contracted in anticipation of the misery she knew so well.

Jake stilled. He said her name on a note of query. Ash did not answer. She could not.

Jake hesitated for just a moment. Then he bent his head. His mouth made a slow, devastating journey from her rigid jaw to the slender trembling legs. Ash held her breath. Easily, gently, he parted her legs. Ash quivered. Then she felt his mouth against her. She could not restrain her instinctive jolt of shock. But Jake was bent on sensuous exploration and Ash realized in dawning wonderment that she was travelling, too. Pleasure, so intense it was almost pain, was drawing her faster and faster into some dark

349

vortex. She was almost afraid of the seismic tremors running through her; but then sheer exultation took over.

She thought, So this is *it*.

And then Jake was inside her and an old, wild rhythm took over. She heard herself cry out. Or was it Jake? Or both of them? At last, *at last*, the thing she had sought, without knowing it, was hers. She flew.

In the morning, of course, it was all different. There was still a dark-haired stranger in her bed. Ash held the sheet to her breast and looked at the sleeping head on her pillow. Her naked shoulders felt cold and different from how they had ever felt before. Crazy, she thought. Did she think that Jake's touch could change her chemically, so that her skin was silkier, her hair, falling against her neck, softer, her mouth more tender . . .

Ash moistened suddenly dry lips. Along with her unaccustomed body, she had given him her heart last night. Had he realized it?

She winced at the thought. A blast of shyness scorched her like forest flame. She could not face him, she realized in sudden panic. Not like this, naked and horribly vulnerable. She needed to get some clothes on. And more, she needed to restore some of that defensive wall of self-containment that Jake had breached so confidently, so easily, last night.

She scrambled out of bed, grabbed some clothes and fled in the direction of coffee. She was bundling down the staircase, settling the tee-shirt over her cotton shorts when the telephone rang.

'Ash?' It was Tim Padgett, sounding less than his usual easy-going self.

350

'Yes. How are you?'

But he had no time for pleasantries. 'Is Dare still with you?'

Ash jumped and went scarlet. She almost looked over her shoulder.

'Why do you ask?' she said warily.

'I'm coming over.' He was grim.

'What? Why?'

'Do you know what he's done?'

Yes, she thought. Changed my life for ever. She rubbed her cheek against the new-awakened skin of her shoulder, surveying herself in the curlicued mirror behind the telephone. The brilliant morning light illuminated last night's ravages all too clearly. All of them: feverish eyes, the newly sensual curve to her soft mouth and small tell-tale bruises. Her pale redhead's skin bruised easily and they had not been gentle with each other last night. A small smile curled the corners of her mouth.

'Ash? Are you there?'

'Yes.'

'He's got a private eye digging into the Planning Committee.'

Ash was not much moved. 'He uses a lot of private detectives.'

'Are you telling me you knew?' Tim's voice rose to a scream of outrage.

'Not specifically . . .'

'He was turning over Council records,' Tim interrupted. She could hear the tension in his voice. 'Minutes, applications, the works.'

Ash was bewildered. 'So?'

351

'I'm coming over,' Tim said again. 'I'm going to have it out with him.' He added, as if on an afterthought. 'Do you know there were people out on the hill looking for badgers last night? Do you think that was coincidence?'

'What do you mean?'

'No badger watchers round here for years. Then Jake Dare decides he wants Hayes Wood. And all of a sudden the watchers are back, looking. Do you think it's coincidence?'

'Of course,' said Ash puzzled. 'Jake isn't interested in badgers.'

'Quite,' said Tim drily. 'He won't get planning permission if there are badgers in residence.'

'Are you saying – Oh, come on,' said Ash.

'God, Ash, you just don't live in the real world.' Tim did not sound quite as amiable as usual. 'You tell Dare I'm coming over.'

He slammed the phone down. Ash turned and went to the kitchen, hugging her arms round her. Jake could not have sent people out to trap the badgers, surely? She tried desperately to remember if she had let her suspicions about the badger set fall before he left Hayes Manor. Try as she would, she could not remember.

She fed a subdued Rusty, then made coffee. Then she sat at the kitchen table, looking at the mug, not touching it. She had known Jake had an ulterior motive. Hadn't she? Or had she always secretly hoped that it was not true?

The kitchen door banged back on its hinges.

'You're dressed,' Jake said displeased.

Ash looked up slowly. He was devastatingly handsome in an old towelling robe that he must have unearthed from

352

the airing cupboard. His hair was wet and spiky from the shower. He had not shaved. It gave him a raffish appearance, like a very tall, thin pirate.

'Good morning,' she said.

His brows rose. 'You're very formal.'

He came across to her. His intention was evident. Could he look like that, so gentle, so *loving*, if he had sent out hunters after her badgers? She could not believe it. And yet what purpose could Tim have in lying?

Ash turned her face quickly, so that his kiss fell on her cheek, not her mouth. He stopped as if he had walked into a wall.

'What's this?'

He took her by the shoulders and held her away from him, scanning her face. 'Regrets?'

Ash swallowed. 'Yes,' she said baldly.

Jake was unalarmed. 'You'll get used to it.' There was a world of gentle amusement in his voice.

'Will you tell me something?'

He sat on the corner of the table, smiling down at her. He reached out and traced her eyebrow. 'Anything,' he said absently.

His touch seemed to set up reverberations through every nerve. Ash quivered in spite of herself.

She said harshly, 'Have you got people out in Hayes Wood looking for badgers?'

Jake was taken aback. His hand fell. 'That's some change of subject.' His tone was rueful. But his eyes slid away from hers.

Ash felt as if the kitchen floor had suddenly fractured and started to slide over a precipice.

'You have,' she whispered.

'Hey, Ash. After what happened last night you want to talk about badgers?'

There was a mirror on the wall behind him. She could see her reflection. Her eyes were huge. Betrayed, she thought. A fist closed over Ash's heart and squeezed it until she couldn't breathe.

'Yes,' she said in a voice she didn't recognize.

He had listened to everything she had said and then he had made his plans. And then, just in case his big-city methods didn't work, Jake Dare had taken out a little insurance. Why else would he have made love to her last night, after all? Ash realized that she felt sick.

'Then I'm here to tell you you've got a lot to learn,' he said caressingly.

She met his eyes then. Hers were blazing. 'No, thank you.'

She felt the shock run through him. His hands fell from her shoulders.

'What?' he said blankly.

'No, thank you, I don't want to learn any more from you.'

His eyes searched her face. 'You're running away again.'

Ash allowed herself a wintry smile. 'No. You will be. I want you to leave, please.'

Jake's eyes narrowed. The thin face closed, all expression wiped off. For an unnerving moment, their eyes locked.

Then he drawled, 'I don't think so. I'm not leaving, darling. You and I have too much to talk about.'

'We have nothing to talk about,' she flashed.

'Oh, but we have.' The mockery was savage. 'We had great sex last night, for one thing. That deserves a word or two, wouldn't you say?'

Ash felt as if he had stabbed her to the heart. She was not going to let him see it, though. She did not have much pride left, but what she had she was going to defend to the death.

She managed a theatrical sigh. 'Jake, you're a clever man and a terrific lover but face it. You've lost the game.'

He drew a jagged little breath. 'What damned game? I didn't go to bed with a wood last night. I went to bed with *you*.'

'Oh, very good,' Ash said approvingly. 'Imaginative too. Why aren't I convinced?'

'You're paranoid.'

She stood up. 'Oh, stop it,' she said. 'We both know what you've been doing. And why. You wormed your way into my house so you could seduce me. You thought then I would agree to your scheme. Can you look me in the eye and tell me I'm wrong? Can you?'

The green eyes flickered. He did not exactly acknowledge his guilt but you could see he did not like it.

She said flatly, 'I'm not going to sell you Hayes Wood. I told you I wouldn't and I won't.' Her voice shook suddenly. 'Not if you gas every badger in the area. So go home and forget it.'

'Not if I – '

Ash sprang to her feet. 'I want you out of my house. *Now*.'

He ignored that. 'Who told you I knew about the badgers?'

355

Ash made a dismissive gesture. 'Someone who cares about them.'

He laughed harshly. 'I'll just bet. Who?'

It was hardly important. Ash shrugged. 'Tim Padgett.'

'Padgett.' He sounded savage.

'He said he was coming over to talk to you.'

'Oh no, he isn't. This is something you and I settle on our own.'

'You're not listening to me. I want you to go.'

His voice became urgent. 'Ash, for heaven's sake. Listen to your instincts for once.'

It was her instincts that had got her into bed with him in the first place. Ash gave a mirthless laugh. He took hold of her fiercely. Ash flung herself away, the chair crashing over behind her. Jake froze.

Ash stepped back, pulling her tee-shirt back into order. It was too late. Jake saw what Ash herself had seen earlier: the faint but unmistakable marks that one body had made upon the other in the act of love.

'Oh great heavens,' said Jake. He was utterly disconcerted.

She whisked away from him. His face looked pinched suddenly. His eyes were nearly black.

'I hurt you.' It was not a question.

For once he did not look like a cool manipulator. 'Ash, you have to believe me. I never meant to hurt you.' He sounded shaken.

That, Ash thought, was probably true. It did not make it any easier to bear.

'You don't know me well enough to hurt me,' she said. It was quiet but the venom was unmistakable. 'Don't let last night deceive you. It takes more than sex to get to know someone, you know.'

Jake drew in an audible breath. There was a charged silence. Then he drawled, 'Oh, I think I know quite a lot about you, Ashley Lawrence. Communication takes many forms. And I have my bruises too, darling.'

Their eyes locked in naked enmity; hers ashamed, his hard and angry.

'Your friend Joanne thinks you and Peter Lawrence were the perfect couple,' he said after a moment. 'I think, after last night, we both know that's not true, don't we?'

It was the last thing she expected. Ash gasped as if she had walked into a flamethrower. Jake's mouth tilted in a smile quite without humour.

'I'll pay for my own mistakes. And gladly. But I'm not taking Peter Lawrence's punishment,' he said. 'I'm not leaving until we have had this out.'

'I hate you,' said Ash with fervour.

Jake was bored. 'Tell me something I don't know.'

And then Tim Padgett walked in.

'Get out,' snarled Jake.

After one hard glance, he did not spare him a second look. Ash did not look at Tim at all. She was as tense as an overwound spring.

Tim said in outrage, 'Ash, are you going to let him talk to me like that?'

'I can't – ' she began, trying to stay cool.

But it was too late. Jake's eyes met hers. They were molten. She knew suddenly that there was nothing he would not say, whether Tim was there or not. She had pushed him too far.

357

Ash's self-control broke. She fled. She knew quite well that both of them were staring after her; both of them furious. It made no difference. If she didn't get away on her own she was going to explode.

She called Rusty and went off to a far stretch of the little river. She managed to stay alone for all of forty minutes. She was crouching on a rather wobbly stepping stone, reaching into the whirling water for weeds that needed clearing, when she heard a step behind her. Determinedly she did not look round. It was no use.

'What the hell,' said Jake Dare, 'do you think you're doing?'

Ash looked over her shoulder. At least he was dressed this time. In fact, he was immaculate even in yesterday's fawn trousers and ivory shirt. He looked tough and handsome and mad as a hornet. Her stone wobbled and she grabbed for the edge of it.

'Go away,' she said breathlessly.

'Get back onto the bank at once.'

Her chin came up immediately at the peremptory tone. 'Don't be ridiculous.'

'You are standing,' he said evenly, 'on impacted mud. It could fall apart at the slightest change in water pressure.'

Ash was startled. She looked down, peering at her foothold. The water swirled and roiled over it but, to her chagrin, she saw he was right.

She was not going to admit it, though. 'What's going to change the pressure of the water? This is summer, you know. We haven't had rain for days.'

'You've heard of dams?' he said politely. 'They build up and the water level rises and then one day the dam bursts and swoosh . . . no more stepping stones.'

Ash swung round and glared at him, her hands on her hips. 'We are not talking about the great, grey, greasy Limpopo river here. This is a relatively small tributary of the Thames. I'm hardly going to drown in a couple of feet of water.'

Jake surveyed her unflatteringly. 'You're talking to me about rivers? I was born in Memphis. We have a class river there. And people still drown in creeks with three inches of water. Get back here.'

Ash stood mutinously where she was.

'Now,' Jake said.

'Go to hell.'

His eyes locked with hers. They were narrowed to slits and green as a cat's. A cat looking for a fight on the roof tops. 'You want me to fetch you?' he asked gently.

'You wouldn't.'

He laughed.

Ash said, 'Haven't you manhandled me enough?' Just for a moment he seemed to wince, as if she had hurt him. But when she looked at him more closely, he was laughing again, that glittery devil's laugh that made him look as if he did not care what anyone thought about him and never had.

Then, before she knew what he was about, he took three steps forward and hoisted her over his shoulder. It was neither dignified nor romantic. But it was undeniably effective.

Rusty came prancing up.

'Down!' said Jake.

At once Rusty sank onto his haunches, panting. Jake

deposited Ash beside her dog. His eyes narrowed to slits.

'Manners,' he said lightly. 'That's what you both need.'

'*Oh!*' Ash sprang to her feet. 'Was that why you seduced me last night? Because you couldn't resist teaching me *manners?*' she spat.

Jake went suddenly very still. 'That must be it,' he said at last quietly. 'And what about you? The seduction was mutual, as I recall.' Suddenly he was mimicking her and it was not gentle. '"So this is *it*!" What couldn't you resist, Ash?'

Ash thought she would go up in flames with fury and pain. She sought for the most hurtful thing she could say and found it. It was a lie and she did not care.

'Oh, I made love to you on legal advice,' she retorted.

His eyes flickered and then went absolutely blank. 'I'm sorry?'

'My lawyer told me you were quite capable of making a really nasty court case about Rusty. So he told me to do anything I had to do to keep you sweet.' She shrugged. 'So I did.'

There was a silence which suddenly made her quail. A muscle worked in his cheek. 'What excellent advisers you have,' he said, too quietly, too courteously.

Ash thought she had never seen such coldness; such contempt.

'It's a real shame you can't think for yourself.' The words bit. 'You might even find it enlightening.'

She was silenced.

'And you don't need to worry about throwing me out,' he added. 'I find I've had all I can take of the local wildlife.'

And he was gone.

CHAPTER 14

Ash flung a handful of sopping river weed after him. It hit the earth with a squashy sound. Jake did not turn round.

But over his shoulder he flung, 'Grow up, Ash.'

His figure got smaller and smaller on the path back to the house. Then disappeared.

Eventually Ash went back. His car had gone. The house looked oddly forlorn. For the first time ever she did not want to go inside. It had been her refuge for so long. Yet looking at it from the terrace, she felt as if it had turned into a prison. A solitary prison.

Ash faced it. Without Jake it felt empty.

In the next few days she found out how totally he had spoilt it for her. Her bedroom was the worst of all. She tossed and turned and, every time she closed her eyes, saw only Jake. In the end she got up and wrapped the robe he had discarded around her. Wearing it, she trailed into the master bedroom and lay down on the bed he had stripped. For the first time, when she laid her head on the pillow she did not feel the shadow of those empty nights with Peter.

She realized that she could barely remember them, or

Peter's accusations; not even his terrible, paralysing coldness. It shocked her. Ash sat up, clasping her arms round her. Was it over then, at last? The regrets, the guilt. Had they been burned away in the flame of a single night with Jake?

In a way, the thought was almost terrifying. Jake had made her feel like a woman, Ash realized suddenly. Not a responsibility, not the unwanted girl-bride, price of a hard bargain; but a woman in her own right. What's more he had made her feel like a woman he wanted. Almost like a woman who was loved.

If only he had not been using her.

'You can't have everything,' she told herself cynically. 'At least you've got something out of this. Use it, for God's sake.'

By the time Em arrived the next morning, Ash had made up her mind what she was going to do.

'I'm going to London for a few days,' Ash said airily. 'To stay with my father. Can you feed the cats, please, Em? I've written a cheque for your wages and a float for the housekeeping.' She handed it over. 'I'll ring you when I know when I'll be back.'

Em took the cheque slowly. 'Your father, is it?'

'He's been asking me for weeks.'

That was true enough. Sir Miles had returned from a Caribbean cruise with a spectacular tan and an attentive widow he was having trouble in avoiding. He had begged Ash to come and rescue him. Ash had laughed. It was not the first time. Her father was equally susceptible and unwise and she had never taken his occasional attachments very seriously. Suddenly Ash had more sympathy for him.

Em sniffed. 'If you say so,' she said unimpressed. 'What am I to say to anyone who rings here? Give them your father's number?'

'No one will,' Ash said sharply.

It was a fantasy she could not afford to entertain.

Disappointingly, Em accepted it. 'Have a good time,' she said.

In Dare's offices everyone knew that Jake's mood was volcanic.

'Keep out of his way,' Barbara advised Tony.

But Jake had summoned him. Disobeying would have been worse. He swallowed hard and went into Jake's office.

Molly Hall saw Bob Cummings driving out of the lane that led up to the animal centre. She waved him down.

'Is it true that you're going to release that badger cub before Ash goes away?' she asked.

Bob smiled. 'Chris getting worried? No, there's no chance of that. He's not strong enough yet. Anyway, we're not even sure there's a badger colony still in the area. You tell Chris, we won't let him go till we're sure there's a reasonable chance of him surviving.'

'But I thought – '

Bob's face darkened. 'You've been listening to Mr Padgett. Very excitable chap, young Mr Padgett. No doubt he means well, but – '

Molly knew the two men did not like each other. She said tactfully, 'What will happen to the cub then?'

'I've just taken it into the centre. Now it's on its feet, it won't be a problem. You tell the boys they can come round and see it any time.'

Roger Ruffin reported to his client.

'I don't know what's going on, and that's a fact. I thought he was out to frighten Ashley Lawrence. Or maybe marry her; she's rich enough to attract a chap like that. But now she's going away and nothing is resolved.'

'It will be,' said the client. 'There's too much money involved for this one to lie down and die.'

Sir Miles's luxury flat in Eaton Square had never been Ash's home. For years he had used it during only the most occasional visits to England.

'In case my father kidnapped me and locked me in the bank,' he used to joke.

There was more than a grain of truth there and everyone knew it. There had been nothing more important to Grandfather than Kimbell's and his only son had been a bitter disappointment. So he had made sure his only grandchild was better trained. Sir Miles had not been strong enough to withstand the old tyrant, but Ash knew he was not proud of the way he had left her to be brought up by her grandfather.

'Darling girl.' Sir Miles embraced her in a waft of sandalwood cologne. He held her away from him. 'You look scrawny,' he said, with a father's frankness. 'Something wrong, my poppet?'

Ash was shocked by his perception. She knew he felt guilty about her. She did not realize he was that sensitive as well.

'Just tired,' she said gruffly.

He patted her hand, taking her into the drawing-room. 'I know. I know. Problems with voles. Beastly developers. You said.'

'Otters,' said Ash. Her father did not share her enthusiasms, but he had got the general idea of the otter project. She had told him weeks ago about the threat posed by Dare's development plans. She had not told him about Jake Dare's betrayal of the badgers. For some reason that hurt too much.

He shrugged. 'Whatever. Don't let it get you down, poppet. Now, tell me what do you want to do in the big bad metropolis?'

Ash thought of Jake's stricture. Her smile was lopsided. 'Grow up!'

Sir Miles was intrigued. But all he said was, 'About time. Oh, this is nice. We'll hit the town.'

Ash hugged him. 'Can you afford to show your nose out of doors?' she teased. 'What about the blonde?'

Sir Miles told her without rancour that she was a naughty girl.

'I shall be too busy to see her while I'm showing my beautiful daughter the town,' he said fluently, adding, 'And getting you some decent clothes. It looks time somebody did.'

He was as good as his word. A life of pleasure – drifting, as bitterly described by his father – had given Sir Miles a very good idea of style and where to find it. He took Ash to a discreet boutique and left her with strict instructions not to come home until she had acquired a basic wardrobe.

'And don't forget something exotic,' he added, nodding

at a swirl of emerald, turquoise and crimson.

Ash was faintly alarmed. 'I'm not the exotic type.'

Sir Miles was annoyed. 'Show her,' he told the sales staff.

He left. They did.

Several hours later Ash met him at his club, as instructed. She was wearing an expression of total bemusement and an understated suit of such exquisite cut that heads turned as she walked in.

Her father rose to his feet, delighted. He was undismayed by the number of packages that the saleswomen assured Ash were essential to restore her wardrobe, and equally undismayed by the bill.

'Present, poppet,' he said when Ash protested. 'I was never able to give you very much when you were younger. Deferred pleasure for me.'

He squeezed her hand almost shyly and they sat. Ash gave a sigh of contentment. She had always loved her father's club; the old leather furniture and the members who were even older; the smell of cigar smoke and good coffee.

Her father leaned forward. 'Got a surprise for you.'

He nodded. Laughing, Ash followed his gaze. Her breath caught and all desire to laugh evaporated.

'Oh, *no*.'

Sir Miles seemed not to notice. 'Jake Dare,' he explained kindly. 'That's your man. I'll get him over and you can bend his ear about voles.' He raised his hand.

Ash watched in something approaching despair as the all-too familiar figure detached himself from his companions and came across to them.

Her father glanced down at her. 'Ash, darling, this is – '

Ash swallowed. 'I know,' she said baldly.

Above her head Jake said coolly, 'We've met.'

Ash murmured something unintelligible.

Sir Miles was pleased. ''Course you have. Come and join us,' he said hospitably, patting the leather sofa beside him.

Jake sat. He did not take his eyes off Ash. She kept her head determinedly bent. Sir Miles looked from one to the other. One eyebrow rose.

'I'll go and see about rustling up some more drinks,' he said heartily, ignoring both the bell beside him and the circulating waiters.

Neither Ash nor Jake responded. He left them.

Jake leaned back in the sofa, one immaculate leg crossed over the other. He looked completely relaxed, one arm along the back of the sofa, the other lying casually on its arm. Or was it casual, Ash thought, watching out of the corner of her eye. Was there tension in the long fingers held so still against the scrolled armrest?

She ventured a quick look at him under her lashes. She had seen him cool. She had seen him casual. She had, God help her, seen him naked and driven. She had never seen him so intimidatingly remote. She suddenly realized, with a little shock, that he was startlingly good-looking. And that he knew it.

How had she forgotten that? When had he become, not a handsome, infinitely desirable stranger but Jake who was her lover? And did he know it?

Her face burned suddenly. The silence stretched between them agonizingly.

367

'You're looking very – polished,' he said at last.

She raised her eyes. 'Grown up at last?' she said with a smile that had an edge to it.

His own smile did not reach his eyes. 'Too right. And then some.'

'Thank you.'

'Is that why you came to town?' He sounded odd.

Ash said the first thing that came into her head. 'No. I'm doing a protection job for my father. He's got a blonde after him.'

'I see.'

Sir Miles returned with a waiter. Jake stood up quickly. 'Nothing for me, thank you. I've got to go.'

Sir Miles looked disappointed. 'Another time, then. Ash wants to convert you to vole protection.'

Jake's smile did not reach his eyes. 'I am aware.'

'I've told her animals are all very well but people have rights, too. Doesn't believe me. You'd better come to dinner and teach her the facts of life,' he said, beaming at Jake.

There was an appalled silence. Jake, understandably, choked.

Ash felt as if someone had poured boiling oil over her. Not just her face, her whole body burned. And underneath the heated embarrassment, there was the cold of shock. She did not *believe* it. She met Jake's eyes and found they were dancing. She, however, could not even pretend to sophistication.

'I shall be delighted.'

Ash clenched her hands in her lap. The knuckles showed white. 'I'm not sure how long I shall be here,' she said rapidly. Jake looked at her under his brows. Behind the mischief there was a steady question – and a dark intent which she refused to recognize. Ash could not meet his eyes. But she knew the question was there.

But all he said was, 'Then let it be soon.'

And, of course, it was.

By Ash's standards it was a large party; by her father's rather small. It could not have been more different from the Hall's friendly barbecue. Jake, in dinner jacket and starched shirt, looked devastating and completely at home. Unlike Ash.

At dinner he concentrated totally on charming a dazzled model. After dinner he lost himself in the crowd. Ash told herself she was glad.

When replacement pots of coffee were brought in, Sir Miles nodded significantly at the balcony. Knowing her duty, Ash took a coffee pot out there.

'Would you like . . .?'

But there was only one occupant of the balcony. Very much at his ease in the patio chair, long legs stretched in front of him. Waiting for her, Ash thought.

She stopped dead, clutching the Georgian silver coffee pot in front of her like a shield. She cast a rapid look back over her shoulder. Nobody in the drawingroom seemed to have noticed – except her father.

Sir Miles was standing in front of the fireplace looking at her. He gave another nod. Ash was almost certain that he knew that Jake was out here and began for the first time to wonder how well they knew each other. She looked back at the lounging figure.

'. . . like some more coffee?' she finished huskily.

Silently Jake indicated a balloon glass of brandy on the table in front of him.

'Ah,' said Ash, relieved. She prepared to leave, 'No coffee.'

Jake leaned forward. 'Sit down.'

It did not sound like a polite guest talking to a good hostess. Ash eyed him warily and did not obey.

'Ashley Lawrence, you surely are a contrary woman,' Jake said softly. 'Sit down.'

'Why should I?'

The hooded eyes lifted. A small smile curled the long mouth.

'Because I've got a lot to say to you and you are wearing high heels which you are not used to,' Jake answered literally. 'You can stand if you like, but your feet are going to hurt.'

Ash glared at him. 'I don't have to listen.'

Jake gave a ghost of smile. 'Oh, yes you do.' He lifted his shoulders in a shrug. 'You can do it out here in relative privacy. Or I'll follow you back in there and you can hear it in front of an interested audience. But hear it you will.'

Ash sat down.

Jake looked at her broodingly. All of a sudden Ash had the disturbing impression that he was angry. Really angry. But when he spoke it was still in that cool, lazy drawl.

'Now, let's talk. I don't know what happened that last day. I do know, I don't like it.'

Ash raised her eyebrows. 'Happened?'

Jake met her eyes and held them.

'When we made love.' His voice was level. '*After* we made love.'

Ash held onto an indifferent expression for all she was

worth. Inside the shaking began. She was right, she realized. He was serious. Behind the still, clever face, there were flames of real outrage.

'Well?' she said.

Jake said softly, 'I've known a lot of ladies in my time. They've never thrown me out without so much as a bowl of cornflakes before.'

The flippancy flicked like a whip. Ash, in her turn, was outraged. She found her fingers clenching painfully round the bone handle of the coffee pot. Hurriedly she put it down.

'Oh?' she said very nastily before he noticed the shaking. 'You expect bed *and* breakfast?'

Jake said with sudden, shocking harshness, 'Don't push your luck. Don't forget I wasn't born a gentleman. Push me and I might revert to my origins.'

Ash stared. Somehow, she did not know how, she had scored a small hit there. It was not much but it was something, since she could not stop shaking, to boost her courage. To have got through that diamond hard skin of his was something.

She sat back in her chair, crossed one gold sandalled foot over the other and gave him a cool smile.

'Caveman?'

There was a ferocious silence.

'You – ' He clamped his teeth shut as if it was an act of supreme will to suppress what he had been going to say.

There was a tense pause. Ash cast a longing look over her shoulder at the oblivious party.

'There's just one thing I want to know,' Jake said eventually. 'Tell me that and you can go.'

Ash did not want to hear. Did not dare to hear. She summoned up all the memories of their night together. How she had loved him. How she had *trusted* him. And then she let herself remember what betrayal felt like.

She said harshly, 'I'm not telling you one damn thing more. I've already told you far too much. And by golly you used it, didn't you?'

His face darkened. 'If this is about those damn badgers – '

Ash almost screamed at him. 'This is about *me*.'

'What?'

'Don't you see, you stupid man? You didn't just set people off hunting those badgers. You betrayed *me*.'

'Ash.' He sounded shaken. 'I never – '

'Oh, stop it,' she said, suddenly weary. 'You meant to betray me from the first moment we met. It's normal in your world, isn't it?'

'My world?'

'I remember you said to me once: "All's fair in love and property deals." I should have believed you.'

'Ash, this is stupid. If you'll just *listen* – '

But Ash was at the end of her tether. She was hardly even listening to him any more.

'If I got hurt, I have no one to blame but myself. You gave me fair warning.'

And rising from her chair she left him alone.

CHAPTER 15

Jake left the party early. Sir Miles raised his eyebrows but did not comment. Eloquently. When the other guests had all left, Ash could bear it no longer.

'Well, go on, Daddy. Say it.'

Sir Miles shrugged. 'What's to say? I'm sorry it didn't work out.'

It was clear that he was not talking about an accommodation between development and conservation issues. Ash closed her eyes wearily.

'Don't see things that aren't there, Daddy.'

'I like him.' He looked at her shrewdly. 'I think you do, too.'

Ash opened her eyes and regarded him levelly. 'How do you know him?'

Her father knew her too well to prevaricate. 'He came to see me. Said he – er – knew you. Said he was concerned that you seemed to have backed out of life, somehow. Said he wanted to know you and couldn't get to first base.'

Ash sighed. 'Oh, Daddy. Matchmaking?'

He was affronted. 'I wouldn't dream of it. You're old enough and clever enough to make your own matches.' He paused and then added deliberately, 'This time.'

Ash bit her lip. 'Don't ask me to talk about Peter,' she said in a whisper.

Her father sighed. 'But – no. No, of course not,' he said heavily.

Jake did not call the next day. He sent her a sumptuous bouquet of hot-house flowers accompanied by a thank-you note of crushing formality. It made Ash so angry that she lobbed the card straight into the bin. The flowers nearly followed. But it was not their fault that they were exotic lilies instead of her beloved roses. So she put them in a vase in her father's study and closed the door on them.

Sir Miles, entering his study unprepared, inhaled one nose full of their overpowering scent and announced he was going to his club.

'For the whole day,' he added firmly. 'Got a couple of people to see. Don't wait dinner for me.'

Ash went home. There was no point in doing anything else. She took her case full of smart new clothes and her heavy heart and left a note on her father's bureau. No one would expect her at Hayes Manor, but she just did not care. She wanted to be on her own.

Jake went to a smart mews house and leaned on the doorbell until a surprised cleaning lady opened it.

'Miss Newman,' he said, pushing past her.

'She's not – '

'Then I shall just have to find out where she is,' he said pleasantly. He went to a table spread with a frilled cover and a collapsing pile of notes and invitations and began to flick through them with fierce fingers.

'You can't do that,' said the cleaning lady, pardonably outraged.

Jake turned a face on her that made her take three steps backwards before she realized it.

'Oh, but I can.'

Rosalind Newman decided to appear.

'Hello, Jake. I thought I heard your voice.' She, too, was surprised by his expression. But she was made of sterner stuff than her domestic. 'Coffee?' she said coolly.

He threw the papers away from him. 'No more games, Rosalind.'

'I don't know what you mean.'

'Oh, I think you do.'

She gave a soft laugh. 'I sent the notice to the papers, Jake. What more do you want?'

'I want to know what is going on at Hayes Manor.'

She frowned. 'I don't think I know the name.'

Jake gave a soft laugh. 'Wrong card to play, Rosie. You should have said it was your father's idea. I might have believed that.'

A faint hint of annoyance crossed the smooth brow. 'I don't know anything about my father's business. I can't discuss it.'

'Your father,' he said too pleasantly, 'is a clapped-out old crook. He made a lot of money when it was easy to make money. It never occurred to him that one day it would be more difficult, did it? That was why he kept on spending. That was why you came looking for me, that day on the polo field.'

She shrugged, meeting his eyes with a hard glint. 'And if I did?'

'You're a clever girl, Rosie. You may not know much about investment but you can see when disaster is coming. Which was more than your father could. Was it your idea to get me on board for the Hayes Wood project?'

She looked away. 'Why not? It's the sort of thing you've done a hundred times before.'

'No,' Jake said evenly. 'I've built all sorts of buildings. I've invested in all sorts of developments in my time. I get the contracts, I get the permissions. I go ahead. Hayes Wood wasn't like that at all, was it?'

Now she was really uneasy. 'What do you mean?'

'I mean you got planning permission for a shopping precinct you never meant to build. Eric Stenson got wind of it and started pulling out. But I was out of the country. I didn't hear the rumours. I damn nearly got dragged in so deep it would have cost me my reputation to get clear.'

Rosie laughed scornfully. 'Why should we bother to set up a project we didn't mean to build?'

'Oh, but you did mean to build. Only not a shopping mall. That only covered a tiny piece of land. You wanted a whole housing estate.'

Rosie snorted. 'You're crazy. We would never have got permission to build a housing estate.' She stopped dead suddenly.

'Quite,' said Jake. 'So you bought yourself a bit of private insurance, didn't you? Local information, local investor and local activist, if necessary. Very clever, Rosie. Your dad would never have thought of it.'

Suddenly she was furious. 'Well, I did. And it worked. That stupid Lawrence woman thinks you're the local vandal. You'll never prove anything else.'

Jake was rather pale round the mouth. 'Maybe not. But I can make sure it goes no further. I give you fair warning, Rosie. This stops here and now.'

She laughed at him. 'Or what?'

He showed his teeth. 'Or I'll suggest to the bank they might want to take a long look at the security for your father's loan. Without Stenson or Dare, he doesn't look such a hot proposition, does he?'

'You wouldn't.'

Jake just smiled.

Rosie said furiously, 'That stupid Lawrence piece. It's all her fault. You've gone soft, Jake.'

He shook his head. 'I think perhaps I've come to my senses.' He looked her up and down as if he had never seen her before. 'I used to think women were all deceivers. I used to think you couldn't help it. You were just born without a sense of moral proportion. Then I met Ash Lawrence. I didn't believe it at first; that a woman could be so transparent. Or so vulnerable.' He gave a soft laugh suddenly. 'It's taken some major battles but I think I've got there. All I have to do now is convince her that she can trust me.'

Rosie sneered. 'Touching.'

'No. Hard work. But worth it.' Jake smiled at her without warmth. 'And before I go you're going to tell me the name of your man on the ground.'

At the office, Tony Anderson said in despair, 'Again?'

'On the phone. Now.'

'Look, we've had protection and surveillance on a number of people in the past but this is ridiculous.'

Jake smiled. 'I don't think so. I've talked to Rosie Newman. She is not pleased with me. She let me think I scared her off but I think it's a ploy to put me off the scent.'

'Jake, I can't tell Eric Stenson you want his private eye to mount a round-the-clock protection on a badger set in darkest Oxfordshire. Once was enough. Ruffin thought you were mad but he did it as a favour. But again!'

'Don't argue,' said Jake. 'If she's going to do anything, Rosie will do it tonight before I do anything serious with the bank.' He gave an impatient sigh. 'Thank God, Ash Lawrence is out of it. She may be mad at me, but at least she's safe staying with her father.'

'Oh, that reminds me,' said Tony. 'Sir Miles phoned.'

'You talk to Stenson,' Jake said. 'I'll call Sir Miles.'

When he had done so, he was a great deal more than impatient.

'Get me Joanne Lambert,' he snapped at Barbara. And when she came on the phone he said without preamble, 'This chap Bob Cummings. Do you know how I can get hold of him? I mean fast.'

Joanne began to bridle.

'Listen,' said Jake, 'I've got no time to explain. I think Ash may be in danger. I thought she was safe in London. But she's bolted again. She's gone back to that damned great house and there's nobody there. If someone decides to do something stupid . . .'

Joanne stopped bridling. 'Is there any reason why they should?' she said sharply.

Jake was grim. 'Yes. It's my fault.'

Joanne said, 'I'll call her.'

'Her father has already tried. The line,' said Jake with

restraint, 'is permanently engaged. A fault, according to the phone company. They'll look into it tomorrow.'

'You mean it's been cut,' interpreted Joanne. 'I'm on my way.'

'So am I. You can come with me.'

Ash was on her own when the door bell rang that evening. She was sitting just inside the terrace windows, looking out over the luxuriant green of the gardens, trying not to remember last night's encounter and utterly failing to eat a salad supper. Desultorily she picked up the entryphone.

'Hello?'

'Let me in, Ash. I've got to talk to you.'

'Tim?' She was annoyed by the interruption. But she could not think of a reason to keep him out. She went slowly to the front door.

'I saw the lights,' said Tim. He sounded nervous, almost distracted. 'I thought you were in London.'

'I came back,' said Ash with something of a snap.

'Yes. Obviously. Look – '

'I'm tired, Tim,' she said untruthfully. 'If you want to talk about planning, can we make it another time?'

He said tensely, 'Did you see Dare in London?'

'And told him that I'm not selling him any land. So don't worry.'

There was an odd silence. Tim looked at the floor. Then he said, 'No. I won't worry.'

He came into the hall, shutting the door behind him. Ash stared, not understanding.

'I'm sorry, Ash,' he said. He sounded it. 'I never meant it to go this far.'

'What do you mean?'

He advanced towards her. For no particular reason that she could think of Ash gave ground.

'It's money, you see. Isn't it always? I thought Peter would lend me money. Then he died. Things were hard. I almost ran out of the stuff. And then Newman came along. My house, the Gate House, the animal centre and the Manor. If you put them all together you can build a sizeable estate. Plenty of money for all of us. Eric Stenson bought the Gate House. The centre was willing to sell even though Bob was against it. There was just you. And your otters and your badgers.'

Ash said, 'But you were heading the protest group.'

He smiled sadly, 'I was keeping an eye on the protest group. And the Planning Committee. To make sure nothing went wrong. I didn't expect Jake Dare to turn up in person. Or a bloody protected species to pop up in the middle of the site.'

Light began to dawn on Ash. 'It was you, hunting those badgers in the wood.'

Tim's smile was bitter. 'It would have been. Only your friend Jake Dare got there first. He bought them some protection, heaven help us. Saturday night there were a couple of serious heavies up there. My mates and I had to back off.'

He picked up the silver rose bowl from the hall table and weighed it in his hands.

'Then some nuts from the university got the place staked out.' He smiled again, unpleasantly. 'I was biding my time over the academics. Then I got a call to say it was tonight or never. So I told them I'd seen badgers on the other side of Latterfield. They'll be well out of the way by the time the boys and I get there.'

Ash said through stiff lips, 'And me?'

Tim hefted the rose bowl from one hand to another. He winced, feeling how heavy it was.

'I'm really sorry about that, Ash. You should have stayed in London.' He sounded honestly indignant.

'And as I haven't?'

Tim lifted his shoulders helplessly. 'What choice have I got? You know everything now. And you're not the type to keep quiet.' He advanced on her. 'Are you?'

Ash found herself wishing that Rusty was not so well-trained. If he was the sort of dog who could bring himself to attack people she could just call him in from the garden and . . .

A thought occurred to her.

Retreating, she said, 'Do you really think you can kill me, Tim?'

He grimaced. 'An accident. That's what – hey!'

Ash had ducked into the kitchen. She flung herself across it, throwing Em's stores in her wake as she did so.

Tim blundered after her. She heard him swear as he skidded in flour and sugar. Thank God for the kittens' inspiration, Ash thought.

She lost valuable time, fumbling with the kitchen bolt. Tim almost reached her. But she kicked wildly at the rocking chair, which juddered across the floor and caught him in the side before he had time to sidestep.

Then she was out in the garden, sobbing for breath and running, running. If she could only get to the rose garden, with its compost heap and tools, she was certain she could defend herself.

She did not hear the car. She did not hear Joanne and Jake call her name or the running steps round the house. She did hear the scream of frustration and fury as Jake dragged Tim to the ground and began to hit him. She stopped dead.

Very, very slowly, the fight went out of her. She leaned against a supporting post of the trellis. She did not think she could move, all of a sudden.

And that was where Jake found her.

'Ash,' he said.

He had lost his jacket and his shirt was hopelessly torn. He had the makings of a black eye and he moved as if his whole body was bruised. Ash thought she had never seen anything so wonderful. She still could not move. She held out her hands.

'You look as dreadful as I do,' she said on a choked laugh.

'Oh, *Ash*.'

He dragged her into his arms and held her. They did not say anything for a long time.

It was later, when Ahmed had arrived with a subdued group of hoodwinked badger minders, and Joanne had provided them all with what supper she could manage in the ruined kitchen, that Ash and Jake were alone at last. Joanne did not even argue with Ahmed. She went to bed, looking strained. Ahmed took the students off.

Jake saw them off and then went out on to the terrace.

'Ash?'

She was sitting on the oak bench. After the shocks of the evening she was feeling very shaky but she was quite determined that Jake Dare was not going to bully her.

'I don't like the way you said that,' she said with spirit.

He was not giving any quarter. 'I'm not surprised. I've been talking to your father and I want to know a lot of things.'

Ash said with disdain, 'I suppose you know what you're talking about.'

'Oh, yes,' said Jake grimly. 'I know all right. I'm talking about the legend of the grieving widow. And how no living man is allowed to touch her.'

Ash flinched. But his tone made her so angry that it swamped her wincing guilt. 'That's hardly true. God help me, you touched me.'

'Did I?'

She stood up and took a furious step forward. 'Don't you dare play word games with me.'

'Is it worse than the games you played with me?'

'What games?' Ash said with contempt.

In the moonlight, his eyes were glittering. He looked more like a pirate than she had ever seen him do before. A dangerous pirate.

'Oh, I'd say somewhere between Joan of Arc and the princess and the frog,' he drawled.

'What?'

'Straight out of a story book, anyway. And a million miles from real life.'

Ash was shaking with temper. Or she assured herself it was temper. 'Real life meaning you, I suppose?'

Jake's smile made her want to hit him. 'Now you've got it.'

'I have not – ' yelled Ash.

She got no further. In a swift movement which she completely failed to predict Jake caught her up by the shoulders. His mouth closed on hers. It was as if they belonged together.

Ash went limp. All the feelings she had dammed up burst out and buffeted her. Under the impact, she staggered a little. Jake's arms tightened. But he did not lift his head.

And then she began to kiss him back.

After a long, long while he said in a thickened voice, 'Welcome back to the real world, Ash.'

Her hair was spilling over his hands, her whole body pliant. But she was still fighting back. 'Is this what you wanted? Why you plotted with my father?' she taunted him.

He sent her an ironic look. He was a little pale, but in full command of himself.

'I'm not much of a plotter, Ash. Your father said you were so hooked on your grief that you wouldn't even talk to me. I – well, I don't buy that. I don't know why you're running away from me. But it sure as hell isn't the perfect relationship you had with Peter Lawrence.'

Ash went very still. 'What do you mean?' she said huskily.

He did not answer but the look he sent her was almost compassionate. Ash pulled away sharply and fled into the shadowed drawing-room. She was aware that Jake had followed her.

She put on a small table light and poured a drink, any drink. She gulped it down. It was neat tonic water. She grimaced. Jake propped himself in the doorway, looking at her gravely.

'There you go again. Anyone mentions his name and you run.'

Ash did not say anything. She searched for mineral water among her well-stocked bar.

Jake said carefully to the back of her head, 'Ash, I made love to you. I'm no mind reader but I'm not a fool either. I don't believe you felt so much for Peter Lawrence you want to lock yourself away for the rest of your life.'

'You have no idea at all of how I felt about Peter Lawrence,' Ash said harshly.

He did not argue. 'Then tell me.'

She found the mineral water. The top was stiff. She tried unscrewing it with fingers that shook pitiably. At least it meant she did not have to look at him.

'I can't. I mean – I haven't told anyone. I don't know how.'

Jake came and took the bottle out of her hands. He unscrewed it, poured a glass and gave it to her. He was scrupulous not to touch her fingers.

'Well, let me tell you what I already know. You were married off at eighteen to your grandfather's heir apparent.'

Ash shut her eyes. 'Put like that, it doesn't sound impressive, does it?'

'No. It wasn't impressive. But it also wasn't your fault. You were young and everyone told you how suitable it was.'

She opened her eyes. They were tearless. 'Don't try writing the speech for the defence, Jake. I wasn't a child. I went into it with my eyes open. I was in love.'

He frowned. 'You thought you were.'

'Whatever. Nobody forced me. I knew Peter wasn't – well, wasn't as committed as I was.' She swallowed. She was going to shock him; maybe even disgust him. She said rapidly, 'He didn't like making love to me. Even though he knew Grandfather wanted us to have children. In the end he could hardly bear to touch me.'

There was a terrible silence. She could not bear to look at Jake. She squared her shoulders.

'I knew it wasn't all my fault. But women are supposed to be able to deal with emotional problems, aren't they? I didn't know where to begin.'

Jake swore, vividly and shockingly. Ash was so startled she forgot she was afraid to see his expression. He was looking thunderous. She summoned up her courage and told him the whole truth.

'The night he died, we'd been fighting about it. Peter said I was so unattractive that nobody would ever want me. He said he'd been trapped by his commitment to Kimbell's. He'd had enough of feeding my spoilt brat's ego. He sounded as if he hated me. I said in that case I wanted a divorce. He said I was a fool and he wasn't going to stay and listen to nonsense.'

Jake did not move. Ash was remembering that terrible evening all too clearly.

'He banged out of the house. It was raining. His car hit the tree at the entrance to the drive. He was injured so badly he died. I went every day to the Clinic but he never recovered consciousness. I wanted him to forgive me. Yet when he died it set me free.'

386

There she had told him everything. Even the things she had hardly borne to admit to herself. Ash waited for revulsion.

It did not come. Instead Jake said slowly, 'You haven't been in mourning for the last three years. You've been doing penance.'

With an inarticulate exclamation he pulled her roughly into his arms. Ash rested against the remnants of impeccable suiting as if she had run a great race. She could feel his heart pounding under her cheek.

'He said it was my fault,' she said in muffled accents. 'I wanted too much. Did I?'

'It sounds to me as if you didn't want enough,' Jake said with conviction. He stroked her hair very gently, as if she were breakable and he had to take the greatest care of her.

She drew a deep breath and said painfully, 'He said I was voracious.'

Jake said blankly, '*What?*'

Ash could not repeat it. Then to her shocked astonishment, she felt his chest began to heave under her cheek. Jake was laughing.

Ash tipped her head back and stared in outrage. He brushed the back of his hand over her damp cheek.

'My darling, do you remember the trouble it took me to get you into bed? You cost me more sleepless nights than any damned takeover bid I've ever made. Strategic planning went wrong. Outmanoeuvred over and over again. I've never met anyone less voracious.'

'*Oh*,' said Ash, whipping out of his arms and retreating a safe distance.

But Jake was still laughing. 'There you are. Living

proof. I've been in the house for ten minutes and you haven't laid a finger on me. Even though you know I'm crazy about you.'

His eyes dancing, he managed to look distinctly wistful.

'You think everything's a joke, don't you?' she said uncertainly.

'Honey, I've had to keep a sense of humour. You said I couldn't talk you into a weekend in paradise. The way you've been behaving I was starting to believe it.'

Ash could hardly believe it. She scanned his face. He was not trying to hide his expression any more: it was naked. He was laughing but there was a deep tenderness there. Slowly, she gave him the small, scared beginnings of a smile.

He drew a shaken breath.

'Ash, I know I rushed you into bed too soon. I'll never forgive myself for that. But I didn't do it lightly. And I didn't do it because I thought you were easy.'

Ash flushed painfully. Jake did not move but he would not let her look away.

'I wanted you. More than I knew I could ever want another person,' he told her. 'Not just for that night but for all the nights to come.'

Ash shook her head. 'I don't believe it. I can't believe it.'

Jake ignored the interruption. 'And don't be deceived by my gentlemanly restraint. I still do.'

Ash saw that he was telling the truth. But he did not touch her. As if they were talking about the weather instead of the most important crisis of her life, he said conversationally, 'I want you to fight with and laugh with and make love with as long as we live. I'll dig your blasted potato patch. I'll clear your river banks.'

Ash said slowly, 'What about my badgers; and the otters?'

Jake laughed ruefully. 'I should have known. I ask the girl to marry me and all she wants to talk about is wildlife.'

'Marry?'

'If it makes you any happier, I've already stopped the project. I should never have got involved in it in the first place. I wouldn't have, if I hadn't been so busy and – well, frankly under pressure from a lady I thought at the time I wanted to marry. I didn't,' he added with feeling, 'begin to know the meaning of the word.'

'*Marry?*'

Jake shook his head. 'Want.'

'But – ' Ash sought for objections and could only find one. She did not know why she had remembered it. 'You said no more engagements.'

Jake grinned. 'That's right. You and I are going straight for the big one.'

Ash spread her hands in disbelief. Her thoughts whirled. 'You can't be serious.'

'Never more so.'

She saw it was true.

'Ash, I know you think all I do is take what I want and the hell with everything. I've done that, I admit. All I can say is, not with you.'

'A scarecrow? A scarecrow that stood in your way?'

Jake winced. 'OK, I admit that too. I had some crazy idea of charming you into selling me that damned land,' he said impatiently. 'I'm not proud of it. All I can say is I was jet-lagged and I wasn't thinking clearly. And I was mad as a hornet at Tony for letting me think that Mrs Lawrence was a little old widow lady. And even madder at the little old lady for driving me wild with lust,' he added with bitter self-mockery. 'So I wanted to turn the tables on all of you. It didn't last.'

Ash raised her eyebrows. 'Lust?'

He took an urgent step forward. 'I want you in my life as my wife and I never thought I'd say that again. But only if you want it, too. Do you?'

Ash hesitated. From somewhere, a great happiness seemed to be welling up. It made her feel stronger than she had ever imagined. Her self-doubt receded sharply.

Jake still did not touch her. The message was plain. It was her decision.

Still she hesitated. The blaze of feeling in his eyes admitted of no doubt what he wanted. Hesitantly Ash took a step forward. It seemed to her that Jake held his breath. Those treacherous doubts disappeared into infinity.

'Yes,' she said simply.

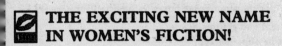

THE EXCITING NEW NAME IN WOMEN'S FICTION!

PLEASE HELP ME TO HELP YOU!

Dear *Scarlet* Reader,

As Editor of *Scarlet* Books I want to make sure that the books I offer you every month are up to the high standards *Scarlet* readers expect. And to do that I need to know a little more about you and your reading likes and dislikes. So please spare a few minutes to fill in the short questionnaire on the following pages and send it to me. I'll send *you* a surprise gift as a thank you!

Looking forward to hearing from you,

Sally Cooper

Editor-in-Chief, *Scarlet*

QUESTIONNAIRE

Please tick the appropriate boxes to indicate your answers

1 Where did you get this Scarlet title?
   Bought in Supermarket ☐
   Bought at W H Smith or other High St bookshop ☐
   Bought at book exchange or second-hand shop ☐
   Borrowed from a friend ☐
   Other _____

2 Did you enjoy reading it?
   A lot ☐   A little ☐   Not at all ☐

3 What did you particularly like about this book?
   Believable characters ☐   Easy to read ☐
   Good value for money ☐   Enjoyable locations ☐
   Interesting story ☐   Modern setting ☐
   Other _____

4 What did you particularly dislike about this book?
   _____

5 Would you buy another Scarlet book?
   Yes ☐   No ☐

6 What other kinds of book do you enjoy reading?
   Horror ☐   Puzzle books ☐   Historical fiction ☐
   General fiction ☐   Crime/Detective ☐   Cookery ☐
   Other _____

7 Which magazines do you enjoy most?
   Bella ☐   Best ☐   Woman's Weekly ☐
   Woman and Home ☐   Hello ☐   Cosmopolitan ☐
   Good Housekeeping ☐
   Other _____

cont.

And now a little about you –

8 How old are you?
Under 25 ☐   25–34 ☐   35–44 ☐
45–54 ☐   55–64 ☐   over 65 ☐

9 What is your marital status?
Single ☐   Married/living with partner ☐
Widowed ☐   Separated/divorced ☐

10 What is your current occupation?
Employed full-time ☐   Employed part-time ☐
Student ☐   Housewife full-time ☐
Unemployed ☐   Retired ☐

11 Do you have children? If so, how many and how old are they?
_____
_____

12 What is your annual household income?
under £10,000 ☐   £10–20,000 ☐   £20–30,000 ☐
£30–40,000 ☐   over £40,000 ☐

Miss/Mrs/Ms _____
Address _____
_____
_____
_____

Thank you for completing this questionnaire. Now tear it out – put it in an envelope and send it before 31 January 1997, to:

Sally Cooper, Editor-in-Chief

SCARLET
FREEPOST LON 3335
LONDON W8 4BR
Please use block capitals for address.
No stamp is required!   DECEP/7/96

Scarlet **titles coming next month:**

RENTON'S ROYAL Nina Tinsley
Sarah Renton is troubled. **Renton's Royal,** her one abiding passion, is under threat. Her rivals for power and success are other Renton women – who each have their own reasons for wanting to take over from Sarah. What these women all discover, in their search for success, is that passion and power make dangerous bedfellows . . .

DARK LEGACY Clare Benedict
Greg Randall haunted Bethany Lyall's dreams . . . and her every waking moment too. Before Bethany could follow her heart, though, she had to conquer the demons from the past and face the dangers in the present. Of the *three* men in her life, only Bethany could decide who was her friend, who was her enemy and who would be her lover!

WILD JUSTICE Liz Fielding
Book One of **The Beaumont Brides trilogy:**
Fizz Beaumont hates Luke Devlin before she even meets him! So Luke Devlin in the flesh is a total shock to her, particularly when he decides to take over her life. Fizz is so sure she can resist him, but then he kisses her – and her resistance melts away . . .

NO DARKER HEAVEN Stella Whitelaw
Jeth *wants* Lyssa. Lyssa wants marriage without romance. Jeth offers excitement and passion, but his son, Matt, offers uncomplicated commitment. Against her will, Lyssa is caught up in an eternal triangle of passion.